Nina Singh lives ju[...] [...] husband, children, a[...] [...]er several years in the c[...] [...]d the advice of family a[...] [...]e writing a go, already'. She's oh[...] [...]ppy she did. When not at her keyboard she likes to spend time on the tennis court or golf course. Or immersed in a good read.

Michelle Douglas has been writing for Mills & Boon since 2007, and believes she has the best job in the world. She lives in a leafy suburb of Newcastle, on Australia's east coast, with her own romantic hero, a house full of dust and books and an eclectic collection of sixties and seventies vinyl. She loves to hear from readers and can be contacted via her website: michelle-douglas.com.

Also by Nina Singh

Her Billionaire Protector
Spanish Tycoon's Convenient Bride
Her Inconvenient Christmas Reunion

How to Make a Wedding collection

From Tropical Fling to Forever

Also by Michelle Douglas

Redemption of the Maverick Millionaire
Singapore Fling with the Millionaire
Secret Billionaire on Her Doorstep
Billionaire's Road Trip to Forever

Discover more at millsandboon.co.uk.

FROM WEDDING FLING TO BABY SURPRISE

NINA SINGH

CINDERELLA AND THE BROODING BILLIONAIRE

MICHELLE DOUGLAS

MILLS & BOON

First Published in Great Britain 2021
by Mills & Boon, an imprint of HarperCollins*Publishers* Ltd,
1 London Bridge Street, London, SE1 9GF

www.harpercollins.co.uk

HarperCollins*Publishers*
1st Floor, Watermarque Building,
Ringsend Road, Dublin 4, Ireland

From Wedding Fling to Baby Surprise © 2021 Nilay Nina Singh

Cinderella and the Brooding Billionaire © 2021 Michelle Douglas

ISBN: 978-0-263-29993-9

09/21

MIX
Paper from
responsible sources
FSC **FSC® C007454**
www.fsc.org

Printed and bound in Spain
by CPI, Barcelona

FROM WEDDING FLING TO BABY SURPRISE

NINA SINGH

MILLS & BOON

To all those who feel they are the odd ones.
May you find where you truly belong.

CHAPTER ONE

"YOU'RE BREAKING UP with me?"

Laney Taytum stared at her phone screen as if it had grown tentacles since she'd answered its ring.

"And you're doing it over the phone? While you're across the country on business?"

Joseph's loud and long-suffering sigh could be heard clearly from the other end of the line.

He'd been her steady and serious boyfriend for the past two or so years.

A status that seemed to be about to change.

Surprisingly, the flush of emotion running through her right now couldn't exactly be described as hurt. More like a stinging sense of disappointment.

They'd never been that kind of couple—the hot-and-heavy, can't-keep-our-hands-off-each-other kind. She'd never really felt that spark that she so often read about in the paperbacks she picked up in the grocery checkout line. But they'd been comfortable with each other. Enough that her weekends weren't spent alone on the couch, eating a pint of Rocky Road.

Maybe not the most exciting setup, but she'd thought it was a beneficial arrangement for them both. Clearly, that had been a bit naive on her part.

"Don't do this, Laney," he said now. "You had to sense this was coming."

She had not.

"But my sister's wedding. The trip to Italy." How could he dump her at such a time? There was no doubt that they'd passed a point on the road that there'd be no turning back from.

Emily's wedding was the very next month, in two weeks to be specific. The trip she and Joseph had booked together was scheduled a couple of weeks after that. How quickly did Joseph think she could move on after their long-term relationship?

It occurred to her then that he probably already had.

Her favorite cousin's voice echoed in her head. *I'm not gonna lie to you, sweetie. He strikes me as a bit of a jerk.*

While the rest of her family gave the two of them the suggestive wink and nod about marriage, Mabel had never taken a shine to Joseph. Apparently, she was much wiser than the lot of them. To think, Laney had felt rather offended at Mabel's straightforwardness at the time.

Looked like she owed Mabel an apology.

And now Laney would have to break the news to them all. While they'd been expecting the announcement of an engagement, she'd instead be attending her sister's nuptials sans a plus-one.

"How will I tell everyone?" The question was more a thought posed out loud as she was trying to process.

Joseph was silent for a beat before he answered, "Your reaction kind of proves my point. I'll try not to take it too personally."

He was trying to not take things personally? Of all the… The man was the very definition of a jerk.

She went from shocked to irritated. Then angry.

"Take it any way you'd like." For the first time, Laney

realized her voice sounded echo-like through the air. He must have had her on speaker. Was he even alone? "How exactly does my question prove your point?"

Perhaps he had the other woman in the room, eavesdropping, making sure he was going through with her dumping. She was probably listening to the whole conversation, egging him on.

Or maybe he was just a coward who didn't even have the guts to do this face-to-face.

"Darling," Joseph began, "I just told you I'm breaking up with you and your first response is to wonder how you're going to break the news to others. Kind of validates that we shouldn't be together."

Well, what did he expect her to do? Grovel? Cry? Tell him how hurt she was?

Before Joseph, her life had been a series of bad dates when she could find the time to break away from her responsibilities at the club. The two of them didn't always agree on everything, but she felt comfortable around him. Secure in the knowledge that she had a steady partner.

But she wasn't the type to do any kind of groveling or crying. Not since she was a child. Growing up in a family like hers, one didn't show emotion if one could help it. So she'd learned to keep hers in check.

For the most part, anyway.

"Aren't you even going to ask me why?" Joseph was now asking.

Like it mattered. Like it made any difference whatsoever.

Knowing his reasoning was not going to change the fact that she had all sorts of logistical and financial issues to now figure out, between the wedding and the trip.

Knowing his reasons wasn't going to change any part of this scenario. Still, she would humor him. Let him get it all off his chest.

"Tell me why, Joseph," she told him on a sigh.

He didn't hesitate to respond. "I'm bored, Laney. I have been for quite some time. And you didn't even notice," he added with an accusing tone.

He was calling her *boring*?

She'd been fully prepared to hear him say they were incompatible, and that they wanted different things in life. She definitely had not anticipated the sudden direction of the conversation.

Before she could absorb it all fully, Joseph continued, "I mean, when was the last time you tried anything new? And I don't mean agreeing to go to the new Vietnamese place downtown."

Then what did he mean? Laney blinked in confusion. Was he referring to the bedroom? Was she being prudish with him? She hadn't really thought so. But clearly, she hadn't been paying attention.

"When your sister introduced us, she couldn't say enough about how unconventional you were. How different."

Ha! Laney wanted to laugh out loud. Different was relative. She was nothing like the rest of her family, so her sister hadn't been lying to him. Then Joseph threw the proverbial and very sharp dagger. "You're just not an exciting woman to be with."

Despite herself, Laney felt the sting of hurtful tears. While she'd seen their relationship as comfortable and easy, he had obviously found it dull and flat.

She'd been such a fool not to have seen it. In that, at least, he was right.

She had to move on past the hurt, focus on the current situation before her. Focus on the facts at hand.

"You owe me for the trip," she reminded him. "I paid for the booking of it up front."

They were supposed to go to Positano and Florence together two weeks after her sister's wedding. Another stab of hurt shot through her. During the planning, she'd assumed Joseph would take the opportunity to propose himself given the timing.

What a fool she was.

Joseph sighed. "About that. I have an offer for you."

Alarm bells went off in her head. Something told her she wasn't going to like this offer of his. "And what would that be?"

"I'm perfectly happy to pay for the whole trip and go without you."

Laney tried not to react. She'd suspected as much. He wanted to go with someone else. Despite the suspicion, his words served as a figurative punch to the gut. How long had he been deceiving her?

"Otherwise," Joseph continued, "I don't plan on paying you for my half. Take it or leave it. That's the only deal on the table."

She was right. She didn't like his *deal* one bit. "Well, I happen to have a counteroffer. Feel free to drop dead!"

Disconnecting the call without waiting for a response, she took a deep breath and steadied herself. She had a long night ahead of her. Friday's were always busy enough at the club. The fact that this past week in Boston had been cloudy gray and rainy would ensure the usual crowd would be even larger with people looking to get out and party and dance.

Being the owner of a rather popular night spot meant she was in a packed dance club night after night, surrounded by a crowd of partyers. Hence, her rare evenings at home were particularly sacred. Especially on a day like this one, where all she wanted to do was lick her wounds.

As tempting as it was to call in and spend the evening at

home in sweats and fuzzy socks, deep into that aforementioned pint of Rocky Road, she wouldn't do that to her staff.

Processing her breakup, including the fact that her boyfriend of two years had just told her she'd been boring him to tears, was just going to have to wait.

He had clearly just stepped into the seventh circle of Hades.

Gianni Martino scanned the crowded dance floor and bristled with impatience. This really wasn't his kind of scene. What a lousy way to spend a Saturday night. He'd much rather be back at the main gym working out or in the ring sparring with Mario. But that afternoon his father, Franco, had reminded him yet again that he still hadn't scoped out the latest site he had in mind for further expansion within the city.

Better to get this over with, and then he could go about his night the way he wanted. This place was going to need a lot of work. All around him, sweaty bodies gyrated and bounced to a resoundingly loud techno song that was ridiculously heavy on the bass, even for a dance song. He groaned aloud in frustration. How did people enjoy this? Although, he had to admit, the scantily clad and heavily made-up women on the dance floor certainly made for enticing eye candy. A couple feet away, a group of female club goers were darting glances his way and giggling to each other. He was accustomed to such attention. He knew he fell into the category of tall and dark, plus he worked for his family-owned chain of gyms, so he was naturally physically fit. A combination that tended to ensure he was never at a loss for female companionship.

He observed the women again. Large diamond studs adorned the ears of one. A sparkly designer watch graced the wrist of another. They were clearly fit and had money.

Gianni thought about handing them all the Martino's free-pass gym coupons that he always carried with him.

One of the eye candies moved in his direction and stepped within inches of where he stood. He could smell the sharp, spicy scent of her perfume. Her brilliant blue eyes flashed at him and her smile widened into a grin.

"Please tell me you're here alone," she demanded in a breathless tone.

He thought about lying. Then decided there was no need. "I am."

She angled closer and pulled up against him, then grabbed him by the elbow. In a display of strength that somewhat took him by surprise, she yanked him closer to the dance floor. "Then you have to dance with me."

He stood firm after the first step. "I'm not much of a dancer, sweetheart."

She chuckled at that, clearly not deterred. If anything, she pressed closer up against him, skimmed her hand up his chest to his shoulder. "Then why are you here? This is the most popular dance club in Greater Boston."

There was no way he was going to get into all that with her. How exactly would he explain that he was actually here on business on a Friday night, just as the evening had begun?

She would never believe it.

He would then have to explain that he was a senior VP at his family's company. Martino Entertainment Enterprises was a global entity, which owned everything from gaming halls to small casinos to fitness centers and boxing gyms. The latter being his very own idea and accomplishment.

"Maybe some other time," he told the woman with a friendly yet dismissive smile.

The woman gave him a mini shrug. "Well, I'll be here for a few more hours if you change your mind," she threw over her shoulder before walking away to rejoin her friends. Any other night, Gianni might have entertained the offer she'd not so subtly thrown at him. A romantic interlude without any attachments was sometimes just what a man— or a woman—needed. But he really was here on business. And he never mixed business with pleasure. It was the reason he was drinking nothing stronger than a cola at the moment.

After about fifteen minutes, he'd seen enough. Logistically, the place was exactly what they'd been looking for. The square footage, the setup of the building and geographical location made it perfect for acquisition. Everything else would need to be gutted.

He'd already surmised that he'd have to make the current owner a hefty offer, one they couldn't refuse. A lot of work and planning had clearly gone into the place. No doubt, it was professionally decorated—with avant-garde lighting and comfortable seating. The dance floor was large and highly polished. A wraparound bar heavily stocked with the highest grade of spirits and wine was currently mobbed with thirsty customers. Four professional dancers performed on an elevated stage in every corner, occasionally jumping off to wrangle those who appeared to be hesitant to enter the dancing fray.

All in all, Gianni figured he would have to commend the current proprietor. They'd done a nice job—created a welcoming, fun atmosphere. Everyone seemed to be having a good time.

Except one. His gaze fell on her at that very moment, right before he'd been getting ready to exit and go about his night. She walked past him carrying a tray of drinks and delivered it to what appeared to be a VIP table just a few feet away.

She looked utterly miserable.

The waitress uniform she had on—a black tuxedo vest and knee-length leather skirt—fit her to perfection. Her dark hair was piled high on top of her head with tendrils of curls framing her face. She looked more like a pop star about to go on stage than a cocktail waitress in a dance club. Even in the dark, her eyes were striking. An amber-gold shade of hazel that reminded him of a summer sunset.

When had he ever noticed a stranger's eyes before, let alone compared them to a sunset?

Gianni found himself unable to tear his gaze away as she handed out the drinks and made small talk, the smile on her face clearly forced and strained. Watching her made him more curious than he could explain.

Maybe she was just tired, maybe it had been a long night and her feet hurt in the lace-up, block-heeled black leather boots she was wearing.

The real question was, why did he want to know so badly?

CHAPTER TWO

SHE COULD FEEL his eyes on her.

And it was becoming harder and harder to ignore his gaze. Laney did her best to focus on the task at hand. All she had to do was deliver this tray of drinks, then head back for the next order. Then repeat.

Simple. She'd done it hundreds of times in the past. But tonight felt different. She'd begun her shift feeling out of sorts because of Joseph's cowardly phone call.

But her discomfort at the moment consisted of a whole other layer. She was beyond aware of the customer sitting alone at the table by the edge of the dance floor. He definitely wasn't a regular. She would have remembered a face like his. Dark, handsome in an angular, sharp-jawed kind of way. Not her usual type at all. The man was clearly fit. By contrast, Joseph had been fair and rather lanky. As were the few other men she'd dated over the years. Whereas this man couldn't be described as lanky at all. Probably not since junior high. Broad-shouldered with toned muscles visible through the long-sleeved Henley shirt he wore, he was the fittest specimen of a man she'd seen. And he seemed to carry it with an air of grace.

She'd never gone for muscular before. Nothing about this stranger should be calling to her in any way.

Why was he here alone? He didn't seem the type to often be lacking in female company.

Even as the thought ran through her mind, a tall statuesque blonde in mile-high stilettos strode over to him from the other side of the bar. That hadn't taken long at all. Laney hadn't thought he'd be standing there by himself for long, and she'd been right. She prepared herself for the show; the lady was no doubt ready to laser blast all her charm on the guy, who was probably all too willing to receive it. Only, upon closer inspection, the expression on the woman's face appeared less than flirtatious. In fact, she looked downright angry. Combative, even.

Before Laney could so much as process what was happening, the woman flung out her arm in a flash of movement. The next instant, the gentleman's shirt was soaked and his face dripping with the evening's cocktail special.

The woman had tossed her drink in his face!

She gave a final humph with a raise of her chin, then stomped back where she'd come from.

To his credit, he didn't react in any kind of anger or frustration. He didn't even look shocked, for that matter.

Laney faltered in her step. As proprietor of the establishment, she had to tend to her customers. All of them.

She made her way over to him, pulling out the tea towel from her apron's waistband. She handed it to him when she reached his side. Luckily, none of the liquid had made its way to the floor to cause any kind of slipping hazard. Or rather unluckily in his case, it had all landed squarely on his person.

"Thanks," he uttered, wiping his face and neck.

"No problem."

He did the best he could with the towel before handing it back to her.

"Just one question," she began, seemingly unable to help herself.

He shrugged. "Sure. Why not?"

"Did you deserve it?"

He had the gall to wink at her before answering, "Probably."

"Go ahead and laugh," Gianni prompted. His skin felt sticky everywhere the cocktail had landed. His reflexes were usually a bit better than that, but he hadn't moved in time to duck the unexpected assault. Too distracted by the cute waitress. The one who stood gaping at him, a slight smile of amusement quivering along her lips.

The perpetrator of the tequila toss had already made her way back to the refuge of her circle of friends. They each took turns throwing disgusted looks in his direction as the drink-flinger sniffled and wiped away a tear from her cheek.

For the life of him, he didn't recognize her. No doubt that was part of the problem.

The cute waitress was still there, clearly trying hard not to smile or laugh at him.

"Probably, huh?"

"Yeah. I'm usually a lot quicker to duck. She caught me off guard."

An elegant dark eyebrow arched up and she bit the inside of her cheek. Such an innocent gesture that somehow shot a surge of longing through his chest.

"Usually?" she asked. "Does this sort of thing happen to you often, then?"

"I'm going to opt not to answer that, if it's all the same to you." He smiled as he answered, then wiped a hand down his face to remove more of the moisture. "The ride home should be fun," he added.

She seemed to peruse him, her gaze traveling from his forehead down to his soaked shirt, then lower to his feet. She chewed her cheek some more, as if considering. Seemingly, she came to some kind of conclusion or decision.

"Here, follow me," she told him. Without waiting for any kind of answer, she turned on her heel and strode across the dance floor.

What choice did he have?

Gianni started after her, careful not to lose her in the throng of gyrating dancers.

He caught up to her at the bar where she took a left and headed toward a narrow hallway.

"Where are we going exactly?" he asked her back.

"There should be a dry shirt or two in the back office. Hopefully, one of them will fit."

They passed the restrooms and a utility door. Finally, she stopped at the last door and pulled a key ring out of her apron pocket. He followed her inside the room without any thought or hesitation. A strange and unexpected thought reared in the back of his mind—if this stranger asked him to, he'd follow her anywhere.

He gave his head a shake. Now he was just being fanciful. Sure, she was attractive. Hair so dark it was striking, olive skin, shapely in a way that screamed sultry. But she really wasn't his type. His type usually fell toward blonds with porcelain skin and yoga-toned physiques. A lot like the woman who'd just flung a drink at him, in fact.

"We always keep some clean clothes back here," she was saying. "For any bartenders or servers who might be having a clumsy night."

"Lucky for me."

She went into what looked like a utility closet and emerged holding a button-down short-sleeved cotton shirt with a band collar. Really not his style, though it wasn't as if he could be choosy at the moment. It would feel good to get the sticky wet shirt off once and for all.

"So, if you don't mind my asking, what brings you to the Carpe D?"

He had to chuckle at her question. He must have stuck out like a sore thumb out there.

"Why do you ask?" Rhetorical question. He knew the answer.

A small smile spread over her lips. "Let's just say you're not our usual niche of clientele. And I didn't see you on the dance floor even once."

He returned her smile. "Trust me, no one needs to see me dance."

"Then why?"

He shrugged, tried to choose his words carefully. Though he didn't want to lie to her, he couldn't exactly tell her the truth and risk the owner getting wind of his intention. Not just yet anyway.

"My brother's been talking up this place since it opened. He was supposed to come with me but something came up and he backed out." It was all completely true. Technically, he hadn't actually lied to her about anything. His *mamma*'s voice echoed through his head, telling him an omission of the truth was still a deceitful lie. But Mamma's strict code of ethics could be taken with a grain of salt given the reality he'd grown up with.

"Something came up, huh?" she asked.

"Yeah. Very last minute. So I figured I'd just check it out finally even though I'd be alone."

Her eyes narrowed on his. She looked suspicious. He diverted by changing the subject. "So, I didn't catch your name."

She gave her head a shake. "Sorry. Very rude of me. I'm Laney."

He nodded. "Laney. Pretty name. I'm Gianni Martino."

"Nice to meet you." She chewed her bottom lip. "Sorry your first time here is ending on such a sour note." She motioned to his wet chest. "If it makes you feel better, my evening didn't start out all that great either."

"Oh?"

She shook her head. "I was unceremoniously dumped. Over the phone, no less. He didn't even have the decency to come by and do it in person." Her gaze dropped to her feet. "He told me I bored him."

There was genuine hurt threaded through her tone. "He sounds like quite the fool."

She lifted her head back up.

He continued, "I know we just met, but that's the last word I would use to describe you."

"Oh? Why's that?"

"Everything from the way you're dressed to the way you make a living tells me you're far from dull. Tell me, what does this ex of yours do?"

"He's an accountant."

Of course. He had to laugh out loud at that. "Just as I guessed, clear case of projection if you ask me."

She tilted her head in question. "Come again?"

He shrugged. "Sounds like he's the one guilty of the accusations he's throwing around. The man probably figured he'd get out before you came to your senses and realized who the really boring one in the relationship is."

She tapped her chin with a perfectly manicured nail. "I see you might have a point. The man's idea of a good time is to play a round of golf, then sit in the clubhouse for several hours after." She looked up at him, blinking. "You're right! I'm not the boring one. He is. Thank you."

"You're welcome. Glad to be of service."

His reward was a wide smile. "Well, Gianni. Typical client or not, I'm glad you came in. Despite the minor scene out there."

She'd surprised him with her admission. "Me too. Drink attack and all."

"I hope you'll come back."

He had no doubt about it. "Definitely. I know I will."

"Glad to hear it."

A heavy moment of silence ensued. She seemed to have a rare magnetism that steadily pulled him toward her orbit. He'd never experienced anything like it before. Gianni grasped for something to say. He couldn't explain his strong reaction to her, not even to himself. An intense electricity seemed to be crackling between them. The term "sparks fly" came to mind. He'd never experienced anything so heady in the presence of a woman he'd just met.

Stop it already.

There he was being all imaginative again. He'd just met the woman for heaven's sake.

"You probably want to get out of that wet shirt."

Grabbing the hem of his pullover, he pulled it off over his head. He looked up to find her studying him, from his waistband over his stomach to his chest, then his shoulders. When her gaze returned to his, something had shifted in her eyes. They'd grown darker, heavy-lidded. She apparently liked what she saw.

He knew raw attraction when he saw it. If there'd been any doubt about the subtle pull between them earlier, there was no mistaking it now. And it was most definitely mutual.

Laney had no way of describing the wanton attraction that seemed to be humming over her skin straight through to her core. And she certainly couldn't explain why she'd confided in him, a mere stranger really, about her breakup. Yet, the way he'd tried to reassure her had sent a curl of warmth from her chest down to her belly. Maybe he had a point. Now that she thought about it, what exactly did Joseph think made him so exciting in comparison? He certainly couldn't hold a candle to the man standing before her now.

Even before he'd taken his shirt off and she'd laid eyes on that washboard stomach and finely chiseled chest. When had she ever gawked at a man before? But here she was now, her mouth not working, unable to tear her gaze away from his bare skin.

Finally, Gianni cleared his throat, pulling her out of her reverie. His gaze fell to the shirt she held in her hands, further jarring her into the present.

"Oh! I'm so sorry. Here you go," she blurted as she handed it to him. What a shameful reaction to a man simply taking his shirt off. She felt the sting of embarrassment heat up in her cheeks.

As he took it from her, their fingertips brushed ever so slightly. A lightning bolt of electricity seemed to shoot from her hand straight through to her very center. She let her arm linger, still touching his hand.

Snap out of it!

What was wrong with her? She was acting like a schoolgirl who'd just been approached by the high school quarterback in the hallway between classes.

Only, when she looked back up to the stranger's face, there was no mistaking the heat behind his eyes. Maybe it was merely wishful thinking on her part, but it appeared her attraction to this man wasn't exactly one-sided. He confirmed that suspicion when he took an ever so slight step in Laney's direction, and her breath suddenly grew heavier. What might happen if she took a step too? They'd be within a hair's width of each other, close enough to kiss.

Did she dare?

A sudden vibrating in her back pocket along with the

sound of her ringtone yanked her out of the moment. She thought about ignoring it, but maybe the interruption had happened for a reason. The atmosphere had grown much too thick with tension.

"Excuse me." Reluctantly, she dropped her arm and reached for her cell phone.

The photo appearing on the screen was her sister's profile picture. What a way to be pulled back to reality.

Gianni gave her a nod, indicating she should go ahead and take the call. In one fluid motion, he pulled the shirt over his head to put it on. What a shame.

"Hey, Em. Can I call you back? I'm working." A fact her sister was very well aware of.

Not surprisingly, Emily didn't heed her request. "Okay. But, just real quick, have you and Joseph signed off on the hotel room?"

Laney swallowed. At some point, she was going to have to tell Emily and her parents that she'd be attending her sister's wedding events solo. Not something she was looking forward to. And definitely not something she was at all prepared to do just yet. Especially not with the tall dark and handsome stranger standing just a couple of feet away.

For one selfish moment, Laney wanted to pretend the call had dropped and hang up on her sister. To return her focus back to Mr. Chiseled Jaw. But it was too late; he was already turning away and heading back out the door. He mumbled something about making sure to return the borrowed shirt over his shoulder as he walked out.

An irrational sense of loss struck at the center of her chest. She had half a mind to call him back. To then say what? How pathetic it would sound to simply ask him to stay. She had no reason to do so. So she just watched as he shut the door behind him and released a heavy sigh. She shouldn't have expected anything to go her way today of all days.

Would she ever see him again? Why did she so badly want to?

"Are you even listening, Laney? Laney? Elaine!" Laney jumped, jarred by the use of her proper name. Her sister demanded an answer through her phone speaker.

"Everything's all set," she responded, lying to her sister because she simply couldn't get into the mess that was her personal life right now. "Don't worry about anything. Your wedding is going to go off without a hitch."

She could hear Emily's sigh of relief over the phone. "Thanks, sis. I know I'm approaching bridezilla level here. I just want everything to go smoothly."

"It's okay. I'll call you later, Em. I really do have to go," she said gently before clicking off the call.

Laney loved her sister, she really did. But Em could be a bit highly strung at times. And her approaching wedding had somehow severely exaggerated that trait. Not that anyone could fault Emily for her type-A personality. Look at how far it had gotten her in life. A steadily advancing career as a junior lawyer, countless accomplishments and awards within her industry, and now her engagement to a seemingly perfect all-American up-and-coming investment banker.

Yep, by all standards, her sister was the very embodiment of success. Everything her parents could have hoped for. Just like Mom and Dad, in fact. Wealthy, established, highly regarded in their field.

Unlike their other daughter.

In contrast to her sister, Laney had dropped out of school rather than go on to earn an advanced degree in law. After leaving school to pursue her dream of becoming a dancer, Laney had been rejected audition after audition. She'd decided to do the next best thing—find a way she could be near music and dancing while she made a living. So, instead of investing the nice nest egg that their grandfather had left them the way Emily had, Laney used hers to open a nightclub. While Emily had followed in their parent's pedigreed and polished footsteps, Laney had taken the road less traveled.

May they one day forgive her for it.

Somehow their differences were made all the worse because Laney was older by two years. But Emily was the one everyone had always admired and looked up to. Even Laney herself. Who could blame her? Unlike her, Em never felt out of place or like a square peg in a round hole.

And now Laney was going to have to go and explain to all of them yet another failure. She was certain she'd dodged a bullet. After all, if Joseph could be so cold and callous after two years of dating, sooner or later that defect in his character was going to emerge.

Still, on the surface Laney just knew it was going to look like she'd somehow managed to foul up yet another good thing she'd had going for her. No doubt, her parents would ultimately find a way to blame her. It would hardly matter that he'd almost certainly been cheating on her. Somehow, she'd be found to be the one to blame for his indiscretion.

Never mind that she was a successful businesswoman who owned a very popular nightclub. In her family of academic highbrow professionals, her chosen professional path was nothing to be impressed by in comparison.

Laney released another deep breath and plopped down in her office chair. No wonder she'd felt so attracted to a random stranger. She was looking for assurance that she was still attractive, that someone could still want her.

She had to admit she was feeling dejected. She really hadn't seen the breakup coming. That Joseph had told her she was boring just added jagged-edged rock salt into the open gaping wound.

* * *

It had started to feel awkward, with him just standing there getting dressed as she talked on the phone. If he were being completely honest with himself, he'd felt a little rattled at the way she affected him. So he made his escape. Some might call that cowardly. Or simple self-preservation. He was going to go with the latter.

It was bad enough she had no clue who he was or why he was there. And as he pulled up into the parking of the twenty-four-hour boxing gym, he still hadn't been able to put Laney out of his mind.

A nagging sensation tickled the back of his mind. During her phone call, the person on the other end had been loud enough that he'd heard part of the conversation. He could have sworn the caller had called Laney "Elaine."

Pulling out his smartphone, he called up his business drive and opened the file on acquisitions to confirm. And there it was in black-and-white on the small screen, just as he'd suspected. *Owner/proprietor of intended property: Elaine Taytum.*

Elaine. Laney. A quick online search of various local business pages verified his conclusion. She wasn't a cocktail waitress at all. She was merely waitressing at her own establishment.

Gianni bit out a sharp curse. Way to complicate things even further given the fierce attraction he felt toward her as soon as they'd met.

All the better that he was here at the gym. A few rounds with a heavy punching bag would go far to settling some of the inexplicable frustration he was feeling.

Something about the woman had triggered a need in him he hadn't even realized he had. Less than ten minutes later, he was changed and pummeling the bag. Only two other men were also present, sparring in the center ring.

Within no time, Gianni's heart rate was pumping and sweat rolled down his face.

Though it took a while, the exertion finally started to temper the storm of relentless angst he'd been feeling since he'd left the Carpe D.

"Thought I'd find you here," a familiar masculine voice bellowed behind him. "You're not answering your phone."

Gianni stopped mid punch and turned to face his brother. Angelo was the complete opposite of him in every way. Fair where Gianni was tan, not exactly short but nowhere near Gianni's six foot one. Angelo's amber-hued eyes changed color with the light, whereas Gianni's were perpetually dark. Angelo was a devoted family man. And Gianni would never follow that path, he was almost certain. Falling for someone meant opening yourself to humiliation and hurt. Hurt that could spread out toward others like ripples in a pond after a boulder fell into it. For two men who were brothers, the differences between them ran surface level as well as far deeper.

They both knew the reason for that—a poorly kept secret that no one dared to talk about.

Still, despite that damning secret and all their differences, they'd always been close as siblings. Gianni would trust his brother with his very life.

"Planned on calling you as soon as I was done," he told the other man, taking his gloves off and reaching for the towel at the nearby weight bench.

"Did you scope the place out?"

"I did. Even met the owner."

"And? Will it work? Dad's going to want a full account in the morning."

Taking a swig from his ice-cold water bottle, Gianni nodded. "It's perfect. The location, the building." He poured a small amount of the water over his head. "Popular place though. Must do well. I don't see her accepting just any offer." He'd intentionally gone on a night he'd known would be busy, to stay as under the radar as possible. Just a regular guy out for a fun night of clubbing.

Angelo shrugged. "Then we'll just make her an offer she can't refuse, won't we?"

Something told him things wouldn't be that simple. From what little he'd seen of her tonight, Laney wasn't going to fold easy about any kind of deal. She was obviously hands-on, to get into the grind of serving as a waitress. And she cared enough about her clientele that she made sure one of them didn't go home in a soaking wet shirt. Efficient and prepared.

What kind of man would have dumped such a dynamic, successful, attractive woman? It made no sense where he was standing. He gave his head a shake. He couldn't go there again. He'd barely just managed to get inappropriate thoughts of her out his mind. "We're going to have to."

His brother clapped him on the shoulder. "Sorry I couldn't come with you. Had a pounding headache that's only just receding."

"Don't worry about it. Glad you're feeling better."

"Probably coming down with what Marie and the kids had last week."

Gianni stepped back in exaggeration and used his fingers to make the sign of an *x*. "Stay back and keep your germs to yourself."

Angelo rolled his eyes. "Ha-ha. Really funny, bro."

"I'm not exactly sure if I'm really joking, man."

Angelo ignored him and continued, "So I'll see you at breakfast tomorrow at Mom and Pop's, right?"

Gianni couldn't resist the temptation to tease him just a bit more. "I was thinking of skipping that. Seeing as those loud and bratty toddlers of yours will be there."

The statement couldn't be further from the truth. Seeing Angelo and Marie's two-year-old son, Gino, and four-year-old daughter, Gemma, was the highlight of Gianni's week every Saturday. He loved being able to spoil them, then hand them right back when the visit was over.

Angelo gave him a fake glare. "More funniness. You know, if working for the family business doesn't pan out for you, you should go out on a comedy tour."

Now, that was the real joke. As if Gianni had any real choice in his place within the Martino empire of entertainment companies. His wasn't the type of family where one of only two sons could easily walk away from the family business. His father valued loyalty and family above all else. Particularly when it came to his older son. Their empire included everything from gaming halls, to small-scale casinos, to fitness centers and gyms. And Franco wanted Laney's location as the next Martino casino. "Maybe I will."

"You do that. In the meantime, you can give the old man a complete rundown of what you saw tonight when we see him at breakfast tomorrow."

Gianni figured he would leave out the part about having a cocktail thrown in his face. And all that transpired afterward with the club's owner. If his brother and father ever got wind of any of that, he'd no doubt never hear the end of it.

"Yeah, yeah. I'll be there," he answered and reached for his bag on the nearby weight bench.

He'd have to get his thoughts in order before the morning when his father would undoubtedly have numerous questions about how to proceed with the acquisition. He'd also have to explain to his brother and father that Laney was probably going to be a tougher negotiator than they'd assumed.

CHAPTER THREE

SHE'D GOTTEN ZERO SLEEP.

It didn't help that the bridesmaid's dress she'd laid out to steam the other day seemed to be mocking her from across the room. She was supposed to be wearing that dress while walking in the bridal procession on Joseph's arm.

How in the world was she supposed to break it to her sister that she'd be attending solo? Emily would have to find somebody to take Joseph's place in the wedding party. Wayne, her soon-to-be brother-in-law, was probably going to have to ask one of his friends to step up. He'd have to explain that Emily's boring sister had been dumped on the eve of her sibling's wedding.

Luckily, her sister had decided the groomsmen should be clad in black tie, which meant standard tuxes. At least they wouldn't have to worry about scheduling a new fitting for someone.

It was all so humiliating. Laney didn't consider herself a particularly prideful person. But this was a bit too much to bear.

Her ex's words echoed through her head. *I'm breaking up with you and your first response is to wonder how you're going to break the news to others.*

Did Joseph have a point? What did it say about her that rather than experiencing loss or sorrow about the end of her long-term relationship, she felt anger more than anything else?

Puffing out a frustrated sigh, she shifted to her side. There was no point in pondering any of it right now. She had things to do, decisions to make. Maybe she should just drop out of the wedding procession altogether. Let Em's best friend Lea take over the duties as maid of honor. That thought had tears stinging her eyes. Even if they weren't particularly close, Emily was still her only sibling.

No, she wasn't going to let a philandering ex mar her only sibling's wedding for her.

One thing was certain, as sleepless as she was, she was going to need a whole pot of coffee to get her through the morning. There was the exercise class to teach—Laney had gotten the idea a few months back that she could use the club dance floor for pop-up fitness classes, having been certified since college as an instructor. It didn't provide for a huge revenue stream, but it made more sense than to let the club just sit empty all day. With the added benefit that she got some exercise and met so many more people.

And she was still working on that cocktail recipe for tonight's house special. She couldn't continue to wallow in bed, no matter how groggy she felt.

With a resigned sigh, she threw her covers off and sat up. In between all she had to do, she would have to somehow rehearse exactly what she was going to say to Emily and her parents.

She could just imagine their distressed, yet somehow resigned, reactions. Here was Laney yet again disappointing everyone. Her parents kept expecting her to fail, and she kept proving them right.

They'd undoubtedly ask if Laney had tried hard enough to make things work, especially given the close proximity to the big event. They'd wonder if she'd been the one to somehow mess things up between her and Joseph. She'd finally found someone they could approve of and she couldn't hold on to him.

At least the recipe for the cocktail was fairly close. A combination of elderflower, sparkling water and orange liqueur, she knew she needed just one more ingredient to bind it all together.

Hopefully, it would be a hit and nobody would get splashed in the face with the concoction through the course of the evening, unlike last night. The scene from the previous evening came flooding back into her mind. Images of the tall dark stranger standing in her office as he took his shirt off. The electricity that seemed to hum between them.

What might have happened if Emily hadn't called when she did?

Perhaps they would have exchanged numbers, and she'd be spending this morning wondering if he would call her today or if he would call her at all.

Laney gave her head a brisk shake. She had to have been imagining the tension that seemed to have existed between them. No doubt her mind was grasping at random possibilities simply because she'd been dumped only hours before a handsome and *very* toned Adonis stood shirtless in her office. After all, if he'd really wanted to get in touch with her again, there were plenty of times he could have asked for her number up until Em's phone call. Or he could have simply hung around afterward. But when she'd walked back out to the club, he was nowhere to be found.

Laney couldn't deny the disappointment she'd felt. She'd never met anyone quite so…well, like him. It was the only description that came to mind. He clearly wasn't some kind of office desk jockey. If he was, the man must spend the rest of the hours of his day just working out. Maybe he was a fitness instructor himself only full time.

Maybe he was a male model. Boston did have several marketing agencies that did business throughout the whole world.

She chuckled out loud. The chances of an up-and-coming male model being interested in her would be considered slim to none. Those types wanted glamour and style. She was neither of those things. As she'd found out when she was rejected again and again from any kind of respected dance company.

What was she thinking, anyway? She'd literally just gotten out of a long relationship. She had no business pondering the prospect of starting another one. Joseph's betrayal was going to take time to heal from. She'd trusted him, only to have him drop her at the most inopportune time, when she needed him to be there for her. Not to mention the whole cheating thing. It would take a while to get past all that.

And the risk of falling for a disastrous rebound fling was all too real, especially given her reaction to Gianni at the club.

No, she had to accept the reality that she was single now and she had to get on with her life. And she had to forget about the dark and handsome stranger who had so briefly walked through it.

Having never gotten around to purchasing a washer and dryer for his own place after a relatively recent move, Gianni made sure to do his laundry at his parents' home every Saturday when he went there for breakfast. That's why he was in possession of a freshly washed borrowed shirt that one Laney Taytum had given him when he drove away from his family's house close to noon. He'd tossed it in a paper bag and thrown it on the passenger seat.

The sooner he returned the shirt, the sooner he could put the encounter with Laney out of his head. Maybe then he could finally start viewing her as the next businesswoman he'd be negotiating a deal with rather than the sexy server who'd knocked the wind out of him.

Given the conversation he'd just had at breakfast with Angelo and his father, there was no doubt Martino Entertainment Enterprises was on a direct course to obtain the property and building that housed the nightclub she owned. It was the ideal spot for the gaming hall slash casino they'd had in development for the past year. Laney's club was situated right off the water on a small peninsula that used to house a lighthouse.

He'd been charged with making it happen.

The Carpe D was certain to be closed this time of day. But he'd noticed a mail drop box mounted on the outside by the entrance when he'd been there last night, and it so happened the club wasn't that far out of his way.

A surprising number of cars sat in the parking lot when he arrived several minutes later. Which made no sense for a nightclub, seeing as it was barely lunchtime. Was she holding some kind of training for the staff?

As he got out of the car, the pounding pulse of bass from a hip-hop song he recognized thumped through the air. A female voice sounded over the loud music.

Curiosity piqued, he approached the entrance.

He'd been mistaken. The club was definitely not closed. About twenty women in spandex and sneakers were bouncing on the dance floor in tandem—along with one solitary gentleman who appeared to be holding his own. Then they all started doing some complicated side-step move, which took them all around the dance floor.

But Gianni's focus was centered on one woman and her alone. And the sight of her made his gut tighten with desire.

Laney stood in front of the group on a makeshift wooden stage about five-inches high. She wore a bright green tank top, which fit her like a glove and brought out the tan, golden hue of her skin. Her toned shapely legs kicked to the music as the others followed her lead.

She was instructing some sort of fitness class and damned if it wasn't the sexiest scene he'd ever laid eyes on.

He stood watching, mesmerized as she thrust her hips forward and back, then did a mini twirl. Gianni swallowed. Exercise classes like this one certainly didn't happen at the boxing gyms his family owned and he frequently visited. Good thing too, since their usual clientele would no doubt drool all over the equipment if they were to witness something like this in the center ring, just like Gianni was on the verge of doing.

He continued to watch as the group came to a stop and the music ended. The next song to come on was a much slower one. He could barely hear Laney's voice but it sounded like she was congratulating everyone on a job well done before starting a cooldown.

She bent down and touched her toes, perfectly bent at the waist. The woman was definitely flexible.

Steady, fella. She's simply exercising. Nothing to get worked up about.

Gianni made himself look away and glanced around him. Thank the spirits above that no one else was nearby as he looked suspiciously like a solitary male in a parking lot gawking at a bunch of ladies—and one man—in tight fitness gear, bouncing around a dance floor.

If he were smart, he'd make a break for it right now before anyone noticed him. The class was clearly about to end. He could always drop the shirt in the mail. He started to do just that, about to pivot on his heel and get back in the car, but he didn't manage to move fast enough. As soon as Laney straightened, her eyes found his through the glass door of the entrance.

She gave him a wide smile, one that seemed to spread

through her whole face. He might even surmise that she was happy to see him. Then she lifted a finger in the universal sign that said, *Give me a minute*.

What choice did he have?

She wrapped up the class in under a minute while Gianni waited, leaning against the hood of his car. Now that he'd been spotted, he felt less like a sneaky voyeur and he allowed himself to fully indulge in the view of Laney going through the steps of her cooldown stretches. If he'd only known he'd be treated to such an entertaining scene when he woke up this morning, it definitely would have given him something to look forward to.

Finally, her muscle-strained students started to trickle out and Gianni made his way inside. Laney waved when he made it to where she stood on the stage.

"Hey there." She was breathless, her cheeks pink with a slight sheen of sweat over her skin.

"Hey. I wanted to return this. Didn't mean to distract you during class."

She took the package from him. "You didn't. We were just wrapping up when I saw you. Hope you didn't wait out there long."

He merely shook his head. She'd certainly been worth waiting for.

Pointing to the bag she held, he said, "It's laundered. Nice and clean and fresh."

"Thank you for doing that."

"Thank you for not letting me drive home sticky and wet."

"You're welcome." An awkward pause ensued where Gianni knew he should walk out and leave but he just didn't want to. He enjoyed this woman's company, chatting with her was easy and pleasurable. Laney finally broke the silence. "You should attend the class sometime," she told him. "You might even have fun."

He spread his hands out and shook his head with exaggeration. "No one needs to see me try to do any of that. I don't think my hips would even move that way."

She appeared to study him from head to toe. "Something tells me you're coordinated enough for a Zumba class."

"Probably for the best if we don't try to find out."

She laughed, lifted the bag. "You know you didn't have to come all the way out here just to drop this off. You could have just brought it next time you came to the club. Unless…"

She didn't need to say the rest. She'd deduced the truth pretty much. That he had no intention of coming back to the club after this. Not to just hang out, anyway. He didn't deny it now. Her lips turned downward once more.

There was no mistaking the disappointment that darkened her eyes.

Laney couldn't deny the surge of pleasure that she felt when she'd seen him waiting in the parking lot.

What effect did this man seem to have on her? Was it simply the need to feel some sort of validation after being so soundly, humiliatingly rejected by her ex-boyfriend?

Something told her it wasn't that simple. Whatever it was, she had to get over it. Clearly, it was one-sided. He'd practically just admitted he'd had no intention of stopping by the club. Which left no doubt that he had no plans to try to see her again in the future. This was simply a coincidence. He just happened to come by during her Saturday morning dance class.

His next words confirmed that fact. "So, this is quite the setup. I didn't realize you also did fitness classes."

She made sure to hide the sinking feeling in her chest. How silly of her to feel so disappointed that he only came upon her by chance. "It's just a side thing. I happen to be certified and have all this space."

"Some added revenue?"

She nodded. "It allows me to up the wages I pay my workers. Not by much but it's something."

"That's very decent of you."

Laney was about to reply that all her employees felt like family—some of them even more so than her true kin. Her employees didn't look at her with clear disappointment in their eyes the way her parents and sibling did. She wanted to ensure all her staff were well compensated for their hard work. But they were interrupted by the sound of the door opening. Laney knew who it was without having to look up. Louise Miller was a regular in her Saturday class and managed to leave something behind almost every time. Last week it was her reusable water bottle.

Sure enough, it was Louise who noisily entered. "I forgot to grab my mat," the blond ponytailed, frazzled mom announced as she ran to the spot she'd occupied for the last forty-five minutes. She usually carpooled to the class with four other women from her neighborhood. "Great class, by the way," Louise continued. "We really enjoyed the music, as usual."

Laney gave her a smile of thanks.

"And sorry none of us could stick around to taste test that drink," Louise added over her shoulder as she ran back out the door.

"It's okay, Louise. Have a good week," Laney answered.

Gianni was giving her a quizzical look when she turned back to him. "You also do drink tastings?"

"Not regularly. I'm working on a new special cocktail for tonight. Just wanted some feedback but no one could stay this week."

A dark eyebrow lifted. "Maybe I can be of help."

"Oh?"

"I happen to be a great taste-tester." He added with a charming smile, "And I do like cocktails."

Well, that was unexpected. "Is that so?"

"Yep. As long as I don't down a full one. Then I'd have to call a car service. But I'd be happy to step in as your official taster."

"You would?"

"Sure. Sounds fun."

"That's great. You definitely don't have to drink a full one. And I can brew you a whole pot of coffee after."

"Sounds like a deal," he said with that breathtaking smile.

Suddenly, her afternoon was looking much more entertaining than the original one she'd planned for, pouring and stirring alone in her bar. She tried to clamp down on her excitement when she answered, "Then give me just a second to freshen up in the back. I'll meet you at the bar in just a few minutes."

He winked at her, just as he had last night, and her knees grew a little weak. It had nothing to do with the repetitive squats she'd been doing earlier during the "legs" portion of her class either. "Don't take too long. I'm pretty thirsty."

Made sense. She got the gut feeling that Gianni was the type of man who wasn't kept waiting too often. Particularly not by members of the opposite sex.

"I'll be there in no time," she assured him. "Just have to make myself somewhat presentable."

"I think you look great."

Was he flirting with her? Or did oozing charm just come naturally to someone like him?

Probably a little of both, no doubt.

Whatever it was, she felt a surge of giddiness rush through her at his compliment. When was the last time someone, a man in particular, had actually paid her any kind of praise?

Joseph was always, oh, so quick with the digs. Her hair was too messy, her dress too short. Her nails were the wrong color if she so much as tried anything bolder than plain beige or clear polish.

To think, he had the nerve to accuse *her* of being boring.

But his compliments had been few and far between. Since her breakup, Laney was beginning to see just how emotionally lacking her past relationship had been.

A parting glance at the man before her as she walked away only served to affirm that thought. As she freshened up in the ladies' room, a far-flung idea began to form in her head. He really was very handsome. And full of personality and humor. The kind of man any woman would be excited and thrilled to be with.

The perfect date to bring to a wedding.

She stared at her reflection in the mirror and gave her head a shake. *Nah.* How would she even begin to ask him something like that? But what was the alternative? She didn't have any really close male friends. And as luck would have it, all her close female friends wouldn't be able to help either. Rachel and Leigh were both only children. Carla had two sisters and Miranda's brother was overseas on active duty. Laney's only alternative was to fess up to her family.

Plus…the idea wasn't without appeal. For one thing, she'd get a chance to see him again. She would have to run it by her sister, of course. But Emily would be agreeable to the idea, Laney was certain. Her sister didn't want the snafu of a missing groomsmen this close to the big day. Still, as far as ideas went, it was loony and harebrained and impulsive.

But it just might work.

CHAPTER FOUR

WHEN LANEY RETURNED about ten minutes later, she'd donned a long-sleeved hoodie and gathered her hair into a neater bun. Her cheeks were still slightly pink, but her face had been scrubbed clean.

She looked downright fetching. For an insane moment, he thought about what it might feel like to unzip the hoodie and remove the spandex underneath.

Don't even think it.

What was wrong with him?

The now-familiar hint of guilt fluttered in his chest once more. He really couldn't say why he'd offered to stay and help her play mixologist. But the way she'd told him about making sure to take care of her employees had tugged at him. How very intriguing that she was so worried about those she employed. He simply wanted to know more about her and what made her tick. It certainly couldn't hurt to learn more about her before offering a deal. He'd simply be doing research, so to speak.

He was going to have to find a way to come clean to her. Somehow. And soon. Plus, he'd have to reassure her that said employees would be taken care of once Martino Entertainment Enterprises bought her out.

But first things first.

"So, I can't decide if it should be vodka-based or gin,"

she was saying now and pulling out several bottles, which she placed on the bar between them. She then grabbed a cocktail tumbler and a small shot glass.

"The other ingredients are elderberry syrup and orange liqueur. Plus, I think it needs something else. I just can't seem to come up with what."

"Wow. Sounds flavorful." He looked on, intrigued as she poured very small amounts of each into the shot glass, then slid it to him across the bar.

He took a small sip. It was good. Really good. But she was right, it did need something else. Something subtle. "Basil," he said, as contrary as it sounded. But he knew he was right.

To her credit, she didn't argue the suggestion but quirked one elegant eyebrow. "Really? An herb?"

He nodded. "Trust me."

With a shrug, she turned her back and pulled open a drawer. She returned with a basil leaf that she pinched between her thumb and forefinger before dropping it into the glass. He tasted it and his instincts were overwhelmingly confirmed.

"Not to pat myself on the back or anything, but it's right on the money." Without thinking, he handed her the glass. She took it and sipped with zero hesitation. Something about watching her drink from the same glass had his muscles tightening throughout his whole body.

Her eyes widened as she swirled the liquid around in her mouth. "It's fantastic! I would have never guessed."

He took a mock bow.

"But how? What made you think of basil of all things?"

"My *mamma* taught me to cook as soon as I could turn the oven on. It's all about intermingling various flavors. I don't see why a drink would be any different."

"Huh." She eyed him with appreciation clear in her gaze.

He'd be lying if he said he didn't bask in it to a degree; he almost wanted to pound his chest like some kind of Neanderthal.

"You appear to be a man of many talents, Mr. Martino."

"You don't seem to be a slouch in the achievement department either, Miss Taytum."

Her eyes drifted downward, the smile on her face flattened. Somehow the fun, lightheartedness of the moment seemed to dissipate in an instant.

"Was it something I said?" he asked. Though for the life of him he couldn't guess what it might have been. He'd just paid her a compliment, after all.

She seemed hesitant to answer. Finally, she looked up and the expression on her face reminded him of a wounded doe. "Let's just say that not many people feel that. That I'd be considered a success. And their thoughts on the matter will be once more affirmed next week at my sister's wedding."

None of that made any sense from where he was sitting. "How could that be? You're the owner of a very popular nightclub. And you're what? Twenty-eight? Twenty-nine?"

"Twenty-seven."

"So explain."

She shrugged. "It's all relative, isn't it? Whereas I dropped out of college, my father is a partner at a major Boston law firm, my sister is a junior associate at that same firm and my mom is a professor at New England Law."

He was beginning to see where she was coming from. Laney, for all her achievements, didn't seem to fit into the peg of her academically-oriented highbrow family. "Sounds like you just chose a different path. Nothing wrong with that."

"I guess." Her gaze darkened some more. "And now I have to find a way to tell them about my latest failure—my last relationship is a bust and that fact will throw off my sister's wedding. He and I were supposed to be a coupled part of the wedding party."

She gave her head a brief shake, handed him a bottle of water, then grabbed one for herself and took a long swallow. "But you don't need to hear about my family woes. Sorry to have gone on like that."

If she only knew. When it came to family dynamics, she wasn't the only one in the room with baggage. It surprised him how tempted he was to confide in her, to reveal his family's well-guarded secret to this woman he'd met just the night before. He'd never even considered sharing it with anyone before. He didn't even openly discuss the truth with Angelo, even though his brother had dropped hints over the years that he knew the truth as well as anyone. The truth being that Gianni wasn't actually Franco's son. That he was the product of an extramarital affair neither of his parents would acknowledge ever happened for their purely selfish reasons.

Not the time.

"No need to apologize," he said instead, seeking to reassure her. "I'm sorry to hear you're dealing with all that. Your ex left you in a pretty bad spot, didn't he?"

Her lips tightened. "He really did. With no regret whatsoever." She proceeded to call said ex several choice words, which would have impressed Gianni's buddies back at the gym.

"There's no one else who can step in?" he asked, thinking of a few choice words himself for the man who had put her in such an untenable position. He had to have known the rather tenuous relationship she had with her family and hadn't cared that he was exasperating it.

"I've been racking my brain and can't come up with anyone." Her eyes narrowed on him. "Unless…" She gave a nervous chuckle. "I don't suppose you're doing anything on the seventeenth? Just for the weekend?"

Huh. He hadn't seen that coming. The look of hope in her eyes hit him like an arrow to his chest. He knew he should say no. Things between them were complicated enough as it was. The attraction he felt for her was not easy to ignore. Given the reason he'd even met her in the first place, ignoring it was exactly what he should be doing. Not that she had any clue about any of that.

Which was the whole problem in and of itself.

Then again, maybe this would be an opportunity. A chance for them to get better acquainted before the deal making began. Nothing said the buyout had to be hostile. They might even be able to work out terms toward some kind of partnership.

Laney clapped her hand to her cheek, her mouth agape. "Oh, my! I really shouldn't have asked. What an awful position to put you in. I'm sorry. Please forget I even mentioned it."

He stood up from the bar stool and pulled his smartphone out of his back pocket and clicked the first icon. "You know what? According to my calendar, I am completely free that weekend. And it's been a while since I've been to a wedding."

Though she thought she'd been prepared for it, Laney still felt the rush of surprise at Gianni's answer. Deep down, she'd really doubted that he would say yes.

"Wait. Really? Are you really saying you'll come with me?"

He bowed slightly over the bar. "I'd be honored to accompany a lovely lady to her sister's wedding."

The relief she felt, straight to her core, was nearly palpable.

"Just one question. Won't they feel resentful later?" he

asked. "When someone they don't really know is going to be part of this monumental day? Part of the photo albums? And all of that."

Of course, she'd thought of that. But given the circumstances, it was something of a moot point. "That's going to be the case regardless of who steps in at this point. Everyone of import in Emily's life or Wayne's is already a part of the wedding party. And look how nonpermanent Joseph turned out to be." He seemed to mull over what she'd said.

"That would be the ex, I take it."

"You would be correct. Plus, I'd ask you to do one more thing, if you're comfortable." She was biting the corner of her cheek nervously again, but she couldn't seem to help it.

"What's that?"

"Could we pretend that we…you know…are kind of in a serious relationship? That it came fast and heavy and we were both taken by surprise? I know it's rather deceiving—"

He cut her off. "Say no more. I find nothing wrong with a little playacting given what's at stake. I'm glad I can be of help."

She released a deep sigh. "I don't know what to say. Aside from thank you. You have no idea how much this means to me." She held up her hands, palms up, hoping that he really understood where all this was coming from. "I hate that I'd be misleading my family, but I think this really would be best for everyone involved. At least until I can explain to them at a better time."

"I get it." He really seemed to. It sent a feeling of warmth and appreciation through her middle.

"You do?"

"Sure. Sometimes being part of a family is letting them believe what they want to believe—untruths they're vested in despite all evidence."

He sounded very sincere. Like he really did understand. Better than she could have guessed.

"You'd be surprised," he told her, as if reading her thoughts.

She waited for him to continue, didn't push when he failed to elaborate further. He changed the subject. "So, first things first, what's the venue? I'm guessing this is a formal affair. I already own a couple of tuxes."

"Yes. We'll need to get into all of that. Plus, I don't know all that much about you. Well, I know nothing about you, in fact."

"Nor I you. That is indeed a problem. We'll need to set aside some time and get into all of the unknowns. How about dinner tonight?"

"I can do that," she answered, then chuckled with a slow shake of her head.

"What?"

"I just can't believe that we're going through with this. That you've actually agreed to go along with it."

She could only hope they both knew what they were getting into.

CHAPTER FIVE

SHE COULD HAVE stumbled into a worse scenario than the one she was about to embark upon. Somehow, through some very random events, beginning with a tossed drink, Laney found herself about to dine with a gentleman she'd barely just met who was preparing a home-cooked meal for her so they could go over how to act like a committed couple. Gianni told her he wanted to show off his culinary skills, so he'd invited her to his apartment for what he called a *made-from-scratch, authentic-Italian meal*.

The thought of it made her mouth water as she walked up the steps to his brownstone. He lived just outside Boston's North End district, an area most other cities would call Little Italy. Even from this distance, the myriad of scents from the nearby restaurants, bakeries and grocery shops hovered in the air and further spurred her appetite.

Not to mention, the aroma coming from Gianni's apartment was just as enticing. She deeply inhaled it all as she pressed his doorbell. He answered within seconds. He wore a waist apron with a cartoon map of Italy. The T-shirt he had on wasn't exactly tight but fit him well enough to accent all those toned muscles of his chest and upper arms.

How did the man manage to look so gosh darn sexy wearing a cartoon apron for heaven's sake?

"Right on time," he said with that devilish smile she

was starting to find so familiar and charming. "Welcome. Come on in."

He stepped aside, opening the door farther. That mouth-watering scent she'd been enjoying outside intensified, a heady mix of spices, garlic and tomato.

"I happen to be running a bit late," he informed her. "Dinner is still in progress."

"You didn't have to go through the trouble of cooking for me, you know," she told him. "But I definitely appreciate it. It smells delicious in here."

"I enjoy cooking, happy to do it."

She reached inside her oversized bag to pull out the host gift she'd brought. Gianni had told her he had the whole dinner planned and would take care of everything from the wine to the dessert. And she certainly didn't want to second-guess an expert Italian cook about any part of an Italian dinner. So she'd brought the only thing she could think of.

His smile grew as he took it from her. "A basil plant. Perfect." He gently pulled off a couple of the leaves. "I'll put this to use right now on the bruschetta."

She followed him down the hallway, farther into the apartment. He had some kind of hard rock track playing in the background, just loud enough to notice but not enough to recognize the tune.

"Is that what smells so divine?" she asked.

"That, plus the tomato sauce is simmering on the stove top."

He really knew what he was doing. "Can I help in any way?"

"Sure. Have you ever rolled gnocchi?"

She shook her head. "Can't say that I have. My culinary skills are limited to throwing some kind of meat in the oven and pressing start on the rice cooker."

He pointed behind him. "Then go wash up and get prepared for a brief lesson on gnocchi rolling. Washroom's through that door."

She did as instructed, and when she returned, Gianni handed her an apron of her own. A full-length one for her. "Don't want you staining that dress," he told her. "That would be a shame." His eyes traveled down the length of her body as he said it and she felt heat spread from her middle clear up to her face. It had nothing to do with the steam coming from the various pots on the stove.

Without responding to his comment, she pulled the apron over her head and tied the straps behind her back at the waist. She took her time in order to try to regain some of her composure after the effect of his words and gaze. She stepped over to the counter. "What can I do to help?"

Several thin rows of some kind of dough sat on the counter, fluffy white flour was sprinkled along the entire surface. Gianni took a large knife and deftly sliced each row into small pieces. He then grabbed a small wooden board with a handle and ridges on one side. "Here," he gently took her by the shoulders as he handed her the board. "Take a piece of the dough, and just sort of roll it down the board. But stop before the dough completely rolls on itself. You need a small gap in the middle."

She started to do as instructed, trying to focus fully on the task at hand. It wasn't easy with him standing so close. He reached inside the drawer for another board to use himself. Her first roll didn't turn out so great. Why was it so hard to concentrate on a simple task merely because he was near?

"You look confused," he said with an amused smile.

"Well, not to sound too uninformed, as I did admit my limited culinary talents earlier after all, but this seems like a lot of work. Can't we just cook the dough as these small pieces?"

He slowly shook his head. "I can't believe what I'm hearing. You need these ridges and the small opening in the middle so that the sauce can get into each nook."

She supposed that made sense. But understanding the concept wasn't exactly helping her with the process. All her pieces looked like mangled small pebbles.

Gianni must have taken pity on her. "Here, let me show you."

He stepped behind her and she lost her breath for a moment. Whatever aftershave he was wearing reminded her of nighttime walks along the beach. The heat from his body behind her seeped through her clothes to her skin. She could feel his warm breath on the back of her neck. Then he took her right hand in his own and proceeded to demonstrate exactly how to roll the small piece of dough down the board in one quick motion.

"See, easy as pie," he said against her cheek. "You think you've got the hang of it?"

Think? Who could think? As if Laney could even register anything but the feel of him against her back.

She nodded lamely and allowed him to continue guiding her.

"You're a natural," he declared.

A shudder ran through her as heat flamed over her skin. His breath was hot on her cheek. It would be so easy to turn her head back just enough to bring her lips closer to his. Would he kiss her? Or would he wait for her to make the first move? Heaven help her, she very likely would. Several beats passed with neither one moving so much as a muscle. The very air around them seemed to grow thick. Her pulse pounded in her ears and she couldn't seem to make her mouth work.

This was wrong. They barely knew each other. She'd just broken up with her boyfriend.

She had to pump the brakes.

As if sensing her thoughts, Gianni released a sigh behind her and it was enough to break the heated moment. Finally, he stepped back. Part of her felt relief. And another much more bothersome part of her felt sheer, stark disappointment.

One thing was certain. When Gianni Martino accompanied her to the wedding as her newest fling, she was going to have absolutely zero trouble pretending to be attracted to him.

He didn't even want to pretend anymore. Not to himself, anyway. He absolutely couldn't deny just how much he was attracted to this woman. Which really was rather inconvenient.

For a moment back there, before he'd regained his senses, he'd come perilously close to reaching for her, then pulling her into his arms. From there, heaven only knew what might have happened. He imagined lifting her up, sitting her on the counter, then pulling her up against him as he finally indulged in the kiss he'd so often fantasized about.

Luckily, he'd somehow managed to resist.

The growing attraction between them was only going to further muddy an already rather complicated situation. He had nobody but himself to blame. Not that there was much he could do about it now. He couldn't very well renege on his commitment to attend her sister's wedding.

He should have never agreed to that. She'd just looked so forlorn and so down when she'd spoken about her family and all the ways she felt out of place within her own clan.

It had all tugged at his heart. They had more in common than she'd ever guess. It still felt a bit unsettling, how close he'd come to telling her about his own situation, as the unwanted and unplanned son of a father who only claimed him to save face. So that he could pretend his wife had never cheated.

Laney didn't need to know any of that about him or his family. What had made him come so close to telling her? He had to wonder if agreeing to go with her wasn't going to end up being a colossal mistake.

Speaking of mistakes—what had he been thinking, stepping behind her and holding her that way? The electricity between them right now practically crackled in the air.

"Am I doing it right? They look better, don't they?" she asked next to him now, finally breaking the loaded moment. She held up the latest gnocchi she'd just rolled.

He pretended to examine it closely. "It's a work of art. My *mamma* would be impressed."

"Ha! Somehow I doubt that."

But chances were she'd never even meet his *mamma*. He was only meeting her family due to a fluky set of circumstances neither one of them could have guessed before they'd laid eyes on each other.

He would have to tell her the truth as soon as their playacting was over. Right after the wedding. He would have to confess that it hadn't been mere happenstance that had brought him into her club that night.

Her reaction was probably going to be far from pleasant. But he would have to cross that bridge when he came to it. By then, he'd be able to prove himself to be someone she could trust, and she'd hopefully see that his heart had been in the right place even if he couldn't tell her.

And if she didn't?

Well, he wasn't going to allow himself to entertain that unpleasant possibility just yet. And he certainly wasn't going to let it spoil what was so far turning out to be a thoroughly enjoyable evening.

After all, what exactly was he supposed to tell her? That he also happened to be the black sheep of the family? But his similar status came about for an entirely different reason. A reason everyone in his orbit had denied and ignored his whole life. He'd only discovered said reason himself thanks to an aging uncle with loose lips when he'd visited Italy as a preteen.

He shook off the useless thoughts and made himself focus on the present. Laney stood staring at him, as if she'd noticed he'd drifted somewhere far away. He hadn't even noticed all the gnocchi was rolled already.

He gently took her by the shoulders and led her to one of the bar stools at the counter. "Enough work on your part. I'm dangerously close to being a bad host here. Have a seat while I finish up." He grabbed the bottle chilling in the ice bucket and poured her a glass of wine.

"If you're sure."

"Absolutely." He pointed to her midsection. "Take off that apron and assume honored-guest mode starting this instant."

She laughed and gave him a mock salute. "As you command, sir."

Within minutes, he had them both plated with the hot steaming entrée, bowls of crispy salad and perfectly toasted garlic bread. He'd done good, if he did say so himself. Laney looked impressed. Her next words confirmed it.

"My mouth is watering. You have outdone my wildest expectations."

He couldn't begin to deny the surge of pleasure at her compliment. It grew stronger when she took a bit of the food and groaned in pleasure. Every ounce of will he pos-

sessed needed to be summoned in order to avoid responding to that groan.

"Mmm. This is divine. Overwhelmingly good. Seriously, I would have been happy with a deli sandwich and
some chips."

"You wound me with your low expectations of my talents."

She tilted her head and raised her wine goblet. "You're
right. I admit to underestimating you. My deepest apolo-
gies."

Gianni tapped his glass to hers. "Apology accepted. So,
tell me, what made you open up a dance club in Boston?
Not a very typical career choice."

She chewed some more and swallowed. "It wasn't my
first choice."

"No?"

Shaking her head, she set her fork down. "I left school
to become a professional dancer."

She was certainly full of surprises. "You did?"

"Yep. Didn't exactly work out."

Gianni felt himself leaning closer to her over the table.
"How so?"

"I tried out and auditioned for numerous companies
and acts. Not a one bit." She gave a wistful shrug before
continuing. "Just didn't have what it took, I kept being
told."

He wanted desperately to go to her, take her in his arms
and reassure her that she was more than enough as far as
he could see. But he couldn't allow himself to do that. Besides, right now it sounded like a simple ear to listen was
all she might need.

"So I came back to Boston with my tail tucked between
my legs. After having let everyone down with my decision
to *throw away* my future, as my mother and father put it."

"But you didn't go back to school."

She took another sip of her wine. "It's not for me. I'm not exactly the studious type. And I'm definitely not the type to sit in an office cubicle making phone calls or crunching numbers."

"So what happened?"

"As luck would have it, my reclusive grandfather left us a small sum of an inheritance. My sister invested her share in the market. And I invested mine in a different direction than the one I'd originally set for myself."

He was fascinated by her. Despite consistent disappointment, she'd somehow managed to find an alternate dream to pursue, then made it come true. "That's remarkable. Consider me impressed."

Gentle laughter escaped her lips. "Impressed? Did you hear the part about my numerous rejections as a professional dancer?"

"Yes. I also heard the much more important part."

Her gaze drifted downward before she cleared her throat, then changed the subject. "So what about you? Tell me about what you do."

His story wasn't nearly as interesting, but he began to tell her. "I work for an entertainment company. We own and run everything from gaming centers to small casinos, and a few gyms."

She raised an elegant eyebrow. "That sounds like quite an empire. What's your role?"

"I'm a VP in the office of the CEO. Who happens to be my father. He's a self-made businessman who started out small with a few gaming halls, which then led to small casinos and other entertainment venues. More recently, we've expanded into the fitness and gym arenas after I discovered kickboxing."

To his surprise, Laney seemed genuinely interested in

the kickboxing piece. He explained his training routine and the various positions, both offensive and defensive. Before he knew it, they were halfway through with dinner.

There was no more delaying the inevitable. Laney apparently came to the same conclusion based on her next comment. "So I suppose we should start to talk about your newly acquired status as my significant other. And exactly what scenario we're going to present to the outside world next week."

She was right of course. But he couldn't help the small twinge of disappointment at the clear acknowledgment that this wasn't any kind of real date.

"I suppose you're right."

She turned in the stool to fully face him, all business suddenly. "We may as well start with the basics. How did we meet? I say we stick as close to the truth as possible."

The sincerity in her tone made it clear just how serious she was about all this going smoothly. How much it meant to her that her family believe she'd found a real and solid relationship after her last one had crumbled.

He could only hope he wouldn't let her down.

CHAPTER SIX

Two weeks later

HERE IT WAS—their first big test. Emily's wedding weekend. And it all started with a merry bash the night before the big day aboard a yacht for a sunset sail. The entire wedding party and a few distinguished guests were being treated to a three-hour cruise along Boston harbor. Gianni had picked her up so that they could drive in together. Laney tried to swallow down the queasy feeling in her throat as Gianni pulled his late-model sports car into the underground parking lot of the hotel that was to house the festivities for the next couple of days.

Between all the last-minute wedding details and her sister's and parents' work schedules, they'd never actually met Gianni. So tonight was going to be all or nothing as far as impressions went. They'd reacted just as she'd expected when she told them about Joseph's sudden rejection. Hence, she'd spared Gianni no amount of praise and compliments as she described him to her family, somewhat softening the blow from the announcement of her breakup.

She glanced at him now as he killed the ignition and gathered his wallet from the dashboard. He was everything a girl would want to bring home to the folks. Handsome, successful, personality in spades. And he could cook! A soft flush of heat warmed her cheeks as she thought about that night two weeks ago in his apartment when he'd stood up so close to her, the scent of him tempting all her senses. The same scent which filled the car right now. That night had been the last time they'd been physically together to try to hash out the plan. Only a handful of phone calls had taken place between them since. Their work schedules just hadn't seemed to mesh.

A curtain of panic dropped over her. Sweet heavens. What if they hadn't thought of and prepared for all the ways this harebrained plan could go, oh, so wrong.

"You ready for this, sweetheart?" he asked.

Laney pressed her hand to her middle to quell the sudden nervous nausea. "Not sure that's the right question."

"No?"

"A better question might be if my family is ready and willing to accept what we're about to try to pull off."

He gave her a warm smile that she was sure was meant to comfort. "Hmm. How about we just look at it as more like simply attending a party together?"

As if she could ignore the true reality of what tonight and tomorrow were really about. "Sure. Let's go with that."

He winked at her. "That's the spirit."

At least one of them had their wits about them. Though Gianni had so much less to lose if everything went south.

Without giving her any warning, he gently took her hand in his and leaned toward her in the passenger seat. "Hey, relax. Everything will run smoothly. We'll be convincing as the budding, infatuated couple we're meant to play."

A voice in her head taunted that one of them would be playacting just a bit more than the other. But that was neither here nor there. Right now, they had a party cruise to get ready for.

"Right. Let's get up to the room, then. I could use time to freshen up a bit and change into my dress."

"You got it."

Before she could so much as unbuckle her seat belt, he was outside her door and opening it for her, then he helped her out and even grabbed her two carry bags.

"I'll let you grab the garment bag with the dress," he said, shifting the seat to give her access to where it hung. "Don't want to be responsible for any wrinkles."

Beyond thoughtful and considerate. Laney had to bite back her longing. Why couldn't this be her reality? Why couldn't Gianni have been the man she'd spent the last two years with in a committed and rewarding relationship?

She could guess at the answer. She wasn't the type to really attract a man like him. Not beyond a surface chemistry. She'd found that out the hard way during her days in New York, then Los Angeles. And again, more recently with Joseph. She had more than her fair share of feeling unwanted for one lifetime.

Gianni was well rounded, smart, successful. And he even had something of an edge. He'd told her that night at dinner that his fitness routine was mainly kickboxing. Mostly with a bag out of the ring. Though he admitted to occasionally sparring with a partner *inside the ropes*, as he explained it. He even went so much as to compete in events sporadically.

Not exactly a noncontact sport. No, he was unlike her in every way, the polar opposite of boring.

She had to snap out of it. This was no time to wallow in self-pity. She was supposed to be half of a newly minted, infatuated couple. She had to look and act the part.

By the time they made it to the garage elevator, she'd managed to convince herself that she could do it without arousing any suspicion. Yes, they really could pull this off, her and Gianni. She just had to relax.

Besides, everyone would be much too focused on the bride and groom to take much notice of her and her new boyfriend. Including the bride and groom themselves.

She was fine. She just had to breathe. It was simply a matter of staying calm, she told herself.

Until she realized she was still clutching Gianni's hand in a viselike grip since he'd helped her out of the car several moments ago.

To his credit, he wasn't attempting to pull it away. Still, they weren't in the company of the others just yet. She had to save such images for when they'd be witnessed. Hesitantly, she pulled her hand away and pressed the button for the ground floor of the hotel.

Turning to Gianni, she cleared her throat. There was one small piece of the puzzle she hadn't wanted to get into, had procrastinated bringing it up until this very moment, in fact. "There's also something else you might want to be prepared for. About my parents."

He simply lifted a dark eyebrow.

"They might be a bit…" She faltered, searching for just the right words. She'd known this was going to be hard, and she hadn't been mistaken. "Let's just say, they're not the warmest, most affable people upon first meeting someone. I'm sorry, I should have mentioned that before."

"Don't worry, *cara*," he told her with another devastating smile. And she was just going to have to ignore the endearment or she might turn into a puddle on the floor. "I think I can handle them."

Laney only wished she could say the same.

She was downright terrified. Gianni wanted badly to simply pull her into his arms and rub out some of the tension stiffening her shoulders.

As far as her parents, Laney seemed to think she was announcing some surprising bit of information. Truth was, he'd long ago surmised her parents as much the way she'd just described. Everything she'd said about them so far gave every indication that they were probably distant and unapproachable.

So unlike Laney herself.

But like he'd just reassured her, he was certain he could hold his own with two staunch and serious professionals who would no doubt decide to dislike him on sight.

Not that it would be easy. Coming from a loud and boisterous family of Italian heritage, he was used to being the recipient of big bear hugs and physical displays of affection and love from everyone—from toddlers to the elderly to frail *zias* and *nonnas* making their feelings well-known whether anyone was actually listening or not.

Gianni stepped aside once they got to the ground floor and Laney began their check-in as part of the wedding party. He found himself watching her as he so often did. Even dressed in leggings and an oversized T-shirt, she managed to appear graceful, elegant. Full of class.

Not exactly how he'd describe himself.

No. He had no illusions about any of it. For all intents and purposes, he was about to enter an alien and unfamiliar world. One where he'd be suppressing a good portion of his personality. While most of these people probably spent their off time in a book or on the golf course, his hobby of choice involved throwing punches in a boxing ring.

A crowd such as the one attending this wedding was sure to look down on such an unrefined, brutal activity. Not many people understood that it was a sport just like any other. One that focused on athleticism and discipline no less than other physical pursuits. He'd be willing to wager that he didn't get bruised and cut up any more than most other non-pro athletes. But he wasn't here to argue about the merits of his workouts. He was simply here to support Laney and in the process gain some of her trust.

The thought took him aback a bit. When he phrased it that way, it sounded conniving and wrong. But that wasn't his intention, to deceive her in any way. He just wanted them to be on better terms when he finally approached her with his family's offer to buy out her building and business.

"We're all set," she said, approaching him now and holding out a key card for the room.

"Thanks."

"Room 709. Supposed to be a great view of the harbor."

He had no doubt it would, along with everything else the Boston Harbor Hotel had to offer. Tourists and businesspeople from all over the world used this luxury hotel as their destination point when traveling to the area. Hardly a surprise that Laney's sister would be holding her wedding here.

Gianni wasn't exactly in the pauper category. In fact, his family was one of great wealth. His father owned gaming halls, fitness centers and casinos all over the world. But Papà had come from nothing—born in a poor remote village in the northern hills of Italy—and he'd fought and scrambled for all the material wealth he possessed. It was very obvious that Laney came from good old-fashioned American money. An entirely different category.

They were in their suite within a couple of minutes, the elevator ride spent mostly in silence. Gianni wracked his brain to come up with something to say that might lessen the tension that was emanating off her like a steady hum.

Then her gaze fell on the furniture in the room and he could practically feel her discomfort skyrocket. Rather than the full-sized couch they'd both assumed would be part of their furnishings—the couch Gianni had planned on sleeping on overnight—the master area of the suite consisted of two small love seats with a center wooden coffee table. He couldn't even help the images that sprung into his mind. The two of them together in the only bed, tangled up in the sheets and in each other. He shook his head to clear it.

"It's okay, Laney. I can sleep on one of those sofas."

She rolled her eyes. "You'd have to sleep sitting up."

"So be it."

"I wouldn't be able to sleep myself, knowing you were out here so uncomfortable."

"Then I'll just drive home if I have to."

She threw her hands up. "That's not any better. How am I supposed to feel knowing you were driving in the middle of the night after partying on board a boat?"

She really was wrapping herself up in figurative knots here. "Then I'll stay. I've slept in worse."

She shook her head. "I hardly think so."

He laughed, trying to reassure her. "You'd be surprised. Go take your shower. It might help relax you a bit."

"I doubt that," she argued.

It was worth a shot.

"Come on, Gianni," she continued. "We can't exactly pretend this isn't a very awkward set of circumstances."

He responded with a shrug. "It doesn't have to be."

As she chewed her bottom lip, it was clear she wasn't exactly convinced of his comment. She glanced at the digital clock hung on the wall by the large flat-screen television. "Well, I guess we'll have to figure it out at some point. The cruise takes off in a couple of hours. I'm going to take my shower. I won't be long."

"Take your time."

When he heard the water come on a few seconds later, Gianni couldn't stop where his mind went. The images of Laney in the stall, steam billowing around her bare skin as she lathered soap all over herself.

Only a slim door separated them. What would happen if he knocked on that door? Asked her exactly what she thought about the notion of him coming in, joining her?

Whoa. Steady there, fella.

He blinked hard and forced the pictures away. He really didn't need the tempting image of her undressed and in the shower. Looked like he wasn't going to need much hot water when it was his turn to shower.

In the meantime, he had to get out of the suite and clear his mind. Some fishy harbor air would do just the trick.

CHAPTER SEVEN

GIANNI HAD BEEN RIGHT. The shower did make her feel loads better. Laney secured the belt of the complimentary terry cloth robe at her waist and wrapped a thick Turkish towel around her wet hair.

When she returned to the suite to tell him the bathroom was all his, he was nowhere to be found. A split second of panic rushed through her center at the thought that he might have changed his mind about the whole thing and just abandoned her. But then she noticed his bags were still sitting on the floor by the coffee table. The rush of relief had her actually chuckling out loud. She should have known better.

Everything she'd witnessed about the man so far had shown him to be honorable and true to his word. There was a lot there to admire. Which was the entire problem, wasn't it?

Gianni was assuming her nerves and anxiety could all be attributed to the show they were about to perform for her family. He was only partly right. Another very large piece of the puzzle as far as her nervousness went was the way she reacted to the man whenever they were together. Never before had she felt so drawn to another person. And it was more than just physical.

But this was no time to even consider or even acknowledge any kind of romantic feelings. She still felt emotionally bruised and battered from being dumped so unceremoniously by the man she was convinced would be proposing on the trip they'd been about to embark on. Hah! She couldn't have been more wrong.

Oh, and there was also the whole fact that Gianni hadn't shown even the slightest indication that he was feeling at all the same way toward her. Aside from a few charmingly quaint compliments.

No, she couldn't risk being so ridiculously incorrect yet again. Her pride wouldn't be able to take it. Nor would her heart.

A knock on the door pulled her out of her musings. Had Gianni forgotten his key? When she peeped through the eyehole, a different familiar face greeted her.

Mabel, her cousin.

A smile instantly formed on Laney's face. Mabel was always fun and pleasant company. And she was a sweetheart. Though three years younger, Mabel always seemed so wise and enlightened. Laney could really use some of that right now.

She opened the door without hesitation.

"Hey, coz!" Mabel threw her arms around her shoulders and Laney enthusiastically returned the hug.

"I'm so glad to see you!" They both spoke over each other, saying the same thing.

"How was the trip up from Vermont?" Mable was doing graduate work at UVM in a very demanding biology program. Which meant Laney didn't get to see her favorite Taytum nearly often enough.

"I came up yesterday to give myself an extra day. You know how much I love shopping in Boston."

"Find any good bargains?"

Mabel nodded with enthusiasm. "You know it!" She

took Laney by the hand and led her to one of the loveseats. "Never mind that. Are you alone?"

Laney nodded. "For now. My date appears to have stepped out."

"Good," Mabel decreed. "You and I need to have a chat."

Uh-oh, Laney could just imagine what this was about. And she wasn't sure if she was quite prepared for it just yet. Mabel was no doubt about to serve up a third-degree-level questioning about the new mystery man Laney was bringing to a monumental family event. She had to find a way to stall. Pointing to her head and robe, she began to argue. "I should really get dressed first."

Mabel held firm, by literally not releasing Laney's hand. "You can do that later. Right now, it's time for you to spill."

Laney started to argue, then stopped short. Perhaps talking to Mabel for a few minutes was just what the doctor ordered. Who better for a practice run than the dear and kindhearted cousin she'd always felt so affectionate toward? In fact, under any other circumstances, she'd confide fully in the other woman. But she just couldn't risk the very real possibility that Mabel would let something slip to the wrong person. She was definitely a talker.

"Tell me all about the new man in your life," Mabel said. "And I can't believe what that lowlife Joseph pulled."

Laney waited for the hurt and outrage that she expected to wash over her when the topic of Joseph came up.

Surprisingly, it simply wasn't there.

What did that mean, that she was over him so quickly? All she felt was a low-level anger at having been treated with such disregard.

"I'd rather not talk about Joseph. Or so much as think about him," she said, realizing perhaps for the first time just how true those words were.

Mabel nodded. "Fine by me. Emily told me you were with someone new. But she didn't know much about him."

Laney made sure not to rush. She had to tread carefully and avoid saying anything that might trip her up later. Or Gianni, for that matter. She had to stick to the thought-out script they'd agreed on.

"He's great, May. I can't wait for you to meet him."

Mabel's grin grew wider. "Me too! Where is he?"

"He must have stepped out for a bit."

"Then tell me all about him. What can I expect?"

"He's like no one I've ever met." Laney felt a warmth spread through her chest as she said the words.

For it was the absolute truth.

When Gianni returned to the suite about twenty minutes later, he didn't need to open the door to know that Laney wasn't alone. The distinct sound of two different female voices floated through the wooden doorway. Though he had his room key, he knocked in order to announce his arrival.

The door opened within seconds. Laney stood across the threshold in a white fluffy robe that looked about three sizes too big and an even fluffier towel wrapped around her head.

She looked downright adorable.

His hands itched to unwrap the towel and let her hair fall over her shoulders, then to run his fingers through the wet strands. He wanted so badly to remove the robe and discover exactly what lay beneath the fabric. So much so, he forgot there was someone else there with her. He took a deep breath to dislodge the wayward thoughts. Then he caught sight of a petite blonde with wispy hair and bright hazel eyes sitting on the sofa. She gave him a small wave and a big smile. The eye color told him she had to be a relative.

"Hey there," he said to Laney, not sure what to do. Should he give her a kiss or something? Hadn't they talked about this very thing? If so, for the life of him, he couldn't remember. In his defense, he hadn't been expecting his first introduction to be a surprise visitor to the suite.

"Just went out for some fresh air," he told Laney, trying to ask her the question silently with his eyes.

It didn't work. Laney stepped aside to let him in. "Did you forget your key?"

"No. Sounded like you weren't alone and I didn't want to intrude."

Both eyebrows lifted and she gave him a dazzling smile, as if he'd passed some sort of test. "See," Laney threw over her shoulder at the other woman. "What did I tell you? He's so considerate." She gave him a small wink. "Come meet my cousin."

The blonde immediately stood and strode to where they both stood.

"Gianni, this is Mabel. Mabel, meet Gianni," Laney said as she shut the door.

Gianni extended his hand, but it was bypassed as the cousin reached with both arms to grip him in a tight hug. So this was clearly one of the few who didn't fit the mold. She was about the furthest thing from standoffish as he could think of.

"It's so nice to meet you," she was saying under his chin. "We're so glad you're here with Laney."

Gianni waited to speak until she let go. To his amusement, it took several beats.

"Thank you. I'm very glad to be here."

To his surprise, Laney took his hand in hers. He had to work hard at not reacting to her unexpected touch. How silly of him to be so affected when he knew full well the gesture was purely for show in front of her cousin.

"Mabel's working on her doctorate in animal science. She's studying to be a veterinarian, specializing in marine animals," Laney explained.

So this one was an academic, as well.

"Keeps her very busy," Laney added. "I haven't seen her in months."

"Then I should leave you two to your visit."

"Oh, no," Mabel protested. "I'm the one who should leave. I need to get ready in any case." She gestured toward Laney with a laugh. "And you do too!"

Without giving himself a chance to think, Gianni pulled Laney up against him, tight to his side. "I think she looks adorable."

He felt her shock as she stiffened next to him. She recovered quickly. She stepped fully into his embrace, wrapped his arms around her waist with her back up against his front. "Oh, he's such a charmer, isn't he?"

Mabel stood grinning at them both. Looked like they were pretty convincing. "I'd say."

"It's easy to be charming with you, *cara mia*," he told her, at the risk of laying it on a bit thick. Throwing the Italian in there might have been a bit much. But it was hard to deny that he was enjoying this—the affectionate banter between the two of them...the feel of Laney in his arms.

If only they didn't have an audience. Which was a silly thought. After all, that was the entire point, wasn't it?

Mabel looked ready to swoon at the sight they made.

He leaned closer to give her a small peck on the cheek. Laney chose that very moment to tilt her head up and back to look at him. They somehow met in the middle. He didn't allow himself to think. He meant to give her a small peck, just to complete the charade, but his mouth seemed to have different intentions. Before he knew what was happening, his lips were on hers. He couldn't even tell which one of them started it.

She tasted exactly as he'd imagined she would. Like the sweetest fruit at its most ripe. Like cream and honey and nectar all in one. He breathed in her scent as he tasted her. A small moan sounded from her mouth into his.

It was over all too soon.

Laney pulled away with a jolt, no doubt remembering there was another individual in the room with them. A fact he'd so easily forgotten.

Mabel had her hands clasped to her chest, studying them with a clearly heartfelt smile. She actually said, "Aw. How sweet." As if she'd just watched a scene from a holiday movie on one of those seasonal channels.

Somehow, when he wasn't looking, he'd found himself playing leading man.

She should have found a way to stop the kiss. Or she should have managed somehow to avoid it altogether for it had left her shaken to the core. If Gianni had been moved by it in any way, there was no sign of it in his expression or his manner. And why should there be? He'd done it simply for show. He'd behaved exactly as she'd asked him to around her family members. She was the one being silly.

Someone in the room cleared their throat. She couldn't be sure, but it might have even been her. Right. They weren't alone. This was just pretend. The kiss that had so shaken her was merely a ruse, a playact. Nothing more. So she'd do well to ignore the quaking sensation in her middle.

"I guess I'll see you both aboard the boat, then," Mabel said as she started walking toward the door. "So nice to have finally met you, Gianni."

"Likewise," he answered, his voice steady and cheery. Not shaky at all, unlike her. She was right. He hadn't been affected by the kiss in the least. Had probably already forgotten about it. What a fool she could be when it came to men in general and to Gianni in particular. How many times could she leave her heart unguarded only to have it bruised?

She didn't bring herself to glance at him as she turned toward the bedroom once Mabel had left. "I guess I'll finally go get dressed. Be out soon."

"I'll be here."

By the time she came out dressed and ready twenty minutes later, she'd managed to steady herself and had only thought about his lips on hers about a dozen more times. Progress. Her dress of choice for the occasion was a silk wrap in a deep navy blue. A color that always seemed to complement her despite her dark coloring and olive skin tone. If she were being fanciful, she could swear Gianni did a bit of a double take when she emerged fully dressed and heeled. The idea had her nearly giddy and she made sure to squash it with haste.

For his part, Gianni had changed into a fresh collared shirt and beige khakis. He somehow seemed to make the casual outfit look stylish and elegant. He could have been a picture out of a magazine cologne ad spread. The man certainly cleaned up well. As if he weren't attractive enough in simple jeans and a T-shirt. Or even a waist apron.

"Ready to go?" he asked.

"As ready as I'll ever be."

They were outside and walking toward the harbor marina within minutes. The afternoon was mild and warm, sunlight filtering through thick white clouds. One had to hand it to Emily. She somehow managed to book a day in which the weather couldn't have been more ideally suited for a city cruise.

Laney exhaled a deep breath once they approached the vessel's boarding ramp. The happy notes of party music sounded in the air. The DJ had started with a bouncy new pop song that featured an accompanying dance. Laney heard the sound of a cork popping. "I guess this is it. The moment we've been prepping for. Ready to meet my people?"

"Ready and able, Captain." He gestured toward the ramp.

A crew member greeted them at the entry way and asked for their names, which she then crossed off a list.

"Go right on up," she instructed, her smile bright and cheery. "You're not late but the party is well underway."

"That's not a bad way to sum up my life in general," Laney found herself saying as they made their way toward the hub.

"What's that?"

"I'm not often late but somehow the party has always started without me," she explained with a small chuckle. But Gianni wasn't smiling when she glanced over at him.

"Do you really see yourself that way?"

She'd meant it as a small joke. Though now that he was asking, she realized how true the statement was.

She gave a small shrug as she answered him. "I guess I do. I always feel like those around me have moved on as I'm perpetually trying to catch up." It could certainly be said about her last relationship, in fact. "I seem to be the square peg in the round hole all too often."

He stopped in his tracks. "I haven't known you that long, but I don't see you that way at all."

"You don't?"

"No. Not in the least."

She was afraid to ask the next question but mustered the courage to do so. "Then how do you see me?"

Something shifted behind his eyes. Something she didn't want to analyze too deeply. "You're bright. You're successful. Fun to be around. As far as catching up to others, have you ever considered that you might just be going in a different direction?"

"Not really."

He inhaled a quick breath. "You chose a different path than the family of attorneys you come from. That says nothing about your accomplishments or success. It merely says you decided to pursue your own goals."

"Guess I hadn't thought of it that way."

"Maybe you should start," he said, then slowly started walking again. Laney didn't move with him right away. Instead, she let the full impact of his words really settle in. Not just the last part, though the statement about her going in a different direction was certainly something to think about. She'd always been the square peg in her family.

But everything he had said before that echoed through her head. He thought she was bright. And fun. Which implied he liked being with her. That he actually enjoyed her company. Given the way Joseph had dumped her a couple weeks ago, the thought that this much more dynamic and alluring man felt that way made for a heady feeling. She'd be lying if she didn't say she felt flattered and…well, validated.

Suddenly, the next forty-eight hours didn't seem so daunting. Not with Gianni by her side. She'd be able to get through this. His words had somehow given her a shot of confidence—something she hadn't felt in a while.

Gianni seemed to finally realize she hadn't kept step with him. He turned and gave her a questioning look. "Coming?"

"I just need a minute."

"Still nervous?"

She wasn't really. Thanks to him. "I just want to gather my thoughts before we venture into the crowd."

"That's fair."

She strolled over to the rail, the sounds of the party still echoing through the air around them. Gianni joined her, and for several moments they remained silent, simply taking in the view of the Boston skyline from the water.

"Also, I just wanted to thank you," Laney eventually said.

"For coming with you? Already told you. I'm just here to enjoy a party with a beautiful woman."

He was doing so much more than that. She shuddered to think what the day ahead of her might have looked like if she'd had to endure it solo. All the questions about why she was there alone. Of course, now there were bound to be questions about the new man she was with. But those would be so much easier to answer with someone by her side.

Even if it was all a lie.

CHAPTER EIGHT

"YOUR DAD KEEPS staring at me."

Gianni took a sip from his frosty bottle of beer and made sure to keep his polite smile in place. The introductions so far had been short and sweet, with Laney's parents assuring him they'd make time later for a longer chat after the wedding tomorrow, when there would be less distractions. Or maybe *threatening* would be a better word to use in this context.

"Don't sweat it," Laney said, swirling her glass of Chardonnay absentmindedly as they sat at one of the side tables. "He's just trying to measure you up a bit."

He had to chuckle at that. "And I'm not supposed to sweat it that he's doing so?"

The soiree was fully underway now. They were past the harbor waters and the city skyline was well off in the distance. Emily had gone all out and chartered a tri-deck luxury yacht with tinted glass walls and a plush luxurious interior big enough to house a dance floor, ample number of tables for guests, and comfy sofas and upholstered chairs for the close to three-hundred guests in attendance. True to form, Emily had succeeded in securing the perfect venue for her first wedding event.

Laney shrugged before answering Gianni's question. "It's not like it really matters, does it? Eventually, we'll have to tell them that you're not in my life anymore."

It was silly of him to feel any kind of offense to what she said, but he did, nonetheless. Funny, up until she'd spoken the words, he hadn't realized just how much he did want to remain a part of her life, in some shape or form. Which might be hard if she wasn't keen on selling her business.

She was right. This was not the time for him to worry about how the business deal might play out or what type of friendship the future might have in store for them. Though, the way she looked in the silky sky blue wrap dress she wore, friendship wasn't exactly the first thing that came to mind. His mouth had gone dry when she'd first walked out of the bedroom wearing it. His skin still itched with the desire to run his fingers over the silky material. If he allowed himself, he could so easily imagine helping her out of it and then carrying her away behind a closed door.

Before he could reprimand himself for those thoughts, a small child darted out from behind a table and practically jumped onto Laney's lap. "Hi, Aun' Wainey."

Laney immediately cuddled the toddler closer to her chest and gave her a peck on the cheek. "Well, hello, pumpkin. I was wondering where you were."

Pumpkin pulled her thumb out of her mouth and pointed at him. "Who dat?"

"This is my very good friend. His name is Gianni."

"Jownee?"

He had to laugh at the pronunciation. "And what might your name be?" he asked.

"I'm Lisbeth."

"Nice to meet you, Lisbeth."

Laney tousled the girl's hair. "Lisbeth is my little cousin. Mabel's niece."

"Yeah? I have a niece," he said, for the benefit of them both, but Lisbeth had already lost interest in them. She left Laney's lap and scampered off without so much as a glance back.

"She's cute as a button," he told Laney when the child had skipped off toward the dance floor. A tall man with blond hair scooped her up in his arms and twirled her around to the music.

"That she is," Laney answered. "With the attention span of the three-year-old toddler that she is. How old is your niece?"

"Not much older. She just turned four. Her brother is younger by about two years."

"You're an uncle, times two?"

"I am indeed. I make sure to spoil them rotten."

She laughed and took a sip of her wine. "Oh, their parents must love that."

"It's no less than what my brother deserves, the way he annoyed me when we were kids. I finally get some payback."

"Revenge by spoiling his kids. Diabolical."

"Yep. And just as they're about to throw the inevitable tantrum, I simply hand them back to Mom and Dad and make my escape."

She held her wine glass up and tipped it toward him. "There's one thing you might not have thought of in all of this."

"What's that?"

"What happens when your brother and his spouse get their own chance at revenge? Like once you have kids of your own?"

Her question was an innocent enough one. But it wasn't one worth entertaining. He'd decided long ago he wasn't the type to play husband or daddy. He had no intention of having a family of his own. Falling in love and having kids weren't for him. Love could make a man swallow his pride so hard that he could pretend the world wasn't laughing at him when it clearly was. Just look at his own pop.

"That's not going to happen," he answered, signaling the server for another beer. "I don't plan on having kids of my own. A family man, I'm not."

She narrowed her eyes on him. "Oh? Why is that?"

He shrugged. "Just not for me."

"That sounds like a vague way to tell me you don't want to really discuss the subject."

A petite brunette waitress stopped by the table with his drink. "There's really nothing to discuss."

"Consider the matter dropped. It's really none of my business."

The conversation was starting to get too deep, and a heavy mood had suddenly settled in the air between them. Gianni didn't like it. Coupled with the repeated speculative looks Laney's father kept sending him, it was all making him edgy and uncomfortable. He needed to step away from this conversation and from the table. He needed a physical outlet.

He stood and extended his hand to her. "Dance with me."

Laney didn't hesitate. Setting her wineglass down on the table, she stood and took his hand. "About time, Mr. Martino. I thought you'd never ask."

Huh. "Why didn't you just ask me yourself?"

She gave a small shrug of her shoulder. "I didn't see you dancing at all that night at the club. I thought maybe you were one of those men who lack rhythm or skill." A hint of a smile tugged at the corner of her mouth. She was teasing him.

"You insult me. I can manage a few dance steps." He pulled her gently to the dance floor. "As you are about to find out."

They moved well together. Laney matched him step for

step, moving in tune to the music. The image had his mind flashing back to the day he'd witnessed her instructing the exercise class in her club. And it was no less tempting now than it had been then.

Only now they were in the company of a literal boatful of her family and friends, which made such thoughts beyond inappropriate on his part.

It didn't help matters when the song switched over and the next number was a slow and sultry one that happened to have lyrics loaded with sensual undertones.

Laney stepped closer to him, a question deep in the depths of her sparkling amber eyes. He pulled her into his arms without a second thought.

Then he didn't allow himself to think at all.

Laney could only guess the number of eyes that had to be on them. She didn't care. After all, this is what they were after, wasn't it? To put on a show of affection. To look as if they were two lovebirds who had just discovered each other and couldn't get enough.

She sucked in a shaky breath. The scary part was that it was so perilously close to being true on her part. She really was growing rather fond of her pretend boyfriend. A shudder ran over her skin as she recalled their kiss in the room earlier. The taste of his lips on hers still lingered, the tingling sensation in the pit of her stomach resurfaced. The pleasure of being in his arms right now as they swayed slowly to the music. Yeah, no doubt about it, she couldn't exactly deny her developing feelings or her ever-growing attraction.

So what was she going to do about it?

Though she knew the risk, knew fully well the hit her soul would take if he wasn't as attracted to her as she was to him, the way she felt right now in Gianni's arms made all of that moot. Sometimes a girl just had to take a chance.

"Do you remember what I told you about my breakup?" she asked, blurting out the words and clearly surprising him with the question.

He faltered his step ever so slightly but quickly recovered. "Not particularly. Though I was rather hoping we didn't have to discuss the ex as I'm holding you in my arms during a slow dance."

Did that mean he had feelings for her that perhaps bordered on jealousy? But his next words quickly relieved her of that assumption. "It's not really great for my male ego." Just his pride speaking, then.

She shook her head. "This isn't really about him. It's about me."

He continued to lead her through the dance, but his attention and gaze was fully focused on her face now. "Oh?"

"I was told I was boring. What do you think that means?"

He tilted his head, studying her. "I think it means he was a brainless, inconsiderate buffoon who didn't know what he had."

She wasn't going to let the compliments go to her head. Gianni was a charmer. It seemed to be an intrinsic part of his personality. She couldn't take his words to heart, even if he thought he meant them. "No, I mean, why do you think he used that particular description?"

His hold on her seemed to tighten. "I couldn't venture to guess, Laney. But does it really matter?"

It did matter to her. It had stung to hear that description about her coming from someone she thought had loved and cherished her. Someone she thought was getting ready to propose. While she'd thought she may have found someone in Joseph who finally loved her and respected her for who she was, he'd ultimately rejected her for someone else.

Gianni leaned his face closer to hers. She could feel his warm breath on her cheek, along her neck. The sensation sent a shiver of longing through her core.

"I thought we established he was just making excuses."

Excuses to justify rejecting her. To toss her aside without guilt.

Gianni continued, "He described you in a way that was a much more fitting description of himself."

Yet that was too simple of an explanation. "Hmm. Maybe."

He sighed. "You don't sound convinced. I see no reason to give it any more thought. Unless…do you still have feelings for him?" he asked, nearly whispering the words. She might have been imagining the rasp in his voice.

"No. Not in any real sense. More a feeling of disappointment in what I thought was real that clearly wasn't."

"So why the questions?"

"I'm just trying to understand. When someone tells you you're boring, that typically means you're afraid to take chances, that you're scared of making a mistake." It was so hard to search for the exact right words. She had to do better. "That you're afraid of asking for what you want for fear of rejection."

An eyebrow raised in question. "Where exactly are you going with this?"

"I guess I'm asking for what I want. Regardless of the consequences." *I want you.*

He inhaled a deep breath and then let it out slowly. "You're going to have to be really clear here, sweetheart. I don't want to be making any kind of incorrect assumptions. Not about something like this."

Maybe she was making a mistake here. One she might regret later. After all, it had been a long day and she'd had more than one glass of wine. Still, at this moment, what she was about to do felt right. And she wouldn't question it any further. Perhaps it was indeed time she simply lived for the moment.

She wanted what she wanted. And she wasn't going to deny herself. "Then I guess I'll spell it out in concrete terms. I'd like to go back to the room soon. And I don't want you to sleep on the couch. Nor do I want you to drive back home."

If he was about to reject her, to tell her what she was saying made no sense, or that they barely knew each other, then so be it. She would find out once and for all that the attraction was one-sided and solely on her part. At least that way she would know that she hadn't chickened out. That she'd taken her shot and gotten her answer.

"I see. And exactly what *do* you want?" The thickness in his voice was unmistakable this time.

"I'd like you to stay the night. With me."

Gianni could tell by looking in her eyes what it must have taken for her to speak those words out loud. She couldn't have any idea the effect hearing them had on him now. His heart pounded wildly in his chest. The urge to lift her in his arms and carry her back to the hotel had his muscles twitching. Somehow, he managed to contain himself to keep from doing just that.

He had to try and think straight here, hard as that was to do. After all, he'd known, hadn't he? All the previous moments of desire and longing had led them here to this very point in time. He couldn't deny that he'd seen it coming.

Laney squeezed her eyes shut and bit out a mild curse. "Oh, no. I've really stepped in it this time, haven't I?"

She'd taken his hesitation as rejection. How far from the truth...

"Gianni, I'm so sorry. Look, if you don't want—"

He silenced her with a press of his finger to her lips.
"Don't even think about finishing that sentence." She hon-
estly thought he might not want her. There was no way he
could let her think that for even so much as a moment. It
was so far from the truth.

She slowly opened her eyes to look back up at him.
"Why?"

"You beautiful, silly fool."

A long and slow sigh escaped her lips. "I thought
maybe... Does that mean you want this too?"

How in the world could he say no? It would be such a
big lie.

He glanced around the room to see who was left still
partying. Unfortunately, all the important family members
still seemed to be lingering about. As expected, Laney's
dad was even at this moment eyeing the two of them. Gianni knew he should care, but he couldn't bring himself
to. "How fast can you say your goodbyes?"

Within moments, they were off the boat and onto the
harbor walkway. Gianni couldn't seem to let go of her, his
arm around her waist, half carrying her.

She pulled him to a stop under a streetlight, turning
him to face her. "I want you to know, this isn't characteristic of me."

"You don't have to explain yourself, Laney."

Her lips tightened. "It's just that I want you to understand. I don't typically ask for what I want. There's just
something about you."

He tightened his hold around her. "Then I'm honored to
have triggered the transformation."

Her response was to pull his face to hers. The kiss sent
a surge of pure pleasure down his chest clear to his toes.
For several moments, he just let himself indulge, to take
her in fully, to taste the sweetness she was offering. Still,

there were things he needed to say. Confessions he needed to make to her.

He forced himself to pull away.

"Listen, Laney. Before we—"

The sound of a loud giggle behind them interrupted his speech. "Get a room," yelled a feminine voice with a teasing, amused tone.

Laney gave the stranger a small nod before turning back to him. "I think she's right. We should get to our room." She took him by the hand and led him toward the hotel. The time it took to get from the sidewalk up to their room seemed to take forever. Finally, Laney swiped the keycard and they were through the door.

Now. He had to tell her now.

But she immediately wrapped her arms around him as soon as they shut the door behind them. Gianni could barely manage more than a low growl of pleasure as her lips found his once again.

He started to speak against her mouth. "Laney, about that night at your club."

She shook her head, continued kissing him. She whispered softly against his lips, "Mr. Martino, I was really hoping to keep the conversation to a minimum."

The thickness of her voice, the sheer longing woven through her tone was his final undoing. When she eventually broke the kiss and took him by the hand to lead him to the bedroom, he could do nothing but follow.

So this was what all the romantic books and movies had been referring to. Laney slowly opened her eyes as thin rays of morning sunlight filtered through the blinds of the large bay window across the bed. She felt languid, more relaxed than she'd felt in a long time.

Images from the night before flooded her mind and she felt heat throughout her entire body.

She was going to take the memory of last night and cherish it for the rest of her life. The way she'd been held last night, the way Gianni had loved her and held and whispered sweetly in her ear, the way he'd simply made her *feel* was an experience she would never forget.

What did it matter that it was only a fling?

She felt him rustle next to her just as a set of warm, gentle arms wrapped around her waist and pulled her closer up against him, her back to his chest. Hard to believe just how right it felt to be lying next to him in his arms.

"Why are you awake? It's got to be early still," he asked softly against her ear before trailing a line of kisses along her cheek, down her jaw and to her neck.

A small purr of pleasure escaped her lips. She could get used to this.

Except she really couldn't. This was just one weekend. A simple fling. After the wedding was over, they'd both go their separate ways. Gianni had given absolutely zero indication that he was after anything permanent. Look how disdainful he'd been last night when talk had turned to family.

She squeezed her eyes shut. She had no business even thinking the word. For one, she had some serious thinking to do herself about exactly what she wanted for herself in the future. There was no way she was ready for any kind of other relationship so soon.

Moot point. She was getting way ahead of herself.

Funny, she'd never considered herself to be the type to indulge in a no-strings-attached fling, but she'd never encountered the likes of Gianni Martino before.

"I was thinking about calling room service," she answered his question once she could find her breath and her focus. His hands were doing very distracting things at the moment. "I for one could use a strong pot of coffee."

"Yeah? Didn't get much sleep last night, did we?" he said with a rather naughty hitch to his voice. It had her giggling like a schoolgirl in response. His lips found hers again and she allowed her hands to roam over the toned muscles of his arms the way she had last night. She couldn't seem to get enough of touching him.

It was much later until they got around to ordering the coffee.

To her delight, Gianni had thought to order a variety tray of pastries and spreads. Dressed in the terry robe again, she tucked her feet under her on the loveseat as she bit into a rich buttery croissant. A steaming cup of Boston dark roast sat on the coffee table beside her.

The cushion shifted as Gianni plopped down next to her. He ate what remained of a cinnamon roll that had originally been the size of a small dinner plate.

"So, how did I do yesterday? Does your family think I'm good enough for you?"

"Wrong question."

"Again, huh? I seem to keep doing that."

She patted his knee. "You are still learning," she announced in a wise sage voice.

He gave a slight chuckle. "What's the right question, then?"

"Whether they think you're good enough for *them*. And they're still deciding by the way." It pulled her up short when she realized how that must have sounded. "I'm sorry. I know that's not really fair."

He took another bite of his breakfast treat. "No problem. I like a challenge." He certainly had a healthy ego. Good thing too. He would need it to get through the rest of the ceremonies, which included an early lunch followed by the wedding vows and finally the reception.

"To answer your question. You couldn't have done any better, as far as I'm concerned."

"Yeah?" He polished off the rest of his pastry in one big bite. "You think so?"

"I do. You were quite charming, a big hit with both ladies and gents alike. And toddlers. Lisbeth seemed taken by you as well by the end of the night."

He grinned at her. "Charming happens to be my middle name."

"Well, it fits."

So did he. He really had fit in yesterday with a group of people he'd only just met. She really had to thank her lucky stars. Central casting at a major movie studio couldn't have picked a better candidate for whom she needed by her side this weekend.

To think he'd just walked into her life at the perfect time.

Just when she'd needed him.

What a mess he'd gotten himself into.

Gianni tried to keep the mood light and amusing for Laney's sake as they ate their breakfast. But inside he was full of conflict. It was tearing him up inside that he was keeping such a big truth from her.

Now, as he listened to her humming while she showered, he cursed in frustration.

He had come perilously close to the precipice of spilling the entire truth to her last night. But the way Laney had told him that she wanted to be with him, the way she'd asked him to stay with her had made it impossible to find any kind of feasible way to even bring up the subject.

What was he supposed to say?

The reason I was even in your club two weeks ago was

because I work for the family business and we'd like to buy
you out. Now, where were we?

Not exactly pillow talk. And how could he possibly tell
her now? He wouldn't be able to live with himself if he ru-
ined her sister's wedding for her. The only reason he was
here was to make things easier for Laney with her loved
ones. Nothing would change if he kept the truth from her
a little longer.

As for last night, he'd like to think that had been inevitable, meant to be. From the moment he'd laid eyes on her,
something deep within him had known they'd become intimate. Nothing had been going to stop what happened between him and Laney last night. The moment they met, they
were drawn to each other in a way that couldn't be deterred.

No. He would have to find a better time to tell her the
truth once this weekend was over. Surely, he'd be able to
make her see where he was coming from. Business was
business. Personal was personal. As a business owner herself, she had to understand that their personal relationship
had nothing to do with any offer he may present her with
in the future.

He realized now he'd missed the best opportunity he'd
had to tell her. The night she'd come over for dinner, he
should have come clean. He'd just been enjoying her company so much he'd actually almost forgotten the circumstances surrounding their first meeting.

Well, there was no use dwelling on mistakes of the past.
It wouldn't do him any good now. Now he had to focus on
the best way to make things right and exactly how to do it.
Laney was a reasonable woman. She'd accept his apolo-
gies for misleading her.

He could only hope he wasn't being overly and naively
optimistic.

CHAPTER NINE

THE WEDDING WAS a big hit. Couldn't have gone better, in fact. A beautiful ceremony had commenced into a massive reception at the grand ballroom of the Boston Harbor Hotel. Aside from sitting down to the gourmet dinner of braised salmon with sautéed root vegetables and fluffy whipped potatoes drizzled with truffle oil, she and Gianni had spent most of the evening on the dance floor. Despite what he'd told her that night at the club, he was a more than competent dancer. Laney had long ago kicked off her heels and removed her bulky gold leaf earrings. A slight sheen of perspiration covered her forehead and the back of her neck.

She was enjoying herself.

Sure, she had plenty of opportunity to dance in her daily life. Owning a nightclub meant it was a large part of the job description, but those times were more of a responsibility, a performance to wrangle clients onto the dance floor if it was too empty for too long. Tonight was different. She couldn't remember the last time she'd danced just for fun, for the sheer joy that moving her body to music brought to her soul.

Now, Gianni twirled her around in a semicircle before dipping her dramatically when the music hit a crescendo as the song ended. She couldn't help the girlish giggle that escaped her lips.

The DJ chose that moment to announce he was taking what had to be a much-needed break. As the music came to a stop and the lights in the ballroom turned up brighter, she leaned into Gianni. "You know, you lied to me the night we met," she teased.

Something shifted behind his yes. "I did?"

She gave an emphatic nod. "You told me you weren't much of a dancer."

He blinked. "Oh, that."

What else did he think she might be referring to? Before she had a chance to ask, he gently took her by the elbow and led her off the dance floor back to their table. "I could use a drink. Can I get you more wine?" he asked.

"Yes, please."

Laney watched as Gianni made his way to the bar. Several of the groomsmen and guests stopped him to chat. Gianni had fit in rather well with the rest of the wedding party. The groomsmen treated him like he'd known them all for ages. His knowledge of kickboxing and the fact that he co-owned a string of gyms had broken the ice quickly with the other men. Including her new brother-in-law. Plus, Gianni had an easy manner that had also helped to acclimate him with the others.

Was there anything the man wasn't good at?

She gave her head a brisk shake. She was dangerously on the verge of becoming besotted. And that would be perilous indeed. Despite their night of intimacy, they hardly knew each other. Though that was changing by the minute.

"Please explain to me what's happened, Elaine." Her mom's voice interrupted her thoughts. Laney looked up to find her parents pulling out the empty chairs at her table. They both sat down and turned to face her head on.

Uh-oh. She'd been caught unaware. Too focused on Gianni, she hadn't even seen them approach. But then again, her parents had a way of being stealth-like, particularly when it came to keeping their girls in check.

It was time for the Gianni third-degree grilling. Nothing she could do about it now.

She really had wished to put it off a while longer. She took a deep calming breath and prepared herself for the onslaught.

"What do you mean?"

Her mother pinched her lips before answering. "I'd think it was obvious. You were on the verge of being engaged yourself to Joseph. And now you're with someone else entirely. Tell me again, how exactly did all that happen so fast? What in the world is going on with you?"

"Now, now, dear," her dad said, patting his wife's hand gently on the table. "This probably isn't the time or place. We are here to enjoy Emily's nuptials." Laney hadn't fully released her sigh of relief when her father turned his intense gaze on her. "But your mother's right. You owe us some answers, young lady."

"It just seems so sudden," her mother continued, without so much as giving Laney a chance to respond. "Why, he's practically a stranger."

Laney cut her off before she could continue with that train of thought. "It's okay, Mom, Dad. You don't have to worry. We're taking things slow." She had to look away as she uttered the last word as memories of their night together rushed through her head. That was just physical. Not that she'd be sharing that bit of knowledge with present company.

"Good," Mom declared. "I'm glad to hear it."

"What does he do again?" her father asked, studying Gianni as he slowly made his way back to the table.

Laney caught his eyes, trying to send him an apologetic

look. His shrug was almost imperceptible, but she caught the slight motion. Her father waved him over.

Don't panic. All is fine.

They'd planned for this moment, after all. Hardly unexpected. Truth be told, she was surprised it had taken her parents as long as it had.

Gianni approached with a friendly smile and was at their table in no time. Charming as ever, he gave her mom a nod first, then shook her father's hand after setting her wineglass down in front of her. He sat down in the remaining empty chair.

"Finally," her father began without any kind of pretense. "A chance to talk."

Laney tried to give Gianni a reassuring smile, but he didn't seem fazed in the least, just sat there calmly sipping his beer before he answered. "Likewise. Laney told me so much about you when we first met. And Emily. You're a lovely family."

Whoa, fella. Try not to spread it on too thick.

Her mom leaned closer, resting her arms on the table. "Thank you. That's a lovely thing to say." She scrunched her face. "We're looking forward to getting to know you better."

Very subtle, Mom. A nice, roundabout way to tell him they didn't know him that well. And they intended to change that fact as fast as possible.

"We were inquiring what it is that you do for a living," her father supplied. The tag team was in full practice now.

"I'm a managing VP for Martino Entertainment Enterprises," Gianni answered. "My father founded the company as a young man upon his arrival to the States three decades ago."

"Martino Entertainment Enterprises. That sounds familiar," her father said, his eyebrows drawn together in thought.

"We own and manage various fitness and entertainment venues. Everything from boxing gyms to gaming halls to smaller casinos."

"Ah, yes," her father responded. "Now it's ringing a bell. I read somewhere you're looking to expand."

Was it her imagination or did Gianni flinch ever so slightly? "Always," he answered with after another swig of his beer. "Got to grow the business. At all costs," he added almost under his breath with another swig of his beer. She might not have heard him if she weren't hyper-focused on the conversation.

He hadn't told her much about his business. Or his family, for that matter. But clearly there was a story there. Maybe he'd feel comfortable enough with her at some point in the future to confide what that story might be.

Gianni hadn't meant to say that last part out loud. Judging by the way she was looking at him, Laney had definitely heard him. Luckily, her father changed the subject. "It's rather lucky, isn't it? That you two met when you did."

Yeah, the new subject matter could be considered equally full of landmines. "Laney tells me you were visiting the club one night, even though you'd never been there before."

He gave her a sideways smile. "Guess it was meant to be." Man, when he finally told her the full story, there was going to be so much explaining he needed to do.

"Yes, I'm glad she managed a plus-one to the wedding, after all," her mother added. Laney's cheeks were growing redder by the second. "Now, she just needs to figure out what to do about this trip to Italy she planned. Positano, then Florence, already paid for." She patted her daughter's hand, but there was zero affection in the gesture. "Yet another impulsive decision on your part that seems to have bitten you in the hind. I don't suppose you can get your money back."

"I have every intention of going still, Mother. Gianni might even come with me."

Whoa. He hadn't seen that coming. Laney looked ready to slide under the table. Clearly, she'd said it without much thought.

He wasn't sure what to say. This whole conversation was throwing him off. He just wanted to somehow get the look of utter despair off Laney's face. He had family in Positano. "I have a great aunt and several cousins in that area. Positano."

Why had he thrown out that fact? It sounded like he was considering actually going with her. Of course, that was out of the question.

"Oh?" her mom said. "Where did you say your hotel was again, Laney?"

She hadn't said, as her mother had never actually inquired about the hotel before. "A seaside hotel on the Amalfi Coast. The Palazzo Positano," she answered.

"Is your family in that area, Gianni?" her mom wanted to know.

Before Gianni could respond, Laney jumped in. "I haven't made any final decisions about the trip. Let's just drop it, okay?"

Her mom gave her a sharp look that bordered on pity. "Of course."

Several moments of awkward silence ensued. Gianni had taken gut punches in the ring that had left him feeling more comfortable. Luckily, fate intervened. Laney's mom suddenly stood. "Well, it looks like they're about to cut the cake." She took her husband's hand. "Let's go, dear."

Laney's sigh of relief was audible as they walked away. "I am so sorry, Gianni."

"Nothing to apologize for. That wasn't so bad." That much was true. Up until the whole Italy conversation, he'd been managing pretty well.

"What I said just now, about you traveling with me to Positano, you have to know it was just for their benefit. So they would just drop the subject. I don't really expect you to come to Italy with me."

Ouch. As infeasible as it was, she made it sound like the idea was preposterous. "Yeah. Go figure."

"I guess I should have seen that coming."

"Hey, the good news is, you have a bit of a reprieve from the paternal third degree. And we're about to eat some wedding cake."

Her lips curled up in a smile. "I suppose so. Guess I should look on the bright side, huh? Silver linings and all that."

He tipped his nearly empty bottle in her direction in a mini salute. "Always."

She picked up her glass and touched it to his bottle. "A toast to silver linings. So, have you ever been, then? To Italy? You said you had family there."

The question brought back a flood of memories. Most of them pleasant and joyful. Except for one moment he'd rather forget.

"A few times. I could recommend some places, if you'd like. If you do decide to go, that is."

She studied his face. "Sure, I'd like that."

Something about her expression made him want to pull her onto his lap and wrap his arms around her. In an alternate universe, this conversation could go a completely different way. He wished things were different. That they really were together and he could take this trip of a lifetime with her. He could show her all the sites in Italy he enjoyed, a lover slash tour guide in one. Then he'd have her meet his family.

He had no business even entertaining such thoughts. He was only here with her to play a part, to help her get through her sister's wedding. They weren't exactly a couple in any sense of the word, certainly not one who'd be planning any kind of international trip together. Though he couldn't deny how much it shook him that he wanted to so badly. To travel with her, to show her his Italy.

Moot point. He couldn't very well change reality, could he? As much as he wanted to. So he'd settle for being able to spend one more night with her before it all had to come to an end.

CHAPTER TEN

ONE OF THESE days maybe she'd learn to stop checking her phone for missed messages or missed calls. It appeared today was not that day. Though why she bothered was beyond her. One week since the wedding and Gianni hadn't contacted her other than a perfunctory reply to her one text thanking him for attending with her.

Well, what had she expected?

Gianni had done her a favor that weekend. Nothing more. She'd asked him to help her save face at her sister's wedding and he'd obliged. And he'd done so in a way she'd be eternally grateful for. Maybe if their paths crossed again, they could form some kind of friendship. As for their weekend fling, that was simply two adults enjoying each other's company under some rather uncanny circumstances. Gianni had never alluded differently. And to be completely truthful, neither had she.

So she was going to resist checking her phone yet again this hour. In fact, she was going to set it to silent and not even look at it until the club opened for the evening. Business calls were a completely different number. And heaven knew, she didn't have anything pressing that was personal.

She had a lot to do before she flew to Italy in a few days No time to constantly interrupt herself, looking for messages that weren't there from a man she should just start to forget. Surely, in time, he would stop appearing in her dreams night after night. But she couldn't deny the truth. Gianni Martino was going to be a hard man to forget and put behind her. The way he'd made her feel, the things he'd said to her. Almost as if he saw her in a way no one else had.

With a resigned sigh, Laney fished her phone out of her pocket to change the setting when a dull knock on her office door stopped her.

"Come in."

Her head bartender poked her head in the door. "Hey, boss. Someone here to see you. One Gianni Martino."

Laney's heart gave a thud, then proceeded to pound wildly in her chest. Gianni was here? She couldn't help the thrill that washed over her. He was actually physically here. That was better than any text message or voice mail. Had he missed her as much as she'd missed him? Another exciting possibility occurred to her that sent a lightning bolt through her midsection. What if he'd decided that he wanted to go to Italy with her?

"Oh?"

"I can tell him you're busy. He said he doesn't have an appointment."

"No!" Laney jumped out of her chair, clearly startling the other woman. "I mean, no appointment needed. He's a friend."

When he stepped into her office a moment later, she realized just how inadequate describing him as a friend was. Dressed in a well-cut gray suit that fit him like a glove, he could have been an image out of a commercial. She itched to run over and give him a hug. But something in his manner gave her pause.

"Hey, Laney." It sounded friendly enough, but his smile was off. No warmth. Not like the man she'd spent a heavenly weekend with just a short time ago. She held off approaching him, any sense of excitement washing away like water down a drain. Instead, she motioned for him to have a seat.

"This is a pleasant surprise."

"Sorry, I'm here without calling first. I hope I'm not interrupting a busy day." Unbuttoning his suit jacket, he sat across the desk from her as Laney took her own seat.

So formal, so…professional. Her senses were beginning to signal a high alert. "What can I do for you, Gianni?"

"There are things we need to go over, you and I."

"Go over? What kinds of things?"

He took a breath before continuing. "Laney, there was a reason I was here that night. One I didn't fully explain to you."

What in the world was this about? "I don't understand. Why exactly are you here?"

He rubbed his forehead. "I'm here on behalf of Martino Entertainment Enterprises."

Laney had to swallow the brick that had formed at the base of her throat. This was all wrong. "To do what?"

"To make you an offer on your property. We'd like to acquire it as the site of our next casino."

Laney's vision blurred. A dull pounding sounded in her ears. She couldn't have heard him correctly. "Please explain."

"I think you'll be happy with the figure. But of course, we'd be up to negotiate."

Her mouth didn't seem to want to work. How was any of this happening? It had to be some kind of joke. He was teasing her, no doubt. But one look at his face made it clear this was no joking matter.

So that's what that weekend was about. The only reason he'd said yes to pretending to be her date. Did he think she owed him now?

And to not have told her the truth from the very beginning.

A horrified gasp escaped her lips before she could stop it. She'd asked him to spend the night with her for heaven's sake! What a fool she'd been.

She had to get him out of here before she made an even bigger fool of herself and began to sob. The tears were perilously close, stinging the back of her eyes and clogging her throat.

Standing, she strode to her office door and yanked it open. "This conversation is over, Mr. Martino."

She heard him sigh deeply. Several moments passed when neither one of them moved. Finally, Gianni stood to face her. "Laney, hear me out."

She shook her head. "There's no need. Save your breath. I have no intention of selling. Not to anyone. And especially not to you." She pulled the door wider. "Please leave."

He inhaled deeply. "Laney, listen. I wish things were—"

But she didn't let him finish. There was no point. Everything was so clear. How many times in one lifetime could she let herself be duped like a naive, clueless child?

He was only after her business. The one thing she was proud of. The one thing she could claim as having done right. Her one true success.

"Please leave now, Mr. Martino."

She'd barely shut the door behind him when the tears began to flow and a sob escaped her lips.

Well, that went well, he thought with bitter sarcasm once he'd left her office.

Gianni entered his car and slammed the door shut so hard

the window rattled. Then, for good measure, he pounded the steering wheel hard about half a dozen times with his fists.

It wasn't enough and he wasn't going to be able to get to the gym for another several hours. Laney wasn't even open to the possibility. He'd tried to sound as professional as possible in there, so that he didn't sway her into making a decision based on what they'd shared personally.

But clearly he had hurt her in the process.

How could he have been so foolish? Wanting to get it over with without too many advance questions, he'd simply shown up at her office to tell her all of it in person. It had backfired.

He certainly could have handled the meeting so much better. First, he'd waited too long to tell her the truth, and then he'd botched it royally when he finally had. Now, it was too late to fix things. She would probably never want anything to do with him after this. He wasn't sure what he wanted when it came to Laney Taytum. But he knew with certainty that he would hate to live with the knowledge that she hated him. Though they had no kind of future together, he had to admit he'd grown fond of her. No. It was more than that. He cared for her in a way he hadn't felt for any other woman before in his lifetime. And look at how he'd treated her. It was unconscionable. She'd told him opening that club had been a new beginning for her, after her dreams of becoming a dancer fell through. How could he have forgotten to take that fact into account?

He had to try to do something. Anything.

Part of him wanted to forget what had just happened and just go pummel the punching bag for a good ninety minutes until all the frustration and disgust he felt with himself poured out. But he had too much to do first. He had to go to his father and demand they stop any pursuit of Laney's property. Gianni knew his father wasn't beyond pressure tactics when he was after a business goal, and he never took the first no as a final answer.

That approach was out of the question in this case. He would see to it personally. When it came to Laney, he wouldn't allow it. No matter the cost to himself.

By the time he got to his father's office, his agitation had only grown. Angelo was there too. That was good. He could make his announcement in one fell swoop—tell them both at once.

His father looked up in surprise when he entered without knocking or so much as announcing his presence. Angelo blinked in question.

"You're back, son. That was quick."

"Hope that means good news," his brother said. "You didn't have to alter too far from our original offer?"

"Not exactly."

His father crossed his arms in front of his chest. "Then why are you back already?"

Gianni loosened his tie and shrugged off his jacket, throwing it behind one of the office chairs. "I've made a decision. You may not like it."

"I already don't," his father responded. Angelo merely raised an eyebrow. When was the last time either of them had directly challenged their father? He couldn't recall. Aside from a rebellious teen tantrum years back, or an inconsequential disagreement about a minor decision, Franco Martino was a hardened man who valued discipline and loyalty, partly because of his background but mostly because of simply who he was and all he'd accomplished. As a result, his sons historically fell in line. Not this time.

"The owner doesn't want to sell. I think we should look elsewhere."

His father rubbed his chin. "I see. Would this happen

to be the owner you spent the weekend with? Attending a wedding, if I recall."

"That's not material to this discussion."

Angelo rubbed a hand down his face.

"So you failed to negotiate a deal. Is that correct?" Franco asked.

Gianni made sure to look his father straight in the eye as he answered. He was fully prepared for the dressing down he was sure to receive. It hardly mattered. "That's correct. She doesn't want to sell."

Angelo stepped toward him, his hands up. "Maybe if we just upped the offer."

Gianni shook his head before his brother could even finish. "I won't ask her again."

Angelo dropped his hands as their father responded. "I see."

Gianni somehow doubted that. "We'll have to find another location, Pop."

"That will set us back months."

"So be it."

His father steepled his hands, elbows on his desk. "That's the location I want, son. I thought you understood that."

"Things have changed."

"What kinds of things?" Angelo wanted to know.

Everything had changed. "You'll both just need to take my word for it."

His father eyed him with contemplation. "Your word is gold as far as I'm concerned. Nevertheless. I'd like to try again, see what we have to do to have her accept."

"Then you'll have to do it without me." There it was, he'd thrown down the proverbial gauntlet. And he'd stand firm by it. Franco wasn't used to his authority being questioned in such a blatant manner. But there was a first time for everything.

Ironic, really. How hard had Gianni tried in life to avoid this very thing? How often had he run himself in circles trying to prove himself worthy of being Franco Martino's son? One of his heirs. Given the reality, who Gianni really was—a consequence of a betrayal—this very moment had been one he'd done his best to never experience.

But now, he knew he was doing the right thing. In fact, nothing had ever felt more right. "I refuse to pursue this venue any further."

Angelo's eyebrows went clear up to his hairline, but Gianni could swear he detected a hint of a smile along his lips. It was probably just his imagination.

His father waited several beats before finally answering. "That's very disappointing, son. Shut the door on your way out."

If she didn't finish packing in haste, she was going to miss her flight. But it was hard to pack when one had to consistently stop to throw things at the wall in anger and regret. Not for the first time—okay, maybe for about the hundredth since she'd decided—Laney thought about canceling the trip. After all, never would she have guessed that she'd be taking this journey alone when she first booked it.

But then what? She would just sit here in her apartment during the days wallowing in self-pity and then spend the evenings delivering drinks at the bar while seething with anger. At least being away might take her mind off things for a while. She might even go an hour without thinking of Gianni Martino.

Ha! As if that were likely.

Shaking off the useless thoughts, she made herself focus on the task at hand. Down to the wire, she was just zipping up her carry-on bag when her phone dinged, signaling the arrival of her ride.

No time to second-guess now. Looked like she was on her way to Italy. By herself.

So distracted by her jumbled, angry thoughts, Laney barely noticed about half an hour later when the driver pulled up to the airport departures area and stopped the car. She was right. The timing was definitely close. By the time she reached the gate and boarded, she wouldn't have a minute to spare.

The adrenaline wore off as soon as she sat down in the cabin. The empty seat next to her seemed to mock her. She'd always credited herself as a strong independent woman but right now, all she felt was alone.

And lonely.

Visiting the Amalfi Coast had been a dream of hers for as long as she could remember. Never would she have imagined that she'd be doing so alone. An image of a ruggedly handsome face with dark chocolate eyes and wavy thick hair popped up in her mind and she cursed herself. How could she even be thinking of Gianni Martino at a time like this? She regretted ever running into him that night. She regretted that she hadn't simply swallowed her pride and attended her sister's wedding alone. It would have been so much better than the empty, battered feeling she was wrangling with right now. He was the last person she should wish could accompany her aboard the flight and to Positano, then on to Florence.

But there was no denying, wish it she did. Foolish to the end.

CHAPTER ELEVEN

IT WAS AN official fact. Even on vacation, Laney Taytum was a creature of habit.

By the third day of her dream trip to the coastal tourist town of Positano, Laney had managed to develop something of a routine. She walked the cliffside pathways to get some exercise in the morning. Afternoons were allotted to a leisurely swim in the ocean followed by lounging on the beach with a packed lunch. In the evenings, she perused the many shops for trinkets and souvenirs, then had a quiet dinner in one of the many restaurants or sandwich delis.

It was an utterly charming way to pass the time even if it was rather solitary. Sure, the locals were very friendly. As was the staff at her hotel. She wondered how much of it was the mere characteristic of being a tourist magnet known worldwide. People knew how to treat visitors here.

So she wasn't terribly disturbed the fourth afternoon when a shadow fell over her, blocking the sun as she was sunbathing. Someone she'd met on her escapades so far was stopping to say hi, no doubt.

Until she opened her eyes. Then blinked twice before doing a double take. And then she blinked again.

"Hey, Laney."

Either she was seeing things, things she wanted to see,

or Gianni Martino was standing over her on the beach. Half a world away from where she'd last seen him.

This couldn't be real. Sitting up, Laney blocked the sun glare with her hand, the hand that was shaking just a tad less than the other. Somehow, she got her mouth to work. "Tell me something. Do you happen to have a twin who lives in Boston?" She couldn't even tell for sure if she was joking.

He laughed and the sound of it gave it away. She'd recognize that laugh anywhere. Scrambling to her feet, "Gianni? What in the world—"

"Surprised to see me?"

If that weren't the understatement of the decade. Or the century.

This had to be some kind of weird coincidence. He'd said he had family here nearby. Maybe some kind of emergency had come up with one of his relatives. But that didn't explain his presence here, on the beach. Where he'd found her. Coincidence surely couldn't go that far. "What are you doing here?"

"I remembered which hotel you said you were staying in. This is the closest beach, so I took a chance."

"Not that. I mean, what are you doing here? In Italy?"

"I couldn't leave things the way they were between us. The truth is, I owe you an apology."

She had to give her head a shake to chase away the fog of confusion. "And you decided to fly across the world to do it."

He had the gall to wink at her, just like that first night, making her heart tug just a tad in her chest and she chastised herself silently for it. She would *not* fall for his charm that easily again. She'd only laid eyes on him again for about two minutes, for heaven's sake. "You couldn't have just called or something?"

He shrugged sheepishly. "It was a pretty big apology. Some things are worth a bit of effort or a long flight across the ocean."

"Yeah. I'd say."

He stepped closer to her. That spicy masculine aftershave she'd gotten so fond of back in Boston drifted on the ocean breeze and made her shudder. How inconvenient that she was still so attracted to this man.

But first things first. "Go on, then. Let's hear this apology you flew to Italy to give."

He rubbed his chin. "I should have been upfront with you from the get-go. I have no excuse. It's just that after we met, one thing led to another, and there never seemed to be a good time. Things just sort of snowballed. I'm usually in better control of my variables than that. I'm sorry, Laney. More than you could know."

Wow. Sounded as if he'd given this some thought. He had to be sincere. He'd gone through an awful lot of trouble to deliver his sorry in person. But she was still nursing her wounds. Transatlantic flight or not. What he'd done back in Boston wasn't insignificant.

She crossed her arms. "What about my club? I take it your family is still after it?"

"I confess that's true. They have their eyes on it, given it's prime real estate near the water and its proximity to the heart of the city. Just keep turning them down."

She squinted at him. "Them?"

He swallowed and nodded. "I've removed myself from the project. And I'll do everything I can to try to get them to look elsewhere. Before getting to know you, I hadn't realized how much the place meant to you. That's not an excuse, I know."

"It's a start."

"I'd like to make it all up to you. If you'll let me."

Her logical mind screamed that she should walk away now. Tell him he shouldn't have bothered coming all this way. But a small yet stronger voice, the one that seemed to always get her in trouble, had other plans in mind. Her curiosity got the better of her.

"How exactly?" She couldn't begin to guess what the answer to that question may be.

"Well, it occurred to me how serendipitous it is that you happened to be traveling to Positano, given how well I know the city. And given the fact that I have family here."

"So?"

"So there has to be some kind of kismet there, wouldn't you say?"

What exactly was he getting at? "You need to spell out for me exactly what you have in mind, Gianni. I'm not in the mood for guessing games."

He nodded once. "Fair enough. Like I said, I know the area really well. And you don't. Let me play at tour guide. Show you a side of Positano only a local would know."

"Tour guide?"

He motioned around him. "This city is like no other. I can make it so that you have memories to last you a lifetime. It's the least I can do to begin to make amends."

"You want to show me around Positano as a way to redeem yourself."

He visibly winced. "In a nutshell. If you say no, I'll walk off this beach and you'll never hear from me again. If that's what you want."

"Huh." It was the only word she could come up with. Her mind was blank. If someone had told her during the flight here that she'd be faced with such a decision on her fourth day of the trip, she would have laughed, then asked which bridge they were selling.

She started to say no. But there was that pestering, obnoxious voice again that always got her into trouble. The voice that seemed to forget all the times she'd been naively foolish enough to think she could have something simply because she wanted it so badly. She started packing up her things, just to stall.

"I think I've had enough sun. I'm going to head back to the hotel."

He nodded, and tried to help her gather her towel before she pushed his hand away. "Can I walk you back to your room?"

Straightening, she studied his face. Those eyes that she'd lost herself in that one fateful weekend. The smile that charmed the socks off her the first time she'd seen it.

She just couldn't do it. She couldn't bring herself to turn him down flat, though she knew it was the only right thing to do.

"I'll have to think about your offer," she said over her shoulder as she walked away.

"You know how to get a hold of me," he said behind her.

She didn't dare look back, too tempted to change her mind and say yes then and there.

Positano certainly seemed to be the land of lovers.

Laney sat down at the solitary corner table at the bistro a member of the hotel staff had recommended to her. All the center tables were full. Most of them occupied by couples, many of whom were holding hands or sharing bites of each other's food. One handsome gentleman was actually spoon-feeding his companion, landing a kiss occasionally between bites. An older couple, one table over from them, raised their wineglasses in a toast.

Laney made herself look away from the romantic scenes and focused on the menu instead. Without pulling out her phone and calling up the translation app, she could only make out a couple of items. One particular dish jumped out at her. Gnocchi.

She certainly knew that one.

Images of the night in Gianni's apartment as he cooked for her flooded her mind. He'd been so charming that night, so attractive in his chef's apron. A warm current ran up her spine as she remembered the way he'd stood behind her and held her arm to show her how to roll the potato dough. A current of ire bolted through her center suddenly. He could have told her then, that very night. Instead, he'd let her continue to think their paths had simply crossed co-incidentally. He'd kept her in the dark until it was too late and she'd grown to care for him.

But he was looking to make it up to her now. Could she really take him up on it? He was here, merely miles away in the same town. She would have never guessed when she'd arrived in Italy three days ago that he might follow her. Hard to deny the fact that she felt rather touched that he'd done so.

Was she actually considering accepting his offer to show her around?

She mentally ran through the pros and cons. Yes, she was still angry. And hurt. But she could be smarter about their relationship now. Part of the reason his admission had hit her so hard was that she'd begun developing feelings for him. She had no such delusions about doing so now.

Nothing said spending time with him had to have any underlying emotional undertones. Not if she made sure to keep her emotions in check this time.

As long as she made clear that the arrangement was nothing more than that. She'd let him accompany her through Positano, let him show her the sights he knew so well. And at the end of the day, they'd go to their separate rooms.

She wouldn't soon forget what he'd done. The way he'd

misled her. But the man had traveled across the world in an attempt to make amends. Would it be so bad to take him up on it? Especially if it meant she wouldn't have to spend the rest of the week all by herself. The solitary tourist thing was getting a little old.

Agreeing to his offer made logical sense, as well. Many of the excursions she'd signed up for and the meals that were part of the package deal were included for two individuals. Though money was the least of her worries at the moment, it was something to consider.

"Scusi?" The server interrupted her thoughts. "You are expecting someone, *si*?" he asked in broken English, taking away the other menu that sat in a center holder.

She shook her head in answer. No, tonight she wasn't expecting anyone else to join her. She'd spend yet another evening by herself. But that didn't have to be the case going forward.

As Gianni had said, the decision was completely up to her.

"Hiking? We're going hiking?"

She wasn't expecting Gianni's first outing for her as a tour guide to be quite so physical. Laney looked down at her open-toed soft leather sandals and her butter-beige newly untagged capri pants. He'd told her to meet him for breakfast at the lobby restaurant of her hotel to discuss what he had planned. Clearly, she should have asked first about proper attire for their day trip.

Gianni followed the direction of her gaze. "Yeah, you might want to run back upstairs and change into more rugged shoes."

"The most rugged pair I brought with me are sneakers."

"That should work," he reassured her.

Now that she thought about it, she remembered reading

about one of Positano's more famous, if not less glamorous, attractions in a travel agency brochure. A hiking trail along the cliffside. Not usually a hiker type, she hadn't given it much thought. Gianni was telling her it was not to be missed. Still, she had reservations.

Gianni had already ordered and had the breakfast waiting for her when she'd come downstairs. She found herself ridiculously grateful that the food was there and ready, particularly the coffee. Laney took a sip of her strong espresso and tore off a piece of the brioche, then popped it into her mouth. "Just how strenuous is this going to be?" she asked.

"You dance every night to bouncy pop songs and carry heavy trays laden with bottles and cocktails. I think you can handle it."

Dancing and delivering drinks used entirely different muscles and skills than the ones required to ascend mountainside cliffs. Nevertheless, she ran upstairs quickly to change into her athletic shoes and a pair of denim shorts while Gianni waited.

When she arrived back down at the lobby, Gianni was loading up the backpack he'd brought with snacks and bottles of water.

"I'm ready," she told him. Or as ready as she was ever going to be. Growing up in New England, she'd visited more than her fair share of mountains and thought herself a skilled and experienced skier. But none of those mountains could be considered anything near cliff-like.

She hoped Gianni knew what he was doing here.

In moments, they were boarding a late-model SUV helmed by a uniformed driver.

"We'll get dropped off at Agerola. And the path will bring us back to Nocelle," Gianni explained as she buckled herself in the back seat next to him. The way he pronounced the names of the cities in a fluid Italian accent sounded alluring and exotic. "Should take about an hour or so to drive there."

"Nocelle?"

"It's the cliffside village right above Positano." He pointed up toward the sky. "We'll be over a thousand or so feet above where we started from."

Well, that implied there was a piece of the overall puzzle missing. "And how do we get down, then?"

"That's the best part." The smile he gave her sent a small shiver down her spine. She wanted to pretend it was due to the adventure ahead of them and nothing more.

"How so?"

"We go down the stairs."

She felt her jaw drop as she took in what he said. "Over a thousand feet of stairs."

"Can you handle it?"

"I'm not sure. That's a lot of steps."

"About fifteen hundred or so."

They were driving around tight roads through commercial shops and street-side vendors. A quaint scene of seaside life in Italy she probably would have enjoyed more if she wasn't worrying about how her legs would handle a thousand plus number of steps after hiking a trail for a couple of hours.

"Come on," Gianni said. "You're pretty fit. You lead weekly fitness classes. The way you carry all those cocktails and bottles. And those fitness classes you teach." He did a move as he performed small double kicks behind the seat in what she assumed was meant to imitate an aerobic workout step. A bubble of laughter escaped her lips.

"That's not quite the same as jumping down miles worth of steps, is it?"

He shrugged. "At least I'm no making you go up the steps. Why I hired a car to get us up there."

She shuddered at the thought. "Well, thank you for that."

"You'll have fun, I promise," he said as he placed his hand on her thigh above her knee. She couldn't even help the images that immediately flooded her mind at his touch. Memories of their one night together after the wedding reception.

Different time. Different place.

She'd learned her lesson when it came to this man. No, she was simply enjoying his company as a friend who happened to be familiar with the foreign city she was visiting. He was helping her to make the most of this trip. There absolutely could not be a replay of the events that had led them into each other's arms. She simply didn't have it in her to deal with the emotional fallout.

As if sensing her thoughts, Gianni quickly removed his hand. He pointed to a spot outside her passenger-side window. "That place has the best gelato this side of the ocean. Remind me to have us stop there at some point."

See, his comment was further cementing her point. She would have had no idea where to go to get the best gelato. Heck, it might not have even occurred to her that she wanted any. And she might have missed going on this hiking path altogether if it weren't for Gianni.

Suddenly, she felt better about her decision to take him up on being her companion for the next couple of days or so. Then she'd be off to Florence for the next adventure. He hadn't offered to accompany her there, and she wouldn't ask him to. He was only here in Positano because he could helpfully show her around the area.

A pang of regret tugged at her chest that she'd be alone once again after she got to Florence. But she shook it off. One step at a time. Starting with the ones that would follow their massive hike.

Pretty soon the shops and vendor carts gave way to a

narrow stone-lined path surrounded by the greenest shrubbery she'd ever seen.

"How long will we be hiking?"

Gianni gave a small shrug. "Depends how often we stop. You brought your camera like I asked?"

She nodded in answer.

"Trust me, you'll want to pause several times to take photos. You're not going to believe the visionary treat that's in store for you."

All right. He had her curiosity piqued. "There's a reason it's called Il Sentiero degli Dei."

"What's that mean?"

"The Path of the Gods."

So celestial. And a little under an hour later, Laney was well on the way to fully grasping exactly why the hiking path had such a divine name. View after view was more breathtaking than the last. She'd taken countless photos. The crystal blue ocean beneath them reminded her of the finest turquoise jewelry, the greenery a color of rich jade she'd never seen before.

A visual buffet of magnificence that had her gasping with wonder as they reached each new vantage point. By the time they reached the massive array of steps over two hours later, she was panting and her midsection felt tight and fluttery.

Gianni noticed. "Are you all right?" He handed her a bottle of water.

She nodded. "All the excitement. Plus, I'm famished. Those granola bars only did so much to tide me over." Funny, now that she thought about it, she realized she'd been hungrier on this trip than she could ever remember being. Waiting for the next mealtime had proven impossible most days, and she'd found herself down in the hotel concierge floor to nab a bite, or stopping in a shop along her way to the beach. Who knew going on a bucket-list trip would so arouse a girl's appetite?

Gianni studied her with concern for a beat, then hoisted his backpack. "Then let's get down these steps posthaste. We'll get you an authentic Italian meal you won't soon forget."

Gianni could barely contain his amusement when he led Laney to the front door of a charming two-story box building, rather than to the entrance of a bistro like she'd no doubt been expecting.

"Where are we?" she asked, as he led her up the steps and knocked on the door. "Did you need to run an errand or something?"

Her voice was on the verge of snappy and she looked mildly annoyed. Like his younger clients at the gym would call it, she was "hangry." He had to get some food in her and soon. This was just the place. "I promised you an authentic Positano meal like no other."

"But this is clearly someone's house," she protested while the sound of footsteps could be heard behind the door.

"Trust me."

The door swung open at that moment and the familiar matronly face of his favorite *zia* beamed at them from across the threshold.

"Gianni! *Mi bambino. Bene! Bene!*"

She stepped out onto the porch and enveloped him in a tight affectionate hug. When she finally let go, she turned her attention to Laney who looked rather shell-shocked. Her expression only grew in surprise when Zia Rosa took her by the arm and led her inside behind her.

"Come in…come in," she said in perfect English, albeit with a thick Italian accent. "We were expecting you tomorrow."

"Change in plans," Gianni answered. "Hope that's okay."

"Yeah, it's okay. You are welcome here any time of day whenever you wish."

He knew that, of course. Laney didn't look convinced, however. He made brief introductions, explaining to Laney exactly where they were and who was leading her to a center table and sitting her down on one of the chairs.

"Dinner won't be for another couple of hours," his aunt announced. "But let me get you some bruschetta while you wait. And there's some soup left from lunch. You are both hungry, yes?"

"Yes. But we don't want to impose, Signora Rosa." She stopped long enough to send him a fierce glare across the table as he took his own seat. "I had no idea we were coming. Unannounced, no less."

His *zia* scoffed, setting a steaming bowl of minestrone and a plate of fragrant bruschetta in front of them both. "Nonsense. Family needs no announcement."

"Rosa spent years studying international affairs in London," Gianni explained. "Her English is more proper than mine."

"I can see that." Laney seemed to have suddenly lost her earlier hesitancy, once the soup and veggie-loaded tray of bread were placed in front of her. His aunt's warmth and hospitality had surely helped, as well.

Rosa turned to retrieve more bread from the pantry. Laney leaned over the table as soon as she left the room.

"We shouldn't have come unannounced, Gianni."

He waved away the comment. "Stop worrying about it. Italy isn't like the States. Friends and family often just show up. Particularly family that happens to be visiting from half a world away."

Her eyebrows drew together, making it rather clear she

didn't quite believe him. "What if she was out? Or if it was a bad time?"

He shrugged. "If it happens to be an inconvenient time, the visitor is just told so. And they wander off to come back and visit another day."

Laney leaned back against her chair. "Huh. You're right. That's completely different from how things are in the States. It's definitely different from the way I grew up."

Yeah, he'd gotten the impression even before her sister's wedding that her family was rather keen on formality and proper decorum. Rules in general.

"Yeah, and there's always food," he answered, helping himself to more. Particularly at an older aunt's house, regardless of the time of day.

Good thing too. He could practically hear Laney's stomach grumbling from three feet away.

She looked right here, at his aunt's small wooden table in her cozy kitchen. As if she belonged. And it felt right, to have her in this house, with him. As if she belonged by his side.

There was no doubt Zia Rosa had already taken a liking to her. He would have gotten some kind of stink-eye look by now if that weren't the case.

Still, he couldn't help but notice the slight dark circles under Laney's eyes, the tight set of her mouth. The way she still hadn't seemed to fully catch her breath. She looked fatigued, weary. He would have to make sure to get her back to her hotel room early so she could rest.

Their long hike and the subsequent trek down the Nocelle stairs had worn her down more than he would have expected.

Just went to show, even when his heart was in the right place, he couldn't seem to do right by Laney Taytum.

CHAPTER TWELVE

THREE HOURS LATER, after yet another scrumptious meal of seafood and homemade pasta, Gianni took her upstairs to sit on the balcony. Between the view of the ocean in the distance as the sun set and the quaint scenes of walkers and playing children in the street below, Laney felt as if she could be sitting in a painting. Straight out of the Italian Renaissance.

Just more affirmation that besides the awkwardness of the situation, she had made the right decision about Gianni accompanying her. By contrast, if she hadn't taken him up on his offer, she'd be alone in her hotel room right now with a paperback or trying to discern the Italian on some random television show.

Heavens, she felt tired though. More so than she'd felt in as long a time as she could remember. Her days back home were rather physical, so it was somewhat surprising that she was feeling so bone-deep exhausted.

"Did we over do it today?" Gianni asked next to her, tilting his chair back on its two back legs, reading her thoughts. But then, he seemed to have a knack for doing that. It hardly even surprised her anymore.

"So I look as exhausted as I feel, then?"

"You always look beautiful, Laney."

Good thing the sun was setting, hopefully the shadows

would prevent him from noticing the slight flush that instantly rushed to her cheeks at the compliment.

"But you do look rather tired," he added. "Sorry if the hike was too much."

She shook her head, wondering how he was managing to not topple backward as far as that chair was tilted. "Probably still some jet lag lingering on top of the exertion of the hike."

He looked concerned enough that she wanted to change the subject. "Your aunt is a lovely woman," she told him. "And quite a cook," she added, rubbing her belly. "I may never enjoy another meal again after that work of art she set in front of us."

"She is at that. It's too bad my cousin is away on business. You would have liked him. He's quite a character."

"Then it must be a family trait. Something in the genes."

She was certain she didn't imagine the slight wince and the sudden lift of his shoulders.

"Aunt Rosa is my father's sister," he said, as if that explained anything.

"I'm guessing you think you take after your mother's side of the family more."

The clang of metal hitting the wooden balcony floor rang through the air as he straightened the chair finally to sit on all four legs.

"You could say that." He stood suddenly. "I'll be right back."

When he returned about a minute later, he held a frosty tall bottle full of bright yellow liquid, along with two bottles of water and a couple of glasses.

"Limoncello," he declared, holding up the bottle. "Homemade by said cousin you have the misfortune of not being able to meet this visit."

As refreshing as the drink sounded, alcohol was definitely not what she wanted or needed at the moment. She could barely keep her eyes open as it was. But the sweaty bottle of water was practically calling to her.

"Maybe later. I will take the water from you though."

"Are you sure? This stuff is made from the ripest lemons grown only in this part of the world."

She absolutely was. "Just the water for now, please."

He tossed it to her with a shrug. "Suit yourself."

Tiny effervescent bubbles floated in the air as he poured himself the limoncello. The aroma tickled her nose and she imagined herself walking through a fruitful citrus garden. She would have to make a note to add a limoncello-based drink at the club when she returned to Boston.

Gianni seemed to have gone silent, sipping his drink slowly and staring at the ocean in the distance. The water was growing a darker, deeper shade of blue as the sun lowered farther into the horizon.

Taking a long drink of her water, she tried to keep the conversation going. "So, tell me about this cousin of yours. He's clearly some kind of drink master."

Gianni scoffed, didn't turn to her as he answered. "He's not really my cousin."

"He's not?"

"No. And Aunt Rosa's not really my aunt. And my father is definitely not—" He cut off the words, took another drink instead. This time it was way more than a sip.

Laney gave a shake of her head. Obviously, she was missing something.

He made the universal sign of sealed lips in a clearly mocking gesture. "But don't tell anyone. No one can talk about it. Even though everyone knows."

Understanding began to dawn. "Oh, do you mean you were adopted?" It was the only explanation that made sense of what he was saying.

"Not quite. I was the product of an extramarital affair."

Laney bit down on her gasp of surprise. Just barely. She could hardly find the words to respond. Exactly what did one say to such an admission?

Several beats of awkward silence ensued until she finally broke it with the truth. "I don't know what to say, Gianni. Other than that, from what I can see, you were born into and grew up in a loving family."

His fingers had tightened on the glass he held. She worried it might shatter in his hand. "That's the absolute truth. Except for one small yet significant detail."

"What's that?"

"The only reason my father calls me his son is because he'd never admit anyone on earth would have the audacity to betray him. Especially not the woman he fell in love with and made his wife."

Gianni couldn't believe what he'd just shared with her.

He couldn't remember the last time he'd talked about his heritage. If ever.

He turned to her now in the ever-growing darkness, fully prepared to see the pity on her lovely face. After all, how would someone like Laney Taytum, with her pedigree of perfect professionals ever understand what he'd just admitted.

But the expression Laney wore was one of clear concern. He wasn't sure that was much better.

"How did you find out?" she asked.

He let out a deep breath. "I can hardly remember. During one of our Italy visits when a distant uncle didn't realize I was rather fluent in Italian. I was fairly young, but not too young to understand what had just been revealed." There'd been no point in anyone denying it wasn't true. His mom had taken off one day, leaving nothing but a note behind that she'd found someone else. Gianni had never been told all the details, but something had made her return to Franco even as she carried another man's child.

"Everyone just sort of ignored it," he told Laney. "And I was just a kid. So I followed along."

"And you've kept it to yourself? All these years?"

"Not really. After college, I visited Aunt Rosa. She was the one person who I knew wouldn't lie to me. She confirmed my suspicions in not so many words."

Laney reached over the arm of her chair to rub the top of his hand. A small gesture, but one he found oddly soothing. "She clearly loves you, Gianni. I can tell just from these past few hours that she loves you deeply. I have three aunts. None of which I can say I'm particularly close to." She pointed back toward the house. "Not like what I witnessed in that house between you and that lady in there."

Huh. Maybe she did understand, after all. Who would have thought?

"Did you ever approach your mother for answers?"

He released a deep sigh. "I tried. My mother wouldn't even breach the subject.

"And you stopped bringing it up."

He shrugged. "What choice did I have? What would have been the point in confronting anyone?"

"How brave of you."

He had to chuckle at that. "How in the world is any of that being brave?"

Her hand tightened around his. "It is. You never hurt either one of your parents by confronting them. You even work for your father."

That last part was almost certainly about to change but she didn't need to know all that. He'd divulged enough to her already.

More than enough.

"We should probably drop it," he said, tilting his head in the direction of the house. "I don't want Zia to hear any of this conversation."

"Of course," she said, immediately dropping his hand. Gianni felt the loss of her touch right down in his center.

He lifted his glass. "Here's to family," he said in a toast that was meant to be ironic. "And to this gorgeous sunset."

Laney took the cue and remained silent for several minutes. For a good part of the hour, they simply sat and admired the changing colors of the sky and the ocean below it. Eventually, the passersby in the street below slowed to a trickle. The sound of children kicking around a ball had already ceased.

It was probably time to call it a night and get Laney back to her hotel. But when he turned to tell her so, he stopped short. She had her arms folded in front of her. Her chest rose and fell in a steady, slow rhythm. Her head lay tilted on her shoulder.

She was sound asleep.

With a sigh, he stood and went to her, then gently lifted her out of the chair, taking care not to wake her. She really had looked tired. The best thing for her now was just to get some rest. Rosa had a spare bedroom she usually kept clean and ready given all the various visitors she was accustomed to. And he certainly wasn't any stranger to crashing on a couch now and again. He knew his aunt wouldn't mind the company.

Walking back into the house, he made his way toward the hallway and back to the spare room. He set Laney down on the spare bed, and threw one of Zia Rosa's hand-crocheted covers over her.

For one long moment, he simply let himself indulge by watching her. They'd known each other only a short time but had gone through quite a bit together already. No wonder he'd felt at ease enough to share his family's deep-seated secret with her. Something about her had called to him from the moment he'd laid eyes on her.

Too bad it couldn't go anywhere. She was the first woman to have him even so much as reconsider his stance about a long-term relationship. Laney Taytum had him thinking all sorts of scenarios he would have previously never considered for himself. But it was all just wishful thinking. They were from completely different worlds. She came from a strong lineage of overachievers and knew exactly who she was. While he was a man who didn't even rightfully belong in his family and had no idea who'd sired him. She was much too far out of his league.

Finally, he turned to leave, taking care to step softly over the creak he knew was there on the wooden floor under the plush rug.

He was about to shut the door behind him when he heard her low voice in the darkness.

"Please stay."

He hesitated for just the briefest second. But then resigned himself. He wouldn't be able to turn her down. Pulling off his T-shirt, he slipped under the blanket and took her in his arms.

He couldn't even explain what happened next. He meant to give her just a small quick peck on the cheek as a good-night. But she turned her head at just the right moment. Or maybe it was the wrong moment. But his lips found hers. Then he was tasting her mouth, a low groan rumbling in her throat. Her arms wrapped around him, her chest tight against his own. He simply savored the taste of her, blanketed in the warmth of her body. Gentle yet untamed. Full of yearning. He might not ever get enough.

It was over all too soon. Gianni didn't even know which one of them pulled away first. Both of them remained silent for several beats, the kiss hanging heavy in the air between them. Finally, Laney released a deep sigh, whether from weariness or regret for the unplanned kiss, he didn't know and wasn't sure he wanted to find out. But she didn't ask him to leave. So he simply held her as she fell asleep, until the morning light woke them both.

So this was goodbye. Gianni cursed under his breath and tried not think about their kiss that night. He'd been a fool for thinking even for a moment that it might have meant anything more than a temporary lapse in judgement. Laney was leaving for Florence. And he would just have to find a way to forget about her.

Easier said than done.

Now, Gianni watched Laney's retreating back as she made her way down the platform at the Nocera Inferiore train station, her dark curls bouncing along her shoulders. Rushing because she was convinced she was late.

On her way to sunny Florence.

Amazing just how fast three days had gone by. During his weaker moments over those days, he'd been tempted to offer to travel there with her. Luckily, those temptations passed quickly. For it was better this way, better to make a clean break. He hadn't spent much time in Florence, thus had no excuse to accompany her as any kind of guide or expert.

He would be of no use to her. Moot point. Not like she'd asked him to accompany her.

Laney Taytum was off on her next adventure. An adventure that had no room for him. He'd set her up to meet one of his distant cousins, just so she wasn't alone when she first arrived. His part in her travels was over. As was any part he had in her life. Anyway, he had to get back to the States. So much there needed to be attended to. For one, he had to figure out a way to buy out his share of Martino Entertainment Enterprises in case he was no longer wanted as part of the company. His father had been eerily quiet since Gianni had so openly defied him about pursuing Laney's club. The gym-and-fitness arm was his brainchild. He'd developed and grown that piece and had no intention of letting it go easy.

Starting over with a competing business was always an option but one he'd rather avoid. He just had to get the old man to agree. He almost chuckled out loud. Piece of cake. Trying to convince that man of anything once he made up his mind was like putting out a four-alarm fire by blowing on it.

So much of Gianni's professional life was up in the air at the moment. Yet another reason he had to forget Laney Taytum existed. Maybe they'd run into each other on the streets of Boston. Who knew? Perhaps next time he saw her, she'd be accompanied by the man she was meant to be with. Someone more appropriate, who would fit better in her world and with her family.

A rage of emotion he refused to acknowledge as jealousy rushed through his midsection at the thought before he shoved it aside. Any regret he may feel was his burden to bear.

Still, he couldn't help the deep longing he felt when she turned back to wave at him one more time, then disappeared from his sight completely. That was it, then. No more looking back for either of them. He'd check with his relative to make sure she arrived in Florence safely and that she was settled in well at her next hotel. His cousin Zara had promised to set her up with a reputable tour company who would make sure she was well taken care of.

He hoped she had the time of her life. And he hoped life for her afterward continued to be adventurous and full of happiness. It was no less than what she deserved.

* * *

He really was a lovely specimen. The perfect man, actually. Every muscle chiseled and perfect. His tall imposing
frame sent a shiver of excitement up her spine. How long
had Laney waited for this moment? Probably her whole life.

Yep, the statue of David was everything she had expected and more.

Just looking at him took her breath away. That had to
be the reason for the quaking in her stomach. Pure adrenaline begotten by finally setting her eyes on one of the
world's greatest artistic creations. Only, it didn't explain
the mild nausea that had plagued her since boarding the
train from the Amalfi Coast. She pushed back the memories that threatened to assault her mind as she thought about
her time there. Gianni hadn't asked her to stay, not even for
another day or so. Nor had he offered to travel with her to
Florence. How foolish of her to think even for a moment
that he might. He'd felt bad about what had transpired between them in Boston and he'd made up for his mistake
by playing tour guide in Positano. Now that his conscience
was clear, he was moving on.

Enough. Laney had to move on too. She couldn't think
about Gianni Martino. She was here on the second part of
her bucket-list trip, darn it. And she was going to make the
most of her time here. Starting with an attempt to sketch the
marvelous work of art that stood before her now. Drawing
and painting weren't exactly her strongest creative skills,
but she thought she had more talent than what was currently being shown. It seemed to be taking a lot of effort
to drag the pencil across the page to form any semblance
of a depiction of the statue.

Maybe she should have had more for breakfast. Being
in Italy certainly made her ravenous.

Visiting the statue first clearly wasn't a good idea. She

should have started with the paintings farther down the hall. The *Madonna with Child* would no doubt be breathtaking.

Child. A nagging suspicion crawled into the back of her mind and she almost swatted the thought away. But it persisted.

It couldn't be.

The sketch pad fell out of her hands. Slowly standing up, she felt the blood rush to her limbs. Several deep, even breaths didn't do much to settle her nerves.

Could this really be happening? The constant hunger, the fatigue, the mild nausea that hit her without warning. All the clues of the past few weeks started coming together. What if her suspicions were founded? What then? It was too much to think about.

Her sketching was going to have to wait. Right now, she had to get back to the hotel and ask about the nearest pharmacy or medical center. Time seemed to flow into another dimension as she slowly made her way out of the museum. Disoriented and scared, she turned the wrong way before fixing her mistake and turning in the right direction.

An hour later, she had her answer. Laney couldn't seem to move, blindly staring out the window at the piazza outside. Her mind was a complete scramble. She had bought two tests just to be sure. Both results were the same. She shuddered at the thought of telling her parents. But she would do so and she would make sure everything that came from now on would be her decision and hers alone. She had more than herself to think about now.

And Gianni. Her heart did a little somersault in her chest as she thought of how she would tell him. One of the first things he'd announced about himself was just how much he wasn't interested in things like getting married or having a family.

She was all alone in this. Same as ever.

CHAPTER THIRTEEN

SHE REHEARSED HOW her end of the conversation might go one more time before picking up her cell phone. Laney had started the practice during her long trip back to Boston. Somehow, all the rehearsing didn't seem to be making it any easier. With a frustrated huff, she threw her phone back down on the sofa. She couldn't do it, couldn't sum up the courage.

How in the world was she going to tell Gianni that she was pregnant with his baby? Would he blame her?

She could only hope he'd be a better man than that.

There was a very real possibility he'd want nothing to do with her when she told him. Or their child. She would just have to accept that and learn to live with it somehow. Though the thought that Gianni would turn his back on her when she was the mother of his child sliced her with a searing hurt.

Only one way to find out. This was going to be the most important and probably the most nerve-racking phone call she'd ever have to make. And she absolutely couldn't put it off any longer. She'd been back in the States three days already.

To think, she'd almost deleted his number from her phone. After he'd dropped her off at the train station and said goodbye as if they were never meant to see each other again, it had seemed the most prudent thing to do. Why in the world would it have occurred to her that she'd need to call that number in a few days? They'd been careful. Or so she'd thought.

Her hand shook as she picked the phone up and called up his contact info. Without giving herself another chance to chicken out, she hit the dial icon. And puffed out a sigh in frustration as soon as it went through.

Voice mail.

Or maybe it was a sigh of relief. She hardly knew her right from her left at the moment. She hadn't even considered she'd get his voice mail. Hormones must be scrambling her brain, given that the possibility hadn't even occurred to her during all those rehearsals she'd gone over in her mind. She practically flung the phone across the room over onto the love seat.

It rang the second it landed on the cushion. She knew without looking that it had to be him, though it was the standard ringtone. Walking with heavy steps to retrieve it, she clicked on the call without giving herself a chance to chicken out. But no words would come out of her mouth.

"Laney? Is that you?" His voice washed over her like the smoothest waterfall. It had only been a few days since she'd seen him, but it seemed so much longer. A lot had happened.

She'd missed him.

"Laney? Did you just call me?" he asked.

For an insane moment, she thought about lying that it had been a pocket dial. But that would just be putting off the inevitable. She forced her mouth to work. "Yes, it's me. Hello, Gianni."

"Hello. Are you calling from Florence? Is everything okay?"

"Yes. I mean, no." Oh, Lord. This call was going so

poorly. "I mean I'm calling from Boston. Just decided to cut the trip short a little bit."

I don't know if everything is okay.

"Oh. I see. Weren't you enjoying your trip?"

Not after we parted, she almost said out loud before she caught herself. "Something came up. Something you should know about. It's why I'm calling. Otherwise, I wouldn't have bothered you."

Nothing but silence came through the tiny speaker for several beats. Finally, he spoke. "Sounds serious. Maybe you should just tell me."

"Well, you might want to sit down. If you're standing, that is." Wow. She really wasn't handling this well at all.

"Laney, tell me, sweetheart."

"Well, it just so happens, that I'm pregnant," she blurted out, just like ripping off the proverbial bandage. An adequate analogy, given the pain she was experiencing. "I found out in Florence."

She heard him suck in a breath. "Our weekend in Boston?" he asked.

"Yes. It had to be."

"Okay. I see."

"I thought you should know."

"And you're absolutely certain?"

What a question. She wouldn't be calling him otherwise. This wasn't the kind of news a woman broke on a hunch or guess, after all. "I took two different tests in Italy. Then confirmed with my doctor once I arrived back in the States."

"Guess that settles it. Are you feeling well?"

"Yes. For the most part." Physically, she was hanging in there. Her emotional state was another matter entirely. "Just hungry a lot. You know what they say about eating for two." She chuckled at her own rather lame attempt at lightening the moment.

"Well, uh, thank you. For letting me know." He paused for what had to be a second. But on her end, it may as well have been a lifetime.

"Uh, you're welcome?" For the life of her, she couldn't come up with anything else to say. She'd been right. This really was the most awkward phone call she'd ever made.

"But I thought we were—"

She cut him off. "Yeah. I did too. I guess not enough."

"Huh. Okay. I see."

He really had to stop repeating that or she was going to lose her mind completely. Only what he said right after was even worse.

"Yeah. So, listen, can I call you back?"

"Call me back?"

"Uh-huh. I'm actually in the middle of a rather important meeting."

A meeting? He wanted to interrupt this earth-shattering news she was delivering because of a business meeting? "Oh. Of course. Sorry." Why in the world was she apologizing? "For interrupting the meeting, I mean."

"Okay. I see."

Laney rolled her eyes. He was clearly at a loss for words. Or maybe he was just really concerned that he was missing his important meeting.

It hardly mattered. She'd delivered the news. The rest was up to him, the ball completely in his court.

"I'll let you get back to it, then," she told him, clicking off the call without saying goodbye.

Tears stung the back of her eyes as she sank down into the floor. His reaction was one she would have never guessed. She'd had less business-sounding calls with her wine supplier.

She was a fool to have expected any different.

* * *

Gianni slipped the phone back into his pocket and braced himself against the wall with one arm. Laney's phone call seemed like some kind of daydream. As if he'd just made it up.

But it was all too real, he knew. A baby. His baby.

The new reality was going to take some time for him to process. The truth was, he hadn't seen this coming by a light-year. He knew he could have handled the call better than he had. He'd just been so shocked by the news. So he'd tried to be very careful with his words, saying less for fear of saying the wrong thing. Perhaps he'd been a bit too straightforward and narrow with his response. But that was better than the alternative. Hurting her somehow or making a statement she didn't agree with.

For all he knew, she might not even want him in this child's life. That thought felt like a slice across his midsection. If that were the case, he'd have to do all he could to convince her otherwise. He couldn't live with himself if his reality was to live his life as an absentee father. Or worse, if he were made to simply stand back and let another man raise his son or daughter.

But he was getting way ahead of himself. First, he had to let it all fully sink in. And he had to check in on Laney as soon as was feasible.

His accountant stepped out into the hallway. "Mr. Martino? Has something come up? Did you want to reschedule?"

Gianni didn't even realize how long he'd been standing out there. It could have been an hour or merely a few minutes. He just remembered jumping out of his chair and running out of the room when he'd realized he'd missed Laney's call. "No. I don't want to reschedule. In fact, there's an entirely different matter we need to discuss."

The man lifted an eyebrow in question.

"On top of the financial documents to present to my father for a purchase offer, I'd like to establish a few trust and college funds with investment to begin immediately."

His accountant didn't bother to question him, simply motioned for him to step back into the room. Good thing too—Gianni wasn't sure how he would even try to explain the additional request that seemed to have come out of nowhere.

Besides, his finance man wasn't the first person he intended to announce the fact that he was going to be a father. The words echoed around in his head, like musical notes ricocheting off the chambers of his mind.

He was going to be a father.

Two and a half hours later, as he arrived at his brother's house, Gianni felt he might have finally absorbed the brunt of the shock. He rang the doorbell and waited for someone to answer, not even sure exactly how to break the news to Angelo. There was a lot to explain, given the circumstances.

His brother opened the door wearing pajama bottoms and a gray T-shirt that had seen better days. "Please tell me you're not here to rile my kids up right before bedtime."

"No. That's not why I'm here, though it's very likely to happen."

Angelo looked upward, whispering some kind of prayer to the deity above. "You gonna let me in, or what? It's starting to drizzle out here."

Angelo rubbed his jaw, as if thinking about leaving him out there. "I suppose I have to," he said as he walked inside, leaving Gianni to step in and shut the door behind him.

"Though you might be recruited to help with a bath and then to read a bedtime story. Don't say I didn't warn you."

Angelo continued walking toward the kitchen where

Gemma could be heard demanding more water in her cup. Gino was nowhere to be seen or heard. Which, based on past experience, did not bode well for anyone.

"Well, that's part of the reason I'm here, little bro," he said to Angelo's back.

"Yeah, why's that?" Angelo asked, throwing the question over his shoulder. "You'll never convince me you actually came here to help with the bedtime routine."

"Ah, that's where you'd be wrong. See, it turns out I might need the practice."

It took an instant or so for his words to register. Angelo stopped in his tracks and whirled around to face him. "Come again? Why would you need practice—" Gianni watched as realization dawned over his brother's features. "Honey," he bellowed in the direction of the kitchen. "You might want to come out here."

"I just found out myself."

"Just found out what?" his sister-in-law wanted to know.

"Looks like our little *bambinos* are going to have a cousin soon."

Marie gasped and nearly let go of the toddler on her hip. Angelo strode across the room, his hand outstretched. Gripping Gianni's palm in his, he gave him a firm, hard handshake.

"Well, don't keep us in suspense. Who is the unlucky lady?"

If they only knew. "It happens to be a bit of a long story."

Marie pointed to him. "Then I suggest you brew some coffee, then come upstairs to help your brother and I get the little ones bathed and tucked in."

Gianni scoffed in mock affront. "You're so bossy."

His sister-in-law nodded. "*Si.* And I'm also nosy. So let's get to it. You know where the coffeepot is."

He'd have to brew it really strong. Telling them the entire story was going to take a while.

Forty-eight hours, forty-seven minutes and however many seconds.

That's how long it had been since she'd spoken with Gianni about her baby. *Their* baby. She hadn't heard a word from him since save for a couple of impersonal texts. No matter. Nothing he could say would make a difference at this point anyway. She was going to be a mother, and if that meant single parenthood, then so be it. She'd find a way to cope.

A small knock sounded at her office door and pulled her out of her thoughts. It had to be her cousin. Mabel was on a two-week break from school. She usually helped out at the club when she wasn't up in Vermont studying and she was here helping now. Thank the heavens for it too. Laney was definitely slowing down, even though it was rather early in the first trimester. This little one was already proving to be rather demanding, between the increase in her calorie count and the sheer exhaustion she often felt.

"Come in."

She pulled the supply order form from under the pile of papers on her desk. Mabel had offered to do the weekly inventory for her. But the footsteps sounded wrong, too heavy. A lump formed in her throat when she looked up.

"Hey, Laney."

How many times in one lifetime could he approach her that way, completely unannounced? Each time felt as if a rug had been pulled out from underneath her.

"Hope it's okay to just show up?"

She did her best to appear unaffected. Inside, she was a shaky mess. "That depends, I guess. What exactly are you doing here?"

"I came to check up on you. Are you feeling all right?"

"I feel fine," she lied. He didn't need to know about the exhaustion or the sudden bout of morning sickness that had come out of nowhere and nearly had her heading back to bed.

"Good. That's good."

Leaning back in her chair, she folded her arms across her chest. "Was that it, then?"

He looked at her in question. "I'd say it's not. Don't you think we need to talk?"

"Oh. So now it's time to talk. No business meetings today, I take it?"

Without asking, he pulled the chair by the wall over and across from her desk and sat down. Laney had half a mind to tell him not to bother, but figured she owed it to her unborn child to hear him out. For now, at least.

"I apologize for that. I was not in exactly a good position to talk at that very moment. Not physically or in any other sense."

Did he think that served as any kind of acceptable excuse? She was convinced he wanted nothing to do with her or their child since she had barely heard from him aside from a few perfunctory text messages. Now, here he was telling her he thought they *needed to talk*.

She summoned a deep breath to try to calm down. Just last night, she'd read in her baby book that stress hormones could have an impact on the baby. It didn't help that he looked as handsome as ever. His hair had grown just enough that it almost reached his shoulders now. He must have been at the gym earlier. He had that glow that came from a good bout of exercise followed by a long shower.

She really had no business imagining him in the shower. *Focus!* "And since then? It's been almost three days since we spoke."

"Didn't you get my texts? Asking how you were?"

If he thought texts were adequate in this situation, he was sorely mistaken. "Texts? You think a few texts were enough?"

"Laney, I didn't want to come and talk until I had everything in order. There were a lot of matters to tie up. Please know that I understand what a huge responsibility this is. One I don't take lightly."

There it was. Responsibility. Loose ends to tie up.

While she considered this baby a blessing to cherish, he clearly saw their situation as just an inconvenience that had to be addressed. Yet another rejection, another let down. Gianni no doubt planned to move on with his life. Who knew if she or their child would even be part of it. And she had no business feeling hurt or even surprised. Given what he'd told her that night on his aunt's balcony, the complicated relationship he had with his parents, she knew it must be difficult for him to find himself an unplanned expectant father.

Still, it was pretty hard to accept. Without warning, her anger suddenly morphed into pure, unfiltered weariness. She didn't have all the answers, and just felt so tired.

Another knock on her door suddenly interrupted them. It was followed by her cousin rushing into the room. "Sorry it took me so long. Had a little spill of pomegranate juice as I was mixing. What a mess. Red liquid everywhere!" She halted when she finally realized Laney had a visitor. Her eyes narrowed when she realized who that visitor was. "Gianni. Wish I could say it's nice to see you again."

He didn't acknowledge the goading nor the tone. Mabel had been the one to hear the alternating angry then sad rants since Laney returned from Europe. "Mabel. Hope you've been well," he answered with a polite nod in her direction.

"I can come back another time?" Mabel directed the question at her.

But Gianni answered by standing up. "I should be the one to go. Can we meet for dinner, Laney? To discuss all this and go over all our options."

He may as well have been speaking about a business negotiation. As much as she wanted to get it over with, delaying this conversation would give her time to get her thoughts together. "I think that's a wise plan."

"I'll see you in a couple of hours."

"Are you okay?" Mabel asked as soon as Gianni had left. "That was pretty intense."

"I'm not sure I'd describe things that way," Laney answered, waiting for her pulse to slow. Seeing Gianni for the first time since announcing her pregnancy was wreaking havoc on her insides. "I'd say Gianni was the opposite of intense just now."

"What do you mean?" Mabel asked.

Laney puffed out a sigh in frustration and pushed the bangs off her forehead. "He's just so… I don't know…flat, and straightforward. As if this is all no big deal." Darn it, her eyes were beginning to sting. She was not going to cry. Not again.

"You want him to be more excited about the baby."

That was it in a nutshell. Funny how she hadn't been able to articulate that one fact. Not even to herself, let alone be able to communicate it to Gianni. "Is that too much to ask?"

Mabel walked around the desk and sat on the edge of it, facing her. "Of course not, sweetie."

Laney sniffled, still desperately trying to keep the tears at bay. She wasn't sure how much longer she could hold out. "My parents could barely hide their disappointment in me. Again. That I'd gotten myself in yet another predicament they see as less than ideal." She squeezed her eyes shut at the memory of the heavy scene in her parents' living room when she'd broken the news to them. "Mom's first words after I told them was to ask how I could have been so careless."

Mabel's lips tightened. "I'm so sorry. As much as I love my aunt and uncle, they can be completely tone-deaf. They've always been the type that had that proverbial stick up their—"

Laney cut her off before she could complete that unseemly statement, as funny as it was. "Well, I seem to be the only one feeling any sense of thrill about this soon-to-be little human."

Mabel patted her arm. "That's not true. You know I can't wait to be an aunt to this little one."

"Thank you for that. I wish Emily had said the same thing when I told her yesterday."

"I take it she was also less than congratulatory."

"You would be correct. If I didn't know better, I'd say she was rather disappointed that I'd be a mother before her. She's the one who just got married."

"Families come in all different ways these days. Plenty of women have babies on their own."

"Yes, I know." Looked like she was well on her way to becoming one of those women. Life as a single parent was daunting, and she couldn't help but feel scared. But she'd do whatever it took to make sure her baby thrived. Having her child's father by her side, in some way or another, would have been ideal. But it didn't seem to be in the cards for her.

"And we both know Emily usually finds ways to feel slighted. She'll come around. And so will your parents."

But her family's reaction was secondary. What mattered more than any of their feelings about her child was the way the baby's father felt about him or her. Judging by what she'd seen so far, all indications implied he felt little to nothing.

"I hope so, May." She patted her belly. "Or else the size of our family is going to be small indeed."

CHAPTER FOURTEEN

MAYBE AGREEING TO dinner at Gianni's apartment hadn't been the best idea on her part. After all, this was where it had all begun. The night he'd cooked dinner for her seemed ages ago. Hard to believe it had been close to two months ago. How different things were between them now.

Laney sighed and pulled her car to park along the only spot left on the street. As she reached the steps, Gianni's door suddenly flew open and a small child ran out onto the porch. A little boy. He looked to be about two or three. The slight resemblance was there if one looked hard enough. He had to be Gianni's nephew.

"Hi!" he declared to her, then stuck his thumb in his mouth. Gianni stepped through the door at that very moment. He lifted the child up and in one smooth gesture lifted him over his head to sit on his shoulders.

Laney had to remind herself to breathe. The image of Gianni with a small child was pushing all the wrong buttons. If he had planned this scene, he couldn't have done a better job.

"Hey. You're here." He gave his nephew a small bounce on his shoulders. "I see you two have met."

She had to clear her throat in order to speak. "Um… We were just getting acquainted."

"Gino won't be here long. Angelo just ran out to get some groceries from the North End."

He motioned her in, then followed her through the door, ducking low as he entered. His nephew giggled when he finally let him down. The little boy scrambled away toward the living room where several wooden puzzles lay scattered across the rug. He bit down on one of the large pieces before trying to cram it into a spot it clearly didn't fit in.

"You're babysitting?"

"Yeah, sorry. He was supposed to be picked up an hour ago. Angelo's just running late."

"No. Don't apologize. I'm glad to be able to meet your nephew."

Gianni glanced at his watch. "Well, looks like you're going to be able to meet my brother, as well. He should be here any minute."

Laney was a grown professional woman. Yet the prospect of meeting Gianni's brother for the first time sent a shiver of nervousness down her spine. What would he think of her? What would his parents think when she eventually met them?

Though she hadn't allowed herself to really dwell on it, she had to acknowledge there might still be some lingering resentment about her unwillingness to sell her business.

All of that had to be water under the bridge, however. They had bigger fish to fry, as the saying went.

"The good news is my babysitting fee is being paid in a very valuable currency."

She had to laugh at the clear humor in his tone. Gianni's natural charm served well to lighten some of the tension. She couldn't help but feel appreciative. "What would that be?"

"Desanti's pizza. Extra-cheesy. Hope you're hungry."

How uncanny. She'd been craving pizza for the past

day or so, never getting around to order any. Usually, by the time she got home, she was so famished and so low on energy that she nibbled on toast while boiling pasta or reheating leftovers.

"It's like you read my mind."

The doorbell sounded at that moment and whoever it was didn't bother to wait for an answer. A slight breeze blew through the room as the door opened and a tall wideshouldered man carrying several large pizza boxes stepped through. The aroma of garlic and cheesy tomato immediately filled the air.

"There he is now," Gianni declared. "About time, little bro. What took you so long? Come meet Laney."

Angelo left with his son about thirty minutes after walking in, taking two of the boxes of pizza with him. Laney had concluded right away that there'd never been any reason to feel anxious about meeting Gianni's younger sibling. The man had an easy demeanor and charming sense of humor. Plus, the teasing banter between the two brothers, where they incessantly and mockingly insulted each other, made for a rather humorous dinner.

And now she and Gianni were alone. No buffer in the form of an adorable toddler or a talkative distracting sibling. Time to acknowledge the real reason for this little visit.

Laney took a sip of her sparkling water, watching as Gianni tidied up the kitchen and loaded the dishwasher. How could a man look so sexy doing tedious housework? And the way he'd been with his nephew, playful and patient. He'd laughed and simply cleaned up when Gino launched a slice of pizza across the table, splattering sauce and cheese everywhere.

Yeah, it was pretty clear Gianni Martino would make

an excellent father, if he only wanted to. That was the part that wasn't quite clear from where she was standing.

He joined her in the living room after drying his hands on a dish towel. "Did you get enough to eat?"

"More than enough. I might have had one full box."

"Hardly counts. You only ate from the plain cheese."

She rubbed a hand along her very full middle. "My tummy definitely disagrees with you. Trust me, it counts."

Gianni chuckled, then turned serious in a rather striking transformation. Looked like it was time to stop avoiding the elephant in the room.

"Listen, Laney." He braced his elbows on his knees and leaned toward her. "I just want to tell you that I take full responsibility for what's happening."

His statement sounded perilously close to an apology. She wasn't having it. "I played a fairly significant role in getting us to this point also, Gianni." After all, she'd been the one to invite him back to the hotel that night after the harbor cruise. Then she'd asked him to stay with her all night. "I was the one who did the asking that night, remember?"

He shrugged. "I wasn't exactly resisting."

There was no point in any of this. So much was being left unsaid while they tiptoed around useless niceties. But darned if she knew how to push past the formality between them now. In many ways, Gianni's demeanor at the moment reminded her of the time he'd shown up at her office to finally admit that he'd been planning on making her a business offer all along. This wasn't the warm, charming man who accompanied her around Positano, then took her to his beloved aunt's house, where he sat with her on the balcony, laying bare his soul. And it most definitely wasn't the passionate and sensual man who had spent the night with her in Boston.

She didn't know how to breach the distance to Gianni Martino in his current alteration.

"You should know I've already started the process of setting up both trust and college funds." She'd expected as much. "I can send you the files with details on all the portfolios," he added.

She shook her head. "That won't be necessary. I trust you know what you're doing. I'll be making my own investments."

"Fair enough. And, of course, I will contribute to day-to-day expenses. I have my accountants sending you documents as we speak."

A muscle twitched along his jaw before he spoke again. His shoulders visibly tensed. "As far as my role, I want you to know that I'll respect your discretion. To a point."

Okay. "What does that mean?"

"I'd like to be a part of this child's life. I'm willing to be flexible, and I'll bend over backward to make sure you're completely comfortable with my level of involvement. But I do plan to be involved."

"I understand." What kind of woman did he think she was? Of course, she had no intention of keeping him from his child. If anything, the more likely possibility was that eventually he would see both her and the child as more of a remnant from a past life.

He'd been so clear and adamant about not wanting a family. Or children of his own. He was saying all the right things now but would he eventually grow resentful that one had been forced on him and turn his back on her and their child?

Pain seared through her chest at that very real possibility. Then she'd have the Herculean task of making sure her child remained sound and whole afterward. Maybe it was the hormones, but the thought of her baby's father simply moving on with his life and leaving them behind as the unintended consequences from his past fling felt like a gut punch. It took all she had not to double over.

"I can have paperwork drawn up which outlines specific details if you like." He was back to being all business again. Not that he'd ever completely stopped.

"I don't think that's necessary. But go ahead if it makes you feel more comfortable, Gianni."

He leaned back against the couch, rubbed his jaw. "There is one other option I feel we should consider."

"And that is?"

"We could always get married."

Laney stared at him as if he'd grown horns atop his head. She gave a brisk shake of her head before speaking. "I'm sorry. I could have sworn you said we might want to consider getting married. I'm sure I must have misheard."

She looked so cute when she was taken aback. Clearly, she hadn't been expecting such a suggestion in the least. But it made sense, even if it was a rather unconventional marriage proposal. He'd thought about it over and over and kept coming to the same conclusion. Despite how he felt about the so-called sanctity of marriage, there was more at play here. He wanted his son or daughter to feel accepted and loved. He wanted this baby to know exactly who they were and who their parents were. If Gianni had his way, his child could grow up in a home with two loving parents. Legally, all the red tape and financial issues would be so much easier to address. Why have a child grow up in a broken home if there was an alternative? All logical. "That is indeed what I said."

Laney cupped her hand to her mouth and chuckled. "Right. Ha-ha."

She thought he was joking. "Laney, I'm being serious. Think about all the ways it makes sense."

Dropping her hand, she slowly shook her head. "You and I know it only makes sense for one reason. The only reason you're even suggesting it. You're only doing this because I'm pregnant."

"I can think of worse reasons for a couple to tie the knot."

She suddenly stood, waving her arm in clear frustration. "You wouldn't have even considered getting married if we didn't find ourselves in this predicament. Why would you change your mind?"

He would have thought that was obvious. "I think you know why."

Her shoulders suddenly slumped. "This isn't the middle ages, Gianni. Couples who are expecting together are perfectly capable of co-parenting without tying themselves down to each other forever through marriage."

Ouch. Quite a strike to his ego. The thought of marriage to him was obviously not a palatable one for Laney Taytum. Not that it should surprise him, anyway. Her thinking made sense. They had nothing in common. He knew full well she was in a completely different league. A much higher one. Still, there was a child to consider now. It wasn't about just the two of them.

"First of all, marriages don't always have to be based on some kind of emotion. Lots of unions are made simply because they're beneficial for both parties."

Something shifted behind her eyes. "I'd like to think mine will mean more than that. Or at least I plan on approaching my own marriage that way."

He didn't voice out loud what he was thinking. Unlike him, Laney appeared to harbor the illusion that love and affection had to be the impetus behind a proposal of marriage. He had no such delusion. "Look, I'm simply putting forth all our options. I think we should be open-minded, that's all. Just give it some thought."

She crossed her arms in front of her chest, studied him up and down. "You really are serious."

He stood too, strode over to her across the room and gently lifted her chin. "Think about it, Laney. We tend to get along for the most part. Think of all the fun we had together in Italy. The spark between us the night we met." He didn't imagine the way her body shuddered. She knew what he said was the truth, so he pushed further. "We certainly seem to be compatible in bed."

Her lower lip quivered and it took all he had not to lean down and take that lip with his own, to kiss her until that strained, incredulous expression melted off her face and all she could think about was just how compatible they'd been. Not the time.

"That's hardly a foundation upon which to start a marriage," she argued.

He dropped his hand from her chin. "Maybe. But it's a fairly strong start, I'd say. More than what a lot of couples have."

Couples like his parents for instance. What good was their intense love for each other when the very crux of their relationship depended on one big lie?

Of all the ways she'd imagined being proposed to—on a whirlwind trip through Italy, over a romantic dinner, maybe during a lazy stroll through gentle waves along a Cape Cod beach—that it might happen sitting in a living room in South Boston amidst a clutter of wooden preschool puzzles hadn't occurred to her once.

"Please don't answer right away. I want you to give it some real thought. In a logical and responsible way."

There was that word again. *Responsible.*

He really thought she might be able to accept a marriage proposal that had only been offered out of a sense of duty. Simply gravy or icing on the cake that they happened to be physically drawn to each other. It was all so wrong.

There was no point in telling Gianni, but she already knew her answer. She'd been living in a loveless family her whole life. She had no intention of starting her own family with a loveless marriage. Especially given that even the mere potential for developing any kind of love was completely one-sided.

The word hadn't so much as crossed Gianni's lips.

"What exactly did you have in mind?" she asked, genuinely curious about just how much thought he'd even given this whole suggestion. "That we find a justice of the peace, sign some papers and then be off on our way?"

He gave a slight shrug of his shoulders. "That seems to be the most feasible way."

He really hadn't given this much thought at all. He was asking her practically on a whim.

He rubbed his jaw. "If it's the thought of missing out on a wedding that you're concerned about, I'm sure we can think of a way to throw some kind of party."

He thought she was worried about a lack of celebration behind their mock nuptials. Granted, they hadn't met that long ago but she'd really thought he knew her better. That did it. For such a smart, successful man, he certainly could be rather clueless. She began to turn on her heel, at a complete loss for words when he gently took her by the forearm.

"Whatever you decide, it won't change anything else we talked about. I plan on being a father to this child in every way that matters."

At least there was that.

"You can be as involved in his or her life as you want to be," she reassured him. "I promise you that."

"Thank you," he said simply. "Just promise me you'll think about it. Getting married."

That much was an easy promise to make. No doubt, she wouldn't be able to think of much else. She could only nod in response.

Gianni knew he had to give her time and some space. But it was really hard to focus on any kind of business—or anything else, for that matter. He'd been so distracted in the ring while sparring this morning he'd failed to duck a powerful right hook and currently sported a nasty bruise right below his cheekbone.

Laney wasn't exactly ignoring him; she responded right away to his texts and calls. But her answers were short and to the point. Bordering on curt. He had no idea if she'd given his proposal any thought whatsoever. It had been close to a week. Maybe the length of time was answer enough in itself.

He picked up his phone with the intention of calling her for the umpteenth time that afternoon only to slip it back into his pocket. He didn't want to pressure her in any way. But the truth was, he had to admit he missed her. An hour didn't go by where he didn't think about her and how she must be doing. Was their baby okay? Was she getting enough to eat?

Weren't pregnant women supposed to be taking some kind of vitamin regularly? He needed to be sure to ask her about that at some point. In fact, he could do so right now. For his own piece of mind, if nothing else. He pulled his phone back out and this time actually clicked on her number.

She answered but not until so many rings passed that he was convinced he was about to land in her voice mail.

"Hi, Gianni. Sorry, I almost didn't hear the phone. It's really loud here."

"Where are you?" And what was all that shrieking in the background? It sounded like she could be in the middle of a rowdy soccer match.

She chuckled softly into the phone. He barely heard it. "Impromptu trip to the aquarium. Mabel had some research she needed to do before returning to school. Asked me to come along." That explained all the noise.

"Sounds very busy."

"There appear to be at least three different school field trips."

"Does that mean you're having fun?"

"Yes and no. Mabel's been in the lab for about an hour now. At the moment, I'm admiring the jellyfish exhibit by myself."

He heard the shriek of a child in the background. Or maybe it was several shrieking children, he couldn't even tell. He couldn't remember the last time he'd visited the aquarium but he certainly remembered how loud it had been while he was there. And also the headache he'd been burdened with afterward. So he surprised himself when he asked her the next question.

"I'm not too far from there. Want some company?"

She paused so long that he peeked at the screen to make sure the call hadn't disconnected somehow. When she finally answered, he could hardly hear for all the noise.

"Sure. Why not? I'll probably have moved on to the penguins by then. I'll see you in a bit." With that, she disconnected the call.

Less than half an hour later, that's exactly where he found her. Leaning up against the rail, staring at the variety of penguins in the faux Arctic below. A group of school-children rushed by them, two very harried looking chaperones fast on their heels. Aside from the crowds and the noise, Gianni remembered the other thing he didn't enjoy about the aquarium—the aroma in this particular area of the building.

"Cute little guys, aren't they?" he said, reaching her side. "If you can ignore the smell."

She tapped the informational plaque in front of them. "It says here some penguin species mate for life."

They'd be the select few. He wondered if any of the penguin pairs ever cheated. The ridiculousness of the question had him chuckling out loud.

"What's so funny?" Laney wanted to know.

"Just penguins in general, I guess," he hedged.

She narrowed her eyes at him. "What happened to your face?"

Gianni touched a finger to the bruise on his cheek. "Nothing. Just a hazard of my sport of choice. It'll be fine."

She studied him some more but made no further comment. "Right. Should we head over to the central tank? They just announced it was feeding time."

That he could handle. The central tank contained large sea turtles and a few sharks. He gently took her by the elbow and led her to the circular ramp that wrapped around the Giant Ocean Tank in the middle of the building that towered over four stories. They stopped to admire a school of zebra fish that swam near the glass.

Crowds of children bustled by them. Hard to believe that in just a few short years he'd have a school-aged child himself. He imagined visiting a place like this, the wonder it would hold for a child seeing it for the first time. The picture in his head included the woman next to him. What that meant exactly he didn't want to examine too closely. But a nagging sensation told him he wasn't going to be able to ignore the implication behind it much longer.

They reached the top of the tank just as an aquarist in full scuba gear lowered herself into the water with a bucket full of fish feed. Unbelievably, the crowds were even thicker up here. How was the place so busy in the middle of the week? They were jostled more than once. Laney didn't seem to mind. Though she'd definitely slowed down as they reached the higher floors. He couldn't begin to imagine the toll pregnancy must take on a woman's body.

Laney turned suddenly to catch him staring at her. "What is it?"

"Nothing. Just admiring you as you admire the sea life."

She blew out a long breath. "You shouldn't say things like that to me, Gianni."

Before he could respond to ask why, she'd already turned on her heel and was heading back toward the ramp. "I think I'd like to go pet the starfish and rays now."

The petting area was all the way back on the first floor and was nowhere near as interesting. But he wasn't going to argue. With a resigned sigh, he turned to follow her just as a small toddler ran smack into Laney's thighs nearly toppling her over. Gianni reached her side just in time to catch her before she tripped over the child.

"I'm so sorry!" A harried-looking woman with a large backpack took hold of the little girl. "She moves so fast sometimes."

"It's all right," Laney responded with a weak smile.

"Thanks for the catch," she said after the mom and tot had left, not moving out of his hold. Was it his imagination or had she gone quite pale suddenly? The circles under her eyes grew darker and her lips appeared to turn blue.

Something was very wrong.

Her next words confirmed it. "I don't feel too well all of a sudden." She barely got the last word out as she slumped against him.

Laney's vision turned black just as her knees went weak. Thank heavens Gianni was there. She felt him gently lift her up and carry her to a bench against the wall.

"Laney? Honey?" Gianni's voice reached her ears as an echo. "I want you to try to take a really deep breath and then do it again and again. Can you try for me?"

She did her best to follow his direction. It seemed to help, if only a little. She managed to find her voice enough to make an attempt at telling him what she needed him to do for her.

"My OB. Contact. My phone."

Through the fog clouding her brain, she realized her attempts had worked. She felt Gianni reach into her cross-body pocketbook and pull out her cell phone.

"They have an office at Mass General," she heard him say.

Yes! He knew what to do. With the relief that realization brought, Laney continued to try to breathe as Gianni had instructed. As if observing through a tunnel, she felt herself being carried out of the building and into one of the taxis that always loitered around the harbor side.

She had no idea how much time had gone by when she opened her eyes to find herself lying on a hospital cot in a sterile brightly lit room with an IV in her arm. Gianni sat next to her, holding her hand.

"Guess I picked a rather inconvenient time to take a nap, huh?"

Gianni's head snapped up. He smiled at her. "Hey there, sleeping beauty. How do you feel?" he asked in a soft, gentle voice.

"Right now, I feel rather lucky that you were at the aquarium with me. Does Mabel know where we are?"

"I took the liberty of texting her after finding her contact information on your phone. I just told her you were with me. Not to look for you."

Not only had he caught her fall and rushed her to get help, he'd thought to notify her cousin so Mabel wouldn't be roaming the aquarium looking for her in vain. Gianni Martino really knew how to come through in a crisis.

A knock on the door preceded the entrance of her regular OB doctor. Laney shifted to try to sit up but then gave up given the effort it took. "Hey, Dr. Zhao."

"Hello, there," the petite woman with the sensible top bun greeted her, then took Laney's wrist to check her pulse. "Feeling better?"

"Yes. But I'm scared, to be perfectly honest. Is the baby...?" She couldn't complete the sentence. An icy dread of fear ran through her veins at even the possibility that something may have happened to her child.

"The baby appears to be fine." She lifted her stethoscope. "Strong and steady heartbeat."

The relief that surged through Laney's core had her shaking. Thank the heavens. Gianni's grip on her hand tightened and she heard his audible sigh.

Their baby was okay. "What happened?" she asked the doctor through dry lips.

"All signs indicate that you were simply dehydrated," Dr. Zhao answered. "The IV is taking care of that right now. Your vitals are good. Getting better as the fluid does its thing."

"Thank you." Laney felt the tear that had built up in her one eye slowly roll down her cheek.

"We're just going to keep you here for a while longer, about half an hour or so. Just for observation."

That sounded fine with her. It would take her about that long to recover from the scare alone.

Dr. Zhao continued, "I'm going to have Tina come in and strap a Doppler on you, so we can listen to the fetal heartbeat before we let you go. Just to be on the safe side." She pulled out a notepad from her lab-coat pocket and started scribbling. "I'm writing down the sports drinks I recommend. Of course, water works just as well. Just make sure to keep drinking. And I'd like you to come back in a couple of days. Just to follow up."

Laney wanted to hug the other woman. How could she have let herself get dehydrated? She could have really gotten hurt back there at the aquarium. If Gianni hadn't been there to catch her, she could have easily fallen and hit her head.

Gianni. She looked over at him as the doctor left. He looked visibly shaken. She'd given them both quite a fright. Any doubt she may have had about whether he cared about this baby was now soundly put to rest. If only she could be as sure he cared for her, as well.

"I'm really sorry," she told him as yet another tear fell.

He rubbed her cheek with the back of his hand. "Hey, you have nothing to apologize for. Well, maybe except for making me hang out in the smelly penguin exhibit for so long."

She managed a small smile at his lame attempt at humor. "Sorry about that, certainly. And also for scaring you."

He gently tussled her hair. "All that matters is that you and the little one are all right, *cara*."

The endearment hovered in the air between them. He hadn't called her that since Italy. The physician's assistant chose that moment to knock and enter. She pushed a cart into the room as she greeted them.

With an impressive efficiency and hands that were rather

cold, the other woman wrapped a strap around her middle. She hooked the other end up to a rather archaic-looking machine.

Laney held her breath until the machine came to life. Then the steady singsong sound of her baby's heartbeat rang through the air. It had to be the sweetest rhythm she'd ever heard.

As the PA left, she looked up to find Gianni staring at her in wonder. Without a word, he walked over to her bed-side and gave her a soft and gentle kiss on the lips.

CHAPTER FIFTEEN

GIANNI DIDN'T KNOW whether to jump up in joy or sink down into the floor. The past hour or so had been the most harrowing of his lifetime. His nerves had been shot, his every muscle tight with apprehension until he'd heard the doctor's reassurance. Then he'd felt the flood of relief in every cell of his body.

Now, listening to his baby's heartbeat as it sounded through the air was an experience he couldn't compare to any other. He'd known he wanted this child from the moment Laney called him that day at his accountant's office. But he hadn't realized just how much until the real fear that something might go wrong.

What a punch to the gut.

And Laney, he had to make sure she was better taken care of. From this moment, he was going to do everything he could to ensure it. If that meant finding a way to be with her more often, then so be it. Starting today.

"You don't have to stay, you know," she said to him, lifting the top part of the bed using the controller. "I'm feeling much better now. I can find my way home."

As if he'd leave her side. Not for anything in this world. Besides, he may never tire of listening to the steady thud of his child's heartbeat. The sound of it brought home just how real all of this was. In a way that hadn't hit him before. "You're not getting rid of me. Don't even think about it."

She smiled, and the desire to walk over and kiss her, really kiss her this time—not some chaste little peck on the lips—had him clenching his fists to resist the urge. He was relieved to see she did indeed look much better. The color had returned to her face, her lips no longer a frightening shade of blue. He was going to run out and buy her cases and cases of sports drinks as soon as he had the chance.

"In fact," he added, "I'd like to come back with you to the appointment."

She looked ready to argue, then appeared to change her mind. "You know what? I'd like that."

The half hour went by quicker than he would have thought. Gianni secured another cab while Laney made her appointment at the front desk.

"Are you warm enough?" he asked. "I can ask the driver to turn the heat up."

"Gianni, it's about ninety degrees outside."

"Then I'll ask him to turn his AC down."

"I'm not cold. But thank you. And you didn't have to ride with me to my place."

She really didn't get it. He wasn't merely seeing her home. He intended to stay with her as long as she would let him. "I told you back at the hospital, I'm not leaving your side."

She gave a small shrug. "Suit yourself. But I don't plan on doing anything but taking a long hot shower and then crawling into bed for the longest nap I've ever taken." She accented the statement with a wide yawn and a long stretch of her lower back.

"I'm afraid not. That won't work."

"Come again?"

"First we're going to make sure you get something to

eat. You missed lunch. We just got you hydrated. I won't risk malnutrition."

She laughed loud enough that it echoed through the back seat. "I'm hardly starving. But you're right. I could eat. My exhaustion was just winning out over my hunger."

"Do you have enough food in your apartment?"

"You know, you would have made a good nurse."

"I can think of a few people I'd like to jab with a needle from time to time."

She chuckled again and he realized, not for the first time, just how much he enjoyed her laughter.

She must have given him an even bigger scare than she thought. After setting her up on the sofa and covering her up with a plush afghan, Gianni was in the kitchen throwing together what he called a *satisfying, nutritious lunch* that both she and the baby would enjoy.'

It was so hard to keep her eyes open but the aroma coming from the kitchen was definitely an incentive to stay awake.

"You know, you don't have as much food here as you led me to believe."

She knew she had plenty. Just not enough that might satisfy a healthy Italian male who worked out regularly by throwing and receiving punches.

"I have all the basics."

"Life is about more than just the basics, *cara*." There it was again, that word. Dear, beloved.

She knew she couldn't look too deeply into the endearment. It was just an expression…one he probably didn't even realize he was using.

Gianni walked into the living room a few minutes later, carrying a tray he set down on the coffee table in front of her. Her mouth watered at the sight of the food. He'd made an omelet that was so loaded it was overflowing at the fold. Next to the plate sat a perfectly browned piece of toast slathered in so much butter it looked downright wet. A tall glass of water with lemon wedges had just the amount of ice cubes she liked.

"Aren't you having anything? I could share—"

He didn't even let her finish. "That's all yours. You need to eat. I had a sandwich as I cooked."

Laney gave him a serious military-type salute and picked up the fork. "Yes, sir."

A burst of flavor exploded on her tongue as soon as she took a bite. Cheese, vegetables, myriad spices she wasn't even aware she owned.

The man was an artist. A girl could get used to this. But that was the whole problem in a nutshell. It would be all too easy to get used to having Gianni Martino around.

She thought of the look on his face when she'd first woken up in the hospital, the way he'd held her hand and squeezed it tighter as the doctor had walked in. Just the source of comfort and strength he'd been for her when she'd faced her deepest fear.

There was no denying it. She was falling for him. Head over heels, impossible to deny, tumbling with no hope of righting herself.

If only the man in question felt the same way in return.

Gianni lifted the tray off Laney's lap when she was finished and carried it back to the kitchenette of her apartment. "I believe you've earned your nap now, madame," he told her upon his return. It was clear she was struggling to keep her eyes open.

"I have one phone call to make and then it's off to dreamland I go for the next few hours."

"What's this important phone call? Anything I can take care of for you?"

She shook her head. "I need to call the club and let my manager know I'm not going to make it in tonight."

What he would have preferred to hear was that she would be telling them she didn't plan on making tonight, tomorrow and for the foreseeable future. But that was probably too much to ask. At this point in time, anyway. "Will that leave them shorthanded?"

"I don't think so. We shouldn't be that busy with two major concerts in town."

He sat down next to her as she reached for her phone, waited while she made the call and finally hung up. "All taken care of."

"For now."

"Yes. I'll eventually have to do more hiring. Especially once all the college kids head back to school. I have several working for me over the summer who won't be around much longer."

A tendril of apprehension curled through his middle. After the scare today, he didn't want to think about Laney overdoing it and risking her or the baby's health. Owning and operating any business took a lot of time and effort, let alone a popular nightclub like the Carpe D.

"Don't you think that's a problem?" he asked her. "Finding qualified service workers is tough enough under the best of circumstances."

"I'll have to move quickly to hire and get them trained. But I do still have several months."

He stood and started to pace the room. He couldn't believe how blasé she was being about this. "What happens when the baby gets here?"

She shifted and tucked her knees underneath her. "Well, for one, I plan on taking some time off, obviously."

"And then what?"

"Then there are several very reputable nanny agencies in the area."

He didn't want to overstep. But it was a fair subject. He had to know her exact plans moving forward. The baby was his too, after all.

"You plan to continue as is, then? You don't feel anything needs to change until the baby is born?"

"I don't think I follow where you're going with this."

"I would hate to have another replay of this afternoon. You can't let yourself get run down. Nothing matters but taking care of yourself now."

She tilted her head and gave him a questioning smile. "I was only dehydrated, Gianni. And my doctor is making sure to monitor me closely. You heard her yourself."

"I still think you should slow down. Take it a bit easier now that you're expecting."

There was one obvious way to do just that. She could go ahead and sell to his father. He knew firsthand what a lucrative offer was waiting for her if she only cared to look. Even if Gianni himself had walked away from the whole fiasco out of respect for her wishes. But that was then. Everything was different now. There was a child to consider.

And if she took him up on his marriage proposal, she could devote all her time in preparation of the upcoming birth.

"I can tell you have something you want to say, Gianni. Go ahead and say it, please."

Despite the question, her tone told him she wasn't ready to hear any of it. He had to pick a better moment. "It can wait. You've had enough of a day already. We'll talk some other time."

She sat up straighter. "No, I'd rather get it out in the open."

"Don't you want to take your nap?"

"I find I'm not all that sleepy anymore."

Rubbing a hand down his face, he tried to summon the right words to make his argument. Marrying him and taking his father up on the sale offer was the ideal solution to their current scenario. When the time was right, he'd do all he could to help her open up again elsewhere. With a club that was newer and better.

"All right, if you insist." He walked over and sat on the coffee table in front of her. "You still have an option you might not have considered."

Her eyes narrowed on him in suspicion. "What would that be?"

"You can still sell. My father's offer stands."

She sucked in a sharp breath. "I see. I take it that's what you would recommend I do, then."

"It makes sense, Laney. It would give you time to adjust to the new reality and get ready for the baby. Think about not having to worry about staffing, or drink orders or handling large crowds. You could just relax and focus on our child."

"So you're trying to convince me to sell because you're concerned about our child?"

He nodded. "Of course. And out of concern for you, as well."

"And that's the only reason? Your *concern* for us?"

The way she emphasized the word sent warning bells ringing through his head. "Why else?"

"Perhaps you could tell me."

For a moment, he was simply confused at what she was getting at. But then realization dawned and he couldn't believe what she suspected. Exactly how little did she think of him? "You think I'm telling you this in order to acquire a building?"

Her lips tightened before she answered, "Aren't you? Isn't there a well-known theory that says the most obvious conclusion is usually the correct one?" She pushed her bangs off her forehead. "I can't believe I've been so naive."

"Laney. You can't possibly think I don't have your best interests at heart here. Yours and the baby's."

But she didn't even appear to be listening. Her jaw suddenly dropped and she stared at him, her mouth agape. "Oh, my God. Is that the only reason you proposed? How nice and tidy. You get legal rights as a father...your family's business gets the property they've been after."

"What? Of course not!" How could she even think such a thing, let alone voice it out loud?

"It's so clear from where I'm standing."

Her doorbell rang before he could respond. Without a word to him, Laney threw the afghan off and went to answer it. Her cousin Mabel stood across the threshold. She threw her arms around Laney and the two women embraced in a tight hug. "I came to check on you after getting your text. Are you okay now?"

Apparently, Laney had filled Mabel in about the afternoon's events at some point.

As he watched the two women, Gianni felt the muscles of his jaw clench in frustration and disappointment. Along with another hollow feeling he didn't want to label—the only word that came to mind was *hurt*. How little credit she gave him. She just assumed the worst of him. At this very moment, he had documents and proposals being drawn in order to walk away from the family business once and for all. A decision he'd made in no small part because of how she'd reacted that day he told her the truth.

The idea of marrying him and focusing on the family

they could have together was so unappealing to Laney Taytum that she would rather believe he was trying to dupe her
for a mere business deal.

It was just as well Mabel had arrived. For he couldn't
stay. Not after what Laney had just accused him of. He had
to get out of here.

With a short and somewhat terse goodbye to them both,
he strode out the door.

Laney watched the door shut behind Gianni and heard
his footsteps grow fainter and fainter as he walked away.
For one insane moment, she wanted to run after him. To
plead with him to come back and convince her that all
the things she'd just said weren't true. To somehow prove
her wrong.

Clearly, he couldn't do that. Or he wouldn't have taken
off in the first place.

Well, so be it. She could do this all on her own. She
knew in her heart that she was going to be a good parent,
regardless of whether or not she had the child's father with
her for any kind of support. This pregnancy and the events
of the past few weeks had taught her one thing: she didn't
need anyone else's validation to prove her worth. Not her
parents' or even Gianni's.

So why had watching Gianni walk away hurt so sharply?
How often could she be so naive when it came to one man?
Here she was, once again wondering what exactly between
them was real and how much of it was her simply being
blind and gullible where he was concerned.

"He certainly left in a hurry," Mabel commented. "Hope
it wasn't because of me."

Maybe it was the hormones, or maybe the harrowing
events of this afternoon. Or maybe it was simply the toll
their argument had taken. But Laney felt a wave of emo-

tion so powerful crest through her core that it threatened
to crash with a fierceness that made her tremble. The next
thing she knew, she was sobbing in her cousin's arms.

"Laney. What is it? I thought you said you and the baby
were okay."

Alarm and fear rang loud and clear in Mabel's voice.
That just made Laney feel worse. "We are. I'm sorry. I
should be grateful for that fact alone. And I am. I really
am."

Mabel led her over to sofa and sat her down, yanking
a few tissues from the box on the counter along the way.

"Tell me," she coaxed. "And then I'll go get the mint
chocolate chip from the freezer."

At her cousin's prompting, the words seemed to pour out
of her in a torrent. Starting with Gianni's proposal a week
ago, to the harrowing scare at the aquarium and ending with
the ghastly conversation they'd just had, which led to him
storming out the door with barely a goodbye. By the time
she was done, her throat felt raw and sore and her breath
came out in raspy gasps.

Mabel blew out a puff of air and handed her yet another
tissue. "So, let me get this straight. The man flew all the
way to Italy to apologize. He took care of you when you
felt unwell. Then he pointed out to you that you had an option that would make it easier for you to take some time off
during your first pregnancy. Before that, he asked you to
marry him. And you were upset because he didn't do it the
right way. So you accused him of trying to fool you into a
sham business deal. Do I have all that straight?"

Well, when she put it that way. "He only proposed because he felt it was the right thing to do, Mabel. When and
if I accept a marriage proposal, I don't want it to be out of
a sense of duty. Maybe I'm being foolish, but I want it to

be born of affection. Of love," she added on a hiccup that sounded pathetic to her own ears.

Mabel nodded with enthusiasm. "Oh, I definitely agree with you there."

"You do?"

"Absolutely. But there's one thing you don't seem to be taking in mind."

"What's that?"

"Consider everything you just told me. I'd say those were definitely the actions of a man in love."

Laney immediately began to protest, but an inkling of doubt began to sprout like a tiny seed. What if her cousin was right and she'd just made a colossal error? "That can't be. He's never so much as said anything to that effect."

Mabel shrugged. "Sometimes actions speak louder than words. And the fact is, he's done more than enough to show you he cares about you, coz."

Did Mabel have a point? A small voice in her head began to nag at her. The facts were that Gianni had agreed to pretend to be her real date for her sister's wedding, he'd flown across the world as a way to apologize to her after upsetting her and he'd been nothing but caring and attentive after finding out she was pregnant. And she'd simply discounted all of those deeds.

"Oh, dear. What if I've made a horrible mistake?"

"I'd say that's a distinct possibility." Mabel gave her arm an affectionate squeeze. "We're gonna need that ice cream."

Mistake. The word echoed around Laney's head and she knew she was simply making excuses for herself. What she'd done was more than a mere error. Rather than just tell him she hadn't changed her mind about selling her club, Laney had lashed out and accused him of selfishly trying to con her out of it.

She'd done it because she was afraid. So afraid of loving someone who might not love her back. Someone who might walk away from her and her child and leave her heartbroken and devastated.

So she'd lashed out. Because losing Gianni would undoubtedly shatter her.

And somehow, she'd probably just caused the very thing she feared.

CHAPTER SIXTEEN

Dad wants to see you.

ANGELO'S TEXT FLASHED on the screen of his smartphone as soon as Gianni arrived at his front door. Great. Just great. As if this day hadn't been enough of a nightmare already. To think, Gianni had only checked his phone in case it might be Laney reaching out. How foolish of him. She'd made it quite clear what she thought about his character.

His phone dinged once more. Angelo again.

Expecting you in his office sometime this afternoon.

The floating dots below the last message indicated there was more.

I wouldn't miss it if I were you.

Missing it was exactly what he wanted to do. But he knew Angelo was right. The sooner he made his intentions clear to his father, the sooner he could move on. He would have his own child soon to focus on. He wanted everything squared away before the little one arrived.

Too bad part of the resolution wouldn't include this child being born into a family with two married parents. But that was overrated. That's what Laney had told him, anyway. She refused to marry him and she thought he was stringing her along for the sake of his family's company.

He cursed out loud as he unlocked his front door and threw his keys across the hallway, not caring that they hit the wall hard enough to leave a small mark in the paint.

He needed a good hour or two alone with a punching bag. Seeing his father was enough of a chore under the best of circumstances. When he told him what he intended, Gianni had no doubt all hell would break loose.

Oddly, he could hardly find the will to care.

Two hours later, after a punishing bout with the bag and a quick shower, he made his way to the building that housed Martino Entertainment Enterprises in Boston's Back Bay.

His brother was there when he reached the top floor and entered Franco's office. Angelo stood immediately and headed to the door. "I'll leave you two to it, then."

"You're welcome to stay, Angelo. This concerns you too."

But his brother gave a brisk shake of his head. "Oh, no. I've got to be somewhere else. Anywhere else." He wasted no time walking out of the room.

Coward, Gianni wanted to shout to Angelo's retreating back as he left and shut the door behind him.

His father leaned back in his chair and motioned for him to sit. "Hello, son. How is your fiancée? And the baby?"

So they were to begin with niceties. "They're both fine. Thanks for asking. But she's not my fiancée. We have no intention of getting married." Not for lack of trying on his part, but his father didn't need to know that.

"I see. That's a shame. Of course, she'll always be family now."

"Of course." That much was certain. He knew his mom

and dad well enough to be confident that neither would see his child as any different from Angelo's kids. For all their faults, he appreciated their loyalty. Even if his father's had come at a cost to him personally, the way he'd never felt as if he belonged.

But this was not the time. It was best to get right to the matter at hand. Gianni pulled out a chair and sat down, loosening his tie in the process.

"I'm glad you called me in to talk."

"Do you know why I did?" his father asked.

Now that the question had been asked, Gianni had to admit he wasn't quite sure. He knew why he needed to speak to his father. But why had Franco insisted on seeing him today?

His father took his silence as an answer. "I've been hearing rumors."

"What kind of rumors?"

"That you've made moves to try and remove yourself as a VP of this company. That you're looking to buy the fitness division and run it independently."

He should have known Franco Martino would be one step ahead of him. He shouldn't have forgotten the wide network of associates and acquaintances Franco enjoyed. "I thought it might be prudent for me to take such steps."

His father waved an arm in dismissal. "You can't buy something you already own, son. This company belongs to you and your brother. I'm looking forward to retiring soon and traveling the world with your mother. She says she's tired of waiting."

Gianni would believe his dad was ready to retire when he saw it with his own eyes. But his mom was a strong woman; her influence with her husband was a force in itself. For all its trials and tribulations over the years, their marriage had somehow held. Gianni couldn't figure out how for the life of him.

Franco leaned over the desk, bracing his arms. "You are part of this family. You have had tremendous success growing the fitness and gyms branch of Martino Entertainment Enterprises."

He had to clear his throat before he could answer—a sudden lump of emotion had lodged at the bottom of his Adam's apple. "Thank you for saying that."

"Gianni, you are my son. Nothing will ever change that."

Gianni let the words sink in, fully and deeply. His whole life, he'd led himself to believe Franco tolerated him for the sake of the woman he loved. But maybe it was more than that. Maybe too much had been left unspoken until now.

Maybe his father had loved him all along. He'd just never been able to say it. "I understand, sir."

And he really did. Finally. Amazing the damage unspoken words could cause.

"Good," Franco said with a finality that made it clear he would say no more on the matter. "No more of this spin-off nonsense. Tell your lady she can hold on to her club if that's what she desires." He reached for the file lying on his desk and opened it. "Tell your brother to come back in here on your way out. I don't understand these numbers he's given me."

Gianni didn't bother to knock on his brother's door before strolling into his office. His mind was a jumbled-up mess. Between the revealing talk with his father just now and the heated conversation with Laney earlier, he felt disquieted and unsettled. For all the teasing and mocking insults between them, his brother had always been a good sounding board. Gianni figured he could use one of that right about now.

"When was the last time you bought me dinner?" he asked unceremoniously as he entered the room. "I'm feeling kind of hungry."

Angelo reached inside his desk drawer and pulled out a granola bar that he threw in Gianni's direction. He caught it with one hand and rolled his eyes.

"Never mind dinner," his brother said. "How did it go with the old man just now?"

"Fine. I think. I believe he just told me, in not so many words, that he cares for me."

Angelo scoffed. "That's it? You mean to tell me you two were having some sort of greeting-card moment? Here I thought it was something important."

His brother was doing all he could to make light of the situation, but Gianni could tell by his tone that both men realized the import of what had just transpired in their father's office. "He may have also saved me from pursuing an objective I didn't need to pursue after all."

Angelo lifted one eyebrow. "Yeah? Might this pursuit have had anything to do with the young lady who happens to be carrying your child?"

"It might. But it hardly matters now. We're having a disagreement about whether she should marry me or not."

"A disagreement, huh? What? She didn't like the ring or something?"

Gianni chuckled. "I never actually got her a ring. Wanted to see what she'd say first."

"You seem to have it backward, bro. Sounds like a pretty lame proposal. No wonder she disagrees."

"It's not like that. Not about the ring."

Angelo leaned back and crossed his arms in front of his chest. "I have no doubt it isn't."

"She just doesn't seem to want to see what's obvious."

His brother tilted his head. "What's so obvious?"

"That she and I make a good team. That we can parent this baby as a united couple. She doesn't realize that I happen to have fallen in—"

He stopped short. Whoa. Where had that thought come from? But he couldn't deny it. He loved Laney Taytum. He didn't even know when it had happened. He may have been well on his way the first night he met her.

"You need to tell her, bro," Angelo said. "The sooner the better."

His brother was right. He'd gone about it all wrong. How foolish and arrogant he must have sounded. Gianni had to let Laney know exactly how he felt. He had to tell her that he wanted to marry her because he loved her. And he had to ask her if she thought she might love him in return. Once and for all, they needed to get all of it out in the open.

He was through letting words left unspoken navigate the direction of his life.

Laney looked up in alarm as a car pulled up to the parking lot and Louise Miller got out. She was quickly followed by three others. The regular Saturday morning exercise crew. This was not good.

"Uh, Mabel? Did you forget to cancel the Zumba class? It looks like people are arriving ready to work out." Which would be a disaster. She was in no shape to do any kind of fitness instruction. Her recent bouts with morning sickness had had her knocked off her feet for a good part of the early day.

What she wouldn't give for a strong cup of coffee. She desperately missed caffeine and hadn't been sleeping well the past couple of nights. Ever since the momentous conversation with Gianni. She had to find a way to say she was sorry. That she should have never doubted him. It was probably going to be the hardest apology she'd ever delivered.

But right now she had a more immediately pressing matter. Louise and the rest of the group were making their way inside. "Mabel?"

Mabel looked up from stacking the clean glasses behind the bar. "Oh, did I forget to mention? I was told not to cancel the class, after all."

That made no sense. "Who would have told you that?" And why would Mabel have taken direction from anyone but her? "I'm in no condition to run a Zumba class right now."

Mabel simply smiled at her. "Oh, I know. It's not Zumba. And you won't be running the class."

Before she could delve into that mystery, another familiar car pulled into the lot. Laney's heart did a somersault inside her chest when Gianni stepped out of the driver's side. Wearing sports shorts and a gray cotton T-shirt, he looked sexier than any man should dressed in simple shorts and a tee.

"Gianni's holding class today," Mabel explained behind her, as if that made any kind of sense.

"Why would he do that?"

"He called me last night. Said he wanted to help out a bit around here. We talked about what a shame it would be if you had to cancel your Saturday classes as the pregnancy progressed."

Laney wouldn't have been more surprised if Mabel had just told her that she'd purchased a unicorn and planned to go live with it in a castle in the clouds. Her jaw didn't seem to want to close.

"Gianni is going to teach an aerobics class to cover for me in my club?"

Mabel rolled her eyes. "Of course not. That would be silly."

Right. As if Laney was the one being silly right now.

"He's going to teach a cardio kickboxing class, of course. I notified all the attendees who signed up about the change."

Sure enough, Gianni walked in a few seconds later with a sweat towel draped over his shoulder. As she watched, flabbergasted, he began the class with a warm-up routine, then continued for forty straight minutes with a pulse raising workout that had her regulars sweating. They all seemed to be enjoying themselves.

Herself included. She rather enjoyed watching him. He'd even thought to bring along a speaker with a pounding playlist to accompany the routine. At one point, he winked in her direction, making her blush like a schoolgirl.

At the end of the cooldown, after the attendees slowly trickled out, he made his way over to the bar where Laney still stood in mild shock. She had trouble making her mouth work. "You are full of surprises, aren't you?" she finally managed to utter.

"You haven't seen anything yet, sweetheart," he answered, leaning in to give her a peck on the cheek.

Heavens, she'd missed him. It had only been a few days but hardly a minute had gone by that she hadn't thought about him and how she might make things right between them. Now, here he was, after having run a kickboxing workout for her class, no less.

"You really plan on doing this every week?" she asked, for lack of a better conversation starter.

"You bet. I'm also taking bartending classes online."

"You are?"

He nodded. "I'll be around as often or as little as you want me to."

Laney rubbed her jaw, as if deep in thought. "I see. Well, I have to say, I've been doing some thinking since we last spoke, Mr. Martino."

"What kind of thinking?"

"Some of the things you said, about focusing on this pregnancy and my becoming a mom in a few short months. I've decided a lot of it has merit."

"What's that mean, exactly?" he wanted to know.

"It means, I've rethought your offer."

His smile slowly wilted. "Laney, you don't have to do that. I'm sorry I ever brought it up again. You don't have to sell. This place is your labor of love. We'll find a way to make it work."

She waved a hand in dismissal. "That's not the offer I'm referring to, silly man."

"It's not?"

"No. I mean the offer to marry you. Does it still stand? Because I'd like to say yes."

He blinked at her. Once, twice. In the next instant, she suddenly found herself lifted in his arms and spun around. When he finally set her down, he took her lips with his in a deep soul-shattering kiss she felt down to her toes. It took several deep breaths to get her oxygen level back to normal.

"I love you, Laney Taytum," he whispered against her ear in a tone so genuine that she felt the sting of joyful tears behind her eyes. "I was a fool not to tell you earlier."

She leaned in close against his chest, felt his arms tighten around her. "You did tell me. In so many ways. I just wasn't listening."

From now on, she would be all ears when it came to her soon-to-be husband.

"I love you," she, said against his chest, echoing his declaration. "And I can't wait for the three of us to be a family."

A family in which she truly felt she belonged.

EPILOGUE

"THE PHOTOS YOU sent are breathtaking!"

Mabel's excited voiced reached her through what sounded like an echo chamber. Laney strained to hear better over the crashing waves in the distance. It was a beautiful morning on the Amalfi Coast. The perfect day to enjoy the Marina Grande Beach.

"But please don't send me anymore," Mabel insisted. "I'm just about racked over with jealousy."

Laney sat up in her lounge chair to get a better view of Gianni and their baby girl splashing around in the water. The three of them had hiked the Path of the Gods yesterday, with Gianni carrying their daughter in a back carrier.

Laney had taken more snapshots than she could count, emailing more than a few to Mabel afterward. "Well, then you have to come here, Mabel. As soon as you get the chance. You'd like Gianni's cousin. He makes a mean limoncello."

Mabel giggled into the phone. "Are you playing matchmaker, coz?"

"Guilty as charged," Laney admitted. Would that be so wrong? Now that she had the family she'd dreamed about, Laney couldn't help but want to spread such happiness around. Her cousin more than deserved it.

"There's the small matter of a doctorate I need to finish up," Mabel reminded her.

"Fair enough," Laney agreed. "But after that's done, the next time we come here on holiday, I'm going to insist you come with us."

"It's a plan."

After they said their goodbyes and hung up, Laney grabbed the large plush Turkish towel sitting on the blanket next to her and approached the water where Gianni and their daughter were splashing around in the gentle waves. He held their precious child tight against his chest.

"All right, you two. You'll both start to prune if you don't come out right now," she chided. This was the third time she'd tried to get them to come out.

Her baby daughter's response was to kick her little feet in the water and send a toothless grin Laney's way. Not for the first time, Laney felt her heart swell with the love and joy that rushed through her whenever she looked upon her child.

"What do you think, Gia?" Her husband asked their little girl. "Is your *mamma* right? Should we get out?"

Of course, the eight-month-old didn't understand enough to answer. But Laney could have sworn she gave a subtle shake of her head.

"I agree," Gianni declared. "I think instead of us getting out, she should come in!"

In a stealth-like move she hadn't seen coming, he reached out with one hand to grab her by the arm and pulled her farther into the ocean with them. She barely managed to hold on to the towel, lifting it above her head so that it didn't get wet.

"Not fair," she teased, wrapping the towel safely around her shoulders to prevent it from falling. "The two of you are ganging up on me."

"Not true," Gianni argued. "You were simply outvoted." Slipping his arm along her waist, he pulled her in closer against the length of him. For several moments, they simply stood in silence, with the gentle waves crashing along their legs and their daughter gurgling happily between them. Laney felt like pinching herself to make sure it was all real. Being here was a dream come true, with the man she loved and the beautiful family they'd created together.

She'd indeed found paradise.

* * * * *

CINDERELLA AND THE BROODING BILLIONAIRE

MICHELLE DOUGLAS

MILLS & BOON

To Mr Ian Malcolm and Mrs Janina Sulikowski,
two wonderful teachers who fostered and encouraged
my love and appreciation for stories and storytelling.

I am forever in your debt.

CHAPTER ONE

THE BABY WOULD not stop crying.

Luca Vieri paced the floor of his motel room, dragging a hand through his hair. He'd made sure the baby wasn't hungry, that his nappy was dry, that he wasn't running a temperature. And yet the boy continued to cry.

Luca completed a full circuit of the room, which, given the room's size and the length of his legs, took no time at all. The room lacked both the size and luxury he was used to. Though he suspected the spectacular view of the beach from the open front door more than made up for it in most guests' eyes. He cared for neither the lack of luxury nor the view. All he wanted was to be able to comfort his son.

'Luca, are you still there?'

The voice at the other end of the line recalled him to the task at hand. Covering his other ear with his hand, he did what he could to focus on the report his assistant had just given him. *'Sì.'*

The baby continued to cry.

His son, it seemed, had a healthy set of lungs.

His son.

He closed his eyes but forced them open again a moment later. Once his phone call was finished, he could again give his full attention to the baby.

Perhaps he could step inside his bedroom, close the door,

and finish his phone call in semi-quiet, before reapplying himself to the task of soothing his son.

But he didn't have the heart to abandon seven-month-old Benito for even the few minutes that would take. He wanted his son to trust him, to realise he was going to be there for him, that just because things might be hard at the moment he had no intention of letting them scare him off.

'There is no issue with any of that,' he said, striding back into the main part of the motel room, his heart plunging to his feet at Benito's red-faced misery. Soon that misery would give way to hiccups and exhausted sleep.

Luca's hand clenched so hard around his phone it started to ache. With a force of will he loosened his grip. 'Reschedule it all to next week.'

'Already done.'

'Good.' He approached the child's cage—*playpen*—but when Benito's cries grew louder, he backed off, his heart burning. He so badly wanted to comfort his son, but they'd known each other for two days. The child didn't know him, didn't trust him…was still a little frightened of him.

Benito only let him feed him when he became desperately hungry and only fell asleep in his arms when he was desperately exhausted. But he'd woken from a nap earlier, had allowed Luca to give him his lunch…yet now whenever Luca tried to give him the bottle of cool boiled water, he batted it away. Whenever he tried to give him the dummy, he turned his head away. Whenever he picked him up, he struggled to be free.

He wanted to find a quick fix for his son's distress, but there was no quick fix for grief. Benito missed his mother.

This wailing, it was grief for the woman Benito would now grow up without and would never remember. Luca's throat thickened. He wanted to wail against the fates too.

'Luca?'

His assistant's voice snapped him back. 'Sorry, Piero. As for my mother...tell her I will speak to her when I return to Rome.'

'Yes, sir.'

Luca made a note to give his assistant a substantial Christmas bonus at the end of the year. 'I know it is asking a lot. I will also text her the same message, but I fear she will continue to hound you.'

'No matter. I can deal with Signora Conti.'

Very few people could, but Piero was one of them. '*Grazie*, Piero.'

'You need time with your son.'

His lips twisted. 'Except a business empire like The Vieri Corporation refuses to wait patiently while I do that.' He'd only been CEO for two years. Today, though, it felt like twenty.

'Your cousin, Signorina Rosetta Vieri, has stepped in to pick up what slack she can. She is doing an admirable job.'

Luca's gut clenched. Rosetta was the only one of his cousins he fully trusted. They'd recently discovered that the corporation had a traitor in its midst, and he hated leaving her to deal with it on her own. 'Have there been further financial irregularities?'

'*Sì*. Nothing too significant but troubling all the same.'

Hunting down the source of those irregularities would be his top priority when he returned to Rome.

Benito's continued crying filled Luca's head, making it throb, making it increasingly difficult to focus on anything else. He seized the teddy bear he'd bought as a gift and danced it along the railing of the playpen, but Benito merely flung himself to the other side, almost falling against the wooden bars in his haste to avoid his father.

Luca's throat thickened. He loved his son. From the very first moment he'd clapped eyes on Benito, a fierce protectiveness had taken up residence inside his chest. He would create a strong unbreakable bond with his son, would make sure Benito knew he was loved and cherished.

He dragged a hand down his face. It was unreasonable to expect that to happen immediately. These early days were always going to be difficult.

He just hadn't realised they'd wring him so dry. He was used to solving problems, not feeling so...*helpless*.

'There is something else,' his assistant said. 'Signor Romano has been calling. He demands you speak to him personally as soon as you can.'

Dio! How had the other man found out about this so quickly?

The baby's wailing was reaching a crescendo in his head. Keeping one eye on his son, he opened the glass sliding door onto the back balcony of his room, welcomed the fresh bite of the breeze on his face. 'You think I need to call him before I return to Rome?'

'*Sì.*'

Cavolo! He would need to tread carefully, bring into play all his tact and diplomacy. And even then it might not be enough. 'Leave it with me.'

He'd promised Bella he would find a way to break off their engagement. Discovering he had an unknown son provided them with a plausible enough excuse. Luca could claim he needed time to adapt to this new reality. Bella could claim she did not wish to become a stepmother so soon.

Except Signor Romano would argue that Benito's existence made no difference. He would argue for the children of Bella and Luca's marriage to become the legitimate Vieri heirs, rather than Benito, and if that could be settled Bella would become reconciled to raising Benito.

What the older man didn't know, however, was that Bella was in love with another man.

And Luca had no desire to marry a woman who did not wish to marry him.

And while he sorely wanted the union between their families, he had no intention of treating Benito differently from any other children he might one day have.

Given time, without Luca on the scene, Bella might possibly reconcile her father to her chosen man. Still, Signor Romano had a fiery temper, and a merger between the two families was his dearest wish. Luca had to find a way to keep the older man onside, while reconciling him to the fact that Bella and Luca would not marry.

His shoulders sagged at the Herculean task Bella had set him. He would not be able to settle the issue, appease Signor Romano and restore peace in a single phone call, but he could begin to lay the groundwork.

If only Benito would stop crying. If only Luca had managed some sleep in the last three days. If only he'd known about his son seven months ago!

'Okay, Piero—' he ground back a sigh '—give me your impressions of the situation.'

He forced himself to concentrate on his assistant's voice, but a movement inside the motel room caught his attention. The black skirt, white shirt and sensible shoes informed him it was a member of the housekeeping staff. He hadn't heard her call out to identify herself over Benito's cries.

He went to move into the room and ask her to come back later, but the smile that stretched across her face when she glimpsed his son halted him in his tracks.

She swooped down towards the crying child. 'Hello, Benny boy! What's all this fuss you're making?'

Benito immediately stopped crying to swing around and stare at the maid. And then his little arms lifted to be picked up, his urgency evident in the way he bounced on his bottom.

Luca's heart stuttered in his chest.

She picked him up, two tiny arms went about her neck and she cuddled him close, rocking him as he snuffled into her shoulder and neck. She crooned to his son in a low voice, but Luca caught, 'Poor, poor baby,' and 'You miss her too,' and 'Beautiful Benny boy.'

This woman had known Anita?

He shook himself. Of course she had. This town was no bigger than a postage stamp. Everyone here would know everyone else.

He stared at the woman and child and an ache rose inside him.

She glanced around at him with clear amber eyes. He blinked and straightened. He hadn't realised she'd known he was there. She gestured towards the sofa and he nodded.

Prising her caramel-coloured hair from Benito's fingers, she started to sing a children's song Luca knew from his own childhood. Benito stared up at her with tear-streaked eyes as if she were the answer to all his prayers, and renewed energy began to trickle into every tired atom of Luca's body.

He longed for his son to look at him like that.

'Aren't you going to sing with me, beautiful boy?' this lovely smiling woman said to the child, and Benito broke into the biggest smile that Luca had ever seen.

His son's smile... *Dio!* It was like sunshine and holidays and the Mediterranean in spring.

'Luca, are you still there?'

'I'm sorry, Piero, I have to go. I will call you back.' He pocketed his phone and stepped back into the room.

The maid sang, Benito made cooing noises as if he were trying to copy her and clapped both of his little hands against her larger one—so happy at that moment it made Luca's heart ache.

Without warning, those amber eyes glanced up into his again. Though heaven only knew what he meant by warning, just…such eyes should come with a warning, surely?

Sing, she mouthed.

So he sang along with the song too. The baby jerked to stare at him, but the magician of a maid bounced her charge on her lap to make him laugh again. When the song came to an end, she clapped her hands. 'Yay! High five!'

Benito slapped his hand to hers.

'And yay!' she repeated. 'Daddy knows the song too! High five, Daddy!'

Luca held his hand up immediately and Benito smacked his hand to Luca's palm with something midway between a smile and a frown.

But the maid—this glorious, wonderful woman—didn't give *her Benny boy* a chance to ponder, worry or otherwise regret the presence of the man who'd taken a seat beside them on the sofa. Instead, she tickled him until he was a writhing mass of giggles.

When Benito was contentedly sucking his dummy and growing sleepy in her lap, the woman made as if to rise, but Luca touched her wrist. 'Please, stay, just for a little longer.'

She stared at his hand and he immediately pulled it back, suddenly aware of how warm and soft her skin felt beneath his fingertips, like silk and sun. The tips of his fingers throbbed, and he curled them into his palm. She smelled like vanilla and lemon, and perturbingly enticing.

He shot to his feet and moved away. 'You knew Anita?' It wasn't really a question.

'We were good friends. She worked here at the motel as well.'

Anita had been a maid? If he'd known she'd borne his son he'd have made sure she'd lived like a princess.

'I've babysat Benny many a time.' She smiled down at the slumbering child. 'We're the best of friends, Benny and me.'

'*Sì*, I can see that.'

She glanced back up at him quickly and he shrugged. 'He will allow me to give him his bottle. He will suffer me to change his nappy. He will only fall asleep in my arms when he is completely exhausted and can fight sleep no more. He does not smile at me.'

'Mr Vieri, it will take time.'

She knew his name? Of course she knew his name. Everyone in Mirror Glass Bay probably knew his name.

She glanced around the motel room. 'This is all so new and unfamiliar to him. And he misses his mother.'

He should have stayed at Anita's cottage, rather than dragging Benito to the motel. It was just... He'd felt as if he'd been invading Anita's privacy. His own discomfort, though, shouldn't have mattered. What mattered was what was best for Benito.

And what was best for Benito was this magician of a maid.

He studied her left hand, noticed she bore no sign of a wedding ring. In fact, she wore no adornment at all other than a pair of silver studs in her ears. 'You have me at a disadvantage,' he said. 'You know my name, but I do not know yours.'

That generous mouth widened into a smile, and she held out her hand. 'Monique Thomas. It's nice to meet you, Mr Vieri.'

He liked her easy frankness, the innate egalitarian attitude that seemed so much a part of the Australian culture. She must know he was one of the richest men in all of Italy and yet she treated him as she would any other person. He liked that.

He shook her hand. 'Please, call me Luca. And the pleasure is all mine.'

The faintest pink tinged her cheeks. She pulled her hand from his and glanced back at Benito. 'I really should get to work.'

'I have a proposition for you, Monique.'

She swung back, her eyebrows disappearing beneath her fringe.

'A business proposition,' he assured her. Though it suddenly occurred to him that such a lovely-looking woman must get other kinds of propositions all the time.

Sexual interest momentarily flared, but he ruthlessly extinguished it. Not the time and certainly not the place. To all intents and purposes, the world thought him engaged to be married. While it wasn't true, he couldn't afford to create speculation or scandal.

Monique tried to quell the ridiculous racing of her heart. Anita had told her Benito's father was handsome, but Luca Vieri wasn't just handsome, he was dynamic, devastating... and drop-dead gorgeous.

She swallowed. 'A business proposition?'

Of course he'd meant a *business* proposition. She wasn't the kind of woman who received indecent propositions from rich, powerful, gorgeous men. And even if she were, she wasn't the kind of woman to accept them.

Little Miss Perfect. Miss Manners. Stuck up and buttoned up.

She ignored the childhood taunts to focus on the man in front of her. He'd moved to stare out of the glass door at the motel's pool and gardens, his shoulders tight. The discovery that he had a son looked to have turned his world upside down.

Either that or he was a very good actor.

The jury was still out on that.

A business proposition? She'd bet he was going to ask her to babysit Benny for the duration of his stay in Mirror Glass Bay. She calculated the number of occupied rooms in the motel at the moment and nodded. That could be arranged. Eve and Cassidy would do all they could to accommodate him.

And it'd give her a bit more time to say goodbye to Benny. Obviously Luca hadn't made the connection yet that she was his son's godmother.

He swung from the window, those dark intense eyes fixing on her again. They made her swallow…and for some reason feel guilty. She had no reason to feel guilty. If anyone should feel guilty it should be him!

She frowned. Except she wasn't sure about that either and she wasn't jumping to conclusions.

'Monique, I would like you to come and work for me. In Italy. As Benito's nanny.'

She stared. She shook herself. 'You know nothing about me.'

'I know that my son loves and trusts you. I suspect Anita did as well if she allowed you to babysit her child. That's a good enough reference for me.'

When she said nothing, he gestured towards Benny fast asleep in her lap. 'I just saw how good and kind you were to him. You love my son, I think.'

Tears filled her eyes. She ducked her head, but suspected he'd seen them anyway. He had the kind of eyes that rarely missed a thing. He named a salary that made her sag. Dear God. With that kind of money she could…

'What do you say, Monique Thomas?'

She pulled in a breath, blinking hard, and then lifted her head. 'Are you aware that I'm Benny's godmother?'

He fell into the sofa opposite as if her words had knocked the breath from his body. 'Godmother?'

She nodded.

'But...' his face lit up '...this is perfect!'

He had an arrogant confidence that should've irked her, but she found it strangely comforting—he wanted what was best for his son, he wanted his son to be happy. That made him powerfully attractive.

She laughed at herself. A man showed a modicum of interest in a child's welfare and she turned to mush?

Really, Monique!

'I'd love to be Benny's nanny and it'd be beyond exciting to visit Italy—' she started to reply.

'Then this is perfect! Let us shake hands on it. I will square everything with your employers, and we can leave as soon as the arrangements can be made. Benito has a passport so we can be quick.'

He rose, tapping a finger against perfectly sculpted lips, his mind racing behind dark eyes that hadn't noticed the sagging of her shoulders or seen the way she'd started to shake her head.

'How long will it take for you to be ready to leave? You will have my entire apparatus at your disposal.'

'I'm sorry, Luca, but as much as I would love to accept your proposition, I can't.' She swallowed down the lump in her throat. 'I'm sorry.'

He sat again, staring at her with those throbbing eyes. It was like being in the eye of a storm—all eerie quiet before the wind picked you up and flung you every which way.

'You say you love my son; you tell me you would like to travel, and I know that financially my offer is an attractive one.'

'Correct on each count.'

'Are you married or in a relationship?'

'It's nothing like that.' At least, not in the way he meant.

He pursed his lips. 'You have a child?'

She hesitated. Not exactly. At least, not yet.

'Your child would be most welcome. He or she would be a playmate for Benito.'

That was a lovely sentiment. However… 'I'm afraid it's not that simple.'

He leaned towards her. 'Can you not tell me why?'

If she weren't Benny's godmother, nothing would compel her to expose her family's dirty linen to a complete stranger. But Benny was her godson and she owed it to both him and Anita to maintain as much contact with him as possible. She might not be able to accompany Benny to Italy, but perhaps Luca could be prevailed upon to let her have video calls with the little boy…and maybe real face-to-face visits in the future.

But that wouldn't happen if Luca didn't think her invested in his son's future. And she would hate for Benny to ever think all of his friends in Australia had forgotten about him.

'Monique?'

Dear Lord, when the man said her name in his beautiful Italian accent like that, it could melt a mere mortal to marshmallow. Absurdly, then, she found herself having to blink back tears.

Except it wasn't absurd.

Rising, she took Benny through to the bedroom and placed him in the cot that had been set up in there. She made sure he had his special favourite plush animal nearby—a giraffe with a long neck perfect for little fingers to hold onto. Anita had dubbed the giraffe Colin. She made a mental note to tell Luca about Colin—the comfort and sense of security it gave Benny—and to warn him to always make sure Colin was near…to be careful not to lose him.

She touched a hand to Benny's hair. 'Oh, Anita,' she whispered. 'We miss you.'

When she returned to the main room, Luca held a cup of tea out to her. 'I did not know how you took it.'

'White, no sugar. But black is fine. Thank you.'

She went to take a grateful sip, but her cup was whisked away before she could. 'There is milk.'

It was returned to her a moment later. She sipped, closing her eyes in appreciation. 'Perfect.'

When she opened them again, she found him staring at her with an arrested expression on his face. He shook himself and gestured her to the sofa again.

'Now tell me why you cannot be Benito's nanny, when it is clear that you would like to be very much. And when I would do anything I could to provide my son with the continuity he needs to settle into his new life.'

She smothered a sigh but pasted on a smile. 'If you want continuity then you need to know about Colin.'

He listened intently as she told him about Benny's favourite toy. 'A comfort toy? Yes, I have heard of such things.' That dark head nodded, the expression a little fierce. 'I will buy another—no, I will buy several—and put them in a safe place in case the original ever meets with a mishap.'

That fierceness pressed into the service of his son's happiness gave her pause. It didn't gel that a man like that, someone so protective of his child, would ignore that child's existence for seven months. Which meant someone else in the Vieri family had to have known. And had kept it from him. Who would do such a thing?

Not that she had any intention of posing the question. It was all just conjecture anyway.

'Now, come, tell me what is preventing you from accompanying Benito to Rome?'

At that moment she almost believed he'd slay any dragons that needed slaying—for his son's benefit, of course. Despite the fact it had more to do with Benny than herself, it was still devastatingly attractive. What a shame, then, that the fire-breathing dragon threatening her peace of mind couldn't be conquered so easily.

She set her tea down and forced her shoulders back. 'I recently started proceedings to contest custody of my young niece.'

His gaze darkened. 'Go on.'

'My sister is an addict—drug and alcohol. So is my mother.'

'I see.'

She doubted that. She doubted drug or alcohol addiction had ever touched this man's rarefied world. And she was glad of it. She wished to God they'd not touched hers either.

'I had guardianship of Fern, my niece, while my sister served a custodial sentence for drug dealing. From the moment she was born, though, Fern spent more time living with me than her mother. Skye would occasionally make noises about becoming more hands on, but...'

She trailed off and he nodded, his mouth grim.

'I really thought that she meant to turn her life around when she was released from prison. I thought she'd learned her lesson. She came to stay with me, and I got her a job here at the motel.'

'You had high hopes?'

She nodded.

'What happened?'

Their mother had happened. She'd blown into Mirror Glass Bay with her insults and her challenges, and with that inexplicable hold that seemed to seduce Skye every single time.

'Did she return to drugs?' Luca asked.

It took all her strength to not drop her head to her hands. 'She stole my credit card and disappeared.' She was still paying off that debt.

'Did you not report her?'

She should have. She could see that now.

He must've read the answer in her eyes. He shook his head. 'Monique…'

Her chest burned. 'My sister was once my world, Luca. When I was a child, my mother couldn't be relied on. But when I was four, she came home from the hospital with Skye. That changed my life, gave me someone to love and something to fight for. Having Skye in my life stopped me from becoming just like my mother.'

He rested his elbows on his knees, the action angling him closer to her. For no reason at all, her heart picked up speed. She took a hasty gulp of her tea. 'She left Fern with me, though, so I figured I'd just keep looking after her and be able to keep her safe.'

'What changed to make you contest custody? You have involved your local authorities, yes?'

She nodded, staring down at her hands. 'Skye and my mother came, with a policeman, and took Fern away.'

His quick intake of breath told her what he thought of that. 'How old is your niece?'

'Three and a half.'

'And how did she react to this?'

The question made her flinch. She shook her head. She refused to put that scene into words. Every time she recalled the way Fern had screamed and cried and clung to her, the hot scald of tears made her throat ache.

She forced her chin up. 'Because I'm not Fern's mother, I have no rights.'

His eyes flashed. 'You have the rights of common decency and to protect those weaker than you.'

She'd not been able to protect Skye from her mother's influence when they'd been growing up. Maybe that was why she was so determined to do all she could to protect Fern now.

'What has happened since this time? How long has it been since this happened?'

'Four months.'

She saw his protest before he could utter it and she held up a hand. 'Please, Luca, I know.'

He snapped his mouth shut.

'I don't believe in taking a child away from their parent except in the direst of circumstances. I hoped rather than believed my sister meant to build a proper relationship with Fern, but the truth of the matter is she and my mother are simply holding Fern to ransom.'

'Explain this to me, please.'

'My sister tells me she will give me custody of Fern in exchange for two hundred thousand dollars.' Her lips twisted. 'I don't have that kind of money. And the bank won't lend it to me.'

'You cannot pay this blackmail because it will not stop! Unless you have legal papers drawn up and—'

She held up her hand again and he halted mid-sentence. 'There's a more pressing concern, Luca. My mother, sister and Fern all live in the same house, and while they're not unkind to Fern they neglect her.'

'You are frightened for her safety?'

Terrified.

'I visit as often as I can.' Surprise visits. She never told them when she was coming. 'They live in a larger town forty minutes away. I take groceries so that Fern has something to eat.' And just so she had a chance to hug her little niece and tell her she loved her and was doing everything she could to make sure she could come and live with her for good.

Her heart started to thud. 'Three months ago, when I dropped in unannounced, the house was wide open, but my mother and sister had both passed out in the lounge room and there was food burning on the stove. Fern had been locked in her bedroom.'

Luca's entire body stiffened. He muttered something in Italian. It sounded like an oath. Whatever it was, she found herself nodding. She hated to think what would've happened if she hadn't shown up. They could've burned the house down, with everyone inside it. 'That's when I called Social Services. They've been investigating ever since.'

'But that was three months ago!'

'My mother knows how to play the system. And it's a big thing to take a child from its mother.'

'But—'

'I know. And I've given up hoping that Skye will become a proper mother. I've had to harden my heart against my sister for Fern's sake. Fern deserves to be safe and she deserves to be loved.'

She knew this man agreed with her. She hesitated, but then stood and pulled her right arm from her cardigan. She angled her body so he could see her arm, could see the scar that ran down its length. 'I don't want this happening to my niece.'

CHAPTER TWO

LUCA STARED AT the burn scar that seemed to go from where Monique's arm met her shoulder to halfway down her forearm and everything inside him started to shake with a rage he'd never before experienced. 'How—?'

He broke off to try and control the fury in his voice. This woman deserved admiration, consideration, not anger and outrage.

'How old were you?' he tried again in a lower voice.

'Nearly five.'

Just a little older than her niece. 'What happened?'

She shrugged her arm back into her cardigan. 'My mother had put chips into a saucepan of hot fat to cook for our dinner. Our oven was broken,' she added as if she saw the question in his eyes. 'She'd set the timer and when it went off, I tried to find her, but she was nowhere in the house.'

'So you tried to take the saucepan off the stove?'

'It was heavier than I thought it'd be.'

She didn't go on and he didn't have the heart to ask additional questions that could only cause her pain. Her mother should be flayed alive for her neglect.

'So you can see that, as much as I would love to come to Italy as Benny's nanny, I can't abandon my niece.'

'Of course you cannot. Your Fern needs you.' And he suspected she needed her Fern.

He was going to fix this. And he didn't care how much it cost him. What was the point in being wealthy if he couldn't do good things with his money?

Monique tossed her head and caramel curls danced about her shoulders. 'Now that you know about my family, I…'

'You…?'

She pressed her hands together. She hadn't taken her seat again after rising to show him her arm, and he couldn't help thinking that she was like a bird poised for flight if he made the slightest wrong move. He made a silent vow to do his best to not make a wrong move.

'I should imagine I'm not the kind of woman you'd want in charge of your son.'

He blinked. 'Why not?'

Her eyes widened. Caramel eyes and caramel hair. This woman would taste delicious.

The thought, odd and unsettling, whispered through him. He realised then that the tension wrapping him tightly hid another emotion besides anger at those who should've kept Monique safe. Desire had become a liquid heat in his veins. This woman tempted his every sense in a way no woman had in a very long time. He wanted to feast on her warmth and her smiles, satiate the need that surged through his blood.

He tried to shake it away. She was nothing like the women from his world.

Which could be why he wanted her.

Or maybe the barriers he normally erected around himself had taken a beating when he'd discovered he had a son, and he hadn't had the time to fix them back into place.

He forced himself to straighten. He would not be dallying with this woman, regardless of how lovely she was. He didn't mix business with that kind of pleasure, and he still had high hopes she'd become Benito's nanny.

Neither could he forget that in the world's eyes he was engaged to Bella Romano. Once the news broke of the cancelled engagement, if he did not wish to alienate Bella's father, he would have to wait a decent interval before his name was linked with another woman's.

He'd go to whatever lengths were necessary to prevent such an eventuality. Signor Romano was crucial to Luca's plans for re-establishing the former glory of the Vieri name and reputation. He'd promised his grandfather that he'd restore the family's honour, and he refused to let the older man down. He owed his grandfather everything.

Monique had still not answered his question about why he should now not wish to employ her. He worked hard to keep his voice pleasant. 'Are you dependent on either drugs or alcohol?'

She drew herself up. 'Absolutely not.'

It was as he'd thought. 'You cannot choose your family so why would I judge you based on their actions and attitudes?' He held her gaze. 'Anita trusted you with her son. She made you his godmother. That is a good enough reference for me.'

Something in her face gentled and things inside him yearned towards it, but he cut them off with a ruthlessness born of need. 'I wish to ask you something. Do you know why Anita never told me about Benito?'

She hesitated. 'It was my understanding that she had.'

His temples started to throb. 'Obviously Benito inherits all of Anita's worldly goods. I, as Benito's father, will hold it in trust for him until he comes of age. I have been over the documentation with her lawyer. It appears Anita came into a large sum of money recently.'

She gnawed on her bottom lip, her eyes losing their sparkle. 'I thought that had come from you.'

He stiffened.

'But it appears Benny's existence has come as a surprise to you.' One slim shoulder lifted. 'I'm sorry. All I can tell you is that Anita told me she'd tried to contact you.'

Ice settled beneath his breastbone.

'She never told me your name, but she always spoke of you with a great deal of fondness.' She smiled, as if remembering her friend's actual words, and that those words had all been good. 'She told me it was a holiday fling.'

That's exactly what it had been—an act of rebellion before he buckled down to the path his grandfather had formulated to win back the family's reputation. He'd relinquished the last vestiges of dreams that had somehow survived—dreams of love and freedom.

He hadn't realised he still believed in such things. He'd thought they'd all been destroyed when he was twenty years old, hadn't realised such sentimentality still had a hold on him.

After what had happened with Camilla one would've thought he'd have learned his lesson. But one bad apple didn't mean every other woman in the world was bad as well. Besides, Camilla hadn't been all bad either, just tempted beyond endurance. She'd taken the money and run. A part of him even understood it.

But it had certainly made him wary. How did one tell real love from fake when they looked so alike?

True love? He bit back a snort. One might as well wish for unicorns and a genie! No, an arrangement where both parties knew exactly what they were getting from the marriage was the smarter choice. That way no one could be disappointed.

Monique's low laugh snapped him back. 'Anita told me it was every dream of a holiday fling that one could ever have, making me wildly envious.'

The words should've been a gift. And yet Anita had betrayed him too. Monique's revelation confirmed the suspicion that had been growing in his mind. 'Someone in my family paid Anita to keep her quiet. She took a bribe.'

Monique's chin lifted. 'She accepted child support that she was entitled to,' she corrected. 'That's a very different thing.'

She'd accepted money in exchange for her silence. She'd kept his son from him!

'Who would offer her such a bribe?' she said.

'My parents. If I'd known she was pregnant, I'd have married her. They'd have known that.'

Her eyes flashed. 'You're very confident. Please, don't be offended if I correct you and say you'd have *offered* to marry her.'

Touché. Perhaps he'd become too used to women throwing themselves at him.

Not you, but your family's money.

'And why would your parents do something so…?'

Heinous? Spiteful? Abhorrent? He shook his head. 'They have previous form.'

Though she didn't move, he sensed her drawing away from him. 'You have other children that they've kept from you?'

'No!' He dragged a hand down his face. 'I mean that in the past my father once paid a woman a substantial amount of money to break up with me. Apparently, he and my mother had deemed her unsuitable.'

The smooth perfection of her brow pleated. 'That's… *awful.*' She swallowed, her hands pressed against her stomach. 'I'm really sorry, Luca.'

He had a feeling she meant every word.

'But you're wrong if you think that's what Anita did. She had integrity, but she also had her pride. She'd accept child support for Benny's sake, but she wouldn't beg you to be a part of his life if she didn't think that's what you wanted.'

'She should've known I—'

'I don't think a six-day fling on a tropical island, even given all you shared, qualifies either of you to claim to know the other well.'

He dragged in a breath. That was true enough.

'Please, don't harbour a sense of injury towards her.'

He could see the thought of it broke her heart. It made things inside him tighten and loosen, both at the same time.

'Please, just accept the fact she was a good person and would never have kept Benny from you knowingly.'

It occurred to him then that with very little evidence to the contrary Monique had believed the best of him. After seeing him with Benito, seeing for herself how much his son's happiness meant to him, she'd made the decision to accept what he said at face value. She was right. It would be pointless to hold a grudge towards Anita. 'All you say is true. Very well, I will simply regard it as…an unfortunate series of circumstances that led to a misunderstanding.'

Her eyes narrowed. 'Due to the interference of third parties.'

He also knew it would be pointless to confront his parents. They'd only deny it. All he could do was cherish Benito from this day forward. 'It will be best,' he agreed, 'to turn my face to the future.'

Excellent plan.' She nodded her approval and then lifted a hand. 'I'm sorry, but I really need to get to work now.'

'If I clear it with your employer, will you be Benito's nanny for the duration of my stay?' He had to work hard to keep his voice even.

'Yes, gladly.' She hesitated. 'At some stage I'm hoping to talk to you about ways I can remain in contact with Benny once you leave.'

'We will work something out,' he promised. 'I will go and speak to Eve and Cassidy immediately.'

Her smile could slay a man where he stood. He left before he did something reckless like press a kiss to the golden skin of her cheek and drag a deep breath of her into his lungs like some hormone-riddled teenager.

He spoke to Eve and Cassidy and Eve's husband Damon about more than hiring Monique in the short term. He told them he wanted to hire Monique as Benito's full-time nanny for the next twelve months. 'She is his godmother, practically family. She loves him and he loves her. It is clear Anita trusted her.'

Eve nodded. 'They were close. We all miss Anita. And we'll miss Monique too if she accepts the position you're offering.'

The two women exchanged glances. One he could interpret with ease. 'Yes,' he agreed, 'there is the matter of her niece.'

Both women blinked.

'She has told me of the situation.'

'She won't leave without her,' Cassidy said from her spot behind the bar. 'She's a mama bear where Fern is concerned.'

Better and better. The more he learned of Monique the surer he became that she was the right person to take charge of his son. 'I mean to do something about that situation.

'Good.' Eve's lips thinned. 'That child should've been placed in Monique's care from the moment she was born.'

Damon straightened from where he slouched against the bar. 'Is there anything we can do to help?'

Luca considered the offer. Damon was a successful businessman with local connections. 'Is there a local lawyer you would recommend—someone smart, hard-nosed and who can think on their feet?'

'I know just the person. What's your phone number? I'll forward the details through to you.'

Luca understood the subtext but gave his number without hesitation. If Monique did come to Rome with him, these people wanted personal access to him, to make sure Monique was treated right. This community looked after their own, and he suspected they considered Benito one of their own too. He liked them all the more for it.

He made the decision then and there to buy Anita's little house. He and Benito would come back here. Often. Or, at least, as often as he could manage. He would provide his son with all the links to his mother that he could.

'If there's anything else we can do…'

'There is strength in numbers,' Luca agreed, 'but in this instance I mean to go in hard and fast and get this done as quickly as possible.'

'Excellent.'

That was Cassidy. She was a very beautiful woman, but there was a dangerous edge to her smile that he didn't understand. 'At some point Monique and I will need to beard the lion in his den. I would not wish to take Benito into that situation.'

'We'd love to look after Benny,' Eve and Cassidy both said at the same time.

'Thank you.'

He turned to leave but found Cassidy at his elbow. 'Let me see you out.'

She had something to say to him?

'Mr Vieri, I heartily approve of what you're doing for Fern.'

'But?'

'Monique has the kindest heart of anyone I know. She's been let down by the people she should've been able to rely on.' They halted by his car and that dangerous smile became more dangerous. 'If you hurt her or mistreat her, I will hunt you down, and once I'm through with you, you won't be capable of bearing another child. Do I make myself clear?'

He stared, momentarily lost for words, but an absurd smile built inside him. Monique was much loved here in Mirror Glass Bay. He could not have asked for a better reference. 'Signorina Cassidy, if I hurt or mistreat the lovely Monique, I will let you find me and will hold still while you do your worst.'

'Perfect answer.' Cassidy's smile lost its edge. 'I'm glad we're on the same page. Have a nice day.'

She turned and sauntered away. For the first time in three days Luca felt the sun on his face, heard the surf rolling up the beach just out of sight, and dragged salt-laden air into his lungs. He had a son, a wonderful son, and for a brief moment everything felt right with the world.

It was amazing how quickly money could grease wheels and make things happen, but it still took the best part of a week to get the necessary paperwork in order. He wanted the contract that would give Monique custody of her niece to be watertight.

While waiting for it to be finalised, he moved himself and Benito back into Anita's house. She hadn't owned it, had been renting, but it was where his son had spent the first seven months of his life, so he bought it. He paid more than the market price, but as far as he was concerned it was worth every penny.

While it might be tiny compared to what he was used to, it was also homely and comfortable. Here he could exist in a bubble away from his usual stresses and responsibilities. He could play on the beach with his son and relax. And threaded through it all was Monique, who smoothed *everything*. Who made everything seem easy. Who brought light and joy to Benito's face.

He'd smiled when he'd discovered Monique lived in the house next door. No wonder the two women had become such fast friends. He couldn't have planned that more perfectly if he'd tried.

He didn't tell Monique what he had organised until the morning they set off for her mother's house. She raised her head from the contract he'd handed her, her eyes dazed. 'You've done…?'

'We are going to remove your niece from her current situation and ensure she is properly looked after.'

'You're offering my sister a ridiculous amount of money…' her eyes scanned the page '…to sign custody over to me?'

He didn't consider half a million dollars a ridiculous amount of money. Not when it would ensure the safety of a child. 'Please, let me do this.'

'I've no intention of stopping you. I want Fern safe too much for that. But I will pay you back.'

He took her hands in his. They were cold and he worked at rubbing warmth back into them. 'If you come to Rome for twelve months as Benito's nanny, I will consider myself amply repaid.'

She nodded, but he could see she was too afraid to hope, afraid that something would go wrong.

If he'd judged her sister correctly, nothing would go wrong. She'd be happy to sell her soul, let alone her only child, for the money he was offering.

'Come, the driver and the lawyer are here.' He'd ordered the driver to collect the lawyer first. 'The lawyer is going to explain exactly how we're to do this.'

* * *

It went exactly as Luca expected. The lawyer did most of the talking and Monique's sister and mother couldn't hide the way their eyes lit up when they discovered the amount of money on offer.

He knew what he was doing was sordid, but the entire situation was sordid. If it would give rise to a good outcome for an innocent child, he was prepared to play whatever ugly games were necessary. Especially now he had a son.

He couldn't bear the thought of Benito being neglected or taken advantage of by anyone. *Dio!* What would've happened if Anita hadn't put his name on Benito's birth certificate? It didn't bear thinking about. What he did know was that Monique would've stood by her godson and given him all the love and care that she could. In return, this was the least that he could do for her.

Monique's mother tried to negotiate for more money but was shut down so quickly by the lawyer that Skye reprimanded her. Skye seized a pen and declared herself ready to sign on the dotted line, as if afraid the offer would be withdrawn.

Monique forestalled her. 'Skye, are you really prepared to do this—sign away all rights to Fern?'

Skye tossed her head, her eyes hard. 'She was always more yours than mine. Besides, this amount of money will change my life. This is a once in a lifetime opportunity. If you think I'm going to let it pass me by, you're stupider than I thought.'

He had to grit his teeth to stop from telling her exactly what he thought. Monique would never part with her niece, not for any amount of money.

'If you continue on your current course, Skye, this amount of money has the potential to kill you,' Monique said in a low voice that throbbed with pain.

Dio santo! He had not considered that.

'Who's this?' Monique's mother jeered, gesturing towards him. He saw it for what it was—a tactic to divert Skye's attention. 'Your fancy man?'

Monique's shoulders snapped back. He stepped forward. 'The contract needs to be witnessed. Which I will do.'

Sharlene Thomas laughed. 'You can act as stuck up as you like, Monique, but you're no better than me or your sister.'

What a piece of work! He'd like to—

'It's not too late, Skye,' Monique said.

But Skye ignored her and signed the document in all the spots the lawyer indicated, and Luca forced himself to remain calm and reserved.

'Looks like you've done all right for yourself.' Skye hitched her chin towards Luca. 'And now I'm going to do all right for myself.'

He sensed rather than saw Monique flinch. He had to fight the urge to put an arm around her shoulders and draw her within the protective shelter of his arms, shield her from the barbs and poison of these people who should love her.

The rest of the paperwork was signed with barely another word exchanged.

'I want to sit in your lap!'

Fern's bottom lip wobbled, and all Monique wanted to do was pull her darling niece into her arms and hold her close. 'But we're in the car, pumpkin, and you know the rules.'

Fern banged her heels against her car seat. Luca had been surprisingly well prepared and had ensured the car had one. She wanted to hug him for his forethought, for the provisions he'd made. She could hardly believe that Fern—her darling Fern—was no longer in danger of the harm neglect could inflict. She couldn't believe Fern was now hers to love and look after and protect *forever*.

Thank you. Thank you. Thank you.

'I hate the rules!' Fern shouted.

She could focus on her gratitude later. For the moment she needed to do all she could to quieten her niece's fears. She leaned in close to the little girl. 'I love you, my Fern. And you are now going to live with me for ever and ever.'

Two little hands went either side of Monique's face. 'You promise?'

The mistrust in the child's eyes broke her heart. 'I promise, sweetie.'

A sob wrenched from the depths of Fern's chest, and Monique's vision blurred. Luca instructed the driver to pull over and stop the car beside a small park. Monique turned to him.

'You need ten minutes alone with your niece. This has all happened so quickly. There has been no time for explanations and reassurances or...' his face became strangely vulnerable '...cuddles. Take some time to lay your niece's fears to rest, Monique.'

She already owed him so much. 'I know how badly you wanted to get back to Benny and—'

'We have time.'

This small kindness won over every last part of her that his actions in ensuring Fern was removed from her vulnerable situation hadn't already won.

She sat on the grass with Fern in her lap, her arms tight about the little girl, and told her that they were going to live together until Fern was all grown up, and that even then they could still live together if that's what Fern wanted. She told her of all the fun things they would do together, and how they were soon going on a big plane to a place called Italy where they were going to live for a year.

Because, of course, she was accepting the position of Benny's nanny. Given all Luca had done for her, she suspected she'd do just about anything he asked of her now.

She didn't know how much Fern understood, but the tension slowly drained from the little body and she relaxed into Monique. Monique dragged in a couple of deep breaths and revelled in the feeling, the sense of well-being...the relief that Fern was now safe.

Fern sat up to stare at her aunt. 'And Mummy?'

She'd been prepared for the question. 'Mummy can come visit us at any time, but she's not allowed to take you home with her. It's the rules.'

Fern had cried then, and Monique had simply held her.

It wasn't until later, once both children had been put down for naps, that Monique and Luca had a chance to speak. She resisted the urge to throw her arms around his neck and plant a grateful kiss to his cheek. The way he held himself slightly aloof told her that one didn't take such liberties with Luca Vieri. 'I don't know how to thank you.'

'It is not necessary. Is Fern...? I don't know how to say it. At ease, unworried, no longer afraid?

She nodded. 'This might sound strange, but her show of temper in the car heartened me. She's never been particularly rambunctious, but when she was forced to return to her mother, she became very withdrawn. Even with me. I lost her trust.'

'I am sorry.'

'Don't be. I'll win it back.' She glanced up and then grimaced. 'I'd also like to apologise for the offensive conclusions my mother drew about you.'

'That was not your fault. Besides, what do I care what your mother thinks of me? I urge you to forget it. I have.'

Beneath her ribcage, her heart thudded. 'Luca, I can't thank you enough. I—'

'There is no need.'

He held up a hand, but she ignored it. 'There's every need.'

The coffee had finished brewing and she poured them both a cup, slid one across to him. He shouldn't look at home in Anita's kitchen, but he did. She gestured towards the back door. 'Let's enjoy the sun while we have the chance.'

She led him out to the café table and chairs that sat beneath the shade of a battered-looking frangipani tree. Honeyeaters chirped in a cabbage palm at the bottom of the garden gathering fibres for their nests. In the distance, beneath everything, was the soothing sound of the ocean.

She pulled in a deep breath and released it, feeling a new freedom in both her body and her mind. 'You've made sure my niece is safe. You've changed her life for the better. It's a huge thing that you've done.'

He hesitated, his cup halfway to his mouth. A strangely vulnerable expression stretched through his eyes before the shutters came down over them. 'I had the means to help. We, all of us, should fight injustice when we see it.'

And since he'd discovered he had a son, she suspected it had given him a different perspective on such matters.

'I wasn't only glad to help, I felt privileged to be in a position to help.'

Those dark eyes with their earnest expression could undo a woman.

'So come. Let's hear no more about it.'

Only he would say such a thing.

She tried to not notice the way his lips touched his mug, tried to ignore the warmth it sparked at her very centre, tried not to imagine that mouth doing…other things. Against her better judgement, almost against her will, things inside her softened. Yet some sixth sense warned her against the softening. She was so grateful to this man, but…

They were from different worlds and she couldn't fool herself—the only place he saw for her in his world was as Benny's nanny. Her sole goal now was to make his life as easy as she could. It was the least she could do, given everything he'd done for her and Fern. Getting a crush on him wouldn't make anybody's life easier.

'You've given me my heart's desire.'

His eyes speared back to hers. For the briefest moment she imagined that heat smouldered in their depths. But then he blinked, and it was gone, replaced with his usual calm detachment.

Her heart thundered in her ears. She had to have imagined it. Dear God, if he wanted her...

No. She had to nip all such fanciful imaginings in the bud right now.

Seizing her coffee, she took a gulp that burned her throat. Boss and nanny, that was the only relationship they were going to have. Anything further would complicate things. Besides, she'd sworn to never get involved with another emotionally unavailable man again.

And instinct told her Luca was as emotionally unavailable as they came.

She set her mug back down. 'Of course—' her voice was too husky but there was nothing she could do about it '—there's now no question of whether I'll come to Italy or not. I'd be honoured to be Benny's nanny for the next twelve months. I'll be his nanny for as long as you want.'

Competing impulses seemed to war with each other in the depths of his eyes, and she found herself holding her breath. He blinked and her heart sank when she saw that it was detachment that had won. Kindness was there too, but also determination.

'Two things,' he murmured.

She nodded, not taking her eyes from his as she sipped her coffee.

'The first thing you need to know is that what I did for Fern was not conditional on your acceptance of the nanny position. That was a thing apart. To put conditions on it would cheapen it.'

The man was honourable. While the Vieri family were rich, the name didn't come without controversy. But Luca Vieri was an undeniably honourable man. 'Thank you,' she managed. 'I appreciate that. And the second thing?'

'I ask only for twelve months, Monique. I want my son to have continuity until he becomes accustomed to his new life. But this is your home...' he gestured around '...and you love it.'

She did. With the salary Luca had promised her, she could buy a house here and set up her own business. It was a dream come true.

'I want you to understand that for the next twelve months your life will not be your own. The reason I offered such a generous salary is because I want you on call twenty-four seven. I also want you to train two nannies to take over from you when the time comes.'

She hadn't considered the practicalities of the position. He was a new parent, thrust into fatherhood with next to no warning. He might look capable and in control, but she knew how intimidating it could be to have sole responsibility for a child. He was asking a lot of her. She glanced at the house where her niece slept. He'd also given her so much.

'Once we're settled in and you've started to train your replacements, you will have free time. But if for some reason Benito should need you, I want to be able to call you and have you return immediately.'

Well, that wasn't so bad. It meant that eventually she and

Fern could do a few hours of sightseeing in the city, along with some shopping.

'Will that be a problem for you?'

'Absolutely not.' Even if it had been she wouldn't have said so. 'Benny is my godson. I love him. It'll be no hardship looking after him.'

'This is also why I want only twelve months of your life.'

It took a moment for her to understand what he meant. When she did her mouth dried. Luca was Benny's father—Benny was Luca's, no one else's. 'Are you going to ask me to give up contact with Benny at the end of all this?'

'No!'

He couldn't have looked more shocked and it eased the burn in her chest.

'I mean to bring Benito back here…' he gestured at the house '…for a holiday every year. I hope you and Fern will still be here, and in addition I hope you will video call with Benito regularly. You are his godmother, Monique. You are a link to his mother. I want him to grow up knowing you.'

She sagged back against the unforgiving wrought iron of her chair. 'That's okay, then.'

'Sì?'

'It'll be a wrench to leave him at the end of twelve months, of course. There'll be tears on both sides when it's time for me to return home, and you need to be prepared for that. But…' A furrow pressed itself into her brow.

'But?'

'I'm not going to guard my heart in expectation of that eventuality. I mean to love him as much as I can. He's the dearest little boy who deserves all the love in the world.' It's what Anita would've wanted. 'So if that's going to be a problem for you—'

He reached across to clasp her hand and her tongue cleaved to the roof of her mouth. He murmured something

in Italian that she didn't understand but which sounded unaccountably beautiful. And then he smiled, and it hit her
then how rarely this man smiled.

'No, it is not a problem for me. You are a courageous
woman, and that is a blessing for my son.' He surveyed her
for several heart-stopping moments. 'So we have a deal, *si*?'

She couldn't help answering his smile with one of her
own. She placed her hand in the one he held out and shook
it. She knew next to no Italian—which was something she'd
have to rectify—but one word she did know was yes. She
nodded. '*Si.*'

They set off for Italy in Luca's private jet a week later. It
was proving hard to get her head around the fact that the
man who now employed her was one of the wealthiest men
in Italy. During the last two weeks he'd simply become
Benny's father—a man working hard to forge a solid relationship with his infant son.

The jet brought reality crashing back.

And had nerves jangling in her stomach.

Returning from checking on the children, who were
sleeping in beds at the back of the plane, she found Luca
tapping away on his laptop. She hesitated in front of him.
'You should get some sleep, Monique,' he said without
glancing up. 'It will help with the jet-lag.'

She couldn't sleep. 'I have some questions.'

He glanced up immediately, searched her face and gestured for her to take the seat opposite. 'Just give me a moment to finish this.' He tapped away on his keyboard for a
full minute, before closing the lid and giving her his full
attention. 'Tell me these questions you have.'

It could be heady being the sole focus of Luca's attention. If a girl let it. She had no intention of letting it do any
such thing. 'You've seen the world I come from…'

'Yes.'

She moistened her lips. 'Look, Luca, I knew you were wealthy, but until I stepped on your private jet, I didn't realise… I mean, these last couple of weeks you've just been Benny's father to me and—'

'I am Benny's father.'

'But you're also in charge of one of the world's largest financial dynasties. You have a name to rival Onassis.'

'This is a problem for you?'

That's not what she'd meant. 'It's a change in mindset. I've just realised that I'm not going to be able to take Benny and Fern to play in the local park, am I?'

Understanding dawned in his eyes.

'Given your fortune, Benny would command a huge ransom if he were kidnapped. And even if he isn't at risk of such a thing, the paparazzi will be clamouring for photos of your *"unknown son"*.' She made quote marks in the air.

He nodded heavily.

'My naiveté is appalling. You must be regretting hiring me, but I assure you—'

'No.' He pointed a finger at her. 'This I do not regret. This I blame myself for. I did not think to warn you, to make explicit the expectations of your role.'

It's no one's fault,' she replied. 'I just need to know all the things I must do to keep Benny safe, and not create complications for you.'

He nodded slowly. 'Very well, yes. You cannot leave the house unattended. You must always take a driver and a bodyguard with you when you do.'

Wow. Okay.

'Benito is not to leave the villa without my express permission.'

Lord, it was going to be like house arrest. Her ears had picked up one rather lovely word, though. 'You live in a villa, not an apartment? Does that mean you have a garden…maybe a patch of lawn where the children and I can play?'

For some reason her question made his lips twitch. 'Yes, there is room for the children to play.'

That was something at least. Though she wondered if their ideas of 'room to play' were the same thing.

'Any other questions?'

'Just one more.' She frowned again. 'Should I be calling you Signor Vieri rather than Luca?'

CHAPTER THREE

HE SHOULD NOD. He should tell her to call him Signor Vieri. He should put into place boundaries that could not be crossed, because his every instinct warned him that with this woman he needed all the boundaries that could be enforced.

But he'd grown addicted to the way she saw him, had grown addicted to her softly spoken *Luca*. Found his ears constantly attuned for it.

In her eyes he wasn't the head of one of the wealthiest families in Italy. In her eyes he was a hero, who had won for her her heart's desire. His shoulders went back.

He had little doubt that when Fern's custody case had finally made it to court, the authorities would've placed her in Monique's care. The only problem was how long it would've taken. As far as he was concerned, even one day was too long to wait.

He'd done nothing heroic. He'd splashed around some money, which had solved the problem. Money he could well afford. Yet no one had ever looked at him the way Monique had.

To tell her she could no longer call him Luca…

'Of course you should continue to call me Luca.'

Her smile and the sweet caramel warmth of her eyes was his reward. She opened her mouth…hesitated.

'There is something else on your mind?'

'I've always been…if not friends at least on friendly terms with most of my previous employers.'

She seemed to choose her words carefully. It made his every sense stand to attention.

Her lips pursed, first to the right and then to the left. 'I fear what I'm about to say will seem unforgivably personal to you and you'll think me impertinent.' She winced. 'And I've no desire to vex you.'

He forced himself to not lean forward. He sensed she needed space, a sense of safety, to ask her question and he didn't wish to crowd her. 'Please, ask your question.'

'A little while ago, as in an hour ago, I did what any normal person would've done when you first offered them a job—I did an internet search on you.'

So that was what had kept her glued to her phone.

She smiled and rolled her eyes. 'Though, of course, my life has been anything but normal these last couple of weeks.'

Not normal, no. He'd given her her heart's desire. It had created gratitude, but also chaos. He suspected she did not mind the chaos, but her life—all their lives—had changed so quickly. What had she discovered that perturbed her so?

'You are engaged?'

Ah.

'Onassis, Vieri… Romano… These names are all so far outside of my reality I feel as Alice must've when she fell down the rabbit hole.' She looked dazed, just as the fictional Alice must have, but still sent him a smile that speared straight into his chest. 'I wish you every happiness, by the way.'

Dear God, this woman and her warmth!

Cassidy's words floated back to him. *'Monique has the kindest heart of anyone I know.'*

Things inside him pulled tight. 'What is your question?'

'What does your fiancée think about this situation?'

Situation? There was no situation! He and Monique were employer and employee. Well, okay, perhaps Monique was more than that—as Benito's godmother she was practically family. And, while he might've won for her her heart's desire, it didn't mean—

'I need to know if she resents Benny or...' Her brow pleated. 'Or if she's ambivalent about this turn of events. I'm not saying that's not an understandable reaction. It's just... I'd rather be forewarned.'

He closed his eyes. She meant the situation with his son. Of course that was what she meant.

'In accepting the position of Benny's nanny, I made a commitment to look after him to the best of my ability.'

She was asking if she needed to protect Benito from his future stepmother. 'Bella would never hurt a child, would never be unkind to one.'

She let out a breath he hadn't realised she'd been holding, her body relaxing back into her seat. He made a decision then to confide in her. She felt she owed him and while he had no intention of taking advantage of that, it did mean he could trust her.

'Thank you for taking the time to address my concerns.' She started to rise. 'I'll let you get back to your work.'

'Please, sit.'

She blinked and sat.

'What I am about to tell you is confidential.'

She made a zipping motion across her mouth that made him smile.

And focus far too closely on the dusky fullness of her lips. 'It will be best if you know what to expect when we reach Rome.'

He told himself it would be in Benito's best interests if she were furnished with all the relevant information.

'It is not widely known yet, but the engagement between Bella and myself has been cancelled.'

Her hand flew to her mouth. 'Because of Benny?'

He shook his head. He could not let her think that. 'The arrangement was not a love match. That is not how things are done in my world. Both families wanted the match for... business reasons.'

Her jaw dropped. She snapped it back into place, swallowed and nodded. 'I see.'

She didn't see. The entire concept was foreign to her. He could see that in the thinning of her lips and the way the skin around her eyes pulled tight. He didn't want to see this situation through her eyes. She had no notion of the pressures and responsibilities that came with being head of a family like his. She didn't know of the promise he had made to his grandfather. She didn't *need* to know those things.

'Bella, however, has fallen in love with another man. One it's unlikely her father will approve of. Bella confided all of this to me the week before I learned of Benito's existence. She begged me to find some way to break off our engagement.'

'Why doesn't she just break it off herself?'

'She is afraid of her father's disapproval. I have known Bella since we were children. We are friends. I respect her and am fond of her.' The marriage would've been dutiful, companionable.

Boring.

He did what he could to banish that thought. 'I am happy to help her however I can.'

Monique shifted on her seat. 'So *you* have to take the heat for *her* decision?'

It took all his strength not to drop his head back to the

headrest and close his eyes. If he was careful, he could pre-
serve the relationship between himself and Signor Romano.
And he would be careful. Very, *very* careful.

Her mouth worked. '*This* is the kind of marriage you
plan to make?'

Her incredulity shouldn't sting. His world was alien to
her. 'In recent times the Vieri name, as you no doubt know,
has been tarnished with scandal and disgrace due to the
intemperance of my parents' generation. They—my parents, aunts and uncles—took and took without thought for
others, often not paying their bills. They sent merchants
and tradespeople out of business with their carelessness,
broke up marriages and took advantage of everything and
everyone. The Vieri name, which was once synonymous
with integrity and prestige, is now—'

He broke off, acid burning his throat. 'They gave nothing back. They cared nothing for the legacy my grandfather
and great-grandfather and his father before him worked so
hard to build.'

She stared at him. 'But you do. You want to honour their
hard work.' Her brow pleated. 'So your marriage to Bella
was a step towards winning back that respectability?'

'Yes.'

'And Benny provides you with a convenient excuse to
break off the engagement as he's now...your heir?'

'It is not that simple. Things are no longer that archaic.'

'Really? They sound positively medieval to me?' she
muttered.

His head rocked back.

She winced. 'I'm sorry, I shouldn't have said that out
loud.'

He let it pass. He could imagine how strange she must
find this situation. 'Each generation fights it out to decide
who will become CEO of the Vieri dynasty.'

'So the fact that Benny is your firstborn doesn't mean anything? Any children you and Bella would've had would have just as much a chance as being the head of the family?'

'Along with their cousins, yes.'

Behind those lovely eyes, her mind raced.

'I can see you have many thoughts on the subject. Will you not share them?'

'It isn't my place.'

'Please?'

He wasn't sure why he insisted, except she'd have an entirely different perspective on this situation, and he welcomed anything that would give him an advantage in this particular arena.

'Okay,' she started slowly, 'I suspect you have cousins who wish to depose you.'

'Cousins and uncles,' he clarified. Though until recently he'd thought he and his cousins were all on the same page. 'And if they could gain the favour of the board they could do so.'

'I also suspect you have cousins who are glad to let you have the job.'

'That too is true.'

'So if Benny doesn't want to be head of the Vieri family fortune, he won't be forced into it?'

Her concern for his son touched him.

'If he wishes to be an artist or an engineer or head of PR, he could do those things instead?'

'Yes.'

She was quiet for a long moment. 'As CEO, I'm guessing you're in charge of the purse strings. So… Does that mean some members of your family…' she hesitated '…from your parents' generation resent you?'

He didn't answer that directly. 'I have curtailed all unnecessary expenditure.'

Each member of the family received generous remuneration from the stock they held in the company, but it was time certain individuals learned to live within their means instead of constantly skimming the company's profits or dipping into the family reserves. Such unrestrained spending would eventually see the Vieri Corporation in receivership. None of them needed another private jet, luxury yacht or yet another holiday villa.

'They were all in favour of your marriage to Bella?'

'Yes.' Because they thought it would bring more money into the coffers and would, therefore have him loosening the purse strings—an entirely erroneous assumption he hadn't bothered to correct.

'For the next few months I need to be very careful. The Vieri and Romano families do a great deal of business together and it would hurt us both if a rift were to occur.'

'You mean if Bella's father were to take offence that you've called off the engagement with his daughter.'

'He's a powerful man.'

'So are you.'

He stared. But her confidence in him made his shoulders go back. 'Signor Romano's and my values align.'

'The broken engagement doesn't mean you can't still work together, though, surely?'

He'd had such hopes... Maybe she was right. Maybe all hope wasn't lost. 'I have spoken to him several times in the last two weeks. He is angry and disappointed.' He'd almost sounded hurt.

He shook the thought off. He was merely projecting. It was his own disappointment speaking. Signor Romano was everything he wished his own father could be. 'Signor Romano has not yet reconciled himself to the broken engagement, so...'

'So?'

'I need to be very careful during the next few months to not offend him…to make sure my name is not linked with another woman's.'

Her face cleared. 'Oh, I see.'

He grimaced. 'And yet I will now be considered fair game, so to speak. Therefore, I must also be careful not to give insult to the daughters of other respectable families.'

'Because that would injure your chances of making this respectable business merger marriage you have your heart set on?'

'Exactly.'

She might not agree with what he planned to do, but her approval was neither necessary nor of any consequence. In twelve months' time she would return to Australia while he had every intention of doing all he could to correct the mistakes of the past.

'As much as I would like to retire from the social scene for a few months, I cannot avoid it entirely. There are at least half a dozen events I must attend if I'm to not give grave offence to my associates.' He had a vision of redeeming the Vieri name and he wouldn't let all his hard work be undone by a broken engagement.

Monique glanced towards the back of the plane and her expression told him she was thinking of her niece. When her gaze found his again, he knew she was thinking about how much she owed him. 'What you need, Luca, is a plus one.'

'I do not know what this means.'

'A woman you trust—a friend or a cousin maybe— who'll accompany you to all these parties and dinners you have to attend, but who won't get the wrong idea, who knows you're not interested romantically. In an ideal world, she'd be a woman all of your associates would realise you're not serious about too, which is why a family member or long-standing friend would be perfect. The way these things usually work is that you also act as her plus one—attend events with her so she doesn't need to go alone. A reciprocal arrangement.'

Everything about this woman intrigued him. 'You have had an arrangement like this with someone in the past?'

She shrugged. 'Sure.'

Why had she needed this plus one? And who had he been?

'A plus one can also act as a watchdog—prevent any other woman from trying to monopolise your time or make a move on you. Though, to be honest, most women will back off when you have a date on your arm. So...problem solved.'

Her words made an alarming amount of sense. 'You make a compelling case for this plus one arrangement.'

She tapped her fingers against those delectable lips. 'What would be perfect is if you could find someone that Signor Romano instinctively knows you're not serious about. That would help to soothe his pride. I imagine he's not a man who would like to think his daughter could be replaced so easily.' She stared at him expectantly. 'Does anyone spring to mind?'

Everything inside of him tightened. There was one woman who fitted that description perfectly.

Monique.

There had to be a hundred reasons against it, though. He needed to think. Ignoring the thundering of his heart, he nodded. 'I will put my thinking cap on. You have given me much to ponder. Thank you, Monique. And now you should try to get some sleep. It's getting late.'

Without another word, Monique moved back to her own seat. He should follow his own advice and try to sleep. Instead, he kept turning her suggestion over and over in his mind. Monique Thomas as his plus one? It could be the solution he'd been searching for.

The Villa Vieri was… Monique gulped. It was the size of a palace!

'I currently live in this wing of the house. It is where Benito, you and Fern will also be established. The house-keeper will show you to your quarters shortly, but first I wanted to show you this.'

Luca led them through a series of unbelievably grand rooms—all generously proportioned and opulent. He carried Benny in one arm, as if it were the most natural thing in the world. Benny, who'd grown used to his father, reached up to pat Luca's cheek and tried to reach for a lock of his father's hair. Monique sympathised with the child's fascination. She found herself staring at Luca's hair all too frequently too, wondering if it'd be as soft and springy as it promised. Luca turned his head at his son's touch and pressed an absentminded kiss to his son's hand. The caress made her stomach turn over.

He threw open a set of French doors and then gestured at the view spread before them. 'This is the garden.'

Her jaw dropped.

He chuckled. 'It will do, yes?'

'Oh!' It was all she could manage.

'You might not be able to take the children to the park to play, but I think you can see that might not be as neces-sary as you once thought.'

'How big is it?' she breathed.

'Only two point four hectares.'

Only? She'd had no idea one could actually have an es-tate in the middle of Rome, but it was clear that was exactly what the Vieris had. As they'd driven through the black wrought-iron gates at the front of the property, they'd been greeted with an avenue of clipped pencil pines and formal rose gardens with a spectacular fountain as a centrepiece.

Thorns and water? It'd made her shudder. Talk about disastrous for small children. She'd crossed her fingers there'd be a scrap of lawn out the back.

A scrap of lawn? She started to laugh. Spread before her, besides a paved terrace and cobbled paths, were grassy terraced lawns and mature trees. The children could run and play to their heart's content. Not that Benny was even walking yet, but it wouldn't be long. She imagined games of football and cricket…they could even fly a kite.

Off to one side was a wilder area planted with fruit trees, perfect for climbing, and flowering shrubs, perfect for hiding behind during a game of hide and seek. 'Oh, Luca.' She clasped her hands together. 'This is wonderful…perfect.' Her smile widened. 'My concerns must've made you laugh yourself silly.'

'A little,' he allowed with one of his rare smiles.

'There you are, Luca! So kind of you to finally grace us with your presence.'

Monique spun around to find a thin, exquisitely groomed woman marching towards them.

'Hello, Mother.'

He kissed the proffered cheek. When the woman turned disdainful eyes to Monique, Fern pressed in close against her legs. Monique brushed a hand over the little girl's hair, resting it there as reassurance.

'Mother, this is Monique Thomas, Benito's godmother. She has kindly agreed to be Benito's nanny for the next twelve months. Monique, my mother Signora Conti.'

'How do you do, Signora Conti?' Monique dutifully managed.

The older woman didn't deign to reply.

'And this is your grandson, Benito.'

The older woman cast a critical eye over the baby and gave an audible sniff. 'At least he's not an ugly child.'

What on earth...? *Seriously?* Every muscle in Monique's body stiffened. That's all Benito's grandmother had to say on meeting the newest member of her family? Her heart started to burn. *This* was Luca's mother? She thought of the little boy he must've once been and wanted to weep for him. Children deserved to be cherished and made to feel loved. Signora Conti didn't look as if she'd ever loved anyone.

'Your father and I demand a meeting with you immediately to discuss the Romano situation. Bella can still be brought to heel with a few judicious assurances.'

'That's not going to happen, Mother.' He handed Benito to Monique, before introducing her to the housekeeper hovering nearby. 'Maria will show you to your quarters. Go and settle in the children. I will come and find you later.'

She didn't say anything, merely nodded. There didn't seem to be anything to say. But he looked so suddenly worn out that she sent him a brief but heartfelt smile. One that she hoped told him she was on his side...and reminded him that while many burdens rested on his shoulders, there was now the delight of Benny in his life too.

Maybe it was fanciful to hope a simple smile could say so much, but she fancied his expression lightened.

She followed Maria back through the house and up a grand staircase, introducing her to the children as they went. The delight in her eyes when they rested on Benny told her all she needed to know.

Fern tugged on her hand. 'Tell me the story,' she whispered, gnawing on her lip as she stared around the vast house.

Monique silently asked if Maria would like to take

Benny—an offer that was instantly and enthusiastically accepted. The housekeeper had him chortling before they'd taken another three steps.

'Once upon a time,' Monique started, swinging Fern onto her hip, 'Princess Fern went on an adventure with her friend, Prince Benny. They travelled across oceans to a faraway land to stay in a palace with a beautiful garden.'

It was a story she'd started days before to prepare Fern for the imminent changes about to happen in their lives.

'When they reached the palace, Princess Fern met a fairy godmother called Maria, who loves children and is the keeper of the cookie jar.'

Maria chuckled and Fern's eyes lit up. 'Cookies?'

Monique nodded gravely. 'I think cookies might feature in the adventures of Princess Fern and Prince Benny.'

Fern rested her head against Monique's shoulder and the little girl's implicit trust had Monique's heart swelling and her throat thickening. She'd do everything in her power to give Fern all the love and security she craved.

As they walked up another set of stairs at the end of the corridor to the third floor, she explained to Maria that she was Benny's godmother and that she'd been a friend of his mother.

The housekeeper clicked her tongue. 'You do not have to explain why Luca—Signor Vieri—has hired you. We do not question *his* decisions.'

But she did those of other members of his family?

'I wanted you to know,' she said when they stopped at a door, 'I've no doubt you and other members of the staff here will love Benny and have his best interests at heart. It's therefore right that you know these things. Also, I may need your help.'

'Help?'

'I'll be here for twelve months, to give Benny some con-

tinuity, before returning to Australia. Luca—Mr Vieri—
has asked me to train two nannies who will eventually take
over my duties. Word of mouth recommendations would
be very welcome.'

The older woman nodded. '*Sì*, this is something I can
help with, Signorina Thomas.'

In that moment she knew she'd made a friend. 'Please,
call me Monique.'

Monique didn't see Luca again until just before the children's
bedtime. He played with Benny and Fern for a little, building a castle with them from wooden blocks, and making Fern
laugh when he balanced one of her small soft toys on the top.
He'd taken great pains with the little girl, and his patience
and gentleness had won her over. The two of them had become fast friends.

Both children fell asleep as Monique read them a story.
She put Fern to bed while Luca put Benny to bed.

'What do you think of your quarters?' he asked when
they'd both returned to the nursery-cum-sitting room.

'They're wonderful.' And thankfully nowhere near as
grand as the rest of the house, which meant she and the
children could relax rather than worry about damaging
anything.

The configuration was ridiculously convenient too. Off
this main room a connecting door led to Benny's bedroom,
with another connecting door beyond it that led to Monique's
room, and then another after that to Fern's room. Each of
the rooms also had a doorway to the corridor outside, but
it meant Monique could leave each of the internal connecting doors open so she could hear if the children needed her
during the night, so the likelihood of disturbing anyone else
in the house was minimal.

'It's a great layout, Luca. The perfect set-up.'

He sipped the tea she'd made. 'You have made a big impression on Maria. She has been singing your praises.'

'I had a strategy before I arrived,' she confessed. 'I've lived in a close-knit community for a long time, so I know how someone new coming in can put people's noses out of joint. I didn't want your staff feeling slighted or overlooked for the role of nanny.'

He blinked as if the thought hadn't occurred to him.

'A harmonious environment will be best for everyone. And now that everyone knows my link to Benny and the fact that I'm only here for a year...' She trailed off with a shrug.

'*Dio!* You have thought much about this.'

'But of course.' Why should that surprise him? 'I promised to look after Benny to the best of my ability. This is me keeping that promise. I want to be an asset to you, Luca, not a liability.'

He stared. 'You truly mean that.'

Again, why should her words surprise him? 'After everything you've done for Fern and me, it's the least I can do.'

He shook his head. 'What I did for Fern... You owe me nothing for that.'

A fire stretched through the dark depths of Luca's eyes and it made her mouth dry. She forced herself to break eye contact. Her heart hammered in her ears. 'You're paying me a generous salary to anticipate any problems. I'm just doing my job.'

He straightened at the mention of her salary. 'I appreciate your foresight.'

While they were on the subject of potential problems... 'I wanted to ask if any members of your family are likely to come up to the nursery to visit Benny?'

He shook his head. 'I will take him downstairs some

afternoons or early evenings so he can become acquainted with his wider family.'

She wanted to ask if she should anticipate any potential problems from that quarter—especially his mother—but his face had shuttered. She stared at the forbidding lines of his face that looked as if they were carved from granite and decided against any further probing.

Asset, remember, not a liability.

She clapped her hands lightly. 'Right, how soon would you like me to start training the nannies who'll eventually replace me?'

'Immediately.'

A spike of hurt pierced through her. He wanted to replace her so quickly? She tamped it down. 'Very well. How did you want to select the candidates? From an agency or would you like me to place an advertisement? And do you want to interview them, or would you like me to take care of that?' She bit her lip. 'I took the liberty of asking Maria if—'

'Yes, she told me.'

She tried not to wince. 'I'm sorry if that was out of line.' It hadn't occurred to her that he might consider it a liberty.

'Not at all. Maria has a niece, Anna, who is a maid here. She knows the family, is a hard worker, and her connection to her aunt indicates loyalty. She does not have formal qualifications but is willing to gain them if I wish it of her. She has many younger siblings so has experience with children.'

She tried to inject enthusiasm into her voice. 'She sounds perfect.'

He stared at her with those dark eyes and gave a nod to some silent question he'd seemed to ask himself. 'I would like you to have an assistant as soon as possible so you are not trapped here all the hours of the day.'

In her world, that's what being a parent meant. And she didn't consider it a *trap*.

'You are allowed some leisure time.'

And he'd like Benny to grow used to her occasional absences. She didn't know why that fact should prick her so painfully. It was a sensible thing to do.

'Perhaps you and Anna could select the second nanny together. I would like the two of them to get along.'

'Of course.'

'But there is no rush for that yet.'

He sent her a look that had all the fine hairs on her arms lifting.

'There is another reason I should like you to train Anna immediately. I have a favour to ask of you, Monique. If you agree, it means someone will need to tend to the children in your absence.'

Her absence? Of course she'd perform any favour he asked. Despite his protestations otherwise, she owed him so much. But... She swallowed. 'Will my absence be... prolonged?'

'No!' His eyebrows shot towards his hairline. 'It is not that kind of absence.' Something in his eyes gentled. 'I would not ask you to leave Fern for more than a few hours. Not at the moment when she needs to know you are near.'

Relief made her sag. 'Thank you.'

'The favour I have to ask of you will mostly take place when the children are asleep.'

She gulped. At night-time?

Oh, don't go there, Monique. That's not what the man means.

'It is you yourself who gave me the idea.'

Dear God. Had he sensed her attraction to him?

'A plus one for all of the events I need to attend. You were right. It is the perfect solution to my current dilemma.'

She willed her pulse to slow. What did the plus one thing have to do with her?

'You are the perfect candidate for such a role. Would you consider escorting me to the parties and receptions that I must attend during the next three months? I have whittled them down to only six. The others I can make excuses for. And I'm hoping that within three months I will have repaired most of the damage that has been done between Signor Romano and myself.'

She leaned towards him. 'You want *me* to be your plus one?'

'*Sì.*'

Those dark eyes bored into hers with an earnestness that had everything inside of her yearning towards him.

In all the wrong ways.

He nodded. 'Please, yes, I would like that very much.'

CHAPTER FOUR

THOSE EXTRAORDINARY CARAMEL eyes turned almost golden in surprise at his request and Luca found himself holding his breath. It surprised him how much he wanted her to say yes.

She moistened her lips and nodded. 'Of course I will. I'll help in any way I can.'

All the muscles that had been clenched in painful anticipation of her answer loosened.

'But...'

The line of her throat bobbed and his muscles clenched hard and tight again. 'But?'

'Are you sure I'm the right person for the job?'

'You have reservations?'

'I'm not from your world, Luca. What if I let you down?' She rubbed a hand across her brow. 'I certainly don't have the wardrobe for it.'

That last was murmured almost to herself and he dismissed it with a wave of his hand. 'Your wardrobe will be taken care of.'

Actually, it would be nice to see her in something other than black and white. For some reason she persisted in wearing the same clothes she'd worn when working at the motel. She didn't need to wear a uniform while she was here. She was so full of colour on the inside it seemed a shame it wasn't reflected on the outside.

'I don't possess the polish or sophistication…or the *posture* of someone like your mother.' Her eyes widened as if his mother's posture was a thing of awe and wonder.

He was grateful she was none of those things. Monique had something much more valuable—sincerity.

The confusion suddenly cleared from her face and she clapped a hand to her chest. 'Of course! That's the point. It'll signal to all of your associates that our relationship isn't serious.'

He shook his head, smiling in spite of himself. 'You underestimate yourself, *cara*.' The endearment slipped out without his meaning it to. 'You have poise, but more importantly you have a natural warmth that will not ruffle feathers or raise hackles.'

She looked far from convinced by his words.

'Also, you will be perfect because you know what kind of marriage I intend to make and understand that your tenure in my household is temporary. I know you will not misinterpret the arrangement.'

She stared at him with those clear eyes. 'You mean I won't get the wrong idea and think our arrangement is in any way romantic…that I won't make the mistake of falling in love with you?'

She was beautiful this woman, and intelligent. And she took no offence at his words when other women would've thrown things at him. If things were different—

But they weren't.

He nodded.

'That at least is true,' she mused. 'I mean I *was* the one who gave you the idea in the first place.'

'And in return you get to attend several glittering society events that hopefully won't be too onerous.' He would do all he could to ensure she enjoyed herself.

Her lips twitched. 'Onerous? Seriously, Luca? Parties

should be fun. I bet these ones will be too and if they're not, you're just not doing them right.'

She made him want to laugh. 'Then that is a yes?'

'Can you promise me champagne and caviar?'

'Only the finest.'

'Then, Luca, that is most definitely a yes.'

Luca glanced at his watch. He'd arranged to meet Monique in the foyer at eight o'clock sharp. He hadn't expected her to be late, but it was already ten minutes past the hour.

He paced for five minutes more before turning and taking the stairs two at a time. When he reached her door, voices sounded from behind it. One remonstrating—and as he didn't recognise the voice, he guessed it to be the dresser he'd hired—and the other more conciliatory. Monique. Her tone might be calm and even, but it had steel threaded beneath it. He tapped on the door.

It was flung open by Monique. One look at her and the breath snagged in his chest. *Dio mio!* In a gown of silk and gossamer she looked like a vision from a fairy tale. He'd only seen her in those sensible skirts and trousers paired with prim blouses, but this dress hugged her figure with the kind of loving care that made his mouth dry.

He'd not realised her waist was that tiny. Or that her breasts… The blood roared in his ears and heat stampeded through his veins. He swallowed and only just stopped himself from running a finger beneath the collar of his shirt. He forced his gaze away from those tantalising soft curves. 'You look a vision,' he managed, recalling his manners.

'Rubbish!'

He blinked. 'But the gown looks as if it were made specifically with you in mind.'

The dresser made a smug sound behind her. Monique glared at the ceiling and he could almost see her count to ten. 'It's not the dress I'm referring to. It's the most beautiful dress I've ever worn.'

He saw then that it didn't hide the burn scar on her arm. He'd given that no thought. How insensitive of him! 'Would you be more comfortable in a dress with longer sleeves?'

'What?' She blinked. 'Oh, my scar? No that doesn't bother me at all.'

He was glad of it. She was beautiful as she was.

Her eyes suddenly narrowed. 'Does it bother you?'

'Not in the slightest.'

She searched his face with keen eyes, eventually releasing a breath and nodding. He sagged when she turned back to the dresser. 'Many thanks, *signora*, for your help, but I can take it from here. I wish you a very pleasant evening.'

When the dresser glanced at him, he gave a nod. They waited until she'd gathered her things and left.

Monique glanced down the corridor to make sure the woman had really gone and then hastened to her dressing table, pulling pins from her hair. 'That woman was an absolute tyrant.'

'What do you mean?'

She froze from where she surveyed her image in the mirror, a cotton pad halfway to her face as if to remove her make-up. Very slowly she turned on her chair. '*This* is how you want me to look?'

Dio. This was dangerous ground. 'What do you mean?'

She gestured to her face, her hair. 'This!'

He did his best not to scowl. She did not look as warm and approachable as was her custom, but in his experience this was the way women liked to present themselves. Far be it from him to criticise.

'I don't look like myself at all! I hate looking so…'

He forced himself to remain in the doorway, painfully aware of the bed in the middle of the room. 'So…?'

'Fake and *plastic*.'

The breath she pulled in made her chest rise in the most intriguing manner, the action captured perfectly by the dress. Fantasies, hot and explicit, played through his mind. Fantasies of slowly removing that dress and kissing every inch of her body until she begged him for release. Of hearing his name on her lips and—

Dio! This was torture. He shook with the effort to remain where he was. Thankfully her attention had remained on her reflection and hadn't strayed to him. He let out a quiet breath.

'I'm not from your world, Luca, so I don't think I should try and look the part. Please give me ten minutes to make some adjustments. I'll meet you in the foyer as promised.'

She'd barely finished speaking before her fingers had gone to her hair to pull out more pins and undo the complicated hairstyle the dresser had created. Caramel hair fell down around her shoulders and all he could think of was running his hands through it and—

He turned and strode down the corridor as fast as he could.

Eight minutes later, she walked down the grand staircase and every pore of his skin tightened. 'Monique, you look magnificent!'

Pink flooded her cheeks, enchanting him almost as much as the caramel hair that curled around her shoulders. That, combined with the myriad colours of her dress—the lightest of champagnes through to golden ambers, with a darker pewter thread here and there—made it look as if the sun shone from within her.

'Magnificent,' he repeated as she came to a halt in front of him. The pink in her cheeks didn't subside and he curled his fingers into his palms to stop from reaching out and stroking a finger down the curve of her cheek.

She frowned. 'I'm not supposed to look magnificent. I'm supposed to look unsophisticated and unpolished...a little gauche, like I don't belong.'

She looked none of those things. She simply looked magnificent. He didn't have the heart to tell her that in removing much of her make-up and reapplying it in her own style, her complexion now looked dewy and fresh rather than flawless. Her eyes looked a tiny bit smoky and there was a hint of warm colour on her lips. In eschewing perfection she'd replaced it with a warm authenticity that was a hundred times more potent.

Every man who saw her tonight would want to worship at her feet. Rather than her protecting him from unwanted attentions, he'd be protecting her. For a moment he questioned the wisdom of this plus one arrangement. He wanted to turn her around and race her back up the stairs and hide her from the rest of the world.

It warred with other impulses, though. In eschewing the style currently adopted by his set, she revealed its limitations. And for some reason he found that heady. She deserved to be belle of the ball.

Her brow furrowed. 'Stop looking at me like that, Luca. It's just a pretty dress and some make-up. I don't know how any woman could help but be transformed by a dress like this.'

He wrestled his customary mask back into place, tucking her hand into the crook of his elbow and leading her towards the door and the waiting car. 'Do not sell yourself short, Monique. You are a beautiful woman. Never doubt that.'

She halted by the car. 'Are you sure about this? I wouldn't blame you if you were having second thoughts. There'd be no hard feelings.'

'Nervous?'

Her chin lifted. 'Not at all.'

'You still wish to help me?'

That chin lifted higher. 'Of course.'

'Then, no, I do not wish to turn back. You will be my shield against a society that wants too much from me at the moment.'

'You want a lot from it too,' she murmured as she slipped inside the car.

That was true. He closed her door and strode around to the driver's side. 'For the foreseeable future,' he said, 'you will help me keep the peace. I am very grateful to you.'

'It's the least I could do.' The casual words were belied by the smile she sent him. 'Okay, now that *that's* settled, shall we embrace our roles and have fun?'

Fun? It wasn't a word he could recall applying to his life—duty, responsibility and hard work had usurped it.

Parties should be fun.

He shook his head. Parties were for networking, for showing off, jockeying for position, and wooing business associates. But he would do his best to ensure, for tonight at least, that this woman enjoyed herself.

As he expected, Monique made quite a stir among his peers when she walked into the party on his arm. Not that she noticed or had the least idea, which was an undeniable part of her charm.

He introduced her to his peers and business colleagues— people he'd grown up with and/or did business with. She greeted them all with her customary warmth. She didn't realise it, but the warmth she generated in return was also given to him by association.

It shocked him. He was used to respect, civility and a certain circumspection from his peers. Not warmth...or friendship. For the first time it occurred to him that his reserve and aloofness might have created a wall between him and the rest of the world.

The thought burrowed into him like a burr that couldn't be shaken. He pushed it away to consider later.

Glancing up, he found Signor Romano staring at him from the other side of the room. He touched Monique's arm. 'Bella's father is here. I must go and speak with him.'

Shrewd caramel eyes glanced up. 'I'll go and powder my nose before joining you.'

He appreciated her tact.

He threaded his way through the crowd to Signor Romano, and the two men shook hands, made small talk briefly before Signor Romano fired his opening salvo. 'This marriage between you and Bella can still take place, Luca. We—'

'I have too much respect for Bella to ask her to take on both me and a child when she's not ready for such a move.'

'She is a good girl. She will do as she's told.'

'She deserves to be happy, Erik.'

'You would make any woman happy.'

Bitterness momentarily twisted inside him. His money and position would make any woman happy, that's what Erik Romano meant.

For no reason at all, Monique's face rose in his mind. His wealth and money didn't impress her. At least, not in that way. Winning her custody of Fern, that was what made her happy. Not wealth, position and a large staff at her command.

'And yet,' Erik continued, 'you will eventually marry. Some woman will become your son's stepmother.'

'Not, however, for the foreseeable future. I want to get to know my son first, build a relationship with him before allowing a third party into our lives. For the time being, Benito is my priority.'

'And yet it would appear my daughter has already been replaced in your affections.'

Luca wanted to swear at the mottled red that had crept up the older man's neck, at the furious flash of his eyes. This was exactly what he'd wanted to avoid.

'I'm sorry I took so long, Luca.'

Monique smoothly moved in to form a third in their party, creating a warm circle with her accompanying smile. She handed both men glasses of champagne. Immediately a waiter appeared at her elbow to proffer her a third glass. She smiled her thanks before extending her hand towards Erik. 'Signor Romano, yes? I am Monique Thomas.'

The older man blinked. 'You are… Australian?'

She turned reproachful eyes to Luca. 'You haven't told Signor Romano about me yet?'

He hadn't had a chance!

She turned back to the older man. 'I am Benny— Benito's—'

'Luca's son?'

She beamed at him as if delighted with him. 'Yes, Luca's son! I'm his godmother—I was a friend of his mother. I've come to Rome to help Benny make the transition. His temporary nanny, if you will. In return Luca has been kind enough to treat me to…*this*!' She gestured at the party. 'As a thank you. It's so terribly exciting.' Her eyes widened and she lifted her champagne flute. 'This champagne is a revelation,' she whispered.

And just like that she won Signor Romano over.

The woman was a witch. And a treasure.

'Thank you,' Luca murmured in her ear fifteen minutes later.

The touch of his breath against her ear lifted all the fine

hairs on her nape. 'For?' She tried to keep her voice calm, but her pulse juddered and jammed.

'For smoothing things over with Signor Romano.'

She refused to glance up into those dark eyes. They were dangerous eyes that could mesmerise a woman…if that woman were stupid enough to let them. Monique might not have a tertiary education, but she wasn't that stupid.

She knew that with just a little encouragement from her she and Luca could become lovers. The idea sent sparks of electricity zapping across the surface of her skin. She'd recognised the male appreciation in his eyes when she'd opened her bedroom door to him earlier this evening. It was one of the reasons she'd removed her make-up—to remind him she wasn't from his world.

Only that appeared to have had the opposite effect!

Appreciation she could deal with. It had been the raw hunger that had flared in his eyes when she'd walked down the grand staircase towards him that had almost undone her.

No! She *would* resist. She'd seen what had happened when her mother and Skye had become mesmerised by men. It had always ended badly. She wasn't interested in perpetuating that cycle.

She glanced around at the party—at the crystal chandelier, the glittering lights and all the beautiful people. She felt like Cinderella at the ball with Luca as her Prince Charming. But that was a crazy lie she couldn't let herself believe for even a second.

She needed to stay rooted in reality. She'd be grateful for what she had—Fern. She wouldn't crave anything more. She didn't *need* anything more.

She certainly wasn't going to give her heart to an emotionally unavailable man. That would only lead to heartbreak. She owed it to baby Benny to keep things in his new world stable, and she owed it to Fern. She pulled in a breath. She owed it to herself too.

'You smoothed things wonderfully,' Luca repeated.

Why didn't he sound happier, then? She glanced up. Why didn't he look happier?

'When you told him you and Fern would be returning to Australia in twelve months' time, it put his mind at rest.'

She couldn't see a hint of attraction or desire in his gaze now. Her fingernails curled into her palms. Her reminder of who and what she was had done the trick. She told herself she was glad of it. 'So what's wrong?'

'He still has hopes that Bella and I will make a match of it.'

He dragged a hand across his jaw and her mouth dried as she followed the action, imagined following it with her own hand and—

Stop it.

'How long do you plan to wait before you start... courting again?' Not that she could call anything so clinical and businesslike 'courting'.

'Not for six months at least.'

She made herself shrug. 'A lot can happen in six months. You've dispelled Signor Romano's fear that Bella can be replaced quickly and easily—he's maintained his pride— and you've bought Bella six months. Signor Romano's disappointment or Bella's inability to grow a spine and fight for the life she wants isn't your responsibility.'

He blinked and she winced, wondering if she'd gone too far, taken one liberty too many. Eventually, though, he nodded. 'That is true.'

He took too much onto his own shoulders. Mind you, those shoulders were deliciously broad, and his dinner jacket highlighted their breadth to perfection.

'It's just...'

She snapped back, closing her eyes and letting out a grateful breath when she realised he hadn't noticed the way she'd been staring at him. She forced her eyes open again and the expression on his face made her heart burn. 'It's just that you like him,' she finished for him.

'He's the kind of man I can look up to…in all the ways I'm unable to look up to my own father.'

He'd wanted Signor Romano as his father-in-law, but did he really think marrying Bella would've made him happy?

Did he even care about being happy?

The thought made her heart twist.

Sipping her champagne, she stared at the crowd. 'Are there any prospective candidates for your future wife here tonight?'

He nodded; his expression morose. 'Several.'

Really? 'Who?'

He bent his head to her ear and kept his voice low. 'See the woman in the dark blue dress beside the chocolate fountain?'

The chocolate fountain she'd ached to sample but hadn't, as she'd been too afraid she'd drip chocolate on her dress.

She studied the woman's face and then glanced up at him, wrinkling her nose. 'Really?'

'Why do you pull this face?'

'She was very rude to the attendant in the bathroom.' She'd had a bevy of lackeys she'd ordered about mercilessly with the kind of entitlement that had set Monique's teeth on edge. 'Unnecessarily so, I thought.' She couldn't imagine a woman like that having patience around small children. *Oh, Benny.*

'You did not like her manner?'

She didn't answer that. 'She's very beautiful and sophisticated, though. The two of you would look good together.'

He gazed bored into hers. 'But?'

'She'll be high maintenance, but maybe you won't mind that.' She paused. 'If you want a wife who has the same poise and polish—' and attitude '—as your mother, then she would be perfect.'

He stiffened. 'I do not like rudeness,' he murmured.

'No,' she agreed.

She made a vow then and there to discover as many of the names of Luca's potential brides as she could and to find out all she could about them…vet them if possible. Benny deserved a stepmother who loved him and would treat him well.

And Luca deserved the same from a wife. Even if he didn't realise it yet.

Yes! Monique grinned her excitement as she read the email. Her first lesson packet had arrived. She could start work on it tonight.

She and the children had been at the Villa Vieri for a fortnight now, and they'd fallen into an easy routine, but she was eager to get back to her studies.

She read through the instructions and then frowned. She'd need to print out a couple of things first. She tapped a finger to her lips, recalled Luca's huge home office downstairs that he used when he wasn't in his office in the city. It had a printer. Surely he wouldn't mind…

She copied the relevant material to a thumb drive and glanced at Anna, the nanny in training. Both children were currently down for their afternoon naps.

'Anna, do you mind if I pop downstairs to run an errand?' She held up her thumb drive. 'I want to print off a couple of documents.'

'*Sì*, Monique.'

Monique tripped down the back stairs—the old servants' stairs, apparently. The soft soles of her shoes were silent on the polished marble tiles as she made her way through several large reception rooms on the ground floor to Luca's study.

She had no idea if he was working from home today, but the door was ajar. She knocked. When no one answered, she peeked inside. Empty.

She hesitated for only a moment. The printer was sitting right there, not being used, and it seemed a shame to waste the opportunity. She wasn't hurting anyone, and she was sure Luca wouldn't mind. Especially once he learned what it was for.

The first document had just finished printing and she was waiting for the second job to begin when Signora Conti, Luca's mother, slipped silently into the room and started towards Luca's desk. She swung around with a violent start when the printer started up again, clutching her chest as if to prevent her heart leaping from her body.

The minute she saw Monique, she drew herself up to her full height, her eyes flashing and chin lifting as she glared down her nose. Monique gulped. Her son had obviously inherited his height from his mother. When one coupled that with Signora Conti's ability to make one feel as if they were something disgusting on the bottom of her shoe, it meant she could do intimidation really well.

'I'm sorry, Signora Conti. I didn't mean to startle you.'

'What is the meaning of this?'

'The meaning of...' *um*... '...what?'

'What are doing. sneaking around in my son's office?'

'I'm not sneaking.' Her shoulders went back. 'I simply came in to print something. I—'

'Does my son know you are using his office?'

What on earth was she insinuating? That she'd come into Luca's office to steal something? She started to shake with the effort to hold her temper in check. 'I can assure you that Luca wouldn't mind me using his printer in the slightest.'

Please, let that be true.

'I believe I know my son better than some upstart foreign girl with dollar signs in her eyes and her gaze firmly fixed on the main prize of my son!'

What?

'And I'm going to disabuse you of such foolishness. I know all about you, Ms Thomas, and I know all about your friend Anita Lang too. Girls like you will stoop to any level to find an easy meal ticket, but in this instance—'

'You can say what you like about me.' Monique's voice shook. 'I don't care what you think of me. But you will not insult Benny's mother like that.'

'I—'

'Anita never used Benny as any kind of weapon or bargaining tool over your son, though she certainly could have. If she'd been after a meal ticket, as you call it, she had one. But she didn't cash it in. She was a kind, loving, honest person who'd have never acted without integrity. You have no right to denigrate her character.'

'You *dare* raise your voice to me?'

She wasn't kow-towing to this woman. She might've promised to do all she could to make Luca's life easier, but that didn't include letting anyone besmirch Anita's memory. 'You dare insult Benny's mother—a woman you never met?' she countered.

Luca entered the room, intent on the papers in his hand. He froze when he realised he wasn't alone, his gaze no doubt taking in the way Monique's chest rose and fell, along with his mother's heightened colour.

Signora Conti lifted her chin. 'This girl is not to be trusted, Luca. I found her sneaking around in here.'

If he gave credence for one moment to his mother's assertion…

He raised an eyebrow, and Monique gulped again. He could do supercilious with the best of them.

'I find that hard to believe, Mother.'

He glanced at Monique. This time his raised eyebrow was encouraging rather than cutting. She drew in a breath and made sure to keep her tone even. 'I came down to print off a couple of things.'

When he held out a hand for the pages she grasped, she gave them to him without hesitation. She couldn't read the expression in his eyes when he handed them back, but she swore warmth momentarily flickered there. Warmth and approval.

'Monique has my permission to use the printer any time she wishes.'

She wanted to hug him.

'But that isn't all,' his mother continued. 'The *impertinent* girl was rude to me. I demand—'

'I find that hard to believe, but if Monique *was* rude to you…' he strode behind his desk and set his papers down, as if already bored with his mother's tantrum '…I dare say it was not unprovoked.'

The tightness binding her unravelled in a rush. She'd known he wouldn't be unfair.

'Luca!' his mother gasped.

Monique wanted nothing more than to sidle out of the room, except Signora Conti stood between her and the door. She'd never get out unobserved.

'What are *you* doing in my office, Mother?'

The deceptively quiet question had Monique swallowing. She turned back to the printer to gather up the rest of her pages, doing all she could to distance herself from the scene.

'I came to have lunch with you. It is not unheard of for a mother to want to spend time with her son.'

'Lunch was two hours ago.'

'But I know how often you skip lunch.'

Did he? He hadn't in Mirror Glass Bay.

'Your concern is touching,' he said with a dry drawl. 'Why did you not ring me first?'

'Because you have a habit of not taking my calls. Forget it, Luca. I have changed my mind.'

With that she whirled from the room. The silence she left behind was only punctuated by the sharp sound of her spiky heels receding as she stalked away.

Monique blew out a breath, rueful as she met Luca's dark-eyed gaze. 'I'm sorry. I didn't mean to cause trouble.'

'My mother?' His brows shot up. 'She is not trouble of your making, Monique.' He tapped a pen against his fingers. 'Did you walk in on her or she on you?

'She on me.'

'I see.'

And then so did Monique. She smoothed a hand down her shirt. 'I'd just finished my first printing job, so it was quiet when she entered. At first she didn't see me.' She moistened her lips. 'The sound of the printer gave her quite a scare.'

His gaze sharpened. 'Could you tell what she was making for—my desk or the filing cabinet?'

'It could've been either, but I think your desk.'

He nodded. 'Thank you.'

Dear Lord. What exactly did he think his mother was up to?

CHAPTER FIVE

IT WASN'T MONIQUE'S place to ask Luca what he thought his mother was up to. If he wanted to confide in her…that was a different thing. *Asset, remember, not a liability.* Asking awkward questions wasn't part of the remit.

She shifted her weigh from one foot to the other. 'Thank you for…'

'For?'

'Sticking up for me. I didn't think you'd mind me using your printer, but I should've asked first. I'm sorry. It won't happen again.

He shook his head. 'I trust you. You're free to use the printer whenever you need to.' The pen tapped against his fingers again. 'One final thing… The door to my office was unlocked?'

'It was ajar.'

His mouth thinned. 'I see.'

Was it supposed to be locked? Her heart thump-thumped as she stared up at him. With his olive skin, black hair and eyes fringed in silky dark lashes, he should look like the Prince of Darkness. But he didn't. He looked…

She searched her mind for the right description. Like a hero? Like a dark-haired statue of David? Like an aristocrat stepping from the pages of a historical novel?

Yes, to all of those. But he also looked like a flesh-and-

blood man with too many cares…who needed more sleep…
who needed to laugh.

It hit her then, the description she was searching for.
While Luca might be as attractively tempting as sin itself,
unlike the Prince of Darkness he didn't scare her, neither
did he threaten her. It was her own wayward desires that
did that.

Luca was undoubtedly a powerful man, but every instinct she had, and the knowledge she'd gained from watching him with his son, told her he would never use that power
for ugly purposes. Unlike his mother, he didn't treat those
with less money and power as his inferiors.

When she'd said he didn't frighten her, though, it's not
precisely that he made her feel safe—he upset her peace of
mind too much for that. But she trusted him. She trusted
he would never treat her unfairly.

Growing up as she had, she knew what a boon that was.

'You are staring at me, Monique, with the most inexplicable expression on your face. What is it you are thinking, I wonder?'

She snapped back to the present. 'Oh, I…' Heat flooded
her cheeks.

Giving herself a brisk shake, she tried to smile. 'Ever
since I was fifteen, I've worked in the hospitality industry. Which means I've had a lot of different bosses with…
different leadership styles—some less than ideal, some
good, and some fabulous. Eve and Cassidy fall into that latter group. They have high expectations but in return they
provide their staff with every support. You, Luca, are like
Eve and Cassidy.' She smiled into stunned eyes. 'And that
is a very good thing.'

Amusement lit his face briefly. 'All this because I stuck
up for you to my mother?'

'No.' Her smile became genuine. 'You had every right

to rake me over the coals, but you held fire until you had all the facts. You decided, based on what you know of me so far, to believe the best rather than the worst.'

His lips twisted. 'While I did the opposite with my mother.'

She hesitated. 'I suspect you based your reaction to her on all of your history together and your past interactions. You've nothing to feel guilty about.'

But his relationship with his mother was none of her business. 'I should get back upstairs before the children wake.' She held up her printed pages. 'Thank you for this.'

'You are studying?'

She'd started for the door but halted and turned back. 'An Associate Diploma in Childcare. I started it four years ago, but…' She shrugged. 'I hope to have it completed by the end of the year.'

Another thought occurred to her. 'I promise it'll have no impact on my duties here. I—'

'Of course it will. For the better. The fact you're studying is admirable. I will organise for a printer to be sent up to your room for your personal use.'

'That's very generous.'

His brows drew together. 'Would you like your own dedicated study? That could be arranged and—'

She found herself laughing. 'Thank you, Luca, but there's no need. I'll be happy to steal a couple of hours in my room when the children are sleeping. But thank you.'

She hesitated on the threshold.

'There is something else?'

Would he think it silly? No, surely not… He'd be delighted, wouldn't he? 'Benny said "Da-Da" this morning, clear as day.'

His mouth dropped open. 'He did?'

And then his entire face lit up, and she wanted to laugh

for the sheer joy of it. She tried to shrug, tried to be casual, but she suspected he saw through her pretence. 'I haven't heard him say it before, and I thought you'd like to know.'

'He begins to know me.'

'He begins to love and look for you,' she corrected.

And then she left before she could do something silly, like kiss him.

'So tell me about this course you are doing.'

She and Luca were sitting in the nursery, sharing a pot of tea that Maria had brought up to them—ostensibly to help them unwind after the mayhem of bath and bedtime with the children, but in reality Monique suspected it was so she could have cuddles with them. Benny adored the older woman, and she and Fern had become the best of friends.

All was quiet now, though, and Monique sipped her tea gratefully. 'What would you like to know?'

'Why childcare? Have you always wanted to work with children?'

'I… Yes. I've always liked children.' She felt suddenly self-conscious under that steady gaze. 'I seem to have a knack with them.'

'That is evident.'

'I enjoy spending time with them. I—'

She broke off.

'You?'

She frowned. 'If I tell you the real reason, I don't want you feeling sorry for me. I don't want your pity. While I wouldn't have chosen the childhood I had, it is what it is. And I like my life now. A lot.'

His brows lifted. 'Then I certainly promise not to feel sorry for you.'

She loved the slight formality of his speech, and the ac-companying seriousness. 'Excellent.' She sent him her biggest smile, before sobering again. 'Given my childhood, there weren't many options open to me in terms of furthering my education.' She'd managed to complete her schooling, which was more than Skye had done, but… 'University was out of the question.'

'A scholarship wasn't possible?'

'My grades were good, but not that good.' What with her part-time jobs and trying to look after Skye, there'd been little time for study. 'Neither did I want to leave town at that time.'

Understanding dawned in those beautiful eyes. 'You didn't want to leave your sister.'

She gave a half-shrug. 'So I kept my dreams small. I worked as a waitress, did a stint as a short-order cook, did housekeeping work in motels, and worked as an assistant in a childcare centre. That's when I decided to work towards my childcare qualifications.'

'So is this…' he gestured around the room '…the kind of work you would like to do?'

'No.' And then she realised how that must sound to him. 'I don't mean I'm not enjoying this. I've loved every minute so far.'

'But it is not the dream.'

In hindsight, his understanding shouldn't surprise her. She wondered what his dream was. 'It's full-time work, the salary will allow me to build up a nice little nest egg, and it's giving me the chance to finish my studies. All while giving me the opportunity to build a relationship with my godson that will last a lifetime. I'm very grateful for this job, Luca.'

'And I am grateful you accepted it.'

She laughed, 'Listen to us being each other's personal cheer squad.'

His eyes warmed. 'I like this analogy.' His eyes became serious again. 'Now tell me about the dream.'

She stared into her teacup. 'The *dream* dream is probably out of reach, but one day I'd love to open my own childcare centre in Mirror Glass Bay.' She glanced up. 'The dream I'm working towards is opening a crèche at the Mirror Glass Bay Motel in the high season.'

'While working as a maid in the low season?'

She nodded.

'Eve and Cassidy…they are amenable to this idea?'

'Very.'

She couldn't read the thoughts racing behind his eyes.

Before she could ask him what his dream was, he said, 'This knack you have with children, how did you acquire it? Was it something you were born with—an innate talent—or is it something that can be learned?'

She almost said she didn't know, but the dark intensity of his eyes stopped her. Her answer obviously mattered to him, so she forced herself to think hard about the question, reminding herself how he'd leapt to her defence earlier against his mother.

It occurred to her that, regardless of her gratitude or anything that had happened between them, she'd tell this man anything he wanted to know. No questions asked.

He leaned towards her. 'My question makes you sad?'

'What? *No!*' She tried to laugh it off. 'As I've told you, I was very involved from the moment my sister Skye was born. My mother, being the woman she is, didn't much take to parenthood. As a result, I grew very protective of Skye. And I guess I just learned from trial and error. Hence the knack I now have with children.'

His eyes burned into hers and the lines around his mouth deepened. 'What went wrong? What happened to cause a rift between you and your sister? Why does she not worship the ground you walk on?'

She stared up at the ceiling for a few moments, before dragging her gaze back to his. 'My mother happened.'

She could still recall the precise moment she'd lost her little sister to her mother's influence with the same painful clarity today as she had eight years ago at the age of nineteen.

Skye and her mother had been sitting on the sofa as Monique had rushed around getting ready for her waitressing shift that evening. 'The lasagne will be ready in forty minutes,' she told them. 'I've set the timer.'

Her mother snorted, already onto her third can of bourbon and Coke. 'Look at Little Miss Goody-Two-Shoes in her maxi skirt and the buttons on her blouse done up to her throat.' She nudged Skye's arm. 'God forbid that one should show any flesh, honey.'

Her mother's mockery had been too much of a constant in Monique's life for it to have much of an effect. She'd spent a lifetime pushing away the pain caused by her mother's insults and criticism, so any hurt she felt now was quickly dispensed with.

She glanced at Skye, who refused to meet her eyes. She knew their mother's attempts to make her an accomplice made Skye uncomfortable. *Oh, honey, I don't blame you.*

She continued getting ready for her shift, making sure all her money was in her handbag, before slinging it over her body crosswise so she couldn't accidentally put it down and have her mother pounce on it and take all the cash.

Or her ATM card. Monique made sure to change the pin number on that regularly. In another couple of months she'd have enough saved to cover the bond on a little place just for her and Skye, far away from her mother's drinking and relentless procession of men.

'What do you think, honey?' Sharlene Thomas persisted.

'It's a bit old-fashioned,' Skye allowed.

'Positively Victorian!'

Her mother rolled her eyes before offering her fifteen-year-old daughter a cigarette. Monique froze. She met Skye's gaze and shook her head. Skye lifted a defiant chin and accepted the cigarette. She lit it, dragged deeply, and then puffed out an insolent stream of smoke—controlled and practised.

When had Skye started to smoke?

'Not a push-up bra in that one's arsenal,' Skye said with a cruel laugh, making her mother cackle. She turned back to Monique. 'Lend us twenty, Mon?'

It hadn't been her mother raiding her purse, but Skye. It was the insolent eyebrow lift that told her. Skye *wanted* her to know.

And *that* was the moment Monique had lost her little sister. She'd fought against it, of course. For months. But Skye had shifted her allegiance to their mother and there wasn't a single damn thing Monique could do about it.

She'd forced herself to keep her chin high, had forced the tears back and refused to acknowledge the chasm that had opened in her chest as she'd fished out a ten-dollar note. It had been all she could afford. 'This is the last time I give you money, Skye. If you want pocket money you'll have to ask Mum for it. Or I can get you some weekend shifts at the restaurant.'

Her sister had blinked, evidently not having foreseen this eventuality. Had she thought Monique had no back-bone at all? She wasn't giving her sister money to waste on cigarettes and alcohol.

'I hate you Mon. You know that? So prim and proper and *good*. Maybe if you lightened up once in a while… But you don't have a clue how to have a good time. Well, you're not going to stop me from having one.'

Vicious, casual, cruel…and she probably hadn't meant

it. But those words had sucked all that had been light and good from Monique's world. 'I have to go or I'll be late. Don't forget the lasagne.'

Luca stared at the devastation stretching through Monique's caramel eyes and wanted to swear, to smash something, to defeat those demons like some gallant knight of old. This lovely warm woman had poured her heart and soul into her sister's care. How could Skye have abandoned her so callously?

Because that's what Monique's poorly concealed devastation revealed—that Skye had repaid her sister's love and care with betrayal.

'What do you mean, your mother *happened*? I did not think she was interested in her children.'

Monique shook herself, sent him a smile that made his heart break a little. 'She wasn't interested in the responsibilities or practicalities of parenthood, but when Skye was fifteen it seemed to amuse her to turn Skye into her best friend…turn her into a mini-me. She encouraged her to smoke and drink, to skip school.'

Cavolo.

'Of course, I couldn't compete with that. I was the person who nagged her to eat her vegetables and do her homework…keep her room tidy and help with household chores.'

He knew without being told that Monique had continued to keep her little sister fed and clothed. She'd probably paid all the household bills too.

'But I was, quote, "only her sister" and I couldn't tell her what to do.' She stared at her hands. 'She'd always craved our mother's love and attention, and while I know she loved me too, the lure of our mother's approval was too hard for her to resist.'

'But you didn't abandon her.'

'I stayed until she turned eighteen. But I didn't have the stomach to watch her destroy her life. A school friend... Anita, actually...told me that the Mirror Glass Bay Motel was recruiting. I applied, was hired, and so I moved there and started a new life. It meant I was close enough in case of an emergency, but far enough away that...' She shrugged and didn't finish the sentence.

She didn't have to. What a big heart this woman had. Despite her sister's betrayal, she was prepared to risk her heart all over again now with Fern.

'With the benefit of hindsight, I realise I should've alerted the authorities to our situation.'

'You were only a child.'

'I was afraid they'd take Skye away from me.'

A fear no doubt reinforced by her mother. 'You were only a child,' he repeated.

'If I'd acted less selfishly, maybe Skye wouldn't have become addicted to drugs.'

'Or maybe it wouldn't have made any difference whatsoever. You are not the guilty party here, Monique.'

She brushed a hand across her eyes. 'I know. These are regrets, not a guilty conscience. But...' she met his gaze '...it's why I refused to take a chance with Fern's welfare.'

'I admire you.'

'Don't be silly. I'm only doing what anyone else—'

'And I am sorry for unearthing such painful memories. It was insensitive of me and not my intention.'

She frowned. 'What *was* your intention?'

It was his turn to shrug. 'I wanted to know how you learned to relate to children so well in an attempt to copy you.'

Her eyes widened and she let slip a laugh. 'Oh, Luca, you goose!'

He blinked. No one had ever called him a goose before, and certainly not in a tone of such affection.

'You don't need to learn anything new. You already have it inside you. Benny's face lights up whenever he sees you. Plus, you've been so kind to Fern, so patient in winning her over.'

He'd made sure to be even-handed with the children. If he brought a treat to the nursery for Benito, he made sure to bring one for Fern too. It only seemed fair. Her wide-eyed surprise and hesitant smiles were ample reward.

Monique's niece was a gentle soul—a little shy and with-drawn, but clever too and with a cheeky sense of humour that delighted him. As soon as she fully trusted her new life with her aunt, he didn't doubt the little girl would blossom.

'I am glad you think so, but...'

When he paused, she leaned towards him and gestured for him to continue.

'I want to be the best father I can be. It is what Benito deserves. I want to know how to do better. I want to know what I can improve.' While he couldn't make up to his son for the loss of his mother, he could do all he could to be what Benny needed.

Her gaze dropped and she shifted back in her seat. His stomach clenched, instinct telling him he wouldn't like her answer, but she merely shook her head. 'The world is full of compromises.'

'Yes, but you must have some thoughts on how I can become a better father.'

'You want my honest opinion?' Those clear eyes lifted. 'Then if you want to be a better father to Benny, you need to spend more time with him.'

He stiffened at the implicit criticism. From Monique, who had only ever looked at him as if he were a hero!

'When we were in Mirror Glass Bay, you spent almost

every minute with him, only dialling into work when he napped or at night when he was asleep. The first week here in Rome you spent a lot of time with him—checking in on him in the morning, often putting in an appearance at lunchtime, and spending much of the evenings with him. This week there have been days when he's seen you for less than an hour.'

'I am a busy man.' He shot to his feet to pace around the room. 'I have many demands on my time.' He couldn't continue to neglect the work piling up on his desk.

'I know.' Her lips turned rueful. 'That's what I meant by compromise. You're not the only parent who has had to negotiate the tricky conundrum of work time versus family time. There're a lot of parents who leave the house before their children are awake in the mornings and don't return until they're in bed in the evenings. Many parents, though, don't have a choice.'

He glanced around at her sharply. She thought he had a choice? He was in charge of a legacy that went back five generations. Even if he was prepared to abandon his birthright, the promise he'd made his grandfather meant he couldn't.

He slashed a hand through the air. 'You do not understand!'

'That's true enough.' She glanced in the direction of the children's rooms. 'But you're wrong if you think I don't understand compromise.'

He blew out a breath, tried to temper his sense of injury. 'Of course you do. Forgive me. That was unfair.'

Those clear eyes met his as if they saw him—truly saw him. It made his heart pound. Nobody had ever looked at him that way. Something inside him battled then to break free, but he forced it back within the boundaries he'd set for himself. But the effort had perspiration prickling his nape.

She shook her head, as if trying to shake herself free from some unwanted thought. 'I've no choice but to work, but you're insanely rich, Luca. You should be able to fashion the world to suit you.' Her brow wrinkled. 'But I can see you feel trapped. I'm just not sure by what.'

He straightened. 'I have a responsibility to the Vieri Corporation, to the Vieri name, to all the hard work the previous generations have carried out. It is my duty to honour and expand on their success.'

The furrow on her brow didn't clear. 'But you don't have to do it all on your own, do you? You have a large family. Surely the responsibility can be shared around? I can't believe every member of your family is as irresponsible as your parents, aunts and uncles. Why do you feel you must do it all on your own?'

Because there was a traitor in their midst, and he didn't know who he could trust.

But once he'd discovered the answer to that mystery, once he knew who he could trust, once calm and order had been restored, could he then rethink the company's internal structure?

'Luca, all any of us can do is try to be the best parents and the best role models for our children that we can be within our means and circumstances.'

The best parent he could be... Discovering he had a son had come as a huge shock and his only thought had been to race to his son's side to claim him as soon as possible. He hadn't thought beyond that or what came after. But now he had to decide what kind of parent he wanted to be.

One thing was certain. He didn't want to be the same kind of parent as his own mother and father—distant, remote, and bent more on their own pleasure and convenience than anything else.

He suddenly became conscious of the time. If she wanted to study…

He rose. 'It's getting late. You haven't forgotten the Gallineri party next Saturday night?'

'Of course not.'

It was a two-pronged affair—a select group of thirty for dinner followed by a lavish party for two hundred afterwards.

'I will have dresses sent over from several of the same fashion houses that Bella frequents. You can choose whatever you like. You'll need another four outfits as well, so—'

'I'd really rather you didn't.'

He blinked, wondering if he'd heard her right. She'd risen too and he tried to not notice the way the curves of her breasts pushed against the soft wool of her thin sweater.

He swallowed. 'Is there a different designer from whom you wish to procure your garments?'

'Heavens, no! The thing is, Luca, I don't want designer dresses. I don't want to sound ungrateful, but I'd rather choose outfits that reflect my true position here. I'm a visitor to your world. I should wear clothes that reflect that. It's a strategy that will allay any lingering doubts Signor Romano might have about me accompanying you to these events.' She bit her thumbnail. 'And hopefully signal to your associates that you're not ready to date yet, which will keep everyone else from feeling slighted. That's the whole point of me acting as your plus one after all.'

It was true, and her strategy was a sound one. His head could see the wisdom but something inside him resisted the reasoning. She should be dressed in the finest silks and laces. She'd looked an utter vision at the previous party.

'I'd like to buy clothes I can wear when I return to Australia.'

He stiffened. 'You will not be paying for these purchases. You would not be incurring such expenses if you were not doing this favour for me.'

He thought she might argue but eventually she surrendered with a nod. 'And to be honest,' she added, 'I'd feel much more at ease not wearing designer dresses.'

The smile she sent him had his skin tightening. She was so beautiful it wouldn't matter what she wore.

'I was so afraid of spilling something on the dress I wore at the last party I didn't eat a thing all night.'

'*Dio!* But you must've been ravenous by the time we got home.'

That made her laugh. 'Let's just say I had a *very* hearty breakfast the next morning.'

He took a step towards her, stretched out a hand as if to touch her, a wave of tenderness nearly toppling him. Her quick intake of breath brought him back to himself and he forced his hand back to his side, the blood in his veins pounding so hard he felt bruised from the inside out. 'Please, Monique, you do not need to go hungry in this house.'

The thought of her going to bed hungry... It hurt something inside him. How often had she done that as a child? She did not have to do that here. 'You are free to use the kitchen, to make yourself whatever you want at any time. Promise me.'

If possible, her eyes grew even bigger. She swallowed and nodded. 'I promise.' She rubbed a hand across her chest. 'Thank you.'

What was she thanking him for? He should've noticed she'd not eaten. He should've taken better care of her!

Her brows drew together. 'Luca, I'm not in any danger of starving, you know.'

He tried to shake himself free from the confusion that had him in its grip. It was just...he'd given her her heart's desire. Her happiness and high regard were swiftly becoming addictive. He found himself wanting to repeat it again and again.

Dangerous. Very dangerous.

It was something he had to resist. To surrender to it would make a mockery of all his grandfather's hard work and all that he owed the older man.

'I would appreciate two further things from you, Luca.'

Anything. 'Name them.'

'The first is an afternoon off to go shopping.'

'You may arrange your work schedule any way you wish. I trust you with it implicitly.' She considered Benito's welfare as important as she did Fern's. As much as he did himself.

'And advice on where to shop. Something along the lines of a large department store…?'

A slow smile spread across his face. 'I know just the place. Is Wednesday convenient for you?' At her nod, he said, 'I will organise a credit card for your use, and a driver.'

'Oh, that's not necessary. I—'

She broke off with a laugh at whatever she saw in his face. 'Very well. Thank you. I appreciate it.'

He wondered what she would say when she discovered the department store he wished to take her to had once been the jewel in the Vieri empire's crown? His hands clenched. And it would be again.

He looked forward to the expression on her face when he told her. First, though, he must organise a snack from the kitchen for her. Never again was she going hungry on his watch.

CHAPTER SIX

MONIQUE TRIED TO stifle the anticipation curling in her stomach as she skipped down the front steps of the villa to the waiting car. In the two and a half weeks she'd been here, she'd only left the estate to attend that party with Luca. But now she had an entire afternoon free.

If she did her shopping in record time, could she sneak in a couple of hours of sightseeing?

She hesitated, before sliding into the front passenger seat. 'I know I'm probably supposed to sit in the back, but I have a favour to ask and—' Her words tumbled to a halt when she glanced at the driver. 'Luca!'

He shrugged; his smile the kind that could slip beneath a woman's guard. 'I decided to play hooky from the office for the afternoon.'

He had? She tried to contain a surge of delight.

'But I have an ulterior motive for coming along.' He suddenly frowned. 'I did not think you would mind.'

'Of course I don't mind.' The breath had jammed in her throat, making it hard to get the words out, making them breathless.

'What is this favour you were going to ask?'

'Oh, it was nothing. Nothing at all.' She didn't want him to think she was unhappy or unsatisfied with her position in his household. There'd be time to sightsee another day.

'Monique, I would wish—'

'I just felt wrong about sitting in the back, that's all. I'm not a member of your family and—'

'I consider you part of Benito's family.'

Oh. She tried to not let his words affect her. It didn't change the essential relationship between him and her. She sent him what she hoped was a cheerful smile as he drove out of the huge iron gates. 'The truth is one gets a better view sitting in the front.'

She couldn't see any landmarks that she knew, but when they crested the rise of a hill at the end of the road, Vatican City with St Peter's Basilica came into view in the distance and her breath left her on a whoosh. 'Look!' She pointed. 'It's as beautiful as I always imagined.'

'You must make time to visit it while you are here. It has a fascinating history.'

'And the ceiling of the Sistine Chapel?'

'Sublime.'

She sagged. She was tempted to pinch herself. Was she really in one of the most romantic cities in the world? This was the kind of thing that happened to other people, not her.

Luca seemed content to drive in silence, without conversation, but it wasn't the kind of silence that was unpleasant, and it gave her a chance to focus on the city unveiling itself before her in all of its complex beauty.

It no doubt gave Luca the chance to concentrate on negotiating the insane traffic!

Which he did with admirable ease.

'You must have nerves of steel,' she murmured when a van pulled out in front of them, only missing them by inches as a Vespa sped down one side of them in the impossibly tiny alley formed by the two lanes of traffic. How it didn't clip a side mirror she'd never know.

'One becomes accustomed to it.' His sudden smile sent

her heart pitter-pattering. 'It's a little different from your sleepy Mirror Glass Bay, yes?'

That made her laugh, and then she gasped, looking beyond him. 'That's the…'

'Acropolis,' he supplied.

She could only nod in dumb stupefaction. 'But it's right here in the middle of the city.'

'*Sì*. You have to understand that Rome is an ancient city, and the modern city has sprung up around it—the old and new are blended together and live side by side. We are a city that embraces both our past and our future.'

'While relishing your present?'

Her question made him frown, as she'd meant it to. From where she was sitting, Luca was too intent on both the past and the future at the expense of his present. She didn't think that was any way to live.

Be an asset, not a liability.

She went back to gobbling up the view outside.

Luca broke the silence a short while later. 'This is our destination.'

He pointed to a grand seven-storey building in red brick. Its mullioned windows in their black frames and iron grillwork and big glass revolving doors gave it an understated elegance. Before she could make out its name, they'd descended to an underground car park, where Luca parked his car in a reserved bay.

'Come! Let us go purchase the things you need.'

She pushed out of the car before he could come around to open it for her. Luca was a gentleman, he observed all such niceties, but those kinds of niceties were wasted on the likes of her. And if she told herself that often enough, she might even start to believe it.

She stared at him over the car roof. 'You're coming shopping with me?' She'd thought he'd dash off to a meeting or to do business somewhere.

Something flickered in the backs of his eyes and a mask slid down over his face as he motioned her in the direction of the elevator. 'It had been my plan, but if you would prefer to shop alone then—'

'No! I just… Won't it bore you silly?'

'Why would you think that?'

They stepped into the waiting elevator. 'In my experience, men hate clothes shopping with women.'

A gleam lit his eyes as he punched in a number. 'That must be because they have not shopped at Gianni's.'

That was the name of the store?

'Gianni Vieri's, if one wants to give it its full name.'

'This is *your* store?'

Her mouth fell open and he laughed.

'Who was Gianni? Your grandfather?'

'Great-grandfather. This store was once the jewel in the Vieri crown.'

No sooner had the words left his lips than the elevator doors slid open to reveal rows of counters glittering with cosmetics and perfume, and she couldn't contain her happy sigh. Glass and brass twinkled and glowed in the warm overhead light from a series of opulent chandeliers. Even the air smelled expensive.

'The old décor has been kept.' She pressed a hand to her chest. 'I feel as if I've just stepped onto the set of an old movie.'

'*Sì.* It is part of its charm.'

'Oh, Luca, it's beautiful. I love it. And I guess you must too.'

'*Sì.*'

But the single word emerged tight and clipped, the lines

bracketing his mouth deepening. 'Come, women's fashions are this way.'

'Oh, but first...'

He swung back to her.

'It's just...' She gestured to the perfume counter. 'We have to spritz something lovely on.' It's what she always did whenever she visited one of the big department stores in Brisbane. She couldn't afford French perfume, but on days like today she could spray a little on and relish the experience.

He laughed, his tension dissipating. 'Very well, lead the way.'

A woman at the perfume counter spritzed a brand-new perfume onto Monique's wrists and explained it had a top note of orchids followed by softer hints of jasmine and citrus.

She pronounced it heavenly and said she'd think about it, that she wasn't shopping for perfume today.

'You do not wish to buy it?'

She smiled at his perplexed expression. She couldn't justify the expense of French perfume, not that she had any intention of telling him that. 'You don't understand. Back home I so rarely get a chance to visit the city. So to come to a department store like this is a real treat. And traditionally I always begin such an excursion fortified with a spritz of something lovely. It just sets the tone and makes me feel...spoiled.'

He frowned. 'I see.'

He had no idea. 'Are you wearing cologne?' She leaned in close and sniffed, drawing a deep breath of him into her lungs. And then realised what she was doing.

She shot back as the scent of fresh soap and warm male skin assailed her senses. Stunned dark eyes met hers before he blinked his usual composure back into place. Dear

God, what had she been thinking? *Act normal.* Maybe he wouldn't notice her reaction if she acted as if it were no big deal.

'Here.' She seized a nearby bottle of cologne. 'Try it. Put some on. It's fun to try something different.'

He blinked but did as she ordered. 'What do you think?'

He angled his neck towards her and her mouth dried. All she could think about was pressing her lips to the strong tanned column of his throat and running her hands around to the nape of his neck and—

Stop it!

She forced herself to lean in a little closer and take a cautious sniff. The warmth of amber and a hint of cardamom spiced the air. She closed her eyes in momentary appreciation.

'You approve?'

'Very much.'

She made herself smile. She made herself take a step back. But dark eyes met hers and their gazes held. Something arced between them—a silent male-female acknowledgement of attraction and…liking? It was the latter of those that gave her pause and made her heart hammer in her chest.

Not her liking him. He'd had her undying *like* from the moment he'd helped her rescue Fern. What she hadn't realised was that he might actually like her in return. As a person.

They dropped their gazes at the same time, and she wondered if her eyes were as troubled as his.

'So…' She clapped her hands and made a show of keeping things light—something that came as second nature to her. It was the strategy she'd used to keep Skye from getting too upset whenever their mother had stumbled home drunk to flake out on the sofa. 'Now that we're smelling gorgeous, we can embark on the shopping for real. And it looks like women's fashions are this way.'

Oddly enough, the tension between them evaporated when they started looking at dresses and pantsuits.

'That is horrible, no?' Luca said when she pulled out a heavily beaded navy concoction. 'It is for a much older woman. What about this one?'

'Those frills…' She grimaced. 'Too fussy.'

He put it back and pulled out another.

'Oh! That one's perfect.'

She'd never realised shopping with a man could be such fun. He gave his opinion with a decisiveness that made her laugh. They argued good-naturedly over the pros and cons of certain necklines and hemlines. She loved every moment of it.

She eventually settled on a beaded dress with a fitted bodice in the most glorious shade of jade, a simple silk sheath in a mouth-watering orange, and a butter-yellow trouser suit that hung like a dream. 'There, that's the up-coming events taken care of.'

He frowned. 'But we have another five parties to attend and you have only three outfits.'

'I can wear these more than once, Luca.'

'*Dio!* No. You must also take the rose-coloured velvet dress and that pretty red cocktail frock. Besides, there may be one or two additional events that come up at the last moment and it is best to be prepared.'

She wanted to argue with him. She'd never spent this much money on clothes in her entire life.

He gave directions to the saleswoman and then turned back to her. 'Do not feel guilty,' he chided. 'All of these together are still less than that designer dress in whose service you starved yourself.'

Gah! Don't tell me that.

'So you see? You are saving me money!'

That made her laugh. 'Now you're spinning fairy stories. This—'

He pressed a finger to her lips. 'You are doing me a favour being my plus one and it is only right I ensure you have the equipment necessary to accomplish the assignment. *Sì?*'

Her mouth had gone dry at his touch, rendering her speechless, so she simply nodded.

'Good.'

He removed his fingers and she could breathe again. 'Luca, I can assure you it isn't a hardship attending parties with you.'

'I am glad to hear it.'

'It's fun.' She said the words deliberately, because fun didn't seem to feature on this man's radar at all and it broke her heart a little.

He blinked and stared as if he didn't know what to say. He had so much money and yet fun seemed a foreign concept to him. She sent him her biggest smile. 'Today has been fun.'

His lips relaxed into a smile. 'It has. But it is not yet over.'

He turned to the saleswoman, speaking in rapid Italian, and although she'd been learning the basics from Maria and Anna, she had no hope of following it.

It became clear, however, when a selection of shoes, purses and wraps were paraded for her appraisal. She chose a single pair of beige heels and a purse to match that would go with everything, deliberately hardening her heart against the crystal studded pale pink heels that were frivolous and totally unnecessary.

Luca spread his hands. 'You need more than one pair of shoes.'

'I have another pair at home. I don't need more than two pairs of evening shoes.'

He lifted his eyes heavenward. 'What am I to do with this woman?' He seized the pink heels and a matching purse and then a sumptuous faux fur wrap in white and added them to the pile. And then gave what sounded like another set of instructions to the waiting sales assistants—they now had three.

She frowned when pretty trousers, tops and capri pants were displayed for her inspection. 'Luca, I don't need any of these.'

'Please, choose a selection to humour me. I do not like all of the black and white you wear every day. It makes me feel as if you are working in a funeral home. It is most disconcerting.'

Her mouth fell open.

'It was your uniform when you worked as a maid and a waitress, and this I understand. But such a uniform is unnecessary when you are Benito's nanny.'

'Why?' It would be safer if they maintained the distinctions of their positions in his household. Those distinctions were in danger of blurring enough already due to their plus one arrangement.

'Because you are more than just a member of my staff.'

Her heart tried to dash its way out of her chest. She was more to him…?

'You have come to Rome out of the goodness of your heart because of your connection to Benito—because you love him.'

She gripped her hands together. Of course he meant her relationship to Benny. Nothing more. It'd be idiotic to think he meant anything else.

'His welfare and best interests are of primary concern to

you. I think you love him almost as much as I do. And as his godmother you are family. As such, that makes us equals.'

The way he stared at her as he spoke invested his words with more meaning than he no doubt meant them to. She kept her hands pressed tightly at her waist and gave herself a stern lecture. Luca was outrageously generous, that was all.

That was all.

'So, please, choose five outfits that you can wear during the day. Outfits that are comfortable, practical and to your liking.'

She stared at the clothes he'd gestured to. All her working life it had been her role to fade into the background. Here Luca was asking her to stand out.

'This will be a sign to the rest of the household staff that where Benito is concerned your word is law, that you have my authority to make important decisions on his behalf.'

She glanced up. Perhaps not just to the household staff, but also his family? She sensed he didn't want her allowing his mother to walk all over her, though he didn't say that out loud. And she certainly didn't ask.

Without another word, she chose trousers, capris and skirts in the loveliest fabrics and a selection of tops— practical, colourful and pretty. 'I've never owned such beautiful clothes,' she said as they wound their way back down to the ground floor after Luca had organised for all the purchases to be delivered to the villa later that afternoon. 'Thank you, Luca.'

'You do not need to thank me. You need a working wardrobe while you are here, and I gave you no opportunity to arrange that before leaving Australia. We supply all our household staff with uniforms. This is no different.'

Except hers wasn't a uniform.

'Now, come, that's enough.' He halted in front of one of the large glass revolving doors. 'Tell me which of Rome's many sights you most wish to visit?' He glanced at his watch. 'We have several hours still at our disposal.'

She tried not to gape at him. Had he read her mind earlier? 'But...what about the business you said you had here?'

'It is completed.'

She'd been his business? She lifted her chin against the sinking of her heart. For all his pretty words earlier, he saw her as nothing more than another responsibility. Today's outing was merely another example of his innate generosity.

What more do you want?

It wasn't a question she dared answer.

'I may even tell you about it later. When we are sight-seeing.'

She gnawed on her bottom lip, but he smiled—a true from-the-heart smile that had double the impact as one saw it so rarely—and she gave up worrying.

'I confess I find myself intrigued as to what you will choose.'

He looked as excited as a little child and she found it strangely endearing. 'You're going to find it horribly trite and touristy, I'm afraid.'

'I would be disappointed if it were not.'

She couldn't resist that smile. 'Okay, then the thing I most want...'

He leaned towards her. 'Yes?'

'Is to eat gelato by the Trevi Fountain.'

His mouth formed a perfect O, before he murmured something in Italian that made her want to close her eyes and purr. 'You are a remarkable woman, Monique.'

The way he said her name... *Dear Lord.*

'You could ask for the stars.' His rich chuckle filled the air. 'And yet all you want is gelato.'

'And the Trevi Fountain,' she reminded him. 'And it has to be *good* gelato.'

'Italy only does the best.'

She laughed at the way he straightened, as if he would fight any suggestion otherwise. 'Then we're in for a treat. The stars can wait until next week.'

Luca tried to not question too deeply his satisfaction when Monique's lids fluttered down over her eyes in appreciation as she sampled her first Italian gelato.

'This is delicious!'

If forced to guess her favourite flavour, he'd have said chocolate, but she'd pointed to a creamy passionfruit instead. Normally he'd choose a coffee-flavoured gelato, but not today. Today he'd selected a rich smooth caramel that coated his tongue in sweet promise.

Her eyes flew open, rooting him to the spot. 'Best gelato ever.'

He couldn't move, couldn't drag his gaze from those eyes, her smile or from the life that radiated from her every pore. As if aware of his scrutiny, as if the warmth of his gaze touched her skin, pink stained her cheeks.

He shook himself. 'I am glad it does not disappoint. And what of the fountain?' He gestured to the fountain in front of them. 'Does it too live up to expectation?'

'I think it magnificent. I need to pinch myself to believe I'm really here and that this isn't just a dream.'

She craned her neck, taking in all she could. As if trying to memorise every detail. He did his best not to notice the way her tongue touched the gelato or the shine it left on her lips. If he kissed her now, she'd taste cool and tangy and—

Not that he had any intention of doing any such thing!

Sì, she was beautiful, but a dalliance with Benito's godmother...? *Dio*, it would be very poor form indeed. Besides, he reminded himself, for as long as he continued to tread delicate ground with Signor Romano, he would not want whispers of any such liaison to reach the older man's ears.

If only those thoughts could dampen the tendrils of desire that curled around him with a gentle but insidious tyranny. He took a big bite of gelato, hoping it would give him brain freeze.

'The fountain and the square are both regal and charming,' Monique finally said. 'I suspect that might sum Rome up perfectly too.'

Except that was all conjecture on her part, and not based on experience. How could he have been so remiss and not shown her a little of what Rome had to offer before now? He'd kept her tied to the villa for the nearly three weeks. She must've felt as if she were under house arrest!

'You sum up my city perfectly.' He handed her a coin and gestured. 'You must, of course, toss a coin into the fountain to ensure you will one day return.'

Her fingers closed around the coin as if relishing the heat it had absorbed from his body. He gulped down more gelato.

Placing her back to the fountain and closing her eyes as if to make a wish, she threw the coin high into the air over her shoulder. It glittered in the sunlight as it turned over and over, landing in the pool with a splash.

He beamed at her. 'Now you will return.'

'I hope so.'

He would see to it. He wanted Benito to know his godmother, and to know her well, not just as a passing acquaintance. He wondered if she and Fern would consent to spend every Christmas with them.

He promptly lost his appetite. That would, of course, depend on his wife and what she wished to have happen at Christmas. Not that he could yet put a face to that elusive woman. It didn't change the fact that such a wife featured in his future.

'So?' She raised her eyebrows.

He raised his too. 'So?'

'You were going to tell me about your business at Gianni's today.'

Ah, that. Resolve settled in the pit of his stomach. Yes, it would be wise to tell her...and to remind himself of all he wanted to achieve. Leading her to one of the small tables that bordered the square, he held a chair out for her; taking the one opposite once she was seated. 'I wanted to walk the halls of Gianni's today as a customer. I wanted to try and see the store through your eyes.'

'Did you like what you saw?'

He nodded. He'd liked it very much.

She frowned as if something puzzled her. 'You're an important man, Luca, but hardly any of the staff seemed to know who you were. I expected... I don't know, more bowing and scraping, I suppose. As CEO I thought they'd roll out the red carpet for you. I mean, if you own the store you'd think—'

'But I don't.' Pain tightened his chest, making the words curter than he'd meant them to be. He tossed what was left of his gelato into a nearby bin.

'I beg your pardon?'

'The Vieri Corporation no longer owns Gianni's. One of the first things my mother and her siblings did when my grandfather retired five years ago was to sell it. Secretly and swiftly before any of the rest of us could do anything about it.'

She stared at him as if his words made no sense. 'But you said it had been the jewel in the Vieri crown. Surely that means...'

She trailed off with a gulp, looking as if she wished she'd held her tongue. He nodded. 'It should be cherished and honoured...kept safe.'

She nodded back warily, as if afraid she'd overstepped a boundary. Boundaries he should strengthen.

'It broke my grandfather's heart.'

She reached out as if to touch his hand, to offer comfort, but pulled back at the last minute. 'I'm sorry.'

She moistened her lips. He refused to allow his attention to linger on their soft curves or to allow the craving to taste them to grow. Monique was forbidden fruit. He would not be another weak-willed pleasure-seeking Vieri.

'Is your grandfather still alive?'

Her question made him smile. 'Very much so. He now lives on a small vineyard in Tuscany where he makes wine and tends his garden.' His grandfather had worked hard all of his life. He deserved a trouble-free retirement. He deserved to have both the Vieri name and Gianni's restored before he died.

'You sound fond of him.'

'My parents had very little time for me when I was a child, but my grandfather spent as much time as he could with me and my cousins—half-days and weekends. He would take us all to his beach house in summer for two weeks.' His grandfather was the only reason his childhood hadn't been a cold and lonely wasteland of privilege. 'I can see now how he fostered relationships between us cousins... so we would always have each other. In that way he gave us a sense of the true meaning of family.'

'He sounds like a fine man.' The look she sent him—warm but piercing—left him feeling suddenly naked. 'I think you must be like him.'

It was the greatest compliment anyone could pay him.

'I'm guessing you're modelling your parenting style on him rather than your parents.'

He was trying to, but... A grandfather's love and care did not make up for a parent's indifference. If he'd lived permanently with his grandfather things might've been different. But that hadn't been possible. His grandfather had been working hard to keep his ungrateful offspring out of trouble and out of debt.

Benito deserved better than a part-time father. Luca needed to find a way to balance his commitments to the Vieri Corporation with fatherhood.

'You don't need to do it all alone.'

Monique's words from earlier in the week whispered through him. He wanted to believe them, but someone needed to be the head of the company. And his grandfather had chosen him.

He pulled in a slow breath and released it. 'My grandfather handed control of his share of the company to me after his offspring sold Gianni's. My cousins and I made a bid for power and ousted my uncle from his position as CEO. We have been working towards re-establishing the Vieri name ever since.'

'So you're all working together—you and your cousins?'

'Sì.'

She frowned. 'Then why do you feel so alone, feel as if you must do it all on your own?'

'Because one of my cousins is working against me, working with the previous generation to undermine my control. And I do not know who it is.'

'Which means you don't know who you can trust,' she said slowly, pressing a hand to her stomach as if the gelato she'd eaten now no longer agreed with her. 'Well, that sucks.'

Her bluntness surprised a laugh from him. *'Sì.* It does indeed, as you say, suck.'

'You'll get to the bottom of it. You're clever and determined.'

Her faith in his abilities touched him. Yes, he would get

to the bottom of it, and he would make things right. But at what price?

'Luca?'

He glanced up at the question in her voice.

'Who owns Gianni's now?'

'Signor Romano.'

Her eyes widened. 'That's why you were going to marry Bella? Gianni's was...what? Part of her dowry?'

Her distaste was plain. 'It is how things are done in my world.'

'It seems so...cold-blooded.'

The hand he rested on the table clenched to a fist. When she glanced at it, he forced himself to relax it again. 'Cold-blooded would be to pressure Bella to go through with a marriage she does not want. Cold-blooded would be to marry a woman I do not like or respect. Cold-blooded would be to marry a woman who would not be kind to my son, simply because I want the respectability her name and family's backing will give me.'

He shook his head, but he wasn't sure who he was trying to convince—himself or Monique. 'I intend to honour and respect the woman I marry. While it might not be a love match, there will be affection, and I have every intention of honouring my marriage vows.'

She met his gaze. He knew he looked fierce and grim, but it didn't seem to frighten her. 'I'm sorry, you're right. It isn't cold-blooded. Not when you put it like that. You're a good man and I shouldn't have made such a snap judgement. As you say, our worlds are so different.'

He was no doubt violating ideals she considered sacrosanct and inviolable—like romantic love. He'd believe in that once too.

'When I was twenty, a woman I imagined myself in love with took money from my father to break up with me. It made me realise that while my wealth provides me with much privilege and a luxurious lifestyle, it also brings temptations and enticements to the people I associate with—envy and covetousness in some quarters too. It is better for me to be realistic about this and not indulge in romantic daydreams.'

Her face fell. 'That's awful.'

Seeing it through her eyes…it was all he could do not to flinch. 'I can, however, make a clear-eyed marriage with a woman I respect, a woman who will not tarnish the Vieri name. It is not a tragedy, Monique. Family is everything to my grandfather, my cousins and me. I will do all I can to make them proud. I will be more than content with that.'

'We're so different.' She managed a laugh and while it sounded genuine enough, he sensed the effort it cost her. 'I mean, you can trace your ancestors back at least five generations…probably more. While neither my sister nor I have the slightest idea who our fathers might be. To us, family feels like nothing more than an accident…a lottery… something to be overcome.'

Her family was the absolute antithesis of the kind of family he needed to marry into, that his grandfather required he marry into, to save the family name.

Her face crumpled and for a moment he thought she might cry. *'Dio!'* He reached out a hand to her. 'What is the matter?'

'I should so wish Benny to marry for love rather than duty.'

Everything inside him protested at the idea. It would be otherwise for his son. Luca would make this sacrifice so Benito never had to.

That pretty chin lifted. 'I need to warn you that's what I'll be advising him to do, despite your thoughts on the matter.'

Her fierceness made him smile. 'It is what I wish for him too.'

Her eyes narrowed. 'As long as he falls in love with the right kind of woman?'

'No. If I make the right kind of marriage now, if I can fix the things that need fixing, Benny will not have to make any such sacrifice.'

With a funny sound—part-growl, part-groan—that was cut off before it could fully become one or the other, she covered her face with her hands.

He stared at her, nonplussed, before reaching over and tugging on one of her hands gently. 'I do not lie to you, Monique.'

'I know.' She lowered her hands, but his words had no effect on the unease swirling in her eyes. 'Will you explain something to me?'

He suspected Monique would champion his son to the ends of the earth. He'd explain anything he could to her. 'I will try, yes.'

'Can you tell me how this respectable marriage you plan to make will help you restore the Vieri name and reputation?'

'If you wish.'

'I'd like to understand.'

'Very well.'

'Would it be okay if we strolled as we talked?'

He felt the sudden restlessness in her as a similar restlessness stole over him. 'Come.' He stood. 'The Spanish Steps are this way. And from there we can walk to the Pantheon. Does that sound agreeable to you?'

'It sounds perfect.'

How he wished her smile would meet her eyes. Dragging a breath into cramped lungs, he tutored himself on keeping his voice calm and his heart steady. This was the path he had chosen, and while he might not be able to meet it with enthusiasm, he would meet it with grace.

He gestured the direction they should take and didn't speak again until they'd reached the Spanish Steps. She clasped her hands beneath her chin, and oohed and ahhed when she saw them, but not with the same fervour that she had the fountain they'd left behind.

'You ask how my marrying into one of the old, respected families will help my family…and vice versa.'

She nodded.

'Currently there are companies that refuse to do business with the Vieri Corporation due to the previous leadership's…*unreliability*.'

Her quick glance told him she understood. Unreliability was merely a euphemism for his parents', aunts' and uncles' unscrupulous and at times dishonest business dealings.

'There are businesses I need to get onside, that I need to convince to work with me, if I am to take the Vieri Corporation into the future.'

She frowned up at him, and he took her elbow to guide her around a woman with a stroller who'd stopped in front of them.

'But if these businessmen know you, Luca, then they must realise you're honourable and reliable.'

'There's a difference between believing me honest and believing me capable of keeping power.'

A sigh whispered from her. 'I see.'

'In aligning myself with one of the big families, it will inject the Vieri name with a level of kudos and respectability I'd not be able to achieve any other way. It's an immediate endorsement from a respected source. While I might not yet have the trust of the wider business community, these big families do.'

'And in aligning yourself with one of them, their respectability and integrity will entice the businessmen you want to work with to trust you?'

'Exactly.'

'What does the old established family get in return?'

'Money. Their family estates are prohibitively expensive to maintain.'

She pursed her lips but remained uncharacteristically silent.

'I get the respectability I need while they get the money to maintain a family estate that goes back centuries.'

He watched her mull that over as they strolled along cobbled streets and past shop windows with enticing displays. He wasn't sure she saw any of it.

'Will marrying into one of these families help you counter the in-fighting in your family? Help you maintain control of the company?'

Every single one of her questions was on point. She might not have had as stellar an education as he, but she had a quick mind.

And a kind heart.

'She has the kindest heart of anyone I know.'

Cassidy's words to him in Mirror Glass Bay floated through his mind now, making his heart clench. If only Monique came from his world. If only—

He had to stop wishing for the impossible. It was his duty to focus only on what was necessary.

'Luca?'

He snapped back. 'The big families might not have the same wealth as a family like mine, but they have many contacts in both the industrial and political spheres. Those contacts will be of much assistance to me.'

'So that's a yes, then.' A tiny sigh puffed from her lips. 'How will it help you get Gianni's back?'

'Signor Romano has promised that if I can redeem the Vieri name, he will sell Gianni's back to me.'

She swung back to him. 'He knows the nitty-gritty of your plan?'

It was as if a cloud had passed over the sun. He glanced up but the sky was as blue as it had been earlier in the day. 'He is one of my grandfather's best friends. It is he and my grandfather who came up with this plan.'

'They *what*?'

'I trust them.'

'I can see that.'

'This plan...' he glanced down at her '...it is a sound one.'

Her sigh pierced all the sore places inside him, but then she slipped her hand into the crook of his elbow and he hugged that small warmth to himself.

'Thank you for explaining it all to me.'

'You are welcome.'

She gave a laugh. 'Wow, a family like mine would really be your worst nightmare, huh? Disreputable and constantly trying to extort more money out of you while giving supposedly in-depth reveals to the tabloids.'

Her words were irrefutable. He did his best to keep his shoulders back and his spine straight. Physically he and Monique might be close enough to touch, but in reality they couldn't be more distant from each other if they tried.

CHAPTER SEVEN

MONIQUE SCANNED THE ballroom after returning from touching up her lipstick. She'd needed a moment to herself to gather the mantle of common sense and self-preservation around her again. She was starting to need such moments more and more frequently.

She'd taken such pains to create walls around her heart, to position each brick carefully and hammer it home with all the reasons she and Luca could never be more than friends. Yet one heated glanced from his dark eyes could have those walls cracking. And if she forgot to brace herself, one of his rare smiles had the potential to send them tumbling down until they were nothing but rubble at her feet.

She scanned the room for his tall frame, finding him easily—those broad shoulders standing out in the crowd and making her mouth dry with longing. Even in a crowd, his magnetism didn't pall.

Stop it.

She'd never allowed herself to dream for the impossible and she wasn't about to start now.

Skirting the edges of the crowd, she admired the women's dresses and jewels, the flowers and decorations that brought the room to sparkling life…the extraordinary champagne tower. It was all so wonderfully over the top she couldn't help but enjoy it.

But her gaze returned again and again to Luca, who stood with a group of other men, no doubt talking business. She knew he'd welcome her into the group immediately if she made her way over to him, but…

She pressed a hand to her stomach and swallowed. She hadn't yet won the fight raging inside her—the one that told her to give in to the physical temptation of becoming Luca's lover and to hell with the consequences. The problem was she knew that anything they started now would *not* end happily. She feared it'd end in heartbreak. *Her* heartbreak.

Her eyes stung. He really meant to sacrifice himself on that altar of duty. A woman like her—an interloper into his world with a nightmare of a family—had no hope of changing his mind.

What really broke her heart, though, was that he understood the sacrifice he was making. His white-lipped determination that Benny would never have to make the same sacrifice had told her that.

'Good evening, Signorina Thomas.'

She turned. 'Signor Romano! It's nice to see you again.'

'You are looking a little serious. I hope nothing is wrong?'

Seriously? He of all men could ask that? When he'd been a co-conspirator of this ridiculous plan to marry Luca off to the highest bidder? For a moment her throat closed over.

In the awkward pause that followed, he said, 'I hear you visited Gianni's earlier in the week.'

It was the perfect opening. And she couldn't resist. 'I enjoyed my visit very much. Luca told me of Gianni's history, his grandfather's distress that it had been sold off, as well as how he means to win it back—the plan you and his grandfather have concocted for him.'

'He told you all this?' Signor Romano's jowls worked

before he thrust out his jaw. 'No doubt you subscribe to more modern views, as my daughter does, and disapprove?'

She needed to tread carefully *and* tactfully.

Asset, remember, not a liability.

But Luca had given her her heart's desire. If she could help him in return, she would.

'It's not my place to approve or disapprove, Signor Romano. As I am younger than you, however, it's perfectly true—and natural, I might add—for my views to be more modern than yours…like your daughter's.'

She met the older man's eyes squarely. 'I've told Luca that if he attempts to pressure Benny into marrying for duty rather than love, I'll intervene.'

'Pah! You all think the new-fangled ways are better, but they no more guarantee happiness than the old ways. My Bella fancies herself in love with a man I consider unsuitable. If she follows her heart, it will be broken.'

'And yet if she follows your bidding, you will break her heart instead.'

His head rocked back.

'Why is this young man unsuitable, Signor Romano? Because he's not from your social class?'

He didn't answer, but the set of his mouth told her that her guess was correct.

'Does he not have a job?'

He huffed and puffed for a moment but then shrugged. 'He has a perfectly good job in the city. From all accounts, he works hard.'

She shrugged too. 'So far so good. Does he have a good circle of friends? That's always a good reference for a man's character.'

Did Luca have many friends? He spoke warmly of his cousins. And yet one of them was betraying him.

'Yes, yes. He plays in a soccer team…keeps in touch

with his school and university friends…takes part in work socials.'

From where she was standing, the man didn't sound un-suitable at all. 'So the only strike against him,' she started slowly, 'is that he's not a billionaire?'

Both of them were silent for a long moment, staring out at the partygoers. 'You want the best for your daughter. You want to protect her from harm and hurt. I understand that. I'd do anything to protect my little Fern from harm.'

When she turned back, the indignation had faded from his eyes. 'You think I should meet her young man?'

'I can't see what harm it'd do.'

'It could get her hopes up.'

She smiled. 'I think you're worried you might like her young man.'

He harrumphed. 'Why do you care anyway? I think, perhaps, you want Luca for yourself.'

Her heart clenched, but she refused to allow his words to rile her. 'Luca's a very attractive man, he has a gener-ous heart…and he's been very kind to me.' She pulled in a breath and made herself smile. 'But I'm not the woman for him. The choices he makes, though, will affect Benny.'

'And you are fond of your godson.'

She loved him. And the thought of leaving him and re-turning to Australia—

She shied away from the thought. 'I expect your Bella is every bit as honourable as Luca and would treat Benny well. And I know Luca would do just about anything to make his grandfather—and you—proud.'

'*Me?*'

She glanced up in surprise. 'He looks up to you in a way he wishes he could look up to his own father.'

'I…'

'I don't think giving Luca a wife he respects but doesn't

love, a woman who will spend her whole life pining for another man, is the answer, Signor Romano. It's a recipe for
misery. Misery that the two of them will do all they can
to hide from you and his grandfather. But it will create a
wedge between you all.'

Good Lord. She hadn't meant to say so much. It wasn't
her place, but... 'If your worst fears are confirmed about
Bella's beau and he does break her heart, at least she can
be certain of your unconditional love and turn to you for
comfort and support.'

He stilled. 'There is a ring of wisdom to your words.'

She tried to smile. 'All my life I've wished for a father
who wanted to see me happy, as you do Bella.'

His eyes gentled. 'And this you do not have?'

'No.' She glanced across at the broad-shouldered figure
across the room. 'Neither, I think, does Luca.'

'His grandfather loves him.'

She turned back to Signor Romano. 'Does he? Not above
everything else. While you are primarily concerned with
your daughter's happiness, Signor Vieri Senior is primarily
concerned with regaining the jewel in his empire's crown.
But who's primarily concerned with Luca's happiness?'

Signor Romano's mouth dropped open.

'It seems to me that Luca has to pay the price for his
parents', aunts' and uncles' greed and recklessness, as well
as his grandfather's mismanagement.'

'Monique!'

She swung to find Luca directly behind them—his eyes
blazing and his face pinched white. Her heart thundered
in her ears, but she refused to lower her chin. 'And I don't
think that's fair,' she finished.

'You have no right to speak of this.'

He clenched his hands so hard his whole body shook. His

voice, low and fierce, stung. She'd overstepped the mark.
She'd known it all along, but she hadn't been able to stop.

She turned back to Signor Romano. 'Luca is right. I
spoke out of turn. If I gave offence, I sincerely apologise.'

Signor Romano shook his head. 'She gave no offence,
Luca. In fact, she gave an old man a new perspective.'

Luca blinked.

'Please, will you both excuse me?'

The older man left, and Monique tried not to wince as
she glanced up at Luca. 'How angry are you?'

Some of the fire in his eyes died. 'I do not know. Signor
Romano seemed almost pleased with your conversation.'
He frowned. 'With you raking him over the coals.'

She pulled herself up to her full height, which was still
woefully shy of Luca's six feet two inches. 'I did no such
thing! He spoke to me about Bella, and I gave him my
opinion. I think now he's going to at least meet the man
she's in love with.'

'How...?' He shook himself. '*Why* would you do such
a thing?'

'To get you off the hook.'

'Monique.' His voice held a note of warning.

'And because I don't want a rift to occur between father
and daughter.' She glanced to where the older man was now
in conversation with a group of people across the room. 'It
must be lovely to have a father who cares for you so deeply.'

She started when Luca's warm hand closed about hers.
'Yes,' he agreed.

She squeezed his hand and sent him what she hoped
was a buck-up smile. 'We'll do better. Benny and Fern will
have at least one parent they can always rely on, who will
always do their best for them. They'll know they're loved.'

His mouth firmed. 'I will do everything in my power to
ensure my son's happiness.'

She believed him.

'Now…' he straightened '…you do not have a drink. Have you had ample to eat? Let me get you a glass of champagne and something sweet to nibble.'

'Are you hungry?' Luca said when they returned to the villa later that evening.

'How can I be hungry when you plied me with food all evening?' Ever since confessing she'd gone to bed hungry—that one single time—he'd brought titbits up to the nursery after dinner every night. She'd been treated to bowls of luscious raspberries, ripe peaches, and decadent mouth-watering pastries.

She wasn't hungry, but… 'I'm going to make a cup of tea. Would you like one?'

'You wish to speak to me about something?'

The man always cut to the heart of the matter. She nodded and he gestured for her to precede him into the kitchen.

'I hope Benito is giving you no cause for alarm?'

'None at all.' She put the kettle on and made tea, pushed a biscuit tin towards him. 'Fern and I made Anzac biscuits today—an Australian speciality. It'll make her day if you try one and tell her tomorrow how much you enjoyed it.'

He immediately reached into the tin, and bit into a biscuit. His eyes widened. '*Delizioso!* My new favourite. I will tell her so in the morning.'

Fern and Luca were developing the loveliest of friendships. She bit her lip. Friendship was fine, but…

Fern had suffered too much loss already in her short life. She couldn't allow her niece to start relying on Luca too much. It might be time to start talking to Fern about all the fun they'd have once they returned to Australia—start reconciling her to their future, a future that didn't include Italy or Luca.

She forced her chin up. It wasn't like they'd never see Luca and Benny again. There'd be visits and video calls. They'd simply become part of the wider landscape of each other's lives. Which was fine. Perfectly fine.

'What did you wish to speak to me about?'

She snapped back and glanced at him, hoping he'd take what she had to say in good part—in the way she meant it to be taken. 'Tonight I met several women who I expect are on the list of Suitable Prospective Brides.' She sipped her tea. 'How well do you know these women, Luca?'

His nostrils flared. 'You are again overstepping the mark.'

She couldn't tell if the words were a reprimand or not. It sounded as if he was simply stating a fact. He looked almost…resigned.

She winced an apology. 'I can't seem to help it.'

She could've sworn his lips twitched at her confession.

'It's just… The woman you marry will affect Benny.'

'You think I would choose a wife who would be unkind to him?'

'Not on purpose.' But men could be stupid when it came to women, and she worried that his drive to provide his grandfather with all that the older man wanted would blind him to other things. 'You knew Bella well, obviously, as you said you grew up together. But some of the women I met this evening are awfully young.'

His eyebrows shot up.

'For example, how well do you know Siena Bianchi?

'I've spent very little time one on one with her, but she has always been bright and personable. I have done business with her mother and was impressed with her. Do you have something negative to say about Siena?'

'Not at all. I had an absolutely delightful chat with her. She's friendly and fun—wanted to know all about Australia as she's hoping to travel there one day. She doesn't have a snobbish bone in her body.'

He straightened. 'This is an excellent reference.'

'Except for one minor detail.'

'And that is?'

'She likes women, not men.'

He stared at her blankly.

'She's gay, Luca.'

'How do you know this?'

She raised an eyebrow.

Siena had made a pass at Monique? Luca nearly swallowed his tongue. Did Monique prefer women to men too? He could've sworn…

'And you?' He couldn't prevent the question slipping from his lips.

She sent him the oddest look. 'I'm heterosexual.'

The pounding of his heart slowed. 'Good.'

Her brow knotted. 'Why good?'

Dio! What was he thinking?

'I didn't think you'd be so…' she edged away '…narrow-minded.'

'No! That is not what I meant. I…' He rolled his shoulders. 'I'm merely relieved my instincts haven't led me astray completely.'

A fraught, awkward silence slammed into place. He could've kick himself for causing it. For making them both aware of the attraction that simmered just under the surface whenever they were alone together. The attraction they were doing their best to ignore.

She moistened her lips. He would *not* notice their shine or acknowledge the siren song they sang to him.

'You aren't going to rush into marriage, are you? You

will take the time to get to know a woman well before you propose to her?'

'Of course.'

But the assurance sounded hollow. This hypothetical marriage had seemed an entirely different proposition when Bella had been his prospective bride. He and Bella were friends, he trusted her. He'd known what he was getting into. Now, though…

When Monique was in the room, he couldn't focus on any other woman, barely saw any other women!

He needed to put an end to this dating arrangement. The ground he and Monique were now treading…the lines had become too blurred. The way she'd spoken to Signor Romano this evening had proved that.

'You wish to select my bride for me?'

She choked on her tea. 'Absolutely not!'

'Then why are you vetting these women?'

'To show you what a crazy idea it is to make such a *practical* marriage.'

Exhaustion swept through him. He wanted to close his eyes and rest his head on his arms.

'Luca, don't you want to believe in a strong and true romantic love that will add happiness and strength to your life? It's what I hope and wish for. It's what most people hope and wish for.'

His heart burned. He couldn't afford such sentimentality.

He recalled her words to Signor Romano and his heart burned all the fiercer.

She glanced down at her hands. 'There are other kinds of love that are just as important, of course. Like the love one has for their child—like the love you have for Benny.'

'And you for Fern.'

She bit her lip, glancing away. 'Having Fern is all I've wanted for so long.'

For the first time it occurred to him that it had been unfair of him to ask her to come to Rome. She should've been free to build her life with Fern away from any complications he and his life could create for her.

But the wage he was paying her, and the freedom she had to now finish her childcare qualifications... Those things would help her provide Fern with security. That had to mean something, surely? And then there was her love for Benny. She'd wanted to help him settle into his new life. She'd needed to see him happy and safe.

'I don't need anything else. I don't want to want anything else.'

Her words hauled him back. 'But you deserve so much more.' She deserved to find the strong and lasting romantic love of which she dreamed.

She glanced up with wide eyes, swallowed and nodded. 'I think you deserve so much more too, Luca.'

Who has Luca's best interests at heart?

The pulse at the base of her jaw fluttered. He stared at it, his mouth going dry.

'I don't think anyone has the right to choose your wife for you. I think you should be free to make your own choice.'

'Why are you so set on changing my mind?' He could tell she thought it would add to his happiness, but why did she care? Because he'd given her her heart's desire and she felt she owed him?

She stared at his mouth for a long moment and then shook herself. 'Because you deserve to have someone on your side.'

This woman! Her lips tempted him, but her words undid him. He couldn't help it. His mouth swooped down to hers before common sense could kick back in. And the moment their lips touched common sense scattered on the four winds.

Her lips were warm and soft, spiced with the sweetness of the tea she'd been drinking, and utterly addictive. After the briefest of hesitations, when she'd bowed under the surprise of his initial onslaught, one of her hands slid around the back of his head to hold him close while she kissed him back with a fervour that made the blood stampede in his veins.

His knee knocked the table as he turned more directly towards her and his elbow too as he cradled her face in his hands and swept his tongue across her lips. Her free hand landed on his knee as if to brace against the barrage of sensations that assailed her as his tongue explored the softness of her mouth, enticing her tongue to dance in a kiss that threw every caution to the wind.

Her fingers curled into the firmness of his thigh muscle as if to hold him there, as if to prevent him from moving away. He wasn't going anywhere! But he needed more, needed to feel more of her.

Hauling them both to their feet, he pressed her close, moulding her curves against him—her softness to his hardness. His hand roved across her back and in response she plastered herself against him as if there was nowhere she'd rather be.

The taste of her…the feel of her in his arms… It was like nothing he'd ever experienced. This woman had found her way into his blood, was now imprinted there, never to be forgotten and always to be craved. Throwing back his head, he sucked in a breath. Her hands moved from around his waist to explore the planes of his chest and shoulders through the cotton of his shirt. Her touch sparked explosions of sensation across his skin.

Dazed eyes met his again and her kiss-swollen lips were

an invitation he couldn't resist. His head dipped and she met him halfway in a kiss that tasted like sunshine and joy, wrapped inside a fierceness to rival a summer storm.

Pressing his lips along the line of her throat, he concentrated on her sighs and the tiny sounds she made in the back of her throat, greedy for more, greedy to hear his name on her lips. He cupped one of her sweet, lush breasts through the thin material of her dress, the nipple hardening against his palm. Her gasp dived straight to his groin.

He needed this woman. He needed her naked and writhing beneath him. Every instinct he had told him he would find heaven in her arms, and he craved that with every fibre of himself. But he could not take her on the kitchen table where anyone could walk in!

Holding tight to her upper arms, he held her away from him a fraction so she could meet his gaze.

'What are you saying?' she whispered.

Only then did he realise that he was murmuring in his native tongue. 'That you are bewitching, magnificent… beautiful. That I want you.'

He stared into those amber eyes. 'You make me feel things I never have before. Please, spend the night with me, *tesoro*. Let me make love to you. Let me—'

Soft fingers pressed to his lips halted his flow of words.

She dragged in a breath that made her entire body tremble. 'You make me feel too much.'

'I want the chance to make you feel even more, *cara*.'

She stared, her chest heaving. 'You're suggesting we have a fling? Like the one you and Anita had?'

Her brow furrowed as she mentioned Anita's name, and ice trickled through him. This was no way to win back the respect and reverence for the Vieri name that his grandfather so craved. He no longer had the luxury of acting the playboy.

It was as if she could see that thought flash through his eyes, because she huffed out a laugh. 'Have you given a moment's thought about what would be said if anyone found out we were having an affair? You know my family is utterly disreputable—the papers would say you were consorting with drug addicts and criminals.'

'I know *you* are not like that, Monique.'

'It doesn't change the fact that you wouldn't want to be associated with a family like mine for even a single moment.'

She stepped away, placing her hands on the back of her chair as if she needed its support. 'Before Fern came to live with me the first time, I had a sort of boyfriend.'

Jealousy pooled hot and dark in his gut. '*Sort of* boyfriend?'

'A friends with benefits type of arrangement.'

Dear God. If she suggested such an arrangement for them... 'What happened?' he asked, grinding his back molars together.

'When Fern came to live with me, he stopped coming around, and he stopped calling.'

The fool!

'And I realised that the friendship part of our relationship had meant nothing at all to him.'

The expression in her eyes made him want to tear this unknown man from limb to limb.

'While I'd considered the friendship the most important part of all.' She glanced up, her eyes unfamiliarly dark. 'I made a vow to myself then that I'd never get involved with an emotionally unavailable man again.' She pressed her hands to her stomach. 'And, Luca, you're about as emotionally unavailable as they come.'

He wanted to protest against this conclusion. But... 'You

are right. I am sorry. Please forgive my lack of control this evening.'

'We both lost control.' She dragged in a breath. 'We just have to do better in the future.'

He made a decision then and there. 'It is time to end this plus one arrangement.'

She hesitated, but then nodded.

He thought hard, came to a decision quickly. 'It will be best if I leave Rome for a few weeks.' If he was no longer in the city, his inability to attend certain events might be overlooked. But even if it wasn't, even if he did cause grave offence in several quarters, it was time to prioritise. He needed to uncover the traitor within the company. There was little point in attempting to win respect through networking when he was being undermined at the grassroots.

And with all the recent changes in his life, it was too soon to be thinking of a wife. That needed to be put on hold until he had everything else sorted first.

'Please pack all that Benito, you and Fern will need for a few weeks. We'll leave on Monday.'

'Where are we going?'

'To my place in Tuscany.'

She nodded but didn't smile. 'I'll make sure we're ready.'

And then she was gone.

He dropped back into his chair and rested his head in his hands. A man of honour would not go after her. A man of honour would stop thinking of her in any other way except as his child's godmother. A man of honour would concentrate on earning back his family's good name and assuring his peers that he was a man who could be trusted.

None of that could rid his body's hunger for her.

Enough! There was too much at stake to risk it on a brief affair. Benny needed Monique. His relationship with his godmother was too important to endanger. And Luca was determined to do better by his child than his parents had done by him.

He pushed back his shoulders. He would do what his grandfather had always done. He'd act honourably.

CHAPTER EIGHT

MONIQUE STARED OUT of the car window at rolling green hills, rambling vineyards and stone farmhouses and told herself to focus and take it all in. This was a once-in-a-lifetime trip. Who knew if she'd ever see this part of the world again? She should be storing it up so she could tell everyone at home about it.

But all she could focus on was the unnatural quiet that stretched through the car.

Luca had told her it'd take roughly three and a half hours to reach his *'little place in Tuscany'*. He'd told her it was a converted farmhouse on a little land. He'd even volunteered the information that a woman came up from the nearby village every day to cook and clean whenever Luca stayed.

That had been the extent of their conversation. Sparkling, right? And with the children dozing on the back seat, the quiet that had descended on the car was anything but comfortable.

She considered instigating conversation but dismissed that immediately. Luca was her boss.

Boss. Boss. Boss.

She tried to stamp that word on her brain. It wasn't her place to chatter away like a darned chipmunk. It'd only annoy him and wear her out. Lose-lose. If he wanted conversation, he could initiate it.

She bit back a sigh. If only he acted like her boss and treated her like the hired help. If only she *felt* like the hired help.

Dragging her phone from her handbag, she snapped a couple of happy snaps of the countryside to at least give the impression she was appreciating it…and not obsessing over that stupid kiss.

He glanced at her, but even before she could consider turning to meet those dark eyes, his gaze had returned to the front again, his attention shifting back to driving, capable hands relaxed on the wheel. She forced her hands to stop gripping her phone so hard. 'It's beautiful countryside.'

'*Sì.*'

Smile.

She folded her hands and gritted her teeth. What the hell had she been about, kissing this man?

He kissed you first. He took you off guard. He—

As if that made any difference! She hadn't discouraged him. She'd kissed him back with an eagerness that should make her blush. It didn't. It simply had heat rising through her in a tidal wave of want again.

She shifted on her seat. Luca's knuckles whitened on the steering wheel and a pulse thudded in her throat. Could he sense her need…her frustration? Did he share it?

Stop it!

She did what she could to unclench her thighs and slow her breathing.

A quick glance informed her that his knuckles remained white so she shifted her gaze from the front windscreen to the side passenger window, where she could spare herself the temptation of surveying him in her peripheral vision. She needed to wrangle her wayward desires back under control and remind herself of all the reasons kissing him was the worst idea in the history of the world.

Top of that list, of course, was Fern and Benny. She couldn't let anything that happened between her and Luca affect them. That would be unforgivable.

She wanted, needed—had promised Anita—to create a lifelong relationship with Benny. She took the role of godmother seriously. She knew the impact one person could have on a life, and she meant to have a good and lasting impact on Benny's. She couldn't do anything that would risk jeopardising that. If things between her and Luca became…messy, if she somehow alienated Luca, there'd be no denying it would impact on her and her godson's relationship. She owed it to Benny, and she owed it to Anita, to prevent that from happening.

She owed Fern her full focus too. Her niece didn't deserve a mother figure who was mooning over some man. Fern needed Monique to be fully engaged in their future life together—to show her how to be happy and trust in their future. Not worrying because she sensed her aunt's unhappiness and discontent.

Not that she *was* unhappy or discontented.

Besides, she deserved better too. Luca had given her so much—he'd rescued Fern, he'd given her this opportunity to strengthen her bond with Benny—and she couldn't help feeling she'd let him down in their plus one arrangement, but there was only so far gratitude could and should extend, and she refused to be a martyr to it.

She also refused to pretend that she thought his plan to marry for practical business reasons a good idea. It had disaster written all over it. As his friend she couldn't pretend it was anything else. Not that he'd ever agree with her. And it wasn't like she was actually his friend either, was she?

A fling with her wouldn't change his mind. And although she knew she wasn't the kind of woman he'd ever consider marrying—could her family be any more opposite to his requirements?—if they became intimate…if they had a fling…

A forbidden thrill raced up her spine. Beneath the security of her bra, her breasts grew heavy and her nipples beaded. She gritted her teeth and concentrated on her breathing.

If she and Luca had a fling, and he still went ahead with his cold and clinical marriage, she'd take it as a personal affront. Even though she had no expectation of him becoming serious about her.

It didn't make any sense!

The one thing she did know was that a fling with Luca would complicate everything.

And neither of them needed the drama and inconvenience of that kind of complication at this point in their lives.

'See that farmhouse on the hill?'

She glanced to where Luca pointed; glad to give her mind something new to focus on.

'That is our destination—Casa Speranza.'

Casa Speranza. She repeated it in her mind, fixing it there so she could look up what it meant later.

'It is my home away from home.'

Just for a moment his face cleared, and her chest clenched in response. Whatever else Casa Speranza might mean, it was clear he loved this place.

From here the farmhouse looked large, but it wasn't the huge castle she'd half expected. Grapevines swept down the hillside and through the surrounding fields, and everything looked rich and lush and full of promise. A sigh eased out of her. It *looked* like a home.

'Do you own the vineyard as well?'

He nodded. 'We grow Trebbiano grapes—a white variety we sell to a local distillery famed for its brandy.'

A snippet from a previous conversation came back to her. 'Is this where your grandfather lives?'

'His holding is ninety minutes further north, but he is away from home at the moment, cruising the Mediterranean as the guest on a dear friend's yacht.'

She shook her head. What a life.

'She gestured at the hill. 'How big is it?'

'Thirty acres. It is only small.'

It didn't sound small to her!

Ten minutes later she walked through the front door into a stone-flagged room with beamed ceilings. 'It's lovely!' It was cool and shady and incredibly welcoming, and as she stood there the tension started to slip away.

'If I could, I would spend all of my time here.'

His shoulders had lost some of their hard edges too. 'Then maybe you ought to arrange it so you can.' His entire demeanour told her how much happier he'd be here than in Rome.

'You have an over-inflated sense of the extent of my freedom, Monique.'

She glanced up and their gazes caught and clashed. 'I've seen your home office in Rome, Luca. I don't see why you couldn't establish a similar one here. Just because your parents, aunts and uncles were such hedonists, it doesn't mean you have to be their polar opposite. You're allowed enjoyment and ease too. You're allowed happiness.'

It wasn't her place to say such things! 'Of course,' she managed to choke out, 'what will make you happy is entirely up to you to decide.'

And don't you forget it.

Wordlessly he led her through to the back of the house to a large modern kitchen with a huge open-plan dining and living space. French doors led out to a paved courtyard with a view that stretched over gold and green hills and fields. In the distance a stand of cypress trees stood dark olive against a blue sky and a river sparkled silver as it meandered through the valley.

She clasped her hands beneath her chin and gobbled it all up with a greed she didn't bother trying to hide. 'It's extraordinarily beautiful. And so peaceful. No wonder you love it so much.'

'More beautiful than Mirror Glass Bay?'

She momentarily froze. Why would he ask her such a thing? 'Different,' she managed, her voice unaccountably husky.

'Come,' he said, all brusqueness again. 'I will show you the rest of the house. The children will wake soon.' They'd set the sleeping children on the sofas in the front room.

There was a downstairs bathroom and laundry room, as well as a formal dining room. He gestured to the right of the front door. 'That is my study.' And upstairs there were four generous bedrooms—one a master with an en suite bathroom—as well as a large family bathroom.

She chose the bedroom furthest from the master for herself.

'I think you'll find we'll all be comfortable,' he said.

He was careful not to meet her eyes. She was careful not to meet his. 'More than comfortable,' she agreed, following him back down the stairs. She'd injected a cheerfulness she was far from feeling into her voice and the words rang out too bright and shiny. Behind his back, she grimaced. For heaven's sake, get a grip.

He swung around when they reached the bottom of the stairs and she did all she could to smooth out her face.

'I assume I can leave you to settle the children and organise their lunch?'

'Of course.'

'I'll bring in the suitcases and then must get to work.' He gestured to the door of his study.

'So this is a working holiday, then?' she called out before he disappeared through the front door.

He turned back, his magnificent physique backlit by the sun. The sight pulled her skin tight across her bones with an ache impossible to ignore. His face, though, was in shade, making it impossible to see his expression.

'This is not a holiday, Monique.'

It wasn't?

'It was merely imperative I leave Rome. It is as simple as that.' And then he was gone.

Released from the intensity of his presence, she slumped. Imperative he leave Rome? Because she'd failed as his plus one? An entirely different burn took up residence in her chest then.

After taking the suitcases upstairs, Luca retreated to his study. Closing the door behind him, he rested his back against it and closed his eyes.

Dio. He had to get the better of this *spell* that had him in its grip. He couldn't look at Monique without wanting to drag her into his arms and kiss her until neither one of them could think straight. He continued to relive those few short moments that she'd spent in his arms on Saturday night, aching to repeat them.

He'd found heaven.

But that particular brand of heaven was not meant for him. Striding over to his desk, he switched on his computer and forced himself into his chair. A moment later he was on his feet again, pacing, eventually halting by the window to glare at the terraced landscape outside with its rows of grapevines marching down the hill.

He'd come here to find peace. For as long as Monique remained in residence, though, he'd find none of that.

Send her back to Rome.

The thought whispered through him, the instant remedy tempting him.

A moment later he slashed a hand through the air. She was Benito's nanny, his *godmother*. He couldn't treat her with such casual disregard simply because he found her presence unsettling.

Benito's godmother.

That thought should bolster his resolve and give him strength. Monique was Benito's godmother—a relationship too important for him to risk in the pursuit of a temporary affair. He would control this hunger in his blood, this craving. He was a civilised man, for God's sake, not a beast.

Besides, while Monique might find him attractive, she'd indicated zero interest in any kind of temporary relationship of an intimate nature. She'd walked away from him on Saturday night with considerable—and enviable—ease.

She was fiercely independent, and she wanted to build a good future for her niece in Australia. He had no business, no right whatsoever, distracting her from such a noble goal. No, he would leave her in peace. He would prove to himself and the world that he was better than his parents.

He spent the afternoon shut in his study. He only emerged to feed Benito his dinner and get him ready for bed. He then took his own dinner into his study and shut the door firmly behind him.

Like a coward.

Not a coward—a sensible man. The less time he spent alone with the delectable Monique, the less likely his resolve was to falter. Besides, she had her studies to occupy her and she didn't need his presence interrupting her.

Eventually, though, he could no longer concentrate on

his computer screen, the four walls of the room closing in on him. Emerging into the living room, he collapsed full-length onto a sofa, resting his head back against the soft cushioning, and tried to will the peace he always found here at Casa Speranza into his soul.

Breathe in for the count of four. Hold for the count of four. Breathe out on the count of four. Hold. Repeat. Again. And again.

Very slowly the tightness in his neck and shoulders began to ease and he found he could draw air deeper into his lungs. It felt like an age since he'd been able to breathe so freely and deeply. When was the last time he'd been for a run? Cardio exercise was good for increasing lung capacity. Tomorrow he would wake early and—

'Casa Speranza… Casa Speranza… *Casa* means home…'

His eyes sprang open at the softly murmured words. Monique. Staring intently at her phone.

He feasted his eyes on her. He couldn't help it. How could she look so fresh and vibrant after that long car journey *and* having kept two demanding children happily occupied for most of the day on her own?

She wore the softest of thin lounge pants that did nothing to hide her beguiling shape and a T-shirt of sky-blue that highlighted the blonde highlights in her caramel hair. Yearning rose through him, swift and fast, piercing every defence he'd been at such pains to erect for the past two days.

'*Speranza…speranza…*' she murmured, still staring at her phone. 'It means…'

'Hope,' they both said at the same time.

She nearly dropped her phone as Luca sat up and placed his feet on the floor. 'I… I didn't notice you there. I—'

She broke off to study him through narrowed eyes. 'You look pale…and awfully tired.' Her frown deepened. 'Are you coming down with something?'

He shook his head. 'I am merely weary from too much work and not enough exercise and fresh air. I have not been sleeping well.' His sleep had been disturbed by dreams of a golden woman beckoning to him, but somehow remaining out of reach, no matter how hard he tried to catch up to her. 'I will go for a run tomorrow and that will set me to rights again.'

An awkward silence ensued.

'Casa Speranza.' She moistened her lips. 'Home of Hope. It's a beautiful name for a beautiful place.'

Her approbation warmed him all the way through. 'I am glad you approve.'

'Well…' she sent him a tight smile, edging towards the stairs '… I'll leave you to enjoy the peace.'

It took all his strength to resist the impulse to ask her to stay. A sudden thought, though, made him stiffen. 'Monique?'

She turned at the foot of the stairs, one hand on the banister.

'You are not worried that…' His throat clenched and he had to clear it before he could continue speaking. 'That I will force my attentions onto you? If you are, allow me to assure you—'

'No!' Her eyes widened and she took a step towards him, before halting and pressing a hand to her abdomen. 'Of course I'm not. You're a man of honour. You'd never—'

She closed her eyes and dragged in a deep breath, before meeting his gaze. 'No, Luca, I am not afraid of that. Not at all.'

He fought a frown. Did that mean she was afraid of something else?

'I merely plan to have an early night. I've not been sleeping well either.'

The pleating of her brow and the pursing of her lips told

him she wished she'd not confessed as much. Had she not been sleeping for the same reasons as him? The dragon he'd been doing his best to lull lifted its head.

Her swift intake of breath and the way her eyes flared in answer to whatever she saw in his face told him she recognised his hunger, and that she shared it. His every atom came to electrified life.

She swung away from him and raced up the stairs, her 'Goodnight' drifting down to him like a taunt.

Dropping his head to his hands, he cursed fluently and swiftly in three different languages. Tomorrow he would punish his body with such a gruelling run it would dull and exhaust all these wayward impulses and help to cleanse him of this inconvenient attraction.

By the time he returned from his run the next morning, Luca ached all over. Monique was already in the kitchen with the children, feeding them their breakfast. He stopped to talk to the children and eat a slice of toast he barely tasted. He and Monique barely exchanged half a dozen words.

He locked himself in his study for the rest of the day. At one point, the children's laughter drew him to the window. He watched them romp and play with Monique, all of them laughing in the warm sunshine. An entirely different yearning rose through him then. This was the childhood he'd wanted for himself. It was exactly what he wanted for Benito—warmth, security, laughter…love. As he watched his son drag himself to a standing position, holding onto Monique's hands, at the way he smiled up into his godmother's face, he saw how much Benito loved her.

Dio. How would he ever replace her?

A daring thought burrowed under his skin and started to chafe him. Maybe he didn't have to replace her? Maybe she'd consider staying as *her Benny's* nanny forever? He rubbed a hand across his jaw. Would she give up her dream of running her own childcare centre for that?

With an oath, he swung away from the window. He suspected the answer would be, 'No'.

Still, there was no denying she loved Benito. She'd sacrifice much to ensure his happiness and security. And yet what kind of man would ask her to make such a sacrifice?

A humourless laugh sounded through him. Besides, how would he ever settle on a wife if Monique remained? He didn't notice other women whenever she was near.

He found no answer to the questions that continued to plague him. He wanted nothing more than to cast them aside and join the happy trio outside for a few short hours and leave the future to fend for itself.

In the same way your parents lived their lives? Like your aunts and uncles?

He clenched his hands so hard his entire frame started to shake. No, he was better than that.

When a ping sounded from his computer to announce an incoming email, he obeyed the summons and forced himself back behind his desk. He needed to focus on what he owed the Vieri Corporation—his grandfather, cousins and the generations that were to follow. He would uncover the defector within their midst and cut out the corrupt heart that continued to beat within the company. Once that was done, maybe then he could reassess his future.

A half-formed hope he barely dared acknowledge had started to form inside him. If he could safeguard the Vieri Corporation's future, strengthen its very foundations, and make those foundations virtually unassailable... Wouldn't that be enough? Wouldn't a dynastic marriage then be unnecessary?

If he did everything else right, maybe he could reconcile his grandfather to a new way of moving the company forward. The thought of disappointing his grandfather, the man who had given him so much, sent a bruise blooming over his soul. However, his grandfather wasn't an unreasonable man and if Bella's father could be brought to see a different path for his daughter, then it didn't seem so impossible that his grandfather could be brought to see a different future for Luca too.

Maybe.

When Luca emerged from his study later that evening, he found Monique curled up on one of the sofas, a mug of tea—he sniffed the air, peppermint—on the coffee table, its steam curling into the air. Her eyes raced over the page of the book she held. She turned the page with eager zeal, read the last few lines of the chapter and then let the book drop to her lap.

Only then did she glance up at him, her mouth forming a perfect O. 'Now, I didn't see that coming! The plot thickens.' She held the cover up so he could see—an old Agatha Christie paperback. 'The bookcase is full of them, and I can't believe I've never read her before. This is brilliant.'

He eased down into the sofa opposite and took note of the title, making a resolution to read it once she'd finished. 'I can't remember the last time I read a book.'

'Because you work too hard.' She shook her head, setting her book on the coffee table and reaching for her mug. 'Knowing all you want to achieve, I'm gobsmacked—completely and utterly gobsmacked—that you—'

She broke off, going bright red.

He stared. What had she been about to say? 'That I... What?'

She wrinkled her nose. 'It was nothing...an utter impertinence. Forget it.'

Now he was really intrigued. 'Tell me.' He kept his voice gentle. 'I promise I will not be angry.'

'Even though it's none of my business *and* far too personal?'

He found himself laughing. 'Why does this not surprise me?'

The smile she sent him was rueful, and then she stared at him as if he utterly baffled her. 'It's just… Luca, I know how driven you are, and I applaud your goal to re-establish the Vieri family's good name.'

'But?'

'No buts, just… How on earth did you find the time to not only have a holiday but a holiday fling while you were at it?' she said in a rush. 'It seems so out of character.'

The weariness he'd been fighting all day beat at him again now.

'See?' she said when he remained silent. 'I told you it was none of my business. You don't have to answer.'

'A week before I took that *impromptu* holiday…'

Her gaze sharpened at his emphasis.

'My grandfather came to me with his plan for Bella and I to marry. Or if I didn't think Bella and I would suit explained why another similarly suitable marriage would not only augment our cause but expedite it.'

She stared at him with troubled eyes.

'That holiday was my last hurrah before I buckled down to duty and responsibility.'

Her face softened. 'Your final rebellion. A farewell to youth and fun.'

'Not fun.' He refused to believe his life would be devoid of pleasure, regardless of what path he took. 'But a farewell to the single life, yes.' He lifted a shoulder in what felt like an altogether inadequate shrug. 'And Anita made me laugh, she was excellent company, and she wanted to live in the moment.'

Monique nodded as if she agreed with everything he said.

'We had no thought that there'd be any consequences to our time together.'

'Yes, her pregnancy was a shock to her.'

He hesitated. 'We have not really spoken about her.'

She glanced at him, biting her lip. 'I didn't want to mention her in case it upset you.'

'While I have not mentioned her for fear your grief is still too raw.'

Her smile, brief but kind, made something inside of him tick harder and faster. 'Listen to us dancing around each other's feelings.'

A moment later he felt as if he'd been skewered on the end of a spear when her eyes pinned him to the spot.

'You had your fling…you said your goodbyes…you let her go. And yet, despite what you promised your grandfather, you'd have offered to marry her.'

It was old-fashioned, he knew, but, yes. He would have offered Anita marriage.

'Which tells me there are things that matter more to you than making an advantageous marriage.'

It would've been the antithesis of honour to abandon the mother of his child.

'Can you imagine yourself married to Anita now, Luca?'

He did his best to remember the dark-haired, dark-eyed woman who had made him laugh and momentarily forget the weight he carried on his shoulders, but he could recall nothing of depth, nothing that carried weight. Which was why it was so important Benito had Monique in his life. Through her he would get the opportunity to know his mother.

'The truth?' he asked. 'Even if it sounds hard and un-feeling? Even though I don't want it to?'

'I don't want pretty lies, Luca.'

'You once told me I didn't know Anita, and that is true. We did not share our worries or concerns with each other, or our hopes and dreams. I do not know what she wanted out of life. All I know is that she liked mojitos, loved to dance, and was friendly to everyone.'

He stared at his hands. 'But, no, I cannot imagine my-self married to her.'

CHAPTER NINE

THE RUSH OF relief that raced through her had Monique closing her eyes. She ought to feel appalled…and perhaps it was disloyal to Anita that she didn't. After all, Luca had been her best friend's lover and was the father of her child.

She did what she could to make sense of the thoughts whirling through her, desperately wanting to make peace with them. She'd loved Anita like a sister, missed her every single day. If she could change what had happened—the car accident that had taken her friend's life—she would in a heartbeat.

Dragging in a breath, she tried to imagine what Anita would say to her now if she were here.

Her friend hadn't been in love with Luca. She'd spoken of him fondly, but she hadn't pined for him, she hadn't turned every conversation round to him, she hadn't shed any tears, moped or sighed over him. In fact, after she'd told Monique about the fling and how much fun she'd had on her holiday, she hadn't mention him again until she'd discovered she was pregnant.

No, if anything were ever to happen between Luca and Monique, Anita wouldn't begrudge her friend that.

Not that anything *was* going to happen. But the knowledge made her breathe more easily all the same.

So did the knowledge that Luca wasn't nursing some secret unrequited love in his heart for her friend. She didn't want his attraction to her to be some kind of sticking plaster or panacea.

He'd admitted he barely knew Anita, but...

Oh!

She saw then what he wanted to know. How had she not realised sooner?

Pulling her phone from her pocket, she opened a folder on her photo app and came to sit beside him. His warmth and scent filled her senses, making every cell come alive, but she ignored it as best she could to angle her phone towards him. 'This is Anita, six months pregnant. You can see how well she looks...and how happy she is.'

He leaned in closer. 'Her smile, it could not be any wider!'

He reached out a finger as if to touch Anita's tummy. 'Was she this well throughout her pregnancy?'

'She had a couple of weeks of minor morning sickness in the early days, but after that she glowed. As soon as she found out she was having Benny she gave up coffee and alcohol. Not that she drank that much of either anyway. She did everything she could to make sure he'd be born healthy and happy.'

She showed him multiple photos of Anita as she'd progressed through her pregnancy, and then moved on to the photos of Benny as a newborn. 'I was Anita's birth partner.'

His jaw dropped. 'You were?'

She could only imagine how much he wished he'd been there, so she took her time describing the experience in as much detail as possible. 'It was the most amazing thing I've ever experienced. It felt like a miracle that at the end of it was this most incredibly perfect baby, with Anita counting all of his fingers and toes and radiating so much love that I cried.'

He handed her his handkerchief, and she realised her

cheeks were wet with tears again now. She dried them, and then showed him the pictures she'd taken of Benny during the first seven months of his life. Some of them were of Benny on his own; others were with Anita, Anita's parents or with Monique. She told him the little stories that went along with each series of photographs. It was a joy to talk of that time, to talk about Anita and remember her with such clarity and affection.

'I have seen some of these photos, or others like them. They were on Anita's computer and I have saved them for Benito, but you have given me the context.'

She met his gaze and suddenly realised how closely they'd drifted towards one another.

'You have given me such a gift. You make me feel almost as if I were there and a part of it.'

He should have been there. He *should* have been a part of it.

'I don't know how to thank you.'

'Not necessary.' Their shoulders touched, their thighs touched, and his mouth was too darned close. She should inch back, but she didn't.

'You miss her.'

He said it at the same time as she said, 'Did you ever find out who intercepted Anita's messages to you?'

They were both silent for two beats. 'Yes,' she said in answer to his question. 'I miss Anita every single day.'

'No,' he said in answer to hers. 'There does not seem to be any point now.' He stared at her. 'I'm sorry you lost your friend, Monique. I wish there was something I could do.'

'Thank you.'

'I didn't realise how close the two of you were.' He hesitated. 'Why were you not looking after Benny when I arrived from Italy?'

A pain, swift and sharp, pierced through the centre of

her. 'Skye and my mother had gone to Brisbane and left Fern with a neighbour. They were only supposed to be gone for a day. When they didn't return that evening the neighbour called me.' All the neighbours had Monique's contact details. 'They were gone for a week. I was afraid of the legal implications if I took Fern home to Mirror Glass Bay, so I stayed there to look after her. It was on my second day there that news of Anita's accident reached me.'

A truck driver had fallen asleep at the wheel and crossed several lanes of traffic to slam head on into the car Anita and her parents had been travelling in. They had been returning from a trip to see her mother's heart specialist. They'd been killed instantly. The truck driver was now facing manslaughter charges. Nothing good had come from the tragedy.

His hand closed about hers. 'I'm sorry.'

She shook herself. 'By the time I returned, Benny was already settled in the care of the local nurse-cum-social worker. She was another friend of mine and Anita's, and as she was staying next door with him and I could pop in whenever I liked…' And as they hadn't known if or when Monique might be called to Fern's aid again, it'd seemed like the best solution.

He nodded. 'I see.'

'That day at the motel when we first met, I'd come to your room to introduce myself and arrange a meeting with you to talk about Benny.'

'I am glad you appeared when you did. I knew Benito had a godmother and I had been meaning to contact you, but…'

'You were overwhelmed and still in shock.' He'd come a long way since that day. He and Benny had formed a loving relationship since then. Benny adored his father.

And if she wasn't careful she'd find herself equally smitten.

It took every ounce of strength she had, but she forced herself to her feet. 'It's getting late. It's time for me to say goodnight.'

The downward tilt of his lips, the way he went to speak and then stopped told her he wanted her to stay.

'Goodnight, Monique,' he said instead, and she fled.

'Did you finish your book?'

Luca strode into the living room the following evening and one look at him set her pulse galloping. She told herself she hadn't been sitting here, pretending to read and waiting for him to appear.

She suspected she might be a liar.

'It was fabulous. I've started another.' She held her current book up to show him.

'Excellent. Then I shall now read it.'

He was going to take the time to read a book? She schooled her features to hide her shock.

'You are surprised.'

The amused twist of his lips did the most dangerous things to her blood pressure. 'I'm merely glad to see you taking some R&R.'

'I have been taking stock of many things while we've been here.'

Just as he had yesterday evening, he sat on the sofa opposite. He wore low-slung jeans and the softest of dove-grey T-shirts that contrasted with his dark hair and olive skin. A bone-deep yearning stretched through her.

'Oh?' was all she could manage.

Instead of easing back against the sofa and relaxing into its softness, he planted his elbows on his knees and steepled his fingers. 'I have told you that someone in the

Vieri Corporation—one of my cousins—is attempting to undermine all my grandfather and I are trying to achieve?'

She nodded.

'I am working hard to uncover the identity of this person or persons. It is why I am here, rather than in Rome. It is more important that I unmask this villain than pay court to my business associates in an attempt to ingratiate myself to them.'

'Are you getting close to discovering the guilty party?'

'Closer.' Those steepled fingers tapped twice against his mouth. 'We are hoping my being here will lull them into a false sense of security.'

'We?'

'My cousin Rosetta and I.'

She digested that piece of information. 'I see.'

'I'm not sure you do.' His gaze sharpened. 'Some of the things you have said to me over the past few weeks have made me stop to reassess what I want to achieve…and how I want to achieve it.'

Her?

'It is more important I discover who is causing this trouble within the company than continue the hunt for a wife my grandfather considers suitable.'

She agreed with that one hundred per cent.

'And do you know why?'

'Why?'

'Because it's the honourable thing to do.'

She couldn't stop her eyes from widening. Had he given up the idea of that marriage plan completely?

'Surely it is only right that I have the company's affairs in order before I ask a woman to share my life. My fate is tied to the company and, therefore, hers will be as well.'

'Absolutely. You wouldn't want to be accused of misleading anyone—especially not your future wife.'

'Exactly!'

He frowned. She bit the inside of her lip. 'Something's bothering you.'

He glanced up. 'I cannot help thinking that if Rosetta and I succeed at rooting out the deviant element within the company…'

Yes?'

'And then work hard to consolidate our position, surely that is proof enough of our intent to the wider world? After all, would we not be proclaiming by our very actions that our intentions are above board and honourable? And not just that, but that we also have the strength to withstand any internal leadership challenges.'

Her heart suddenly beat too hard and it was an effort to keep her voice steady. 'It makes sense to me.'

'Rosetta is extremely competent, and the company matters as much to her as it does to me. I've started to wonder why, when she's eighteen months my senior, my grandfather didn't make her CEO instead of me.' His eyes grew troubled. 'I begin to suspect the only reason I am CEO is because I am male.'

She could see the idea disturbed him.

'That is not fair, neither is it honourable. When the traitor in our ranks has been found and dealt with, Rosetta and I are going to restructure the current leadership model and become joint CEOs.'

She couldn't stop from clapping her hands. 'What a perfect solution!'

He smiled, true amusement lighting his eyes as he finally collapsed back against the sofa. 'I knew you would approve. It means that, in sharing the role, I will be at liberty to spend more time with Benito.'

'Both you and Rosetta will have the opportunity to have

a family life alongside your careers. I think that's wonderful, Luca.'

A shadow crossed his face. 'My grandfather comes from an earlier generation when things were done differently. If he were to object to Rosetta's appointment as CEO, I would disagree with him. If he were to demand Rosetta make a marriage to shore up the Vieri name, I would fight against that.'

Everything inside her stilled. 'Are you saying what I think you're saying?'

He leaned forward again. 'What do you think I'm saying?'

She leaned forward too. 'That you recognise the hypocrisy of asking such a thing of yourself.'

Dark eyes throbbed into hers.

'That you're rethinking this plan to make a cold, business-like marriage because you recognise the cost is too high…and that ultimately it's unnecessary.'

'Sì…' The word was drawn from his slowly. 'I must, of course, discuss all this with my grandfather at his earliest convenience. My cousins and I owe him everything. He worked hard and expanded the Vieri Corporation until it become one of the most successful entities in the world, and yet he taught us what it means to be a family too. Without his influence…' He broke off and shook his head. 'I don't like to think of what kind of man I'd be today if it wasn't for him. I might be as grasping and selfish as my parents.'

She doubted that. His grandfather had given him and his cousins not just an amazing financial legacy but something even more important—love. Like Signor Romano, though, the older man would be set in his ways. Still…

'He loves you, Luca, and he knows you love him. When

you explain how you feel, he'll understand. Just as Signor Romano did with Bella.'

'I hope you're right.'

'You say he taught you the value of family. If that's the case I don't think you have anything to fear.' He and Signor Romano were good friends. They shared the same values and outlook. Once Luca had a chance to talk to his grandfather all would be well.

'Your words are wise and they give me hope.'

His smile, brief and dazzling, momentarily blinded her. She swallowed and forced her mind back to the conversation. 'If you can discover which of your cousins is double crossing you, surely that will prove your worth to your grandfather.' She hesitated before giving voice to a growing conviction. 'I think you ought to trace who intercepted the messages Anita sent to you, Luca. It might lead you to the traitor you're looking for.'

One eyebrow lifted. 'You are most anxious I discover that culprit.'

'It was a wicked thing they did.' They'd stolen seven months of his son's life from him. She'd loved every moment she'd spent with Benny, had loved being Anita's birth partner, but she didn't want any of that at the expense of the man in front of her. He should've had those experiences, not her.

'Then I will see what I can find out.'

He thought it was his parents. Instinct told her he also thought his parents were in league with this rogue cousin. That was why he was so suspicious that day he'd found his mother in his office. Maybe the one would lead to the other.

In the meantime, she wanted to rid him of the bitterness stretching through his eyes. 'I'm glad you're fighting for the life you deserve, Luca, and the marriage you deserve.'

She knew it made no difference to him and her. Their

lives were too different, too incompatible. They had no future together. She knew that, but… 'You're a good man. You deserve to be happy.'

Her warmth and sincerity should have sent a corresponding warmth spreading through him. And it did. But it also unleashed a fierce heat into his blood. The heat didn't race through him like a bolt of lightning, but its inexorable progression was like a wall of water flattening everything in its path. 'How can I consider marriage, *cara*, when I can think of no woman but you?'

Her eyes widened. 'Oh, Luca,' she whispered.

Dio. 'I should not say such things.' He shot to his feet. 'I promised that you would be safe from my attentions and I meant it. I will bid you goodnight.'

He'd not taken two steps before soft fingers circled his arm, pulling him to a halt. He dragged in a ragged breath. 'Monique, what are you doing?'

'I don't know. I…'

Her eyes reflected both his turmoil and his hunger. 'I can promise you nothing,' he growled. 'You should run from me as fast as you can.'

Her chin lifted. 'Can you promise me friendship?'

He stilled. 'Always.'

She reached up on tiptoe then as if to kiss him, but he held her off. 'Do you know what you are doing?'

'Following my instincts…my desires. Now that you've removed the spectre of the other woman—and, yes, I know she was hypothetical, this woman you talked about marrying, but she still felt real to me—it leaves me free now to do what I've been longing to do. To kiss you, Luca. And more. Without guilt.'

His hands curled about her arms. He had to fight against the urge to draw her near. 'You deserve more. You—'

'What if I don't want more?' she whispered. 'Luca, both of our lives are in flux at the moment. Neither one of us is in a position to make those kinds of promises.'

Did she mean that? He tried to concentrate over the stampede of hunger her words sent raging through him. What if *he* wanted more?

'No promises beyond friendship. And no regrets.'

If they had friendship; if they had trust…what more could he want? He was so tired of watching his every move, weighing his every action, and more than anything he wanted to lose himself in this woman and live in the moment.

She drew back, uncertainty flickering in her eyes. 'If I've made a mistake, misread what you wanted, I'm sorry. I thought—' She broke off, swallowing. 'How awkward. If I've made you feel uncomfortable, I apologise. I—'

He reached out and touched a finger to her lips. 'You're not mistaken, *il mio cuore*. I want you with every fibre of my being, but I am no longer an impulsive youth. Also, I keep feeling the need to pinch myself. I keep thinking I'm going to wake, and you'll be gone.'

She stared so deeply into his eyes he felt she must touch his very soul, and then she smiled, and his heart stopped beating for a moment before giving a giant kick. 'I'm not going anywhere, Luca.'

He allowed himself, finally, a totally male, totally wolf-ish smile. 'I am going to make such love to you that your knees will go weak and your bones will turn to water.'

Her breath hitched and quickened.

'I hunger to hear your name on your lips when—'

It was her hand on his lips this time, halting his words, and she gave a shaky laugh. 'Shut up and kiss me already.'

In answer, he lifted her into his arms and started for the stairs. 'Once I start kissing you, *cara*, I do not want to stop. And while the sofas are comfortable, if Fern were to come looking for you...'

'Good point.' She pressed a series of kisses along his jawline and the light sensual touch drew his muscles tight. 'I don't want Fern knowing about us, Luca.'

He halted halfway up the stairs to stare at her.

'She's only three and she's had more upheaval in her short life than anyone should ever have. I don't want anything to upset her current equilibrium.'

He nodded slowly. Their children's welfare must come first. 'I would never do anything to purposely hurt or upset Fern.' He'd grown increasingly fond of the little girl.

'I know.'

She tunnelled her fingers through his hair and this time her touch was neither soft nor tentative. It was sure and urgent. And somehow carnal. It had him imagining those hands on his body and—

He stumbled.

'Maybe it's me who'll make your knees weak,' she murmured, her teeth tugging gently on his earlobe.

Gritting his teeth, he made it to his bedroom and set her gently on her feet before closing the door silently behind them. Turning back, he went to gather her in his arms, but she held him off. 'I want to see you.'

Her voice was a husky whisper that brushed against nerve-endings already taut with need and he had to bite back a groan, but he submitted to her request without murmur. When she seized the hem of his T-shirt and lifted it, he raised his arms and let her draw it over his head.

She dropped the shirt to the floor, took a step back, one hand going to her mouth. Moonlight flooded the room from the two enormous windows on the adjacent walls and he watched her eyes widen in awed appreciation and couldn't stop his shoulders from going back and his chest from puffing out. When she looked at him like that, he felt he could take on the world.

Kicking herself forward again, she unbuttoned his jeans and eased them and his briefs down his hips and legs. He stepped out of them and she rose, staring, her eyes roving over his body before she lifted her gaze to his face. 'You're beautiful, Luca.' She moistened her lips. 'The most beautiful man I've ever seen. Beautiful all the way through.'

It took all his strength not to drag her into his arms and ravage her then and there. First, though, he wanted to see her naked too, but he sensed an edge of shyness in her that made him curb his impatience.

Pulling her gently to him, he pressed kisses to the corner of her mouth, working his way along her jaw to the line of her neck, taking his time until her head dropped back on a sigh to give him as much access as he desired. Only then did he ease the T-shirt from the waistband of her shorts and pull it over her head. Flicking open the clasp of her bra, he eased it from her body as he bit gently down on her earlobe.

Rather than reaching for her breasts and cupping them in his hands, he splayed his hands across her back and pressed her against him, the friction of their bodies feeding the wildfire of desire burning between them. And as she slowly turned to him more fully, he felt a sense of privilege he'd never before experienced.

Her hands explored the shape of his shoulders, the muscles in his back, and all the while she pressed kisses to his collarbone and the base of his throat. His entire frame started to shake with his effort to hold himself back. He refused to gobble and devour like a greedy wolf. Instead, he danced his fingers down her spine to her waist. When he and Monique finally came together, he wanted her as hungry and mindless as him.

Her mouth closed over one of his nipples and his body

jerked, the sensation shooting straight to his groin. *Dio*, this woman! Sliding his hands up her sides, he grazed her nipples with his thumbs.

Her gasp and the way she arched into his touch encouraged him to repeat the action, again and again. 'Luca, please...' His name seemed to be drawn from the very depths of her and only then did he cup her breasts, lowering his mouth to lathe the tight buds of her nipples with his tongue until she was clinging to his shoulders, her breath sawing in and out.

Easing back slightly and trying to steady his breathing, he caught her gaze. Lowering his hands to the waistband of her shorts, he very gently eased them over her hips. Kneeling before her, he pressed a kiss to her stomach as he lowered her panties down her legs as well. Lifting each foot by the ankle, he eased her clothes away so she wouldn't become tangled in them.

He knelt there and gazed up at her. '*Cara*, you are exquisite.'

She stared up at him with wide eyes full of need and a vulnerability that almost undid him. 'I've never wanted anyone the way I want you, Luca,' she whispered. 'Please tell me you have protection.'

Her words were breathless and raw, and he gave up fighting the need pouring through him. 'In the bedside drawer,' he growled, lifting her onto the bed and falling down beside her. Their mouths finally met in a kiss of fierce ardour and equally fierce tenderness. That tidal surge of desire picked them up in its current and hurtled them into a maelstrom of pleasure and sensation.

He explored her every inch, and she explored his—with hunger, delight...joy. Their cries and moans mingled until he didn't know where he finished and she began, but all the time they moved closer and closer towards a pinnacle higher than any other he'd ever before scaled.

Until, with a cry, Monique hurtled from its heights, her body arching into his, her muscles clenching around him, and he followed, soaring into an explosion of colour and sensation that left him floating gently to earth and feeling as if he'd been remade into a new man—one of steel and diamonds and sunlight.

He rolled them over, shaping her to his side. *'Dio!'* He could barely catch his breath. He told her he thought her beautiful, amazing, magnificent.

Her soft laugh was warmth personified. 'I've no idea what you're saying, Luca. But I suspect I agree. That was... There aren't words in the English language adequate enough to describe it.'

She nestled into his side and Luca drifted off into a dream-free sleep, wondering if he'd ever before in his life felt such a complete sense of well-being.

Luca woke to soft morning sunshine and the sounds of birds chattering in the vines outside. Without opening his eyes, he reached for Monique, but his arms came back empty. He sat up with a frown.

Her side of the bed was empty. Monique had gone.

Rubbing a hand over his heart, he forced himself back down to the pillows. It didn't mean anything was wrong. It didn't mean she regretted last night.

One of the children might have needed her. He swallowed. Or she might simply prefer to sleep in her own bed.

Friendship and no regrets, that's all they'd promised each other. He stared at the ceiling, replaying last night's lovemaking in his mind, and slowly his tension eased. Monique wouldn't regret what they'd shared. She'd hold it close—a cherished memory—just as he did. As for friendship, surely that had only been strengthened by what they'd shared.

Monique wouldn't go back on their promises. Yet none of that eased his disappointment at not waking beside her this morning.

If he'd needed reassurance, the smile she sent him when he walked into the kitchen a short while later gave it to him, as did her cheery, 'Good morning.'

He checked the impulse to kiss her. Both Fern and Benito were at the breakfast bar, eating their breakfast. He swooped down to give his son a kiss and ruffled Fern's hair before planting himself on the one remaining stool and pulling a packet of cereal towards him. Monique handed him the milk and nibbled a piece of toast.

'What do you three have planned for the day?'

Monique started and a faint pink stained her cheeks. Had she been remembering last night? How long did he have to wait before he could have his wicked way with her again?

'We thought we might go exploring.'

'I want to go down to the river,' Fern told him solemnly.

River? 'Do you mean the stream at the bottom of the hill?'

Fern nodded her little head hard. 'I want to go swimming.'

'It's not deep enough for swimming, I'm afraid. It's only ankle deep.'

She cocked her head to one side. 'So I could paddle?'

'You can paddle,' Monique agreed.

'It's further than it looks,' he warned.

'I'll pop Benny in his stroller, then. The path down looks sturdy enough.'

True, but her arms would get tired, pushing it back up the hill again. And what of Fern and her little legs?

'Would you like to join us?' Monique asked, as if reading his mind, her eyes dancing, and he had to fight the urge to reach across and drag her mouth to his. 'Or do you have to work?'

'I have to work.'

Her face fell.

'But maybe I could work this afternoon instead and take the morning off.'

Her smile and Fern's cheer were his rewards. After all, he told himself, it'd only be for a couple of hours. And Monique might need help with the children.

Ninety minutes later he found himself sitting on the bank of the little stream in the shade of a linden tree. Fern happily paddled while Benito sat on the blanket beside Monique, attempting to eat a banana but mashing most of it between his fingers.

'I missed you this morning,' he said in a low voice as Monique wiped banana from Benito's leg.

She glanced up. 'I'm sorry. I just thought it'd be best if I slept in my own bed.' She glanced at Fern. 'In case someone came looking for me.'

It made perfect sense. It shouldn't chafe at him so.

'Is everything okay?'

Her soft question snapped him back. '*Sì*, it is perfect, *cara*.'

'Auntie Mon, when will Benny walk properly so he can paddle too?'

'Probably not for another couple of months, pumpkin.'

The little girl frowned. 'And he's too little to swim yet.'

'Ah, but think of the fun we'll have when Benny's older and comes for holidays to Mirror Glass Bay. You'll be able to teach him to swim.'

When she returned to Mirror Glass Bay? He fought a frown. Of course she would eventually return there. It was her home.

Fern jumped up and down, clapping her hands. 'Come and paddle with me, Luca!'

He shot to his feet. Somewhere along the line, Fern had won him over with her shy smile and enchanting sense of humour. He was hers to command as she pleased.

Monique stripped Benito to his nappy and soon followed.

He allowed Monique's laughter, Benny's squeals of delight and Fern's chatter to ease the burning in his soul. He didn't know what the future held, but for today he would simply live in the moment.

CHAPTER TEN

THE REST OF the week and most of the next passed in a haze of fun and sensual delight. Monique had never known such peace and happiness. Luca continued to work, and work hard, she suspected, but he'd do his best to spend at least a morning or afternoon each day with her and the children. They'd amble around the vineyard, discovering hidden nooks, and have picnics beside the grapevines. Other times they visited the nearby town and ambled along its cobbled streets, eating gelatos.

And at night she and Luca made love—learning each other's bodies, discovering what gave the greatest pleasure, and talking into the wee small hours. She hadn't known a lover could be as giving as Luca, as patient and sensitive...as skilled.

She swallowed. For as long as they remained here at Casa Sperenza—Home of Hope—it felt as if nothing bad could ever happen. It felt as if they were contained in their own little bubble where the real world couldn't touch them.

It was an illusion. A foolish fancy. As was the hope that had grown in her heart, despite her best efforts to prune it into submission.

Casa Sperenza—Home of Hope—and she had a heart of hope. It would all end in tears—her tears. Yet she couldn't find it in her to regret a single moment of her time with Luca. It's not as if she'd meant to fall in love with him.

In her weakest moments she'd imagine Luca finding a way to fit her into his world. After all, he'd found a solution to Fern's situation so easily. Couldn't he do the same for them?

If he wanted to, he could.

She made herself face that fact with eyes wide open. If Luca wanted to pursue a permanent relationship with her, he could.

But, despite all her romantic foolishness, she was a realist. Just because he'd decided against making a cold marriage of convenience, it didn't mean he'd be prepared to marry a girl with the kind of family Monique had. Her mother and sister would be a thorn in his side forever— wanting money, threatening and probably giving entirely false exposés to the tabloids.

God! The thought made her own stomach churn and she had nothing left to lose at their hands. But Luca had everything to lose. He was trying so hard to redeem and reclaim his family's good name. Marrying her wouldn't help him achieve that. In fact, it'd probably hinder it.

'Impossible,' she told herself for the hundredth time. Anything beyond a temporary affair was impossible.

'It's all set,' Luca told her, late in their second week. 'The trap has been laid and now all we need to do is watch and wait. Soon we will know who the guilty culprits are.'

Everything inside her drew tight at his words, at the determination gleaming in his eyes. She knew then, even before he spoke again, that their idyll at Casa Speranza was at an end. 'That's excellent news.' She made herself smile. 'Once you've dealt with the culprits, you and Rosetta can finally move forward.'

He nodded.

'I'm happy for you, Luca.' And she meant it. 'You've worked hard to uncover this conspiracy. When do we leave for Rome?'

'In the morning.'

'I'll make sure we're packed and ready.'

She played with the children. She kept the smile on her face. She refused to let her internal disquiet ruin the peace and contentment they'd all found here. But that night their lovemaking took on a desperate edge.

Afterwards, when they were lying side by side, both panting from their exertions, he gripped her hand. 'When we return to Rome...'

He didn't finish the sentence, but she knew what he wanted to say. Only he didn't know how to say it. She took the initiative from him. 'If we want to continue our affair—'

'I most definitely do. Do not be in any doubt of that, *cara*.'

So did she. If she were a sensible woman, she'd end it now. But apparently she wasn't a sensible woman. 'Then we keep it just between us. We keep it secret.'

He didn't say anything for several long moments. She wanted him to argue. She wanted him to make their relationship public...official.

'Yes,' he finally said. 'Secret. Our business and nobody else's.'

Her heart sank, though. She was a fool for wanting more. She refused to let her chin drop. He had enough people already pressuring him into taking this direction or that. She refused to join their number.

'It'll be for the best,' she forced herself to say. She didn't need anyone else to witness her humiliation and heartache when the time came.

'I wish we could stay here forever.'

It wasn't the same as wanting her forever, though, was it? 'Me too,' she found herself whispering back anyway.

They made love again—fierce, hungry, wild love. To-night, though, she didn't wait until he fell asleep before she left his bed.

Monique and the children barely saw Luca over the course of the next five days. Oh, he popped up to the nursery for an hour each evening. And two of the five nights he'd taken her to his room, where they'd made love with as much fervour as ever, but she couldn't help feeling he was slip-ping away from her. The real world—*his* real world—had started to reclaim him.

And she missed him more than she could say.

Not that he took up all her thoughts. She loved spend-ing her days with Fern and Benny. The children could be a handful—they were growing fast—but they were an abso-lute joy. Her life was blessed. She reminded herself of that over and over, counted those blessings every single day.

The garden was their favourite haunt. They spent much of their days tumbling on the lawn, exploring the gardens and playing. To stop Fern from missing the delights of Casa Sperenza too keenly, Monique had created a game that was a combination of croquet, skittles and basketball, though they used soft mallets and foam balls, plastic rather than wooden skittles, and a waist-high basketball hoop.

It was Fern's favourite game, and as Benny's favourite thing was crawling after Fern, it kept them entertained for ages. Especially when she taught Fern a couple of Italian songs and they sang them as they played. Benny clapped his hands and joined in the best he could.

They were in the midst of one such fast and furious game when a voice—full of laughter and longing—said, 'You look as if you're having the most splendid fun.'

Luca.

Benny crawled over and demanded, 'Up! Up!'

Fern raced over and flung her arms around his legs.

He picked Benny up and rested a hand on Fern's hair, glancing down with a smile so gentle Monique's heart clenched at the picture they made.

At the picture *he* made.

Would he one day re-create this idyll of family and belonging with another woman, a woman from his world? The thought was a knife to her heart.

Fern handed him the croquet mallet. 'Come and play too.'

Snapping to, Monique settled her game face into place and pointed to a ball. 'First you have to negotiate the croquet course before knocking down all the skittles, and then shooting a hoop.'

As Luca played, his usual seriousness gave way to a sense of playfulness that had both children chortling and wanting to be close to him.

'Benny's too little to play it properly.' Fern's little shoulders drooped on her sigh.

'But it's a game we can play when we're back home in Mirror Glass Bay,' Monique reminded her.

The little girl brightened. 'So we can play it with him when he's a big boy of three like me.'

Behind Fern's back, Luca frowned, but Monique did her best to ignore it. That frown meant nothing. 'Exactly! Which will be loads and oodles and gazillions of fun.'

'Oodles and gazillions!' Fern giggled, before rounding back on Luca 'Teach us a song,' she demanded. 'Please,' she added as a hurried afterthought when Monique raised a pointed eyebrow.

He started to sing, but Fern interrupted him. 'Auntie Mon has already taught us that one.'

He turned to Monique, that tantalising mouth dropping open, sending a giddy rush of excitement surging through her.

'In Italian?'

'*Sì.*' She nodded. 'Let's show him, Fern.'

They all sang the song, and then Luca taught them another. Benny had started to rub his eyes, his head drooping before starting awake again. Monique was about to suggest it was time to return to the house when at that exact moment a fat raindrop landed on her head.

She glanced up and gulped at the dark clouds that had gathered overhead. More fat drops fell. They'd been so intent on their game she'd not noticed the sky darkening. They were at one of the furthest points from the house too. They'd be drenched before they reached it.

'Come on.' Luca reached down and pulled her to her feet, thrusting Benny into her arms and catching Fern up in his. 'The summerhouse is nearby. We can shelter there until the storm passes.'

'It's locked,' Fern told him.

He grinned. 'But I know where the key is kept.'

Fern had been dying to get inside the summerhouse with its indoor pool visible through the myriad windows ever since they'd discovered it. Monique owned to a sliver of anticipation too. It had looked wonderful from the outside when they'd peered through the windows.

'Princess Fern has been wondering how to get into the enchanted glass palace.'

Luca reached above the doorframe for the key, unlocked the door and ushered them all inside. 'As long as Princess Fern has her Auntie Monique with her, she can visit any time she wishes to.'

Monique couldn't help smiling when Fern cheered and wriggled to get down.

'I love you, King Luca,' Fern yelled as she raced towards the pool.

'No running,' Monique called after her. 'And be careful near the edge. I don't want you falling in and taking an unnecessary dip. Promise me?' she persisted. Her niece could be a little monkey when it came to the water.

'I promise, Auntie Mon!'

Only then did Monique fall down onto a banana lounge and try to control the pounding of her heart. *I love you, King Luca.* What had she been thinking, allowing Fern to grow so close to Luca? She thought she'd been doing enough, reminding Fern that their time in Italy was finite, that they'd be returning to Mirror Glass Bay…without Benny and Luca.

It obviously hadn't been enough. She should have been more vigilant! How could she have let this happen? Fern had suffered enough separation in her short life.

She eased back as Benny snuggled in against her chest. He'd be asleep in two minutes flat. She glanced across at Luca, who still stood by the door as if frozen to the spot. Her heart pounded. She had to mitigate the damage. Somehow.

Luca swung towards her, his eyes dazed, before he lowered himself to the lounge beside her. *'Dio…'* he murmured. 'Did you hear what Fern said to me?'

All too clearly.

She nodded. The stunned expression in his eyes made all the sore places inside her ache.

His mouth worked. 'Are children always so reckless with their hearts?'

'Not reckless, generous,' she corrected. She glanced at her niece, her heart aching. 'They haven't learned to be guarded yet.'

'It is terrifying! How do we keep them from getting hurt?'

'We can't. It's impossible.' Though her heart clenched

at the thought. 'Nobody gets through life without getting their heart bruised.' She made herself smile. 'We just do our best to be a soft place for them to land.'

She fought the urge to reach across and clasp his hand. 'We do our best, Luca. That's all we can do.'

He stared at her and she had to swallow the temptation that trickled through her. Now wasn't the time to get caught up in the shape of his lips or the breadth of his shoulders. Or that lazy slumbrous look in his eyes.

She forced her gaze back to Fern, who was busy making a circuit around the summerhouse to stare out of each window in turn. She moistened suddenly dry lips. 'While we're on that subject…'

He leaned towards her, and his amber scent drifted across to play havoc with her senses. 'Yes?'

'When I return to Australia there'll be a lot video calls to keep us all connected, yes? So Benny doesn't forget me, so he knows I haven't forgotten him.'

'*Sì.*'

'I'll always make time for him.'

'I know this, yes. You love him.'

'I have a favour to ask. When Fern and I first return to Australia, will you make a little time for Fern? I know you've no legal or moral obligation to her.' She smoothed a hand down Benny's back, pressed a kiss to the top of his head before meeting Luca's gaze again. 'But she cares about you, and I don't want her feeling hurt or abandoned.'

'I care for her too! I…*love* her.' His words were low and vehement. 'I will always make time for her.' His gaze softened at whatever he saw in her face and he reached across and took her hand. 'This I promise you, Monique.'

It would help to mediate the damage already done, but it wouldn't undo it completely. She needed to start curtailing the amount of time Fern and Luca spent together.

'I had fun playing your game earlier.'

He kept hold of her hand and it made her blood dance through her veins.

He frowned, as if trying to work out a difficult puzzle. 'It would not be that fun with anyone else.'

His words startled a laugh from her. 'Of course not. Fern and Benito are the best children in the world.'

'I meant you.'

The look he sent her made her heart falter.

'I meant no other woman could have made that game so much fun.' His frowned deepened. 'No other woman could ever love Fern and Benny the way that you do.'

Was he saying what she thought he was saying? Her heart beat so hard it almost hurt.

'Stay,' he said, turning to her with an earnest intensity that smashed through every barrier she'd tried to erect around her heart.

'Stay?'

In what capacity? Her heart thundered in her ears. Had he found a way to make a relationship between them work? Had he—?

A sudden splash broke the silence. Before Monique had even registered that Fern had fallen into the pool, Luca was on his feet and had dived into the pool, fully clothed, to lift up a spluttering Fern.

The little girl blinked water from her eyes. 'Why did you dive in wearing all your clothes, Luca?'

'To rescue you.'

'But I can swim. See? The water's warm, Aunty Mon!'

Monique subsided back into the banana lounge, re-adjusting Benny against her shoulder. Her mind was a whirl of confusion as Luca ushered Fern out of the pool, found towels and dry clothes for them—a sweater that came down past Fern's knees—and snacks. Soon Fern had fallen asleep on the cushions she'd piled beside Monique's lounge.

Luca had dressed in tracksuit pants and a T, and he looked casual and virile and more tempting than ever, but a storm to rival the one outside raged in his eyes.

Because he wanted her to stay? She couldn't prevent the leap her heart gave.

'Dio!' he bit out, his voice low, his hands clenched. 'I thought Fern...'

She suddenly realised the emotion in his eyes was fear. And it wasn't for Monique but for Fern. There was nothing of the lover in his gaze, nothing of...

How many different ways could she call herself a fool? With an effort she swallowed and nodded. 'I'm sorry she frightened you.'

'Frightened? She terrified me! I thought...' He seemed to rein himself in before letting out a long breath. 'She can swim?'

'I live near the beach. I've been getting her lessons since she was six months old.'

He was silent for a long moment and then nodded as if coming to a decision. 'I meant what I said before. I want you to stay.'

Reality rose up to smack her in the face with cold, hard sense and her heart shrivelled to the size of a cold, hard pebble. 'You want me to stay as Benny's nanny.' It wasn't even a question.

'You love Benny and care for him as no other woman could. And if you stay, I can keep an eye on Fern, keep her safe and—'

'No!'

His head rocked back at her vehemence. 'What have I done, *cara*? What have I said wrong?'

She tried to rein in her raging emotions. What she

needed to do—the solution that had been staring her in the face since Fern had told Luca she loved him—hit her now. She just hadn't wanted to face it. 'I can't stay, Luca. I'm sorry. In fact… I can't stay here in Rome any longer. I need to return to Australia immediately.'

His eyes went suddenly wild. 'What do you mean? You promised me a year. There are months yet before your scheduled return to Australia.'

'Benny is settled and happy here. He loves you and Anna is great with him. He'll be fine without me.'

'But—'

'Fern has come to rely on you too much and I need to nip that in the bud now, before she's in danger of being hurt even more.'

'That is not necessary. It—'

'Do you see a future for us, Luca?' She broke in over the top of him. 'You and me and the children as a proper family?'

He paled and she could see it wasn't a scenario he'd considered. 'We made no promises to each other,' he said in a low voice.

She made herself smile, even as her heart shattered into a million jagged pieces. 'We promised friendship and no regrets, Luca, and if I'm to keep that promise I need to call a halt to all of this and return home.'

'Can you not give me time to consider what you're asking? I…'

She'd started to shake her head even before he trailed off. 'If I stay, Luca, I'm going to start wanting more from you. I'm going to fall in love with you.'

He flinched. She hadn't thought she could hurt more than she already did. That flinch proved her wrong. 'Look, the storm's passed.' She refused to focus on the pain. She didn't want to break down in front of him. She pushed to her feet. 'It's time to take the children back to the house.'

Luca strode into the grand perfection of the Villa Vieri, but the dwelling held no more cheer for him now than it had when he'd been a child. In another two days Monique and Fern would be gone and what happiness he'd started to associate with the place would likewise be gone.

His hands clenched. He didn't want her to go, but that didn't mean he loved her. *It didn't.* He'd been mistaken about love once before. Camilla hadn't loved him and yet he'd been so sure and certain. He didn't *think* Monique would try to manipulate him, but wasn't her declaration just another form of manipulation? Just as Camilla's had been?

He refused to trust his instincts. And before he did anything as earth shattering as propose marriage to a woman, he needed to speak to his grandfather and reconcile the older man to *everything*.

At least he and Rosetta had uncovered the traitor within their ranks. Today they'd finally emerged victorious. Only victory hadn't tasted sweet. The fight had been dirty, ugly... and far from edifying.

Nonetheless his parents, one aunt and uncle, and a perfidious cousin who'd been cowed by his parents, had resigned from the board. Once the lawyers had provided the guilty parties with the evidence of their culpability, a collection of the various contracts bearing forgeries of Luca's signature, not to mention the recorded conversation Rosetta had made—Rosetta, who they'd thought they'd won to their side—they'd had no option but to step down or risk facing criminal charges.

Rosetta and he were now joint CEOs. From this day forward they would share the burden, responsibility and privilege of leading the Vieri Corporation into the future. He should be happy, over the moon, exultant.

Instead, he felt flat, demoralised…exhausted.

When he entered the nursery, he found Monique holding a sleeping Benito in her arms, tears pouring down her cheeks.

'I'm sorry,' she hiccupped when she saw him standing there. 'I can't seem to stop.'

Friendship and no regrets. *He* could at least keep *his* word.

Very gently he took the baby from her and placed him in his cot, and then pulled her into his arms, stroking her back as silent sobs racked her. His heart clenched. She had always understood how difficult the parting would be from her godson, but that had not stopped her loving him with her whole heart.

She could stay. She didn't need to leave. He—

He shook the thought off. He couldn't ask her to stay. He owed his allegiance to the family corporation and his grandfather. And she deserved more than to be a guilty secret he kept hidden away. She was right to want to leave.

'I wish I could make this easier for you, *il mio cuore*.'

She pulled away, wiped her eyes, and gave him a brave smile that had a groan rising through him. 'What does that mean…*il mio cuore*? I keep meaning to look it up.

'My heart,' he murmured, his collar tightening about his throat. 'It is like saying sweetheart or darling in English.'

'My heart,' she repeated. 'Such an expression should be more than a casual endearment.'

Something deep inside him tensed. Would an honourable man, a truly honourable man let this woman go?

Or would keeping her merely prove that he was made in his parents' image—selfishly taking want he wanted without a thought for who it might be hurting?

He took a step back. He refused to be that man. Monique was right to leave. He and Benito would be perfectly fine without her.

'I need to thank you. You organised drug and alcohol counselling for Skye and my mother. While my mother has declined the offer, Skye hasn't. She emailed me to let me know.'

He blinked at the change of subject. 'Something you said made me realise I'd thrown my money around recklessly. I wanted to do what I could to mitigate any potential damage I'd done.'

He was an honourable man. And he had every intention of remaining that way. 'Is there anything you need? Anything I can do to help?'

She searched his face, but very slowly the light in her eyes died and her gaze dropped. 'I don't think so, but thanks for asking.' She gestured at Benito, who was starting to stir. 'I'll leave you to have some quality time with your son.'

With those words she turned and left.

And he refused to call her back.

Luca's grandfather arrived ten days after Monique and Fern left. Luca had done his best to shore up the hole that yawned through the centre of him with their absence. It would take time to adjust, he told himself for the hundredth time. That was all.

But how much time would it take? It'd already been ten days and yet his yearning for Monique continued to grow.

'Your cousin will eventually marry and have babies, Luca, and her mind and attention will wander,' his grandfather said over breakfast the next morning. 'No good will come of this, I warn you.'

Luca brushed a hand across his eyes and forced his mind back to the discussion at hand. 'What if it is my mind that is wandering because of Benito? I want to spend more time with my son.'

For the first time it occurred to him how much his grandfather had sacrificed in ensuring the Vieri Corporation's continued success. 'How much time did you spend with my mother and her siblings when they were growing up, Nonno?'

Did he regret the sacrifices he'd made?

'There was no time for that. Men did not concern themselves with such things. I made sure my family wanted for nothing! That was my job, and I did it well.'

Luca's heart started to thump. Before he'd discovered he had a son, before he'd experienced the love a man could have for his child, he might have believed his grandfather's words, but now...

'As soon as you find a suitable wife, you too will be in a better position to once again focus all your energies where they're most needed and get your priorities into order.'

'Benito *is* my first priority.'

The older man's face darkened. 'You were a fool to get that girl pregnant, Luca. We could've kept everything so simple.'

He stared at his grandfather and his heart started to pound. Cold, hard dread flooded his chest. 'It was you.' The words were out before he could stop them, but the realisation had him abandoning his customary caution.

'What are you talking about?'

'It was you who paid Anita off.' As he spoke the words, he knew his suspicion was right.

His grandfather looked as if he was about to deny it, but in the end he merely shrugged. 'I did what was necessary.'

'How did you find out about Benito?'

'Piero. He intercepted the emails and sent them to me. You forget he was my personal assistant before he became yours. He knew I would know how to act for the best.'

'For the best?' Luca started to shake in an effort to contain the rage that threatened to burst from him.

'Do not look at me like that. I had only your best interests in mind. You and Bella were so close to marrying!' He spread his hands as if that explained everything. 'As soon as you were safely married, I had every intention of telling you about the child. Benito's mother was insisting on it. I only got her co-operation when I explained to her how important this marriage was.' He huffed as if pleased with himself. 'She did not wish to create trouble in your life.'

Monique had been right about Anita. She'd had integrity and honesty and decency. And his grandfather had taken advantage of it.

'I made sure she had the means to support both herself and the child in the meantime.'

He'd thought his grandfather had loved him, but now...

His grandfather's face turned purple as if he read that thought in Luca's face. 'We were working so hard to bring Gianni's back into the fold, where it belongs. I know you want that as much as I do!'

Luca rose to his feet, his mind racing. 'You who have spoken to me so often of honour... What you've done is the antithesis of honour.' He had to battle the nausea churning through him. 'You don't care about honour or respectability. You just want the appearance of it.'

The older man slammed his hand on the table again. 'It is the same thing!'

Luca realised he had been in danger of following a set of values that beneath their pretty veneer were rotten to the core. In making a good marriage, he'd been trying to buy a family name...to buy respectability. But what was respectable about such a cold-blooded exchange?

Nothing.

Not one of the people here at Villa Vieri—not his parents or his grandfather—cared what Luca wanted or what would make him happy. The only person who'd cared was Monique. And he'd let her go.

His heart pounded. Had he left it too late?

There was only one way to find out. He turned and strode from the room.

CHAPTER ELEVEN

THE WAVES ROLLED up onto the shore of Mirror Glass Bay's glorious beach with the mildness of a grandmother handing out cookies to apple-cheeked children. Monique scowled at it. She wanted tempestuous thundering surf and sand-blasting winds. She wanted the beach to reflect the turmoil roiling within her.

For the four hundred and eighty-third time since arriving back in Mirror Glass Bay nearly a fortnight ago, she told herself she had no right to such emotions. What, after all, did she have to complain about? She had everything she'd wanted—or had said she'd wanted—two months ago.

She had Fern.

What was more, she had two part-time jobs that paid the bills, and was working towards a qualification that would lead to financial security and career satisfaction. What more could she want?

She kicked a hank of seaweed. *Luca*. She wanted Luca. How stupid was that?

'Not stupid,' she muttered, stomping in the water and trying to spray it as far and wide as she could. It was out of season, so she practically had the beach to herself. Which meant she could stomp as much as she wanted without inconveniencing anyone.

It wasn't *stupid* to want Luca. The man was a Greek god,

a Renaissance work of art, a masterpiece of masculinity—
broad, lean, powerful and magnetically handsome. Plus, he
was a lover unlike any other. What red-blooded heterosexual
woman wouldn't want him?

Except her want went so much deeper. She missed
Luca—the man she could talk to, joke with and sit silently
with—in the same way she'd miss a limb. A constant gnawing ache sat like lead in her chest, a persistent reminder
that he no longer featured on the everyday landscape of
her life. And adjusting to that felt like adapting to having
lost an arm or a leg.

It made no sense. Yet it made total sense.

It was the man inside the beautiful packaging that she
truly hungered for. The man who rarely laughed, but when
he did managed to light up an entire room. The man who
saw an injustice and moved heaven and earth to fix it. A
man for whom honour and duty weren't just empty words.

She halted, covering her face with her hands.

A moment later she forced them back down to her sides.
The cold hard truth was that Luca didn't feel the same way
about her. If he had, he wouldn't have let her go. But he
had. So easily.

Tugging her T-shirt over her head and shrugging out of
her shorts, she strode into the water and dived under an ir-
ritatingly gentle wave, the water temperature too mild to
steal her breath. She closed her eyes and tried to let the gentle swell ease the burn in her soul. For a little while it did.
The rhythmic ebb and flow, the rise and fall of the waves
and the absence of a breeze soothed and hypnotised. Until
a playful wave splashed her face.

Opening her eyes, she glanced shoreward and saw a
lone dark-haired figure moving along its length towards
her. Everything inside her stiffened. *Luca?*

'Oh, for goodness' sake.' She made her voice deliberately mocking. 'Now she's seeing him in every dark-haired man who crosses her path.'

She started swimming parallel to the shore. An exhausted body helped her sleep at night and swimming for forty minutes a day certainly qualified as exhausting.

She allowed herself the briefest of smiles. She'd thought heartbreak was supposed to make you either fat from all the ice-cream-consuming comfort eating you did or emaciate you with grief. Not her. She was going to be disgustingly toned and healthy.

Which was just as well, she lectured herself as she stroked through the water, trying to find a rhythm that would momentarily quieten all the noise in her mind. She was the legal guardian of a young girl. She needed to be a good role model.

Her strokes slowed. A young girl who was constantly asking when Benny and Luca were coming to visit.

There'd been a couple of quick video calls—Luca was as good as his word. And Monique had been doing her best to keep Fern's mind occupied so the little girl wouldn't pine. The effort left her exhausted most evenings, but she did what she could to push her own heartbreak to one side. It was Fern's welfare that mattered most.

And the heartbreak was Monique's own fault.

Although Fern missed Benny and Luca, she'd adjusted to being back in Mirror Glass Bay remarkably well. Monique had worried her niece would fear Skye arriving to take her away again. Fern had checked once that her mother wasn't coming for her, but after Monique's assurances to the contrary it seemed the little girl had banished such fears from her mind.

Which was great. She was glad Fern had started to feel so secure. Now she just had to work on reducing the number of Benny and Luca questions that continued to arrive daily.

She forced herself to keep doggedly ploughing through the water and *not* notice the man on the beach. As he drew closer, though, she darted another glance in his direction and nearly sank. He even walked like Luca!

Halting by her clothes and towel, the man pulled his shirt over his head and shucked off his shorts to reveal swimming trunks that hung low on his hips and clung to strong, powerful thighs. Her mouth dried. Every red-blooded cell sprang to life. Dear God. That *was* Luca!

She hadn't been imagining anything! That was Luca. *In the flesh.* Oh, and what flesh…

Her feet touched bottom, but the sand kept shifting beneath them. Luca strode into the water and dived under a wave. He reached her in less than a dozen easy strokes of those powerful arms, biceps flexing in a way that made her dash cold seawater on her face. Except there wasn't water cold enough to dampen the heat rising through her.

Before she could temper her shock or the desire raging through her, he stood in front of her.

'Hello, *cara.*'

'Hello, *il mio cuore,*' she whispered, the endearment slipping out as if it were the most natural thing in the world. But those words—*il mio cuore*—had featured in her dreams and she was powerless to stop them.

He smiled, one of those rare, beautiful smiles, and it took every atom of strength she had not to fling her arms around his neck.

'It is good to see you, Monique. My eyes have been hungry for the sight of you.'

'You…' She swallowed. *Keep it together.* 'You saw me just a few days ago on our last video call.'

'Pah!' He waved a hand, his nose wrinkling in disgust. 'That does not count.'

It didn't? Her heart raced and she gave up trying to get

it back under control. 'What are you doing here, Luca? I—'
A terrible thought hit her. 'Benny? Is Benny—?'

'Benny is happy and healthy and currently sleeping in
his old room a few streets away, with Anna keeping watch.'
His eyes darkened. 'I had to come.'

'Why?'

'I wanted to make sure all was well with you.'

'You didn't have to travel halfway around the world to
do that.'

One finger reached out to trail a path down her cheek.
'I needed to see your face when I told you I missed you.'

Her heart pounded so hard she was amazed that agitated waves weren't rippling all around her. 'Me or Benny's
nanny?' If he thought they were one and the same—

He smiled. 'I miss you as Benito's nanny, it is true. But
mostly I miss you as my lover.'

She leaned towards him, tried to read the expression
in his eyes. She told herself she'd be a fool to believe him,
but… Luca had never played games with her. He'd only
ever been kind and honest.

'Really?' She reached up to touch his cheek, but a wave
pushed her into him, and her hands splayed across his chest
instead. 'Oops, I—'

His hands went about her waist to steady her and her
words dried.

'Yes, really,' he answered, as if their proximity had no
effect on him at all.

The tight line of his jaw betrayed otherwise. She stared
at the pulse thumping in his throat in fascination. If she
touched her lips to that spot, would he show her how much
he'd missed her?

'I want to be the good man you think me, Monique.'

She blinked herself back into the moment, frowned.
'You're already a good man.'

'I know we promised friendship and no regrets…' his hands tightened on her waist '…but I regret letting you go, *tesoro mio*.'

He regretted…? Her brain short-circuited. She opened her mouth, but no sound came out.

'And I wanted to know if you too maybe had regrets and if, maybe, you missed me a little?'

Her heart beat so hard she could barely hear the surf over the roaring in her ears. 'I regret not making love with you one last time.' She'd ached for just one more memory to hold close to her heart. Even though she knew just one more memory would never have been enough.

The fingers at her waist tightened further, sending spirals of sensation circling through her and making her shift restlessly. He said something low and growly in Italian and then lowered his mouth until his breath caressed her ear. 'I am going to make such love to you, *cara*, you're going to think you've died and gone to heaven.'

Her nipples hardened to instant tight buds and her fingers dug into the hard muscles of his upper arms. 'When?' She didn't care how needy she sounded. She wanted this man and the sooner the better.

'As soon as I can get you alone.'

She closed her eyes on a groan. 'I have to collect Fern from pre-school in an hour.' Fern attended two mornings and one afternoon a week. 'And Benny will wake soon from his nap.'

'*Sì*. It is the way with family life.'

The smile he sent her made her heart expand until it felt too big for her chest. 'I regret not telling you I loved you before I left,' she blurted out.

His entire muscle electrified. 'You love me?'

She nodded, her heart pounding.

He wrapped his arms around her waist and spun her

around, his whoop of delight sounding all along the shore-line. And then his mouth was on hers, hot and demanding, and she wrapped her arms around his shoulders as wave after wave of emotion buffeted her.

He lifted his head, long minutes later, his hands cupping her face, speaking a rush of words in his native tongue.

'What are you saying to me, Luca? My Italian isn't that good.' And every instinct she had told her she wanted to know what he was saying.

Luca smoothed the hair from Monique's face, staring down into the eyes of the woman he loved more than life itself. 'I am telling you that I love you too.'

Her eyes filled with tears and he saw the hope shining there, but then it vanished. 'You don't have to say it back. I'm a big girl, Luca, and—'

'I say it only because it is true. Every person who should have loved and cherished you has let you down—me included—and it has made you maybe afraid to trust again. But I am going to love and cherish you every day and in every way I can think of until you no longer doubt it.'

Her whispered 'Oh!' speared straight to the centre of him.

The water gently caressed their bodies, the swell pushing her against him, tantalising him with her soft lushness. But there was still so much to say. 'I was planning on taking things slowly, not overwhelming you with a declaration of love immediately. I was going to woo you. But you tell me you love me, and I lose control.'

'I like it when you lose control.'

The impish light in her eyes had a groan rising through him. How could she make him laugh and want, both at the same time?

'I was also telling you how much I want to build a life

with you. You, Fern, Benny and I—we are the perfect family. I want you to marry me. Please, say you will marry me?'

Her jaw dropped and every insecurity he'd ever had rushed to the fore. He swore. 'I have made a hash of this.'

Lifting her into his arms, he strode out of the water and onto the beach. Setting her on her feet, he dropped to one knee in the shallow water in front of her. 'Monique, you make my heart sing. Will you do me the honour of making me truly the happiest man in the world and marry me?' He frowned. 'There is a ring back at the house. I didn't bring it because I didn't think it would be—'

She cupped his face. 'The ring doesn't matter.'

Of course it didn't. Not to a woman who delighted in a simple gelato by the Trevi Fountain, preferred to buy her clothes off the rack rather than be clad by famous designers, and who would choose the rustic peace of a Tuscan farmhouse over a Roman *palazzo*. 'I love you, *tesoro mio*. Marry me and I will do everything in my power to make you the happiest woman on earth.'

Confusion clouded her eyes. She leaned down to peer into his face. She was hesitant, this woman. And careful. As she had every right to be. But he would win her trust.

She bit her lip and he realised he'd been staring at it, wondering when he could have another taste. His gaze lowered. The way she leaned towards him gave him a perfect view of the generous curves of her breasts in her swimsuit. His mouth dried and his heart started to thud.

'Oh!' She straightened, pink flushing through her cheeks and down her neck. That's when he noticed her hips were now at eye level and the gently flared curves made his breath catch. He wanted to peel that swimsuit from her body and—

'Stop looking at me like that, Luca!'

'You look good enough to eat, *cara*, and I want to—'

Soft fingers against his mouth shushed him. 'I can't think straight when you look at me like that. And before I answer your question, I need to think.'

He did his best to leash all his baser instincts. He would give her all the time she needed.

'Come on.' She hauled him to his feet. 'We both need to put on a shirt at the very least.'

He swallowed his disappointment that he would not be getting an answer to his question today. *Patience*, he ordered.

Her shirt clung to her wet skin, creating dark patches where her swimsuit was. He pulled his shirt over his head and did what he could to ignore the uncomfortable prickle of his skin contained against cotton when it so hungered to be unfettered.

She spread her towel out and sat at one end, gesturing for him to sit at the other end. He did as she bade, resisting the urge to haul her into his lap so he could nuzzle her neck.

'Luca, I'm so happy you changed your mind about marrying for any other reason than love, but it's still a leap to ask me to marry you.'

She pressed her hands together and he wanted to take them and press them to his lips. 'I love you, Monique. This is why I wish to marry you.'

'But my family is the antithesis of respectable. And I know how hard you've been working to win back the Vieri family's good name. I know how much you want to do that. I know what it means to you.'

He glanced down at his hands for a moment. 'It has taken me a long time to realise that respectability and honour are two very different things.'

He told her then of what his grandfather had done. How he had pressured Anita to remain silent rather than create trouble in Luca's life.

'Your grandfather? But... Oh, Luca, I'm so sorry.' The expression in her eyes told him she knew how betrayed he must feel.

'He didn't plan to keep Benito a secret from me forever. Only until I'd made a suitable marriage.'

'But didn't he know how much it would mean to you? Couldn't he see—?'

She broke off, looking as if she wished she hadn't spoken, and his heart swelled. She didn't want to cause mischief. This woman was only interested in spreading kindness, not spite or trouble.

'Once I learned those facts, I understood that not only did I not want to follow in the path of my parents, but that I did not wish to follow the one my grandfather had trodden either.'

Her eyes never left his face and he ached to kiss her. He resisted the urge. He needed her to know everything.

'I know now that if I want to win my peers' respect and trust, I need to earn it by my actions, by acting with integrity. The only way to re-establish the good name of my family is for all of my generation to show they are people to be respected—to act with honour rather than paying lip service to it and merely giving the appearance of it.'

He lifted her hand to his lips. 'A good man, an honourable man does not let the woman he loves walk away from him without a fight. I let you walk away, and I have never been sorrier for anything in my life. My life has never been so barren.'

She opened her mouth, but he carried on over her. 'There is nothing disreputable in my marrying you, and if anyone thinks otherwise then they are not the kind of people who I either wish to know or want to do business with.'

Her smile, when it came, lit up the entire beach. With a soft cry, she moved towards him and straddled his hips, her hands cupping his face. 'You're going to forge your own path, be your own man.'

'I want to be the best man I can—for my family, for Benny and Fern, but mostly for you, *tesoro*. You make me want to be the best man I can be.'

Her eyes shone. 'You're the best man for me, Luca. That much I do know. And, yes, a thousand times. I would love to marry you.'

And then her arms were around his neck and he was holding her close and nothing had ever felt more perfect in his life.

Eventually, though, she eased back and gave a squeak. 'We have to go and collect Fern!' She shot to her feet, pulling him up with her. 'She's going to be so excited to see you.'

He couldn't wait to see her either.

'And I can't wait to cuddle Benny.' She shook the sand from her towel.

'My family,' he murmured, unable to believe his good fortune.

'Yes, we're a family now, Luca, and the rest of our lives starts right here, right now.' She held her hand out to him. He didn't hesitate. He reached out and took it.

'I'm going to make you all very, *very* happy,' he vowed.

'And we're going to make you very, *very* happy too.'

He gave her a brief blistering kiss. 'I love you, *cara*.'

She smiled back at him with all of that golden caramel warmth that left him in no doubt of her feelings. 'I love you, *il mio cuore*.'

He was her heart, and she was his. And he would cherish her to the end of his days.

* * * * *

COMING SOON!

We really hope you enjoyed reading this book.
If you're looking for more romance, be sure to
head to the shops when new books are
available on

Thursday 14th
October

To see which titles are coming soon, please visit
millsandboon.co.uk/nextmonth

MILLS & BOON

THE HEART OF ROMANCE

A ROMANCE FOR EVERY READER

MODERN

Prepare to be swept off your feet by sophisticated, sexy and seductive heroes, in some of the world's most glamourous and romantic locations, where power and passion collide.

HISTORICAL

Escape with historical heroes from time gone by. Whether your passion is for wicked Regency Rakes, muscled Vikings or rugged Highlanders, awaken the romance of the past.

MEDICAL

Set your pulse racing with dedicated, delectable doctors in the high-pressure world of medicine, where emotions run high and passion, comfort and love are the best medicine.

True Love

Celebrate true love with tender stories of heartfelt romance, from the rush of falling in love to the joy a new baby can bring, and a focus on the emotional heart of a relationship.

Desire

Indulge in secrets and scandal, intense drama and plenty of sizzling hot action with powerful and passionate heroes who have it all: wealth, status, good looks...everything but the right woman.

HEROES

Experience all the excitement of a gripping thriller, with an intense romance at its heart. Resourceful, true-to-life women and strong, fearless men face danger and desire - a killer combination!

To see which titles are coming soon, please visit

millsandboon.co.uk/nextmonth

MILLS & BOON

Coming next month

THE WEDDING PLANNER'S CHRISTMAS WISH
Cara Colter

Alexandra firmly held out her hand. "Come on, we have to find your nan."

The tiny minx actually looked like she was considering darting the other way, but then, with a sigh of surrender, she took the proffered hand.

There was that feeling again, as Alexandra's hand closed around the warmth and sturdiness of the little girl's smaller one. She felt almost dizzy with longing.

This was ridiculous! She spent all kinds of time with her nieces and nephews and didn't feel as if she was being freshly immersed in grief, as she did now.

The child obviously knew her way around this tiny wood very well. She led Alexandra straight out and to the path.

A man's deep voice, edged in desperation, penetrated the silence of the woods. "Genevieve!"

The child giggled.

"That's you, isn't it?" Alexandra asked.

She nodded.

"It's not nice to frighten people," Alexandra said firmly. "It's quite naughty." They stepped out of the shade of the trees and onto the cobblestones.

A man was standing just outside the double oak doors at the top of the sweeping staircase that led into Parker and Parker, his gaze anxiously scanning the grounds. Even from a distance, and even though he was obviously agitated, it was apparent he was an attractive man.

A very attractive man.

He looked to be about midthirties and was dressed with the casual and utter sophistication that those comfortable with wealth were able to pull off: a dark gray sweater over a crisp white shirt and narrow-legged dark denims over boots.

He was tall, probably an inch or two over six feet, and beautifully proportioned, with wide shoulders, a broad chest and the flat stomach of the very fit. His legs, encased in those denims, were long and powerful-looking.

"Who is that?" Alexandra said on a breath. Obviously not nan!

"That's my daddy."

Continue reading
THE WEDDING PLANNER'S CHRISTMAS WISH
Cara Colter

Available next month
www.millsandboon.co.uk